Praise for Patrick Taylor's Irish Country Novels

"Gentle humor, deeply emotional stories drawn from everyday life—Taylor's books are what Garrison Keillor might have produced if he'd been born in County Antrim."
—*Kirkus Reviews*

"Taylor is a bang-up storyteller who captivates and entertains from the first word."
—*Publishers Weekly*

"The author laces his heartwarming moments with liberal doses of whiskey and colorful Ulster invectives."
—*Chicago Sun-Times*

"Wraps you in the sensations of a vanished time and place."
—*The Vancouver Sun*

"Taylor masterfully charts the small victories and defeats of Irish village life."
—*Irish America* magazine

"Both hilarious and heartwarming."
—*The Roanoke Times*

An Irish Country Love Story

PATRICK TAYLOR

A TOM DOHERTY ASSOCIATES BOOK
NEW YORK

This is a work of fiction. All of the characters, organizations, and events portrayed in this novel are either products of the author's imagination or are used fictitiously.

AN IRISH COUNTRY LOVE STORY

Copyright © 2016 by Ballybucklebo Stories Corp.

Maps by Elizabeth Danforth

A Forge Book
Published by Tom Doherty Associates
175 Fifth Avenue
New York, NY 10010

www.tor-forge.com

Forge® is a registered trademark of Macmillan Publishing Group, LLC.

ISBN 978-0-7653-8274-0

Our books may be purchased in bulk for promotional, educational, or business use. Please contact your local bookseller or the Macmillan Corporate and Premium Sales Department at 1-800-221-7945, extension 5442, or by email at MacmillanSpecialMarkets@macmillan.com.

First Edition: October 2016
First Mass Market Edition: August 2018

Printed in the United States of America

0 9 8 7 6 5 4 3 2 1

To Dorothy

ACKNOWLEDGMENTS

I would like to thank a large number of people, some of whom have worked with me from the beginning and without whose unstinting help and encouragement, I could not have written this series. They are:

In North America

Simon Hally, Carolyn Bateman, Tom Doherty, Paul Stevens, Kristin Sevick, Irene Gallo, Gregory Manchess, Patty Garcia, Alexis Saarela, and Christina Macdonald, all of whom have contributed enormously to the literary and technical aspects of bringing the work from rough draft to bookshelf.

Natalia Aponte and Victoria Lea, my literary agents.

Don Kalancha, Joe Maier, and Michael Tadman, who keep me right in contractual matters.

In the United Kingdom and Ireland

Jessica and Rosie Buchman, my foreign rights agents.

The Librarians of: The Royal College of Physicians of Ireland, The Royal College of Surgeons in Ireland, The Rotunda Hospital Dublin and her staff.

For this work only

My friends and colleagues who contributed special expertise in the writing of this work are highlighted in the author's note.

To you all, Doctor Fingal Flahertie O'Reilly MB, DSC, and I tender our most heartfelt gratitude and thanks.

Author's Note

Welcome back to Ballybucklebo, or, if it is your first visit, *céad míle fáilte,* a hundred thousand welcomes. Here it is, number eleven in the Irish Country Doctor series. If it is your first visit don't worry. You can start and enjoy this series in any one of the books.

This is a departure from the structure of telling concurrent stories set in different decades, which I have used for the last two books: telling Fingal O'Reilly's backstory as a naval surgeon in the Second World War while continuing to follow the doings of the citizens of Ballybucklebo in the 1960s.

This work, apart from a short trip to Marseille, is almost entirely set in Ballybucklebo in the first months of 1967. While it is not a complicated book, one or two matters about it do require some explanation, which is of course the purpose of an author's note. I need to discuss love, characters, and accuracy, and make a small admission.

Although its title implies that it is a single love story, it is rather a collection of intertwined love stories. It is not simply a romantic novel. Love according to the ancients could be expressed in three ways: *eros, filia,* and *agape.* All are here aplenty.

Certainly the ongoing stories of Barry Laverty and Sue Nolan, Fingal and Kitty O'Reilly, Jack Mills and Helen Hewitt, and the will-they-won't-they affair between Lars

O'Reilly and Myrna Ferguson, the marquis's widowed sister, are true manifestations of *eros*.

But love is not always sexual. There is great *filia*, deep affection, between Sonny and Maggie Houston and their dog, between Fingal and Kitty O'Reilly and their home, and Lord John MacNeill and Myrna for the Ballybucklebo Estate, which will face crippling taxes when his lordship dies. The love of a young woman for a father stricken by a heart attack is true *filia*. Nor is there any lack of *agape*, compassion, from the doctors for their patients and their two sick colleagues, from a young Colin Brown for a friend's misfortune, and from the entire village and townland when it comes to rallying support for a respected member who is under threat.

And ever-present and underpinning all is the unspoken but deeply abiding love, I believe reflecting my own, of the Ulsterfolk for their beautiful little corner of the Emerald Isle. A place soon tragically to be riven by thirty years of internecine strife.

Most of the characters are fictitious, but there are some real people in these pages. Doctor Harold Millar was a distinguished neurologist in Belfast who had a special interest in multiple sclerosis and epilepsy. He taught me this aspect of the field of internal medicine. Doctor, later Professor, Gerald Nelson was head of haematology at the Royal when I was a student and houseman. His son, Peter, went on to be an A&E (accident and emergency) physician. The four wildfowling doctors who owned the Long and Round Islands on Strangford Lough—Taylor, Bowman, and the Sinton brothers—were known very personally to me. Jimmy Taylor was my father, Jamsey Bowman was my GP, and I knew the Sinton brothers, in the fashion of Ulster then, as honorary uncles Jack and Victor. I spent many happy Saturdays on the

Long Island. And the Club Bar, home away from home for preclinical medical students, was owned by Mister Mick Agnew.

As ever, I have striven for historical and medical accuracy. My knowledge of Marseille in the sixties is first-hand, having spent three months there in the summer of 1962 as an *externe des hôpitaux,* a junior medical student with limited clinical responsibilities. The city was a fascinating place where I was meant to improve my French. Was meant to. I am deeply indebted to Christianne Pharand, who corrected my execrable use of a beautiful language.

Doctor John Ward of Vancouver kept me right about the details of pernicious anaemia. Thanks, John.

A purely chance suggestion accompanied by a link to the *County Down Spectator* about the loss of a black Labrador in the Holywood Hills, and the immense effort made by the people of North Down to find him, gave me the plotline for the missing Jasper. In the second great coincidence in these books (there is a gastro-pub in Holywood called the Dirty Duck, which was not there when I started writing about the Mucky Duck), the storyline that came to be about Sonny Houston's missing Jasper was sent by Belfast native Jenny Houston. Thank you, Jenny.

Finally, I must confess my sins. When O'Reilly is explaining to Kitty about the founding of the village of Helen's Bay and the building of Helen's Tower, he attributes these to one of John MacNeill's ancestors. In fact, the village was created by the real Marquess of Dufferin and Ava, Lord O'Neill, whose son had Helen's Tower erected in honour of his mother, Helen Selina Blackwood, the Lady Dufferin. I hope the O'Neill family will forgive me.

I trust these explanations will add to your enjoyment of this novel.

PATRICK TAYLOR
Saltspring Island
British Columbia
Canada
July 2015

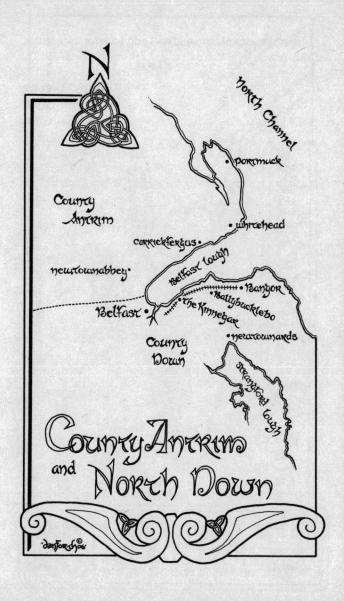

N

North Channel

County
Antrim

• Portmuck

• Whitehead

Carrickfergus •

Newtownabbey •

Belfast Lough

• Bangor

Belfast •

The Kinnegar

• Ballyhucklebo

County
Down

• Newtownards

Strangford Lough

County Antrim
and North Down

danforshos

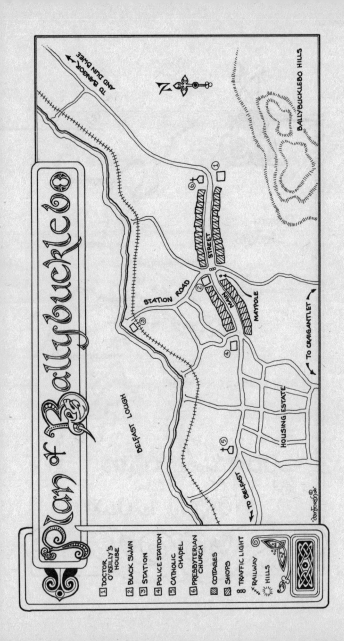

An Irish Country
Love Story

1

In Perils of Water

Brisk," said Doctor Barry Laverty, standing on the shore and watching his breath turn to steam in the chilly, early-January air. The tang of the sea was in his nose, a fair breeze on his cheeks. "Distinctly brisk. Cold as a witch's ti—" No. Out of deference to one of his companions, he'd not make the allusion much loved by his senior partner to the frigidity of a wisewoman's breast. Tucking his neck down into the collar of his overcoat, he held more tightly to Sue Nolan's gloved hand. The young schoolteacher, Barry's fiancée, was spending the weekend at Number One Main Street, Ballybucklebo, before returning to her exchange-teaching work in Marseille.

"Brrrr," she said, despite being snuggled into a sheepskin coat and fur hat. Barry's old six-foot-long British Medical Students' Association scarf was wrapped in layers round her neck. She pretended to chatter her teeth and smiled at him, the light sparkling from her green eyes. Her Mediterranean tan looked out of place on this wintry Ulster afternoon. "In some ways I'll not be one bit sorry to be going back to the sunny Bouches-du-Rhône on Monday." She must have seen Barry's look. "And don't worry, silly, I'll be home for good in March, with the added qualification of having done a six-month teacher exchange. And a much better command of French. I'll be getting a pay raise *aussi*." She pecked his cheek.

He felt her lips, cold on his chilled skin. "And a wedding to look forward to," Barry said. He loved this girl with the long copper hair, distinct political views, and very tasty kisses. Two months wasn't that long to wait. Not really. "Our wedding." He hugged the idea. And mercenary though his thought seemed, her increase in salary would help out with the housekeeping. Becoming a full partner in O'Reilly's practice last January had been very good for the ego, but with what Barry was paid it was unlikely that he'd soon be up there with the Rothschilds or the Rockefellers.

"Our wedding," she said, squeezing his hand, and her smile was radiant. "Yours and mine, *mon petit choux*."

Barry smiled at the French endearment, although why being called a little cabbage should be thought affectionate was beyond him. He held her gaze, then his visions of their soon-to-be married life became entangled with the real world as two little boys dashed past. One, pursued by a scruffy mongrel, yelled, "Happy New Year til youse all," but before Barry could reply, Colin Brown and his dog, Murphy, had juked round a small crowd of folks enjoying a stroll in the Saturday sunshine.

"Hi lost. Go on out. Hey on," Doctor Fingal Flahertie O'Reilly said to his big black Labrador. Typical of the man, he was hatless and wore a tweed sports jacket over a woollen sweater. No overcoat for him. Barry was convinced that O'Reilly, despite his colourful expressions about the cold, was impervious even though his bent nose and boxer's cauliflower ears were red.

Barry watched a tennis ball thrown by his senior partner fly over the damp ochre sand and splash into the waters that lapped Ballybucklebo Beach. A kayak was hauled up above the tide line. Its owner must have gone to get something because there was no one near the little craft, and unless the paddler came back, the soon-to-be-rising tide might carry the boat out to sea.

Arthur Guinness charged past the kayak, his paws leaving blurred prints on the beach. What must be very chilly water didn't seem to bother the big dog as he swam out, grabbed his ball, turned, and headed snorting for the shore. It would be for him no worse than making retrieves, for which he and his clan had been bred, when he was with his master wildfowling on nearby Strangford Lough.

Barry didn't know Strangford well, but he was at home here on Belfast Lough. He'd grown up in Ballyholme and its waters had been his playground for canoeing, sailing, fishing, swimming.

Arthur came ashore, stopped, stood with splayed legs, and shook, the water droplets spraying away to shimmer in the winter sunlight.

"Happy dog," Barry said.

"And happy Barry, I hope," said Sue. "I have loved the sunshine in France, but truly, March can't come soon enough for me, pet."

"I know. And I couldn't be happier. Just look out there." He pointed to a sailing dinghy whose shining white sails gently pushed the boat along in a fair breeze rippling the blue waters. Here and there was a chalk mark of white foam where a wave had broken. "I love the lough. And you know I love sailing." The little sailboat was only about a hundred yards from the tide line. The 16 sail number told him that his pal Andy Jackson was out in his *Shearwater*. "One of my friends. He must be daft. Out in this weather?" Barry said, but well remembered winter sailing before he'd gone to medical school. "It'll be cosier on that big one out there." In the shipping channel, an oil tanker made her way to Belfast, a pilot boat keeping the great vessel company. "I'm happy because I have a great job here in County Down. I could never leave the sea or Ulster for long." He bent and said into her ear, "And I'm happy because most of all I love you, Sue Nolan." And he didn't need her to parrot his words. He knew now how she felt, although until she'd come back from France for the Christmas holidays he'd had his reservations.

"Good boy." O'Reilly took the ball from the grinning dog's mouth and threw it again. "Hi lost."

Barry watched Arthur run and again noticed the kayak. It triggered a memory. "See that kayak, Sue?"

She nodded.

"I tried one once years ago. Couldn't get it to do anything but go round in circles and then I dropped the paddle and tipped myself right into the sea trying to retrieve it. Don't trust the things. Never tried again. I much prefer something bigger, like a Glen-class yacht."

"And so do I when I'm sailing with you, but once I'm back for good I'm going to get you to try kayaking again. It's lots of fun."

"You know how to paddle one of those things?"

"I do, and—don't get huffy now—but my friend Jean-Claude . . ."

"Ah, yes, Monsieur Hamou." Barry recalled the awful feelings of jealousy he'd wrestled with when her letters from Marseille had arrived, filled with mentions of the fellow teacher who was showing her the sights. A lot of worry about nothing. Jean-Claude Hamou had just been a friendly colleague who had taken Sue under his wing and made her feel at home in a strange place. "Water under the bridge."

"Good." She gave him a wide smile. "He persuaded me to take kayak lessons and it's great fun. I can even do a screw roll."

"A what?" He chuckled. "Any relation to a jam roll?"

"No, silly. A screw roll's the simplest type of Eskimo roll to right a capsized kayak while you're still sitting in it."

"I'm impressed. I really am." He shrugged. "All I could ever do was paddle a kind of Indian canoe. It was more beamy than that one. And less cramped." He pointed across the lough. "Look over there." She and O'Reilly turned and followed where his hand pointed. On the far shore, the solid, blue, eternal Antrim Hills rose above the grim granite face of Carrickfergus Castle. Its name meant Fergus's Rock. "When I was fourteen I had a canoe made of wood and canvas. I took it from Bangor to Carrickfergus and back one day."

Her eyes widened. "That's quite a way for a youngster."

"And," said O'Reilly, who had taken the ball from Arthur and told the dog to sit, "what did my old shipmate, your dad, have to say about that?"

Barry laughed. "My father, as you should know, Fingal, believes in discipline. He was, as I believe Queen Victoria said to a minion who had told an off-colour story, 'Not amused.' He thought I'd been very reckless."

O'Reilly laughed, a deep rumbling. "And so you had. I'm sure he wasn't at all amused." He patted a smiling Arthur before adding, "And it is reported that she also said it after watching Gilbert and Sullivan's *H.M.S. Pinafore*." He frowned. "I must say I like the piece, but I

prefer *The Mikado*. Councillor Bertie Bishop, worship-
ful master of the Orange Lodge, committee member of
the Ballybucklebo Bonnaughts Rugby Club, et cetera, et
cetera, holds so many offices he reminds me of one of
its characters, Pooh-Bah."

Barry shook his head. "Sometimes, Fingal, I worry
about your store of minutiae. I really do. You're a sort of
idiot savant, or at least the first half of one." Inside, despite his words, Barry felt a deep sense of comfort. Three
years ago, when he had applied for his first job after
qualifying as a doctor and completing his houseman's
year, he'd been terrified of O'Reilly. Now he was completely at his ease with the big man and never hesitated
to tease him.

"Less of your lip, Laverty," O'Reilly said, but he was
smiling.

"Anyhow," Barry said, "Dad put his foot down. No
more cross-lough forays. When Dad said 'no,' he meant
'no.'"

"How's about youse, Doctors, Miss Nolan?" The
speaker, a buck-toothed young man, lifted his duncher
by the peak as was proper when a lady was being addressed. The shock of hair beneath was carroty red.

"We're grand, Donal," O'Reilly said. "Giving Bluebird her run?" He nodded at a greyhound, the recent
mother of pups. She was exchanging sniffs with a tail-
wagging Arthur Guinness. They had been friends for
years.

"Wasn't it dead sad about your man Sir Donald
Campbell and the real Bluebird?" Donal said.

"It was," Barry said. "I saw the film on TV. The speed-
boat did a back somersault and he'd nearly broken his
own water speed record."

"And no sign of the body," O'Reilly said.

"Very sad," said Sue.

"Right enough. He was a brave man, so he was. Just like his da, Sir Malcolm." Donal patted his dog's head. "Don't you worry your head, girl. Nothing's going til happen til you because you share a name. But we've got to get yiz back into condition and then," Donal lowered his voice, "come here til I tell youse . . ."

Oh oh, Barry thought, that meant Donal was going to impart some secret.

His left eyelid drooped. "Me and your man Dapper Frew are—"

"No," said Barry. "Oh no, Donal." Barry and O'Reilly had been involved in too many of Donal Donnelly's hare-brained get-rich-quick plots with dogs and racehorses. "Tell us when it's over. Doctor O'Reilly and I are going to be busy." Indeed they were only able to be out together today because the new assistant, Doctor Nonie Stevenson, who had taken over from Jennifer Bradley, was holding the medical fort. It was going to be interesting to see how she worked out in the months ahead. Barry had been in her year at medical school and had some reservations about her suitability, but she'd been fine so far.

"Fair enough, sir," Donal said. "What the eye doesn't see, the heart doesn't grieve over, if youse get my meaning."

Barry nodded and couldn't hide a smile. Donal was incorrigible, but in local parlance he had a heart of corn.

"And how's the family?" O'Reilly asked, clearly, like Barry, not wanting to become involved in another of Donal's ploys.

"Julie's got some more work modelling for that Belfast photographer man and wee Tori's growing at a rate of knots. And," he glanced at Sue, "I hope you don't mind, Miss Nolan, but I'd like to tell my doctors that me and Julie think we're . . ." He hesitated then the words tumbled out. ". . . up the builder's again." His blush was nearly as red as his hair.

"Wonderful," Sue said. "Congratulations."

Barry wondered at the numerous Irish euphemisms for pregnancy.

"Great news," said O'Reilly. "Now you tell her, Donal, that we'd like to see her before the end of her third month. Get her care organised."

"I'll do that right enough, and this time it will be a wee lad because—"

The calm of the day was interrupted by shouting. People were rushing to the water's edge, gesticulating, pointing out to sea. Barry stared. Andy Jackson had managed to capsize his dinghy, and *Shearwater* lay on her side, sails in the water. Andy, in yellow oilskins, was trying to clamber onto the keel, obviously hoping to right the boat. Trying and failing. He fell off with a great splashing and thrashing. Andy Jackson had never learned to swim.

Barry turned to Donal. "Donal, run like blazes round to the harbour. See if any of the fishermen can get a motorboat round here quick."

"Right." Donal took off with Bluebird at his heels.

Out at sea, Andy had stopped floundering and was clinging on to the keel.

"Hang on," bellowed O'Reilly, waving furiously, "we're getting help."

Barry, his eyes fixed on Andy's boat, sent up a silent prayer for his friend. "Hypothermia was common on the North Atlantic convoys during the war," said O'Reilly. "At fifty degrees Fahrenheit, a man develops it pretty quickly and just might stay alive for an hour. Near freezing, people die in fifteen minutes. That's about how long the swimmers from *Titanic* survived." He pursed his lips. "This time of the year the water's going to be close to fifty degrees. It could take nearly an hour before Donal finds someone and gets them here. I'm going to go look for that kayaker. See if he can help."

"The nearest lifeboat's at Donaghadee away down the coast," said Sue. "They wouldn't make it in time. I can help, though." She shrugged out of her sheepskin coat, unwrapped Barry's long scarf, and tossed them higher up the beach on the dry sand. "Barry, give me a hand." She headed toward the beached kayak. "I'll take the bows. You take the stern." She was very much in charge.

"Sue," he said, "what in hell's name are you up to?" He glanced out to sea and saw Andy still clinging to the dinghy. Not waiting for an answer, he picked up the little boat and saw that the twin-ended double paddle was aboard. Sue was running to the water's edge and Barry had to sprint to keep up, following her into the sea, feeling the freezing water fill his shoes. "Put the boat down." She bent and Barry followed suit. "But you can't," Barry spluttered. "You can't drag a man into a kayak. If he panics, he could capsize you. I'm not letting you go. It's far too risky."

Sue grinned. "No, it's not, and that man, and we know it's Andy, is in real trouble." She strode toward the little craft's stern, grabbed the port gunnel, and dragged the kayak out until it was well afloat. Sue turned back. "I've done this before. They made us take turns in the kayak and in the water." She smiled. "I preferred it in the boat. Now, if Andy can hang on to my stern or if I can get a rope round him, I can drag him into shallow water. Get him ashore."

Barry hesitated, glanced out to sea again. Thank God, Andy was still afloat, clinging to the dinghy's keel. But hypothermia would sap his energy quickly. "All right. Do it," Barry said, conceding defeat. "But for God's sake be careful. Please."

"You weren't the day you dived in to fish me out. I'm off. Wish me luck." She put a hand on either gunnel to steady the boat and with an obviously well-practised skill, hoisted herself into the cockpit, sat legs outstretched, grabbed the paddle, and with strong rhythmic strokes set off.

Barry watched. She had to cover the hundred yards to the capsized dinghy before Andy's strength gave out and he slipped into the sea. Silly bugger that he was. Sailing without a life jacket when you can't swim. Barry scowled and dug the toe of his shoe into the soft sand. The human capacity for ignoring the obvious sometimes took his breath away. And here was his dear Sue risking life and limb to safe the daft bastard. He loved her for it. Barry took a deep breath. Please, please be careful, Sue. I couldn't bear to lose you.

2

A Cold Coming They Had of It

"Barry. Barry?" It was O'Reilly. "I couldn't find that kayaker but it doesn't matter now. Here. The tide's rising. Take Sue's things. Your brave girl will need dry clothes when she gets back."

"Right, Fingal." For a moment the two men watched Sue in silence, paddling like a professional and making good time crossing the hundred yards of choppy sea. Then O'Reilly thrust Sue's coat and scarf at him.

"I'm going to nip home," O'Reilly said. "Get blankets, hot water bottles, hot sweet tea. The sooner we can start getting him warmed the better, and I'll send for the ambulance, but they'll probably not be here for at least thirty minutes. I'll drive the Rover onto the beach."

He took off in a lumbering and remarkably, for a man his size, fast run, Arthur Guinness close behind. Barry, ignoring the rest of the little crowd watching from the shore, turned back to see that Sue had still a ways to go to the capsized dinghy.

He remembered the day two summers ago when he'd been sailing on *Glendun,* a heavy keelboat, and a fourteen-foot dinghy Sue was crewing had capsized nearby. He'd thought she could swim, but she'd sunk beneath the surface like a stone and he feared she'd been hit by the boom. Despite constantly being taught "never leave a boat for a man in the water," Barry had dived over the side. He'd been able to grab Sue's long hair and, damn it, it sounded so melodramatic, but he had saved her from drowning. He hadn't started to shiver until he'd been back in *Glendun*'s cockpit. Cold and delayed shock, he'd supposed, because he'd not stopped to think what he'd been doing and the adrenaline had kept him going. That same kind of instinct was driving Sue today, and he admired her for it and hoped that at least for a while the exertion and the stress hormones would help keep her warm.

She arrived beside the capsized dinghy, manoeuvering her craft to place its pointed stern near Andy.

He could make out a rope being passed. It looked as if Andy was trying to get it under his armpits. There was a flurry of foam. Barry could see thrashing in the water, Sue's higher-pitched voice calling something, but what, he could not tell.

"Dear God, she's going til turn turtle," a man standing beside Barry said. It was Lenny Brown, Colin's father. He had his hand on Colin's shoulder. Murphy sat at the lad's feet, his front paws restlessly kneading the sand as if he wanted to be out there helping. Barry knew just how the dog felt.

The kayak assumed a frightening list to port and Barry gasped. All three of them, including the dog, leaned forward, willing the little craft upright. As best as he could tell, Sue had tied a rope around her waist and somehow to Andy. He had slipped off the keel of his boat and his weight must be pulling Sue down. Now she was paddling as hard as she could. Barry exhaled. He hadn't realised he'd been holding his breath. He and the little crowd moved to their left as the breeze pushed the kayak and, Barry hoped, the survivor along the coast. At least Andy's head was above water and the boat's list was less.

Lenny, who might have been cheering on his soccer team, was chanting, "Go on, you girl, yuh. Go on. Go on."

Colin imitated his daddy with shrill cries of encouragement.

Ten yards from the shore the kayak shuddered to a halt. Had she hit a rock?

"Your man's grounded, I think," Lenny said. "Look. He's trying til stand up."

As Barry watched, Andy struggled to his feet then pitched forward on his outstretched hands. Barry could tell his friend's lips and ears were blue.

Sue untied the rope and stepped into mid-thigh-deep water. Barry felt the chill for her and shivered. Damn it, he thought, Andy's a big man. Fifteen stone at least. She'll not be able to support him by herself. "Here." He started to hand her clothes to Lenny, who shook his head and said, "Not at all, sir. Stay you here. We'll need a fit doctor on shore, so we will. I'll go." He dumped his coat and jacket, pulled off his shoes, and raced for the water. Lenny Brown was a big man, used to hefting big chunks of metal in his job as a shipbuilder. He'd probably be able to oxtercog Andy unassisted.

Now a young man with a wild head of long blond hair, warmly dressed, trotted past. "It's my kayak," he called. "I'll see to it." At least, Barry thought, that's one of the two abandoned craft looked after. He glanced out to sea.

Farther out, the capsized little dinghy drifted down the wind, helpless, alone, and, if she had a soul as Barry sometimes imagined boats did, as terrified as a winged mallard.

Barry heard a car engine, a slamming door, and a bellowed, "Get to hell out of the way." O'Reilly was roaring in his best quarterdeck voice. "Out of my bleeding way."

A more blasphemous Moses and the Red Sea, Barry thought, turning to see the crowd break apart. O'Reilly had an armful of bath towels. The big old Rover was parked nearby on the sand, engine running to keep the car heater going at full blast.

O'Reilly handed Barry a towel. "Here," he said, "you see to Sue. I'll look after the sailor. Sue'll just be a bit cold and wet, she's only been in the water a few minutes, but the other fellow may have hypothermia."

Barry, whose own soaked feet were afire with pins and needles, understood that very well.

The crowd began to applaud and cheer. Barry turned back. Sue, her soaked jeans legs dark and dripping, was walking from the water's edge toward him. He started forward, wrapped her in her sheepskin coat, and said, "You stupid, headstrong woman. You could have been drowned." His anger was like a flash of summer lightning, quickly gone, and replaced with relief that she was safe. "God, that was brave, and I love you for it, darling." He cupped her cold face and kissed her.

She was shivering, still short of breath from her exertions, and said nothing. Just leaned into him and snuggled more deeply into the coat.

Barry heard O'Reilly calling to the crowd. "And you lot. Quit your rubbernecking. Let the dog see the rabbit. Give us a bit of privacy because I'm going to have to strip your man on the ground. Lenny, lay him down there."

Barry was happy to let O'Reilly take charge of Andy.

"Right," Barry said to Sue, "let's get you out of those damp trousers. Lean on my shoulders." He knelt, undid her waistband, and pulled the sodden pants down her slim, shapely legs. Goose pimples marred her otherwise smooth skin. "Pick up a hoof."

She lifted one foot so he could take off her shoe and sock and get the pants leg over her foot. "Other one." Now she was stripped below the waist, all but for a pair of lace-edged, peach nylon knickers. Still kneeling, Barry grabbed a pink terry bath towel and began towelling her left leg from ankle to groin. The higher he went the more aroused he felt himself becoming. He looked up at Sue and saw she was smiling and had one eyebrow raised. It took all of his professional training for Barry to stifle the erotic impulses, especially when she cupped her hands around his head and leaned into him, and concentrate on drying her other leg. "Right," he said, straightening. "Right. Now wrap that towel round you like a sarong in an old Dorothy Lamour film and let's get you to the car."

"Thank you, Barry. I—I do feel chilled."

"But you're okay?" he said, trying, but failing, to keep the anxiety out of his voice.

"I'm fine, Barry. Really I am."

O'Reilly was kneeling beside Andy, stripping off his oilskin jacket, and telling Lenny Brown, who was standing nearby, "Out of those soaked pants, Lenny Brown. Get yourself dry." The oilskin jacket came off and O'Reilly started on Andy's sodden oiled-wool Aran sweater.

"Sure, Doc, it's only a wee bit of wet, and don't I just live round the corner? It's only a wee doddle."

O'Reilly threw the sweater aside. "You nearly finished with Sue, Barry?"

"I am."

"Can you hang on for a couple more minutes, Lenny?"

"Aye, certainly."

"Good." O'Reilly was unbuttoning Andy's wool shirt. "Sue, quick question before you go to the car," O'Reilly said. "Did you notice anything unusual with Andy when you arrived beside him?"

She nodded. "He said his hands were useless so he couldn't hold on to the kayak, and he had trouble knotting a rope round him. I was scared for a minute I wasn't going to be able to help him after all, and I could see how much he was shivering."

Loss of coordination and shivering, Barry managed to recall, were the two cardinal signs of moderate hypothermia. Not fatal, but not so good either. If it hadn't been for Sue . . . "You did very well, pet," he said.

"Right," said O'Reilly, chucking away the shirt and hauling a string vest over Andy's head. "Barry, you get his oilskin pants and whatever's underneath off. Lenny, help Miss Nolan to my car. The heater's on."

As Barry was worrying at Andy's oilskins he heard Lenny say, "Take my arm, Miss Nolan, and come on. Colin, bring Murphy and we'll away on home. Your mammy'll have the fire on and I'll get warm there soon enough. Have some hot chokky."

"Wheeker," Colin said, clearly relishing the coming treat of a cup of hot chocolate.

"Thanks for your help, Lenny," Barry said as the oilskins came free.

"Away off and chase yourself, Doctor, sir," Lenny said. "You didn't think I'd just stand there both legs the same length with a fellah drowning. There's got to be some advantages to being as strong as an ox. I'm no learnèd man, but I can heft a fellow around, like. And, no harm til yiz, Miss Nolan's a very brave wee girl. What you done was dead on, miss, so it was. Dead on. I seen a man taking pictures. I'll bet youse there'll be a write-up in the *County Down Spectator* next week."

"Thank you, Lenny," she said, "but I hope it doesn't get in the papers. Especially with me only in my knickers." She laughed, but as Barry started on the waistband of Andy's pants he could tell she was embarrassed.

"What? You don't want to be famous?" said Lenny with a laugh. "Come on, miss. Let's get you til the motor."

God, but Barry was proud of her. He ignored his own chilled feet and bent to his task.

As he worked towelling Andy's back and chest, O'Reilly asked, "Can you hear me?"

"I can." The voice was quavery. "I'm f-f-f-f-foundered."

"What day is it?"

"I don't give a d-d-d-damn. I just w-w-w-want to get warm."

"Son," O'Reilly said, "I'm a doctor. You're bloody nearly freezing to death. I'm trying to help you. Now. What—day—is—it?" As he spoke he was taking Andy's pulse.

"Saturday, January seventh, 1967."

"And where are you?"

"On Ballybucklebo Beach. My dinghy cowped."

"I'm glad you know that," O'Reilly said. He stuck a thermometer under Andy's tongue.

Barry had hauled off Andy's sodden pants and Aertex long johns. And all the while Andy shivered. His wet skin was frigid and pale in contrast to the blue tinge to his fingers, lips, ears, and nose.

"Here." O'Reilly gave Barry a towel. "He has a pulse rate of one hundred, a bit fast, his temperature's ninety-five degrees Fahrenheit; should be ninety-eight point four, of course. You can see he's shivering and has the blue of cyanosis at his extremities, but he knows where he is in time and space. The experts classify hypothermia into mild, moderate, and severe." He spoke to Andy. "I'd say yours is moderate. And I've got what we need to give first aid for a moderate case in the car."

Andy, modesty thrown to the winds, struggled to rise. He tottered on his feet.

O'Reilly wrapped a towel round the man's waist. "Help me, Barry, then nip back and bring his clothes and put them in the boot."

"Right."

Barry and O'Reilly supported Andy for the short walk and helped him into the backseat, which was covered with a heavy blanket. They bundled him in and O'Reilly got in with him.

Barry fetched the wet clothes, dumped them into the boot, got into the driver's side, and closed the door. The heat in the car was stifling. He bent to take off his wet shoes and socks and dry his own feet. When he had finished he sat up, relishing the hot air coming into the car.

Sue, looking quite recovered, was sitting with her legs crossed and hadn't noticed that the towel had ridden up to expose most of her thigh. Barry looked away, not in modesty but because if he didn't, he'd want to kiss her. And this was neither the time nor the place. O'Reilly in the back said, "Now you—"

"The name's Andy Jackson, sir."

"All right, Andy, I want you to put one of these"—Barry saw O'Reilly rummaging in the seat well—"hot water bottles that my wife made up for you, under each of your armpits and wrap you in this eiderdown." When he had finished, O'Reilly produced a thermos flask and a mug, and poured. "This is hot sugary tea. We'll get it into you. Two or three cups."

"Thank you. Dear God, but these hotties are grand."

Barry turned in the seat to see his eiderdown-draped friend sipping hot tea. Already his shivering was not so violent.

O'Reilly took the cap of the thermos, filled it, and handed it to Sue. "You have a drink too."

"Thanks, Fingal."

"You all right, lass?"

"I'm fine, Fingal."

"Didn't strain anything? He's a big man and probably felt like a dead weight."

"I'm fine, truly I am. I think I had a bit of help from the wind."

"Huh," said Barry. "Tea. I'd have thought a wee hot half would have been just the ticket."

"It doesn't happen often, Doctor," O'Reilly said, "but this time you'd've been dead wrong. It's the core body temperature that's important for keeping vital organs warm. Alcohol is a vasodilator; it diverts blood flow to the skin and that increases heat loss. While you'd feel warmer you'd be making yourself worse."

"I'll remember that," Barry said, and heard a familiar approaching *nee-naw, nee-naw*. A Northern Ireland Hospitals Authority ambulance bounced over the sand toward them.

"Great," said O'Reilly. "I'm afraid it's the Royal Victoria Hospital for you, Andy Jackson. You'll need to be kept under observation until they get your temperature back up to normal."

Something caught Barry's eye out to sea. A fishing boat that he recognised as belonging jointly to Jimmy Scott and Hall Campbell was approaching the dinghy.

It had made good time. The fishermen would know to put a painter on the little craft and tow her to harbour. "You probably can't see it, Andy," Barry said, "but a couple of locals in their motorboat are getting ready to rescue *Shearwater*."

"Thanks, Barry, for telling me," Andy said. "I was worried about her."

A man in a blue uniform and peaked black leather bus conductor's cap was tapping on the window. O'Reilly opened the door. "We're ready for til get your patient intil our ambulance, sir."

"Grand," said O'Reilly. "Tell the admitting doctor that Mister Jackson here has a moderate case of hypothermia, treated with external warming and hot sweet tea. No medications. Initial temperature ninety-five degrees Fahrenheit."

"I'll do that, sir, and we'll keep on warming you up, Mister Jackson, in the ambulance. We've everything ready and the heater's on. Now, can yiz walk, sir, or should we get a stretcher?"

"Give me a hand and I'll make it there." Andy was still shivering, but his voice was much firmer. He struggled out of the backseat, still wrapped in the eiderdown, but leaving the blanket behind. He stood and, unaided, opened Sue's door. "Thanks for fishing me out, Sue. I thought I was a goner."

Barry shook his head. "You eejit. If you can't swim, Andy, why don't you wear a life jacket?"

"Barry, you know life jackets get in the way on a dinghy."

"Then learn to swim, for God's sake."

"I will, Barry, I promise."

"Good man. I'm glad you're safe," said Barry.

"And there's no need for thanks, Andy," Sue said. "I just did what had to be done."

You did much more, Barry thought, and I am so proud of you, Sue Nolan. You'll not admit it, but you did risk your own life out there. Please don't ever do it again.

3

I'm Leaving on a Jet Plane

Barry knocked on the door of the attic bedroom that had been his when he first joined O'Reilly as an assistant in 1964.

"Come in," Sue said. She was dressed for travelling: sensible shoes, slim black stirrup pants, a loosely fitting powder blue turtleneck sweater. Her copper hair was done up in a single long plait. Pale lipstick and no other makeup. She didn't need it. Her engagement ring shone on her left ring finger.

"You," he said, "look ravishing."

"Thank you, kind sir," she said. "I've just finished my packing."

He enveloped her in a hug and kissed her long and hard. "I love you," he said, "but I don't do teary goodbyes at stations or airports." Another lingering kiss. "That will have to do for now."

She smiled. "It'll have to do until March—"

"Unless my revered senior partner will give me a week off in February."

"Do you think he might? Oh, Barry. That would be wonderful."

"I can ask. Now we've got Nonie Stevenson, she and

Fingal should be able to cope. I should have thought of it before."

Sue kissed him again. "I hope you can come. I'd love to show you around, the Canebière, the Vieux-Port, the Corniche, the Château d'If. It would be great fun. Build memories for rainy days when we're together again here in Ireland."

"I agree," he said, relishing the idea of them as a married couple having shared memories. "But," he said, pointing at his watch, "that's in the future. You've a flight to catch in Belfast today. I want to get you to Aldergrove Airport in good time."

"We'll be far too early, but if you want to go . . ." She shrugged and smiled.

"Sorry," he said, "about my being a bit obsessive about punctuality. I think it has to do with my time as a trainee obstetrician. Time, tide, and a baby wanting to get born wait for no man. I believe that applies to planes too."

"Eejit," she said, "I do love you."

He held her tightly, kissed her one last time, said, "And it's not good-bye, it's only *au revoir*." He bent and picked up her two suitcases as she slipped on her coat. "You go first. I've got the car at the front."

And, following her downstairs, Barry Laverty felt a great warmth in his heart—and a lump in his throat.

When they reached the ground floor, Mrs. Kinky Auchinleck, lately Kincaid, née O'Hanlon, was backing out of the dining room carrying a tray of dirty breakfast dishes. She came to Number One Main Street five days a week now to answer the telephone, prepare meals, and do the housework.

As usual her silver hair was done in a neat chignon. She turned and beamed at them. "So is it off you are,

Miss Nolan?" Her Cork accent was as strong as it had been the day, as the recently widowed Mrs. Kinky Kincaid, she'd left the fishing village of Ring to come north in 1928. She had been housekeeper to old Doctor Flanagan and had stayed on with O'Reilly when he'd bought the practice from the late doctor's estate in 1946. "I wish you a safe journey, so, and if you can wait a shmall-little minute I have something for you in my kitchen." She trotted off along the hall past the waiting room. Barry put the cases down, looked at Sue, and shrugged, turning out the palms of both hands. What had Kinky got for a going-away present?

Across from where they stood, the door to the surgery opened and Doctor Nonie Stevenson appeared, showing a patient, who Barry recognised as Aggie Arbuthnot, out through the front door. Aggie was holding a hanky to her nose. Nonie, who had been on call last night, had not appeared at breakfast and must have gone straight from her bed to the surgery in what at one time had been the old house's downstairs lounge.

"Morning, Doctor Laverty," Aggie said. "Miss Nolan." The "Nolan" sounded like "Dolan." Aggie probably had a cold. It was that time of the year.

"Morning, Aggie," Barry and Sue said together.

Nonie, her thick auburn hair cut in a fashionable bob and wearing a long white lab coat over a knee-length dress and high heels, closed the door, leaned back on it for a moment, and headed back in the direction of the waiting room.

"Morning," Barry said, not altogether approving of white coats. He thought they smacked of a certain insecurity among physicians who felt the need to emphasize their status and put up a barrier between doctor and patient. He noticed bags under her bright green eyes. "Bad night?"

She rolled her eyes, exhaled through her nose, and managed a smile. "But I've had worse doing obstetrics."

Barry nodded. He knew all about that.

Nonie went into the waiting room along the hall and reappeared with Melanie Ferguson and her husband, Declan, in tow. His eyes looked teary and his nose was red. Another patient with a head cold, Barry thought. No doubt general practice had its share of routine work. Although O'Reilly's neurosurgeon friend Mister Charlie Greer had operated on Declan two years ago, the operation to help his tremors had not been entirely successful. Declan was walking as fast as he could, but his progress was slow. Nonie was shaking her head, pursing her lips. Barry could practically hear her thinking, Get a move on. He knew how she felt. He'd been impatient himself when the waiting room was packed and every delay seemed like an eternity.

Kinky reappeared clutching a brown paper parcel, which she offered to Sue. "I have never been in an airport," she said, "but if the food is anything like it is in railway stations . . ." She hunched her neck into her shoulders and shook her head so hard her double chins wobbled. "I've fed better to pigs, so. Here's a couple of ham and cheese sandwiches with some of my homemade chutney, a pickled egg, and a slice of my almond cake."

Sue accepted. "Thank you, Kinky," she said. "I'm going to miss your cooking."

Kinky grinned and said, "And we're going to miss you, Miss Nolan. Travel safely and come back to us and Doctor Laverty very soon."

"Thank you," she said. "I will. I promise."

"And here, Kinky," Barry said, "I thought you were going to say 'may the road rise up to meet you, the wind be always at your back—'"

"Doctor Laverty, bye," Kinky said, one hand on her hip, "I am not some half-baked *amadán* on the stage at the London Palladium pretending to be Irish. No. Ham sandwiches and a pickled egg are all the blessing I have to give."

"No one ever suggested you're an idiot, Kinky," Barry said with a laugh, "but I'm starting to behave like one. It's time to go." He bent and picked up the cases. "Come on, Miss Nolan," he said, "your magic carpet ride awaits."

Kinky opened the door for them. "You go safely, pet," she said to Sue. "And you, Doctor Laverty, bye." Her voice became stern. "Try to be home in time for lunch."

"Mulligatawny soup, and one of Kinky's chicken pot-pies to follow," O'Reilly said from his place at the head of the dining room table. "Feast fit for a king. I wonder what's keeping Nonie?"

"She told me she was running late. Cold and flu season," Barry said.

"I suppose. There's not a lot we can do for a cold or flu, and yet people keep showing up hoping we suddenly have a cure." O'Reilly laughed and took a gulp of soup. "If anything can cure a cold, it would be this soup."

Barry had taken a small helping and had toyed with his potpie. He'd waited with Sue at the airport until she'd waved good-bye from the boarding gate, then walked across the tarmac. He felt the beginnings of something that felt almost like flu settling into his bones. Driving home, he'd sensed an emptiness in the little Volkswagen and, more sharply, within him. Damn it, he'd told himself, stop swooning like a lovelorn swain. The weeks will pass. And here he was picking at Kinky's excellent food.

"So, lad," said O'Reilly, attacking his second piece of chicken potpie, "now Sue's gone back to France how are you going to fill the shining hour?"

The older man, Barry realised, was trying to cheer him up.

"There's work."

"Always that," said O'Reilly. "Like the poor, with us always."

Barry didn't feel like giving the sources, Saints Matthew and Mark. "I want to finish building that nineteenth-century frigate model, and I'm going to see more of Jack Mills. He's still walking out with Helen Hewitt, you know. She's studying medicine now."

"Alan Hewitt's wee girl is making her old da very proud. And he approves of young Mills," O'Reilly said. "Thinks he'll go far. It's been going on for a while now with Mills, hasn't it?"

Barry chuckled. "I think it's a world record for Jack. I might suspect that he's getting serious. About time, too."

"And now you're going to settle down with your lovely Miss Nolan, you reckon your friend should think about marriage too?"

"Like the fox who lost his tail and wanted all the other foxes to lose theirs?"

O'Reilly chuckled. "I'm no fox," he said, "but when it comes to being married, it gets my full support. And Kitty would agree too." He fished out his briar and lit up. "And I suppose there'll be planning for a wedding."

"I'll not have much to do. Sue's family will take care of that. And her mum, Irene Nolan, seems a capable woman."

"And after the honeymoon," said O'Reilly, "you and Sue can certainly live in your present quarters, but you might want to think of looking for a house or a flat of your own now."

"I've been thinking about that and—"

The door opened. Nonie Stevenson, without her white lab coat, came in and sat opposite Barry. "Sorry I'm late for lunch."

O'Reilly said, "Busy surgery?"

"Paddy's market," she said. "Every cold and sniffle in County Down." She looked over at the sideboard. "Is that soup tureen on a hot plate?"

"It is," said O'Reilly, rising. "Let me get you some."

Ever the gentleman, Barry thought.

O'Reilly set a filled plate in front of her. "Get that into you," he said. "You'll soon feel better."

"Thank you," she said, and ate several spoonfuls. "You told me, Fingal, when I applied for the job, that one of Kinky's meals would keep me coming back for the rest of my life. You were right. This soup is wonderful. Just what I needed. I missed breakfast. I delivered one of Fitzpatrick's patients. I only had time to wash my face and go straight to the surgery."

Barry nodded. This wasn't the Nonie Stevenson he recalled from their student days who would have skipped a teaching clinic if she'd had a late night. Good for her.

"Thank you," O'Reilly said. "Everything went smoothly with the confinement, I hope?"

She took a spoonful of soup, swallowed, and said, "Second baby. Normal delivery. As news bulletins are fond of saying, 'Mother and child are doing well.'" She yawned.

Barry, feeling guilty about how much time he'd had off while Sue was here, said, "Look, Nonie, it was decent of you doing the weekend, and the surgery this morning so I could run Sue up to Aldergrove. Would you like me to take your well-woman clinic after lunch?"

A spoonful of soup on the way to her mouth stopped. "Would you?"

"Of course."

"I really would like to lie down," she said.

"I'll do it," Barry said. At least being busy would keep his mind off missing Sue. His model ship could wait.

"You're very sweet, Barry. I'd appreciate it. I really would. In fact—" She finished her soup. "—I'll pass on the second course and head up now." She rose.

"Sleep well," said O'Reilly.

"I will," she said.

"Barry and I will cope tomorrow," O'Reilly said. "All right by you, Barry?"

"Sure."

"You have the day off, Nonie."

"Thank you, Barry, Fingal," she said, heading for the door.

The door closed behind her.

"Decent of you, that, Barry," O'Reilly said.

"Och," Barry said, "I've had lots of time off while Sue was here. Nonie's only just started with us. Let's give her a chance to settle in."

"Agreed," said O'Reilly. "Let's do just that."

4

They That Are Sick

You, my dear," Kitty said as she poured O'Reilly a second cup of tea, "are becoming a regular gentleman of leisure. Here." She handed him the cup and saucer, passing them across his plate, on which lay the wreckage of a pair of breakfast kippers.

"Thanks." He spread his favourite Frank Cooper's Oxford marmalade on a slice of toast. "And it is pleasant to have more time off. Nonie's doing the Friday-morning surgery, Barry's out making a couple of home visits, and all I have to do is sit here in case of a real emergency. I can sup my tea and enjoy the company of the best-looking woman in Ulster until Barry comes back and then, if the lovely off-duty Sister O'Reilly would like, I'll take her to lunch at the Culloden."

"Great idea, Fingal. I'd like that very much," Kitty said. "So we have Nonie to thank for this more leisurely pace."

"We do."

"How is she working out?"

"Fine, I think. She doesn't have the even temperament of Jenny, but she's a first-rate physician. The customers seem to like her and she's a hard worker. I think she's fitting in well."

"I'm glad to hear it." Kitty sipped her own tea. She cleared her throat and said, "Look, after lunch could we nip down to Bangor? We really need to buy some new curtains for this room. They're getting threadbare."

"Excuse me." Kinky came in carrying an empty tray. "I'll just tidy up then get back to my kitchen, so, to see to the other doctors' lunches. I did not mean to eavesdrop, but I did hear you say, sir, that you would be taking Kitty out to lunch?" She began to clear the table.

"That I will," said O'Reilly, and bit into his toast.

"More power to your wheel, sir. It does me good to see yourself having a bit more free time." She started loading her tray.

"Thanks, Kinky." O'Reilly frowned and turned to Kitty. "I don't see the need for new curtains. The old ones have stuck the pace bravely ever since I bought the practice."

"Exactly," said Kitty. "They'd not have been out of place . . . what year was this house built? I've always thought it looked Georgian."

"Back in 1818."

"I was right, and I'm sure they've been here since King George III ruled all of Ireland. They are positive antiques."

"But I like these old curtains. I don't want to spend more money buying new ones." History repeating itself, he thought as he took a healthy bite of toast and washed it down with tea. Of course he wanted Kitty to feel at home here and make it her own, but he saw no need for added expenditure. "Kinky, what do you think of them?"

Kinky abruptly stopped lifting a plate from the table and cast a speculative eye from O'Reilly to Kitty. "Well, sir—"

"Dear Fingal, don't put Kinky in an awkward position."

"No, I'd like to know her opinion. Kinky is the soul of practicality. She'll know if the dining room needs new curtains. Kinky?"

"Well, sir, in truth, they do look a bit the worse for wear, so. And you know how her ladyship liked to climb them when she was a wee kitten. I hadn't really noticed until Doctor Stevenson said—"

"Doctor Stevenson, is it? That's why you're suddenly so eager to redecorate, Kitty—"

"Redecorate? Nonsense," Kitty said, a steely look in her grey eyes. "I just think the dining room needs some new curtains. I'd got used to them too, but Doctor Stevenson mentioned them to me after the last time she was in here."

"I see." He could feel the tip of his nose turning cold and probably white. Nonie Stevenson was a member of his practice, a professional colleague, but she had no business meddling in the affairs of this house, and he'd tell her so the next time he saw her.

"I'll be running along, back to my kitchen," said Kinky, quickly finishing loading up her tray and leaving without a backward glance.

"Thank you, Kinky," Kitty called to the woman's retreating back.

Kitty, Nonie, and even Kinky seemed to be ganging up on him. Lord, he thought, preserve me from this monstrous regiment of women. Then he grinned. Don't be such an old bear, he told himself. In a minute he'd be growling "Bah, humbug" if he wasn't careful.

"Really, Fingal. Doctor Stevenson just mentioned in passing to Kinky and me what a charming old house it was and were the curtains original. It was a joke. There was no malice in it, but it made me think. And while I'm quite sure you do like them, they are going. And don't forget, I earn my own keep. I'll be happy to pay for the new ones."

The front doorbell trilled. Unusual, he thought, taking a sip of his tea. Patients normally came to the waiting room door at the side of the house unless there was some crisis. "I'm very fond of those curtains," he said. "I don't think they need to go at all. In fact I'm sure of it."

He heard Kinky's voice and some other very familiar female tones.

Outside the window, flakes were dancing and whirling, clinging to the branches of the old yew trees in the churchyard across the road, lying on the windowsill, and sticking to the glass of the panes. "Would you look at that," he said, pointing out through the window. As far as he was concerned, the subject of new curtains was closed. "First snow this winter."

"Brrr, I hope it blows over soon."

Kinky peeked into the dining room, looking from Kitty to O'Reilly. "Sorry to disturb you," she said, "but I do have a very anxious Maggie Houston and one of their dogs in the hall, so. You've known Maggie forever and Doctor Stevenson does not. I think the poor woman needs to see a friendly face. Would you speak to her, sir? She'll tell me nothing."

Through the years, Kinky had become a triage officer par excellence, and if she thought a patient should be seen at once O'Reilly knew better than to demur. "Bring her in here," he said.

"I think I'll go and get a tape measure," Kitty said, and made an obvious wink to Kinky, "and measure the windows here when Maggie's gone."

Maggie MacCorkle, as she had been before she'd married Sonny Houston, had been one of the first patients O'Reilly had introduced to young Barry three years ago, when she had been complaining of headaches—two inches above the crown of her head. She was certainly eccentric, but the fact that she'd not confide her troubles to Kinky, when everyone usually did, boded ill, O'Reilly thought. He fished out his half-moon spectacles and perched them on his nose.

Kinky opened the door to the dining room. "Here's Maggie." She ushered the woman into the room, followed by a large dog. The ungainly animal looked like a cross between a Labrador, a standard poodle, and something with long droopy ears.

"Morning, Maggie," O'Reilly said. "Have a pew." He pulled out a chair.

Maggie sat sideways. Wellington boots peeped out from under her voluminous black skirt, itself half-hidden under a heavy overcoat. A blue felt hat perched on her grey hair. The wilted flowers that she customarily wore in her hatband had been replaced by a sprig of holly with fresh red berries. Her usually bright ebony eyes were lifeless.

The dog flopped to the floor at her feet, regarded O'Reilly with doleful eyes, and began sweeping its tail back and forth and drooling onto the carpet.

"This here's Jasper," Maggie said.

"Morning, Jasper," O'Reilly said, and smiled. Rural practice had its moments. The dog wasn't the first animal to be brought to Number One Main Street. Not by a long chalk. Miss Moloney the dressmaker had sought his opinion on the health of her African grey parrot, and just before Christmas, Colin Brown had brought in his pet white mouse, Snowball, the little beast that had got loose at Kinky's wedding. He did not, however, think Maggie wanted an opinion about the dog. "And what can I do for you, Maggie?"

"Och, Doctor O'Reilly," she said, and sniffed.

O'Reilly took a chair opposite and leaned forward. "What's the trouble?"

She sighed, placed a huge handbag on the dining room table, and said, "It's Sonny, so it is. He's not well." A tear trickled down one wrinkled cheek.

He could tell this was an informal occasion. She was not wearing her dentures.

"The ould goat refuses to see a doctor. Said he'd bar the door if one came til the house, so he did." She snatched a short hiccup of a breath. "I don't know what to do. I'm at my wits' end, so I am. He doesn't even know I'm here. I took the bus. Said I was going shopping." She rummaged in the bag, fished out a large linen hanky, and blew her nose with a ferocious honk. "This buck eejit," she pointed at the dog, who made a strange *Aaaarghow,* "followed me til the stop and wouldn't go home. And see that there Sticky Maguire? Him that's the bus conductor with Ulsterbus? Says he til me, he says, when the bus pulled up at the stop, 'No dogs allowed.' And just because your man's got a uniform and a peaked cap, he's standing there on the platform like a wee Hitler." Maggie looked at her handbag. "Says me til him, 'Away off and chase yourself, Sticky Maguire. You let me and Jasper here on or I'll—I'll . . .'" She pursed her lips then inhaled deeply. "I was so cross. I had til get here til see a doctor and I didn't want til miss the bus. And poor Sonny sick, so I took this," she picked up her bag, "and I said, 'See you, Sticky, let us on or, or I'll hit yiz with my handbag, so I will.'"

Fighting words, O'Reilly thought. She must be really worried about Sonny. "And?"

"Shooey Gamble and your man Fergus Finnegan, the jockey, was on the bus. The pair of them starts chanting, 'Let her on, Let her on,' and soon everybody joined in." She smoothed her skirt. "And here I am." She replaced the bag on the table.

"And here you are," said O'Reilly, who was well used to the solidarity shown by Ulster country folk when one of their own was threatened. "And you're going to tell me about Sonny."

She swallowed. "He's not well and I'm dead afeared."

"Don't be scared, Maggie. You've done the right thing, coming to us," O'Reilly said. "Now, what do you think's wrong with him?" He immediately regretted his phrasing. Maggie Houston folded her arms across her chest and snapped, "If I knew that I'd be a doctor myself now, wouldn't I? Finding out's your job, so it is."

O'Reilly smiled. He'd not made that elementary mistake with the literal-minded Ulster folks for years. "True. Let's put it this way. What seems to be troubling him?"

"It's hard to say." She frowned. "You'd need for til ask him. But he won't see a doctor. Says he doesn't need one."

Which, O'Reilly thought, could make things tricky. He hid a smile. Good history-taking was supposed to avoid asking leading questions, but so far he'd learned nothing of use beyond the well-known fact that Sonny Houston was a stubborn man. "Is he in pain?"

She shook her head.

O'Reilly waited. He guessed if Sonny had been bleeding, Maggie would have asked for a home visit at once or dialled 999 for emergency services, so that probably wasn't the cause.

She stared at the carpet.

"Maggie, I really want to help you, but you have to try to help me." Just about what he'd said to Andy Jackson last Saturday.

"I don't know what ails him. He's just, just, och dear, he's just not at himself, so he's not."

"Can you describe in what way?" O'Reilly knew the sixty-one-year-old Sonny suffered from arthritis of his hands and mild congestive heart failure that was usually controlled by low doses of digitalis and a hydrochlorothiazide diuretic.

"He gets awful tired, short of breath and . . ." She started to wring her hands.

Typical of heart failure, O'Reilly thought. Sounds pretty straightforward. Perhaps he needs an increase in dosage.

"I'm ashamed, so I am, til tell yiz the rest." She stared at her boots.

"Come on, Maggie," O'Reilly said, speaking softly, but feeling the rising impatience in his shoulders and neck. "You can do it."

She sniffed, pursed her lips, and screwed up her eyes. "Except for til discipline his dogs," she looked down accusingly at Jasper, now sound asleep and snoring gently, "Sonny Houston's never raised his voice in anger til a living soul. Except maybe that great glipe Bertie Bishop over the roof business." She looked down at her hands, which were gripped tightly together in her lap, then looked O'Reilly in the eye. The words came out in a rush. "This morning I spilled milk when I was putting it on his cornflakes. He—He—" She shook her head. Silence.

O'Reilly leant forward, put a hand on her arm. "Come on, Maggie," he said, "you can spit it out if you try."

She inhaled, paused, and said, "He shouted at me. Called me a clumsy oaf. A stupid old woman. He was fit to be tied. Yelling at me. Spittle flying." She lowered her voice to a whisper. "He put the fear of God intil me, so he did, and that's not the first time lately, neither. That's why I come here. He's not my old Sonny."

O'Reilly sat back. "That doesn't sound like Sonny," he said, while trying to recall what, if anything, he knew about the significance of sudden and completely out-of-character changes in behaviour. They sounded more like some psychiatric disorder. Whatever it was, it needed sorting out, and soon. "I know that's what's got you worried most, Maggie, and I can understand why, but I still need your help. Have you noticed anything else wrong? Anything at all."

She nodded. "He's getting awful forgetful, and he has headaches and he says his hands and feet are numb."

"Mmmm," said O'Reilly, stroking his chin. Those symptoms were not usually associated with heart failure and sounded more like a disorder of the nervous system. That and the sudden outbursts? O'Reilly was still at a loss. "Anything else?" he asked.

She shook her head. "No. But he's not right, so he's not. I'm scared he might—he might hit me or, or hurt himself. I think he's losing his mind and I don't want til see him locked up in Purdysburn."

It was a distinct possibility that Sonny Houston was going to require psychiatric help in the province's asylum, Purdysburn Hospital, but although O'Reilly could not formulate a working diagnosis now, perhaps there was an underlying physical cause that might be amenable to treatment?

Maggie was crying quietly when she said, "I want yiz til do something, Doctor O'Reilly. Give me something til make him better. Please?"

"Give me a minute," O'Reilly said, trying and still failing to arrive at a diagnosis or at least a list of possibilities. Despite patients' beliefs that the examination was all-important, the physical findings in most instances simply confirmed what had been suspected by analysis of the symptoms. Not in this case. O'Reilly knew that all he could do was take a thorough look at Sonny and hope something helpful turned up. Either that or, and it was something O'Reilly disliked doing unless absolutely necessary, admit he was out of his depth and simply refer him to a specialist at the Royal or Purdysburn. But which specialist? "Maggie," he said, "I know your husband doesn't want to see a doctor . . ."

"He'll not let you near him. You know how pig-headed he can be." She was wringing her hands. "What'll I do?"

Jasper woofed once and got to his feet as the door opened.

O'Reilly turned to see Barry in the doorway. "I just got in. Kinky told me Maggie was here. Morning, Maggie."

Maggie sniffed. "Morning, Doctor Laverty."

Barry said, "And that you had plans to take Kitty out. Can I help? I am officially on call now. Is Maggie sick?"

O'Reilly shook his head. "It's Sonny."

Barry frowned. "But he's not here. I don't understand."

"Maggie," O'Reilly said, "I'm going to ask Doctor Laverty's opinion."

"Fire away, sir," Maggie said.

"Sonny has a number of symptoms that have got Maggie worried. I'm afraid they don't quite add up. I'm not sure what's going on."

Maggie's sniff was huge. She dabbed her eyes with her hanky.

"And he's refusing to see a doctor." O'Reilly whipped off his spectacles. "Typical Sonny Houston. Gets a bee in his bonnet and ten strong men wouldn't move him. Huh. Well, he's not the only bloody-minded man in this village. Yes, Doctor Laverty, I would like you to take over Sonny's case, but a bit later." He turned to Maggie. "Doctor Laverty knows a lot more of the new medicine." He saw Barry smile at the compliment. "And sometimes two medical heads are better than one." He looked out the window to see snow falling more heavily. "Maggie, wait here with Jasper for a wee while until I come back for you. Doctor Laverty, it's your case, but what was called in the navy 'a ship of force' is sometimes required. That's me. He'll see me or else."

"Fair enough."

"The Rover's in the garage. Barry, get your coat on again and your Wellies and go on out to the car. I'll nip upstairs, tell Kitty where we're going, then come back and we'll put snow chains on the tyres. I'll tell you what I've found out about Sonny while we work and on the drive out."

"Right," said Barry, and left.

"Sit tight, Maggie," O'Reilly said, then rose and left to climb the stairs.

"How is she?" Kitty sat in an armchair before a fire where Arthur Guinness lay stretched out. Lady Macbeth was on Kitty's lap, along with an open magazine.

"Maggie's worried about Sonny, and I'm not sure exactly what's wrong with him. He's refusing to see a doctor. Both Barry and I are going out to see him. Sorry about that, but . . ." He stared out at the blizzard. "I'm not sure we'd have made it out for lunch anyway." He thought of the dining room curtains. Nor would they get to Bangor. Inwardly he smiled.

"That's all right," she said. "Now drive carefully. I'll let Kinky know there'll be two more for lunch."

O'Reilly bent and dropped a kiss on the top of her head. "I'm off," he said, heading for the door.

As he went downstairs he felt regret about missing lunch with Kitty but an even greater curiosity to find out what the devil was wrong with Sonny Houston.

5

And They Ran Awa'

Hellfire and damnation," O'Reilly yelled as the final clip on the tyre chain snapped shut—and skinned his knuckles. He reflexively sucked them.

"You all right, Fingal?" Barry asked.

"I'll live," he said. "Time we were off, and I want you to drive."

"Oh?"

"That hill up to the Houstons' can be a bugger when it's slippy," O'Reilly said. "You drive and if needed I'll get out and push."

The two men got in and Barry reversed out of the garage.

As they drove up to the front of Number One the snow was falling fast, whirled into spirals by a vicious northeaster. Although it was only midmorning, the steeple of the Presbyterian church opposite Number One was difficult to make out, and the old yews were bowing under the weight of the damp flakes.

"I'll go and get them," O'Reilly said when Barry had parked. It really was as cold as a witch's tit, he thought as he hurried along the short path and on into the house. "Come on, Maggie, and bring Jasper."

On the way back to the car the gormless animal kept bounding and clicking his jaws, trying to catch snow-flakes in his mouth.

"In you get," he said, holding the back door open and closing it behind them. He climbed in the front. "Off we go."

Barry pulled away from the kerb and drove along roads where the few vehicles caught out in the storm crept along. Nobody in their right mind would be driving in this unless they had to.

"Can yiz no' go any faster, Doctor Laverty?" said Maggie from the backseat. "I'm main worried, so I am. We're only hirpling along like an ould snail with rheumatism."

"I'm going as fast as I can, Maggie. There's a lorry up ahead and I can't pass him in this lot."

The swirling snow was barely kept at bay by the windscreen wipers.

"Poor Sonny's all alone, bless him," Maggie said, "but for his dogs. I hope til God he's had enough wit til get a fire lit. It would skin you alive out there."

"I'm sure—" O'Reilly began, but Maggie continued. "Och, but I don't know. The last wee while I've had til remind him til brush his teeth. Comb his hair. I telt him yesterday he'd forget his head if it wasn't screwed on his shoulders."

Memory loss, O'Reilly thought, emotional lability, and the loss of temper she'd already described? He knew they occurred with toxic confusional states or—and please don't let it be—dementia. But how did that relate to numbness of the extremities and shortness of breath? O'Reilly shook his head and stared at the red taillights of the lorry that Barry was using as a pathfinder through the blizzard.

"Maggie," O'Reilly said, "I've been telling Doctor Laverty most of what you've told me about Sonny. I'm going to tell him the rest now."

"You fire away, sir, but don't make the young doctor slow down any more."

"I'll not," Barry said.

"Right. I've told you Sonny's physical symptoms, but there was also an instance this morning where Sonny lost his temper with Maggie, and yelled at her when she spilt some milk—"

"Och, it was only a wee yell."

"She said she was worried he might hurt her—"

"Not at all," Maggie said. "My Sonny's gentle as a lamb, so he is. He'd never take a fit of the head staggers like that. Not at all."

Ahead the lorry signalled for a left turn, slowed, and made its departure. Now the road ahead was empty.

"Maybe I'm making a big fuss out of nothing, Doctors?"

Barry glanced back, trying to reassure her. "Maggie, if a body's worried enough to come to us in the middle of a snowstorm, it's our job to—Look out!" he yelled.

O'Reilly saw at once that the momentary distraction had made Barry miss a bend. He'd tried to correct, turned the steering wheel too violently, and skidded.

Maggie moaned with the passion of the banshee. Jasper the dog yodelled, O'Reilly muttered, "Bloody hell," and Barry simply muttered, "Hang on."

The car juddered, jolted, and shuddered to a halt with a distinct list to starboard.

"Lord Jasus, are we near all killed? Jasper, quit your noise. I'll never get home to poor Sonny now. I'll need til get out and walk. Will youse for the love of God do something, Doctors?"

O'Reilly began, "Beëlzebub's blue, bleeding, blasted, blazing, brimstone . . ." He took a deep breath. "Sorry, Barry. It could have happened to a bishop in these conditions. I'd better get out. Take a shufti. There's a torch in the glove compartment. Maggie, sit tight and don't let that dog out."

"Just get a move on, sir. Please." Her voice quavered. "I want til go home, so I do."

About an inch of snow had fallen. O'Reilly felt the chill on his face and was glad of his overcoat and gloves. He switched on the torch and ploughed past the front of the car. One of the front wheels was sagging over the ditch. "We," O'Reilly yelled, "are somewhat bollixed, but put her into reverse. I'll go and push. See if we can get her back on the road."

"Right."

Barry had opened the window, presumably so he could hear any instructions.

O'Reilly marched to the front of the car, found a secure footing, and put his shoulder to the radiator grille. He yelled, "Try her now," and heaved. Spinning tyres whined, but there was no movement.

"Hang on," O'Reilly said. "We'll have to lighten the car. Ask Maggie to get out and stand aside. Leave the dog inside."

"Right."

Maggie, muttering something about Captain Scott's polar expedition, clambered out. The dog bounded past her and despite her screeches of "Come back here, Jasper," the animal was soon out of range of the headlights and heading at great speed into the whiteness.

"Never mind the bloody dog," O'Reilly yelled as he bent to push again. "He'll probably be home before us at this rate. Try her again, Barry."

The tyres spun, but then O'Reilly felt them catch and the car lurch back. Deprived of the support of the radiator, he fell forward, knocking off his paddy hat. "Holy thundering Mother of—"

"One more shove and I think we can get her out," Barry called from the car.

O'Reilly heard Maggie wailing, "We're doomed. I'm going to start walking. I have to get home to Sonny." And off she set, Wellies crunching through the snow.

"Let her go. We'll catch her up," O'Reilly called as he tried to stand. Still muttering imprecations, he struggled to his feet, dusted the snow from his hair, grabbed his hat, and crammed it on his head. He was panting like a hunted stag and his breath hung in the air. He put his hands on his knees and yelled, "Give—me—a—minute." His breathing was easing. He took two paces forward, lowered his shoulder, and yelled, "Now."

Barry inched the car backward. O'Reilly plodded after. He was gasping and his chest was heaving.

Barry shouted, "She's back on the road."

"Thank—Christ—for—that." O'Reilly tramped around to the passenger door.

"You all right, Fingal?"

"No. I'm colder than a stepmother's breath." He started to clamber aboard. "And from the sound of it I think the car heater's gone on the blink—again. But there's only about a mile more to go."

They'd not gone far when the headlights picked out a solitary figure heroically plodding on in the direction of her home.

Barry pulled up alongside, stopped, and called, "Hop in, Maggie."

She climbed in and shut the door. "Sonny'll have a carniption when he finds out I've lost one of his dogs."

"Never worry," O'Reilly said. "Most dogs are pretty good at finding their way back home. We'll not stop to look for him. We need to get to your place, Maggie, get warm, and see to Sonny."

"Can you not hurry up?" Maggie asked as soon as she was settled in the backseat.

"Maggie," O'Reilly said, "in five minutes we'll be at the bottom of your hill. If Doctor Laverty takes a run-race at it like a bull at a matador's cape we'll skid. Now just bide, hold your tongue, and we'll get you there." He said to Barry, "Take her up the slope in second. You'll get better traction."

Barry dropped the car into the lower gear and soon they were over the hill's crest.

"Well done," said O'Reilly. "And, you didn't need my assistance on the hill after all. Remember, I just came to help us get here, and get Sonny to see you. It's your case. You're the one on call."

"Thanks, Fingal. I appreciate your confidence."

"Pah," he said, shaking his head. "You managed on your own when Kitty and I were on holiday in Barcelona last year, and I want you to take on even more responsibility this year."

"Fine by me," Barry said. "I'll enjoy the challenge."

That was something O'Reilly admired about Barry. He never shirked his responsibilities. He was, in local parlance, a sound man.

"And speaking of holidays," Barry said as the lights of the Houstons' house came into view, "how'd you feel about giving me a week off in February to go and see Sue?"

"As long as Nonie and I can cope, I don't see why not." Good for him, he thought. The lad deserves a holiday.

"Great," Barry said as he slowed down to stop beside the gate at the end of the path. "Now let's go and see the patient."

⌘

From up in the Ballybucklebo Hills, the distant waters of Belfast Lough should have been visible, but the swirling snow blotted out everything. O'Reilly remembered walking along this path two summers ago when Barry had kicked a cloud of downy seeds like miniature parachutes from a goat's-beard weed growing between two paving stones. It was impossible even to make out the path now.

When they reached the doorstep, a loud chorus of barking came from Sonny's dogs. The flap of the letterbox halfway up the front door opened. O'Reilly bent and looked into a pair of eyes peering out.

"Who's there?"

"It's me and the doctors, dear," Maggie called. "We're getting foundered out here. Open up and let us in, like a good man."

"I thought you were going shopping. Meddling old woman. Go away. Go away."

"Sonny, for goodness' sakes—" Maggie fumbled with her house key.

"No. Go-a-way. I told you, I neither need nor want a doctor."

She managed to get the door unlocked, but when she tried to push it open, it was stopped by a door chain.

O'Reilly took a deep breath. "Sonny Houston," he roared. "It's Doctor O'Reilly. I'm worried about you. Open up. Now."

Nothing but the barking of dogs.

"Sonny, put the silly beasts in the kitchen and open the door."

"Don't want to, Maggie."

"Sonny, for the love of God, it's freezing out here."

"All right. Wait a wee minute."

O'Reilly saw the door being shut. The sounds of barking receded. An inside door slammed. Barry looked at O'Reilly, who shrugged and tried the front door. It swung open.

"Come on on in," Maggie said. "He'll be putting the dogs away." She led, followed by Barry.

O'Reilly brought up the rear and shut the door. Kicking off his Wellingtons and taking off his overcoat, he quickly took in the black-and-white photos of Petra on the hall wall. Sonny had been there on an archaeological dig in the 1930s. His oar, with the names of his Cambridge college's rowing eight in gold on the blade, hung nearby.

At the far end of the hall the kitchen door stood resolutely shut.

"I'll kill the ould goat," Maggie said, then raised her voice. "Sonny, would you come away to hell out of there? Nobody's going to hurt you."

"Don't want to. Shan't." He sounded like a petulant child. "Leave me alone. And this door's locked now."

This was more than stubbornness. Sonny Houston was behaving irrationally. But why?

"You two, into the lounge," O'Reilly said. "Leave this to me."

Maggie opened a door ahead and to Barry's right. He followed her.

"Bring the ould eejit into the parlour when you've got him til stop acting the maggot, Doctor," she called.

"Now, Sonny," O'Reilly said, keeping his voice low,

steady, "it's Doctor O'Reilly and I want you to open this door."

"Och, no. Go away." But Sonny's voice had lost much of its earlier hectoring tone.

"Sonny, I'm big enough to break down this door, you know that, but I don't want to."

No other sound but barking dogs.

O'Reilly took a deep breath. "Sonny, I really do want you to come out." O'Reilly let an edge creep into his voice. "Either that or I'll arrange a consultation with a psychiatrist friend of mine in Belfast at Purdysburn as soon as the ambulance can get here to take you there." O'Reilly knew full well the terrible stigma such a consultation would bring. Clearly, Sonny was not so deranged as to be unable to make a rational choice.

The door crept open. Sonny slipped through, keeping the barking, yelping dogs in the kitchen, then closed the door and turned to face O'Reilly.

The man's usually well-brushed iron-grey hair was untidy and there was an egg stain on his woollen cardigan. He wore neither collar nor tie. His face, which usually had a slatey-blue tinge because of his heart failure, was alabaster pale and twisted into a scowl.

"Come on," O'Reilly said. "Maggie and Doctor Laverty are waiting for us in the lounge."

"Oh, all right." Sonny shuffled along beside O'Reilly.

When they arrived Maggie tutted and managed a smile. "There you are, you silly ould fool. You've had me worried sick. My heart's been in my mouth, so it has." She shoved a huge one-eared, one-eyed ginger cat off an armchair. "And you, General Sir Bernard Law Montgomery, get away to hell out of that and let your betters sit down."

The scowl vanished and Sonny hung his head. "I'm

sorry, dear, but I don't know what all the fuss is about." He inhaled. "It's just a touch of the collywobbles and I do not wish to be poked and prodded—" He stopped and gasped.

O'Reilly said, "I've brought young Doctor Laverty with me. He's going to look after your case." He nodded a go-ahead at Barry.

"Hello, Sonny," Barry said. "Not feeling so hot? Doctor O'Reilly tells me that among other things you get short of breath."

Sonny nodded. "I'd like," he said and pulled in a shallow breath, "I'd like to sit down."

Barry stepped forward, took him by the elbow, and helped the man into the armchair recently vacated by General Sir Bernard Law Montgomery.

"Thank you," he said, plucking a tuft of cat hair from the chair and turning a slightly accusing eye on Maggie.

"I'm sure youse doctors would like peace and quiet til look him over, so you will. Now, you do as you're bid, Sonny Houston. I'll go and get my hat and coat off, and I'll put on the kettle and cut a few slices of my plum cake."

O'Reilly's heart sank at the prospect of having to face Maggie's overstewed tea. He had once described it as being fit only for stripping paint off a destroyer, and her cake as tough enough to patch a shell hole in the same ship.

"Now, Sonny," O'Reilly and Barry said in unison.

"I have agreed to be examined, Doctors, and you have told me that Doctor Laverty has that privilege. Very well, Doctor. I'll submit to your ministrations."

"Fair enough," said O'Reilly, sitting in another armchair. "I'm just going to sit here, both legs the same length." He hoped Barry'd not be blinded by Sonny's mild heart failure. While it certainly caused shortness of breath, so did other things.

Barry draped his overcoat on a chair, set his bag on the floor, and took out his stethoscope. "This won't take long, Sonny," Barry said, picking up the man's wrist. O'Reilly watched his partner's head nodding as he counted the heartbeats. "Your pulse is nice and regular and running at ninety beats per minute."

All right. A bit fast, and compatible with heart failure—or a host of other things.

"Look up," Barry asked, and pulled down Sonny's lower eyelid.

O'Reilly could see that it was pale pink when it should have been scarlet because of the blood cells in the capillaries that lay just beneath the conjunctiva, the transparent membrane lining the eyelid and covering the eyeball. That was a sure sign of anaemia, the marker of a family of blood diseases often overlooked by the sufferer until it became severe. Then other people began to notice how weak, breathless, short-tempered, and forgetful their loved one had become. O'Reilly thought back to his own father's blood disorder in 1936.

"Stick out your tongue, please."

It looked smooth and red raw. Oh-ho. This was beginning to add up. There were few causes of that sign.

O'Reilly waited as Barry quickly completed his examination, stuffed his stethoscope into his jacket pocket, and began explaining his findings to his patient. "I think I've a pretty good idea of what your trouble is, Sonny, and it's not your ticker. Your lung bases were clear, your heart rate's not irregular, blood pressure's fine. Some of the things I've found might be due to it, like being short of breath, being tired, fast pulse, tiny bit of ankle swelling, but I'm pretty sure your heart failure is under control."

"That's good," Sonny said. "I am relieved, I'll admit it." He drew in a deep breath.

"Numbness in your feet and fingers, and headaches don't go with that condition, though."

"I see." Sonny nodded.

"Doctor O'Reilly, did you notice how smooth Sonny's tongue is?"

"I did," said O'Reilly, "and his conjunctivae're pale too."

Barry nodded. "And I can feel your spleen, Sonny. That's an organ under your ribs on the left that normally gets rid of old, tired red blood cells."

Sonny forced a smile. "I feel like an old tired blood cell myself these days," he said.

"And," Barry said, "you've lost your knee and ankle jerks, and you didn't feel the vibration when I put a tuning fork on your insteps and ankles."

The door opened. "Can I come in yet?" Maggie was carrying a tray. "Tea and plum cake," she said. "For when you've finished, Doctors."

"Come ahead," O'Reilly said. "Doctor Laverty's going to tell us what he thinks is wrong and what we need to do next."

"Your ticker's under control, but I'm almost certain you have thin blood. The trick is going to be to find the exact cause. There's quite a few to choose from, although even now I can make a pretty good guess at which one it is."

"Can you fix it, Doctor, dear?" Maggie asked.

"We'll have to get some blood tests to be certain of what we need to treat."

O'Reilly hoped that a painful bone marrow biopsy and an uncomfortable gastric fractional test meal could be avoided.

Barry continued, "But yes. I think so. Now my dad likes to say, 'Never make a promise if you're not sure you can keep it.' I'm not promising you I'm right."

Good lad, O'Reilly thought.

"We understand," Maggie said. "We'll leave being infallible to your man with the pointy hat in the Vatican."

Barry smiled. "Thank you."

"Excuse me," O'Reilly asked, "and I'm not interfering, just asking, wouldn't it be simpler to ask Doctor Gerry Nelson, the haematologist at the Royal, to see Sonny?"

Sonny coughed. "Now look here. I'm sorry, sir, but I'm only seeing you two medical men under protest. I hate hospitals. I insist the young doctor look after me here." Then Sonny's stiff posture and superior tone gave way and he looked at Barry. "Please, Doctor Laverty." His supplicant manner would have softened Pharaoh's hard heart.

Barry stopped writing out the lab requisition forms and smiled. "I can spare you a consultation with another doctor for now, Sonny, but I can't do the blood tests here. And you shouldn't be driving in your state. You could pass out behind the wheel. I'll arrange for an ambulance to take you down to Bangor hospital tomorrow, have the blood work done. We'll have the results next week and I'll pop out to give them to you." He handed the forms to Maggie.

O'Reilly nodded his approval.

"I'm pretty sure with the right treatment we can get rid of your tiredness and shortness of breath. I'm sorry, but I don't think I can fix your feet and fingers. Once a nerve is damaged I'm sorry, but that's it. It's gone for good. But I reckon we can stop it getting any worse. I'm working," he said, "with a diagnosis of pernicious anaemia, failure of production of red blood cells because of the body's inability to absorb vitamin B$_{12}$ through the gut."

"Pernicious?" said Maggie. "I don't like the sound of that."

"It was called pernicious in 1800-and-something when it was first described," Barry said. "Now, don't be scared when I tell you that back then doctors could make the diagnosis but had no idea how to treat it. The patients died, I'm afraid."

"Boys-a-dear." Maggie jammed a fist against her lips and stared at Sonny.

Barry hurried to add, "But in 1920, doctors found a cure." He decided against telling Maggie and Sonny that before vitamin B$_{12}$ had been identified and synthesised in the 1950s, the cure had been to eat raw liver every day.

"Hallelloolyah, that's a relief," she said, clearly reassured.

O'Reilly chuckled at the Ulster pronunciation with the extra "lool" syllable.

"Thank you, Doctor," Sonny said. "I am reassured by your findings, and—" He hesitated. "I'm sorry, Maggie, for yelling at you, and you doctors for my being bloody-minded. I don't know what came over me."

O'Reilly was relieved they did not have to consider dementia any longer. "No need. Being grumpy's caused by the disease too."

Maggie, who must have popped in her false teeth when she was in the kitchen, grinned so widely her hooked nose almost met her chin. "There, you ould goat," she said. "You're forgiven for barging at me, going up one side and down the other this morning, and you and your 'I don't want no doctors.' Buck eejit." But she bent and kissed him—and the room was filled with forgiveness and love.

She pointed to the tray. "Now, sirs, tea and cake."

"That would be really lovely, Maggie," O'Reilly said, "but the snow is still falling thick and fast out there and we must get back to Number One."

Barry picked up his coat and bag. "The ambulance will be here for you tomorrow and I'll call round to give you the results next week." He followed O'Reilly, who was making for the door. "We'll see ourselves out," O'Reilly said as he hauled on his boots. He was proud of Barry for having worked out a difficult clinical problem, and nearly as proud of himself for gracefully avoiding Maggie's tea and cake.

On the way to the car through the continuing blizzard, O'Reilly said, "It's downhill on the way home. I'll drive." He got in. "Well done, Barry," he said, manoeuvering the big car away from the kerb. "I was getting worried. It was looking like Sonny might have a blood disorder. I have very personal reasons for fearing them. My father died of leukaemia in 1936. But pernicious anaemia is much less serious."

"I'm sorry, Fingal. He must have been still a relatively young man."

"Och," said O'Reilly, heading for the Bangor to Belfast Road, "he was. Only fifty-eight, same age I am now. That was thirty-one years ago, but it was hard at the time. Particularly on my mother. Do you think there's a chance Sonny might—?"

"Have a leukaemia? The blood tests'll give us a better notion, but I hope not."

"Time will tell," O'Reilly said, slowing behind a lorry spreading sand and salt on the road, "but for now let's get back home." The prospect of a warm fire in the lounge and one of Kinky's hot lunches in the dining room filled his heart with gratitude for Number One Main. "I wonder," he said, "if Sonny's Jasper has found his way home yet?"

6

Pregnancy Humbles Husbands

Someone was knocking on the door of Barry's quarters. He looked up from where he sat at a small inlaid walnut table under an Anglepoise lamp. He was assembling the mainmast on his model of HMS *Rattlesnake* and would be until it was time to accept Fingal's earlier invitation to go upstairs for a predinner drink. "Come in."

Nonie Stevenson, who was taking the Monday afternoon clinic, stuck her head round the door. Tasty cooking smells wafted in from the adjacent kitchen. "My," she said, pointing at the miniature square-rigger, "that's pretty finicky work. I'm impressed. Are you sure you haven't missed your calling—say, neurosurgery?"

Barry smiled. "Modelling's been a hobby of mine for years. Can't say the same for neurosurgery."

She struck a pose with one foot at right angles to the other, knee bent so her heel was off the floor. With her left hand on her hip, and her right hand behind her thrown-back, half-turned head, she curved her full lips into a slight pout.

Good God, she could have been posing for *Vogue*, Barry thought. Even in the white lab coat and knee-length skirt, she exuded a kind of elegant eroticism. He smiled and felt a flicker of temptation. He smiled again. Well, he was only human. He swallowed. Down boy. Think of Sue.

"Modelling, that kind of modelling, wasn't a hobby with me," she said. "I did it professionally when I was a student. Helped pay my fees. I worked for the Stella Goddard Agency." She dropped the pose.

"I'll be damned. I had no idea. I don't think I ever saw your picture anywhere—"

Nonie laughed. "And you wouldn't have. It was mostly just damned hard work, not the least bit glamorous. But it was easier than waiting on tables." She ran a finger lightly over the tiny ship's foredeck railing and looked at him thoughtfully.

Somehow the modelling didn't fit with her professional image, and yet, she was a damn attractive woman. He wondered if she was still posing when she looked down, pursed her lips, and said, "I need a favour."

He frowned. "Sure."

"Can I sit down?"

Barry pointed to a chair.

She sat and crossed her, he had to admit, shapely legs. But as his dad used to say, "A cat can look at a king as long as it doesn't think the king's a mouse." She said, "I had a blazing row with my boyfriend last night."

It was a comfort to know she had a man in her life. And yet there was something provocative about her, sitting neatly in the faded plaid armchair, her hands restless in her lap. Something flirtatious. Perhaps she was one of the new women who were simply less reserved than their more traditional sisters and enjoyed a bit of flirting. "Nothing too serious, I hope."

She pursed her lips again.

"Want to talk about it?"

She shook her head. "Thanks, but not in gory detail. He was mad because I kept him waiting for half an hour. I'd had a nap in the afternoon and slept in."

Barry stifled a grin. As a student she'd been a great one for snatching forty winks at the slightest provocation.

"He yelled at me." She sighed. "God, I'm dying for a cigarette. Anyway, one thing led to another . . . I really don't want it to break up."

Barry relaxed and waited.

"I'm meant to meet him tonight at six in Belfast at the Ritz cinema, and the clinic's running late. I'd best not be late." She looked Barry straight in the eye. "I didn't want to ask Fingal to help out. I've only been here a couple of weeks, you took over for me last Monday because I was bushed, and I don't want him to think I'm a shirker always asking for cover, but . . ."

"Hang on," Barry said. "First of all, Fingal's out, and second, you didn't ask me last week. I offered."

Her smile was full of gratitude.

"Would I see your last patients?" he said. "Is that it?"

"Would you?"

"Sure." Barry rose and so did she. He'd been on call all weekend and it had been a busy one, but seeing a couple of cases wouldn't be much trouble. "You run on. Good luck with your boyfriend."

"You are a sweetheart," she said, moved firmly against him, hugged him, and kissed his cheek.

Barry stepped back. A peck between friends was one thing, but that hadn't been just a peck. He felt himself start to blush. Don't be stupid, he told himself. She knows you're engaged.

"There's only a couple of customers left. I'll run on." She was already stripping off her white coat as she fled.

Barry cocked his head. What had she meant by that

kiss? Come on, he told himself, don't let your imagination run riot. He laughed. Nonie Stevenson was probably just an affectionate young woman, and one who surely needed her sleep. Forget it, Laverty.

He headed into the kitchen, where Kinky was kneading rough white objects shaped like scones. "Cobbler topping," she said. "Just finishing them off so Kitty can put them on top of the beef stew when it's finishing off in the oven. Archie will be here to pick me up at five. We're going to the British Legion in Bangor tonight, so."

The trip to the ex-serviceman's club, Barry thought, accounted for the smart dress under her apron and her best green hat on a chair. "Have fun," he said. "See you tomorrow."

He looked into the waiting room with its mural of floribunda roses on one wall. He heard a chorus of "Afternoon, Doctor," from the three people in the room. Donal Donnelly sat with his wife, Julie, and a young woman in her early twenties whom Barry did not know. "I'm sorry," he said, "but Doctor Stevenson has been called away."

" 'At's all right, Doctor Laverty," Donal said, but the young woman rose and said, "No harm to you, sir, but I really wanted to see the lady doctor."

Barry recalled a line from Sir William Osler, a famous late-nineteenth-century Canadian physician: "There are three sexes, men, women, and doctors," but smiled and said, "That's perfectly all right. She'll be here on Wednesday afternoon and unless it's urgent . . ." The recognition that some women did prefer being seen by another woman was, after all, one of the main reasons Nonie had been appointed to replace Jenny Bradley.

"Thank you, sir. I'll come back." The patient let herself out by the side door.

Barry felt a flicker of irritation. It hardly seemed fair that the stranger should be inconvenienced because Nonie had wanted to get away early, but then in fairness the patient could have seen Barry if she'd wished.

He smiled at Julie. "Come on, you two," Barry said, and waited for the Donnellys to follow him. "I know why you're here. Donal told us when we were on the beach a couple of weeks back. A little brother or sister for Victoria?" He ushered them into the surgery.

They sat on the two hard wooden chairs and he took the swivel one in front of the old rolltop desk.

"And this is your third pregnancy, Julie."

"Yes, sir, you'd remember," Julie said. "I lost the first."

"I do indeed," Barry said. Hadn't he run her up to the Royal in his own car when she'd miscarried her first? "But then you had wee Tori."

"She's at her granny's so we could come in and see you," Donal said.

"I appreciate that," Barry said. Consultations without the pleasure of the company of active toddlers always went more smoothly. "Now," he said, crossing to the filing cabinet where records were stored, "let's get some details." Barry went through the routine questions so familiar to him now as to be second nature. "Right," he said, doing Naegele's calculations in his head, "that makes you fifteen weeks today." He knew what Julie's greatest fear would be, so added, "Past the time most miscarriages happen."

"That's a relief," she said. "I'd not want to lose another one."

"Not likely now," Barry said, "and your due date's July the twelfth."

"Wheeker," said Donal with a broad grin. "The anniversary of the Battle of the Boyne. If the wee lad arrives on time, we'll call him William after King Billy of glorious and immortal memory, so we will."

"Donal," Julie said. "It might be another wee girl."

"Will it be a boy or a girl, I wonder." A frowning Donal looked at Barry as if he might know the answer to the question.

"Yes, it will," said Barry. "I can promise you that."

He could see by the way Donal's face screwed up that the truth of the statement was taking a moment to sink in. Then he chuckled and said, "No harm ti yiz, sir, but you're so sharp you'll cut yourself, so you will, Doctor Laverty."

Barry laughed, and said, "Exactly, Donal. I'm a doctor, not a fortune-teller." He rose. "Come on, Julie, let's get a good look at you."

She stood and handed him a small bottle containing amber fluid. "I brung my specimen," she said.

"Thank you. I'll test it while you're getting ready." He pulled back the screens round a new examining couch that Nonie had suggested was needed the day she'd been interviewed last year. Barry smiled. Fingal was a good man and he could not have asked for a better partner, but when it came to spending money, the man would wrestle a bear for a halfpenny, as they said in Ballymena. But he had been persuaded to make the purchase when Nonie had pointed out that the costs could be a deduction from his income tax.

"Just be a minute." Barry worked over the sink. The reagent-impregnated cardboard sticks were a great advance over having to mix stinking chemicals with the urine. He was happy to see that none of the Dipsticks had changed colour. "Urine's clear," he said, rinsing out the bottle. He went in behind the screens.

A complete physical examination confirmed that Julie's

uterus was of the correct size and its top had already risen into the abdomen. It was too early to listen for a foetal heart. He had detected no unusual signs except that her systolic blood pressure, the pressure in the arteries at that point in the heart's cycle known as systole, when the great pump contracted to push the blood round the body, was 130. It should be 120, but it was a well-known phenomenon that the stress of merely visiting a doctor could affect the systolic pressure. Of more import was her diastolic pressure, that which occurred when the heart relaxed to fill up with returned blood. It was only 80, and with a pregnant woman the doctor's alarm bells should only start to ring if the level was 85 or higher. But he made a note on the chart. It would bear keeping an eye on at subsequent antenatal visits. Julie finished dressing and together they went back from behind the screens.

"I'm pleased to say that everything seems to be spot on." Not entirely true, but concerning her now about what was probably a finding of no consequence would serve no useful purpose. "I just need to give you the lab forms to take to Bangor hospital." He kept some already filled in for routine antenatal care and simply had to add her personal details. Work of but a few moments. He gave her the requisitions.

So far progress was essentially normal, but of course that was the thing about obstetrics. No pregnancy was low risk until the bairn was in the crib and the mother doing well. "Everything looks fine. No reason you can't have the wean at home. Off you trot now, and come back in three weeks or if anything worries you," Barry said.

"Thank you, Doctor Laverty," she said.

Barry walked with them to the door of the surgery. "Safe home," he said as they left the house.

Barry stood for a moment, then turned and surveyed the slightly shabby, old-fashioned room with its brand-new examining couch. New life was growing inside Julie Donnelly and the thought gave him a sharp thrill of delight. Midwifery was fun. Nearly all the time you ended up with a healthy baby and happy, grateful parents. It made up for some of the more depressing times, dealing with fatal or crippling diseases, which fortunately were not common in general practice. Julie was going to be fine. Second, third, and fourth pregnancies usually were.

And Nonie and her antics? He grinned. Nothing to worry about. Not a damn thing. He started to climb the stairs.

He was looking forward to that jar. O'Reilly was probably home by now. He'd had to go to Bangor for something this afternoon and had, as was ethical, suggested to Barry that as he'd be passing the Houstons' he might just pop in even if the lab results were not back yet. Barry certainly had not objected. He was well aware of his senior's propensity for keeping an eye on his more vulnerable patients.

7

He Is Lost to the Forest

"It is quare and decent of you til pop in like this, Doctor O'Reilly," Maggie Houston said as she fondled the remaining ear of her cat, General Sir Bernard Law Montgomery. "You're holding your own, aren't you, Sonny. He's still not at himself, but he's no worse than he was on Friday, and now that them tests have been done, it's easier to bide til we see what's what. But it's a shame about Jasper."

"It is, Maggie. It is." O'Reilly glanced out the window to the threatening skies as he tugged the blood pressure cuff from Sonny's arm. Maggie pursed her lips, inhaled, then brightened. "Doctor, are you sure you'd not like a cup of tea in your hand and a bit of plum cake for your sweet—"

"I am truly sorry the animal's not home yet," O'Reilly said with some feeling, hoping his remark might waylay Maggie's question. "I don't like to think of him out there on his own." He wound the tubes of his sphygmomanometer into a coil around the cuff and tucked it into his bag. All of Sonny's vital signs were good, and he thought the man's colour was better and his breathing a little less laboured.

"Aye," said Sonny, "I'm worried too. You know, Doctor, I've always had a wheen of dogs. Some of them wander off once in a while, particularly if there's a bitch on heat around, but only in the summer, and they always show up in a couple of days."

"But Jasper's eyesight's going. So's his hearing," Maggie said. "I don't think the poor thing has been able to find his way in the snow. Maybe he can't pick up scents no more neither. He'll be lonely, and scared, and cold."

"Getting old stinks," Sonny said. "Look at me."

"For a man of your age, Sonny Houston, you're not in bad shape at all," O'Reilly said, "and Doctor Laverty will have you in fine fettle very soon." As soon as Sonny's test results were in, Barry would get right on top of things and O'Reilly would not interfere. The young man was fulfilling his earlier promise of being a first-class GP.

"I hope so." Sonny moved in his chair to make more room for a rotund little dog, Missy, who had whelped last May. One of her pups, Murphy, was Colin Brown's now. "At least I've all kinds of people looking after me. Poor old Jasper has nobody. Got him when he was just a wee pup. I was walking through the Ballybucklebo Hills one October day and there he was hiding in a culvert. I took him home, called a few people. I went over to my next-door neighbour Mister Doran . . . I'd heard he'd got a pup." Sonny shrugged. "I got told in no uncertain terms to mind my own business. Asked if I was insinuating he'd abandoned the wee pup."

"Used to be a patient of mine," O'Reilly said. "There are more civil men in the townland." He curled his lip. "I'd not put it past him to have done that."

Sonny nodded, inhaled. "So I advertised in the *Spectator*," he said, "but nobody claimed him. That was sixteen years ago now. I've had him longer than any of the others. Ordinarily I'd have gone looking for him by now, but . . ." He shrugged.

"I understand," O'Reilly said, and felt a squeeze in his heart for his old friend and patient. Sonny and Maggie had married late in life, too late to have a family, and the dogs were like children to them. It would be hard to be ill, forced to face your own physical limitations, and have the worry about a dog you loved.

"We've phoned the police and the animal welfare folks, but we've heard nothing back," Maggie said.

"And we've rung up our friends and neighbours, of course, but no one's seen him."

Sonny looked down at the little dog on his lap.

"I suppose I could spread the word in the village and if any of the doctors are out on home visits to farmers we could ask," O'Reilly said. "Would you like that?"

"We certainly would," Sonny said. "Doctor O'Reilly, you are a grand man for helping folks. That's what twenty-one years here has made you. You're our Doctor Fix-It, whether it's medical or not." The man grinned and reached up to dash a tear from one of his eyes.

"I promise I'll do what I can. Now I must be running along."

"I think, sir," Maggie said a few minutes later when he was putting on his boots in the hall, "that you don't care for my plum cake." There was a pointedness in her voice and her look was stern.

"Now that's an awful thing to say, Maggie Houston. Look at me," he said, patting his stomach. "Do I look like someone who would turn down good food freely offered? But it's five thirty, nearly my teatime. We're having one of Kinky's beef stews with cobbler topping, and we've invited Doctor Laverty in at six for drinks before dinner. So I must be on my way."

As he walked to the car, a thought struck O'Reilly. Where else to spread the word faster about Jasper but in the Duck. A trip there before dinner was definitely indicated.

⬚

O'Reilly caught up with Barry halfway up the staircase.

"Evening, Fingal," Barry said. "How was Bangor?"

"Got a couple of boxes of twelve-bore shotgun cartridges. Wildfowling season finishes at the end of the month and I'm hoping for one more day out on Strangford Lough with Arthur before then. I popped in with Sonny and Maggie. He's not much changed, that's no surprise, and their blooming dog's still missing. Poor Jasper. I know how Sonny feels. I'd go daft if Arthur disappeared." He preceded Barry into the upstairs lounge, where Kitty, back from her job as a senior neurosurgery sister at the Royal Victoria Hospital in Belfast, was already ensconced in her usual chair. "We're home," O'Reilly said, and brushed her shoulder with his hand. "How was work?"

"Bloody," she said, "if you must know. It's so good to be home. I'm well and truly knackered. Thank God I've got a day off tomorrow. Your pal Charlie Greer can be a right old targe when things don't go right. He always apologises afterward, but it was pretty fraught for a while. And today that combination of demanding families—and there were two today—and the regular needs of the patients was just too much. I know we're meant to understand why they're demanding—they're worried, I do understand, of course. But honestly, sometimes."

O'Reilly leaned forward and began to massage her

shoulders. "Kitty, you're human, not a flaming saint. It's all right to get irritated once in a while, isn't it, Barry?"

"Absolutely," Barry said. "A good rant with folks you trust around you is very healthy. Excellent for bringing raised blood pressure down."

"Thank you both," she said, slowly moving her head from one side to the other, "and don't stop that massage, Fingal. It's heavenly. We had a sisters' meeting too. Interminable. You know how I hate meetings."

"I do indeed." O'Reilly kneaded away. "What you need is a gin and tonic. Barry, will you do the honours?"

"Of course." Barry moved to the sideboard and O'Reilly heard the clinking of bottle and glass. "And as your medical advisor, I prescribe it be taken according to doctor's orders . . . in a hot bubble bath."

"You are incorrigible, Fingal O'Reilly, and I know you. You're taking Barry to the Duck, aren't you?" There was no rancour in her voice. She chuckled.

"Reads me like a book, Barry," he said. "You'll find out soon enough."

"I'm looking forward to it," Barry said, and handed Kitty her drink.

"And we have a good reason to go."

"You always do," Kitty said, still smiling. "Its name is Guinness. And the *craic*."

"No. Honestly. Not this time. The Houstons' dog, Jasper, is still missing."

"Aah. Now that's a shame," Kitty said. "Poor old thing."

"I promised we'd spread the word and where better to start than—?"

"—at the centre of the male universe of Ballybucklebo. You two trot along. I bought a brand-new bottle of Badedas last Saturday, but"—she inclined her head and fixed O'Reilly with her gaze—"please don't be late for supper."

〽️

Same old comfortable Mucky Duck, O'Reilly thought, as he and Arthur Guinness followed Barry inside. The warmth, the fug, the tobacco fumes, the beery smells and dim lights. Most of the tables in the single, low-ceilinged room were occupied. Men in Ulster overcoats, mufflers, dunchers, or paddy hats were lined up along the bar. A hum of conversation that sounded as if the room was filled with industrious bees rose and fell the while, punctuated by occasional caws of laughter, clinking of glass on glass.

"... No harm til yiz, but away you off and chase yourself, Mister Bishop. See your man Colonel Hogan. See him? He's never going to let the Nazis transfer Colonel Klink and Sergeant Schultz away from the camp, so he's not. They're far too important to Hogan's plans. You mark my words." Dermot Kennedy, who clearly took the TV programme very seriously, stabbed the tabletop with one index finger.

Since his heart attack, Bertie Bishop had taken to dropping into the Duck for his daily permitted one pint. Constable Malcolm Mulligan, who must be off duty, and his friend Mister Coffin, the undertaker, nodded in agreement.

"I've been watching *Hogan's Heroes* since it started on BBC in '65," Bertie said. "And I think them two characters is gettin' stale. That there Sergeant Schultz is a few too many clowns short of a circus if you ask me. I think Hogan needs more of a challenge."

"How's your Bluebird, Donal?" asked Fergus Finnegan,

the Marquis of Ballybucklebo's jockey and captain of
the Bonnaughts rugby football team. "I know you
stopped racin' her because you couldn't get decent odds
no more, but the word's out you're training her up again."
He, Donal, and Dapper Frew were sitting together.

"Coming on a treat, so she is."

Donal winked at Dapper.

What were they cooking up?

Barry said, "Can you order the drinks, Fingal? I want
a quick word with Dapper."

"Go ahead."

Barry made his way to the estate agent's table.

Lenny Brown and his pal Gerry Shanks were leaning
against the bar where it turned at right angles near the
door. "How's about youse, Doctors?" Lenny called loudly.

Conversation stopped as if someone had thrown a
switch. All eyes turned on O'Reilly, who said, "Good
evening to this house."

A chorus of greetings filled the room.

"Don't mind us," O'Reilly said, "not until we've a jar
in our hands and a drop into ourselves. But then I'll
want your attention."

"Don't like the sound of that," muttered Gerry
Shanks.

"Och, hould your wheest," Lenny said. "If Doctor
O'Reilly wants til tell us something I'm sure it'll be all
right. Now move over, you bollix, and let the doctor
order."

Conversations were resumed throughout the room.

O'Reilly moved to the bar, where Mary, the owner
Willie Dunleavy's plump daughter, was drying a glass.
"Two pints, please, Mary."

"And a Smithwick's for Arthur?"

"Aye. Please."

"And there's a wee table just come empty at the front there now, so if youse'll have a seat, I'll bring the drinks over," she said.

O'Reilly noticed that the table in question, which had been occupied when they'd come in, had been vacated. He grinned. Rank did have its privileges.

"Under," O'Reilly said, sitting and pointing to show Arthur the way.

Barry came back and plopped into a chair with a sigh. "This place feels like home." He unbuttoned his overcoat and pulled off his cap.

"It is part of your home, you eejit," O'Reilly said.

Barry smiled. "That's what I was talking to Dapper about. He says there's a lovely bungalow that's not even on the market yet. He's going to phone me when I can see it."

"A house? You mean for you and Sue?" said O'Reilly.

"No, Fingal. I thought I'd do a spot of real estate speculating to augment my meagre income."

"Less of your lip, you young pup. If it suits, I hope you get it, but I have to say we'll miss you around Number One, Main."

"And I'll miss you and Kinky and Kitty, believe me. But it's not far away, and I want Sue and me to start off our married life together in a bit of style."

"Fair enough. You'll keep me posted?"

"Of course."

"Your pints, sir." Mary set two black Guinnesses with creamy heads on the table. "I'll bring Arthur's in a wee minute."

"Thanks, Mary. Here you are." O'Reilly paid the six shillings and thruppence with exact change, hoisted his drink, said *"Sláinte,"* and took a pull. "Mother's milk," he said, wiping foam off his upper lip.

"Cheers," Barry said, and drank.

Mary reappeared and shoved Arthur's bowl under the table.

O'Reilly heard a rumbling "woof," and a happy "yip." He looked under to see Arthur lapping from one side and his friend, Brian Boru, Mary's feisty and sex-mad Chihuahua, from the other.

All right, O'Reilly thought. Let's get this done. He rose, stuck two fingers in his mouth, and let go a whistle that might have challenged one on a steam locomotive. "Listen, everybody—"

". . . and your man says—" Donal, the last to realise that O'Reilly was demanding attention, cut himself off in mid-sentence. "Sorry, Doc."

Silence. Every eye was on O'Reilly.

"You all know Sonny and Maggie Houston. One of their dogs, Jasper, an old Labrador-poodle cross with floppy ears, has got himself lost. I'd like everybody to keep an eye out, ask their neighbours to do the same, look in your outbuildings."

A chorus of "Och, dear," and "That's ferocious, so it is," and "Poor wee doggy."

"He jumped out of my car just before the hill up to the Houstons' and took off like a liltie into the blizzard on Friday. No one's seen him since."

Bertie Bishop rose, put his thumbs behind his coat's lapels, and said, "Youse all know me and Sonny have had our differences . . ."

O'Reilly heard the murmurings of assent.

". . . but we've buried the hatchet. Sonny Houston is very fond of all of his dogs. I think we need to do more than just look in our own backyards. I think we need a search party." Bertie Bishop was a congenital organiser.

The crowd roared approval. Voices clashed as suggestions flew.

Now there's an idea, O'Reilly thought. "I agree," he said, and was happy to sit back and let the other men make the arrangements. O'Reilly reckoned he and Barry had time to finish their first pints and start on a second while matters were being sorted out.

Finally Bertie said, "We'll meet tomorrow morning, nine o'clock. Under the oak tree at the crossroads at the bottom of the Ballybucklebo Hills. Anyone with a dog that can hunt, bring it. Doctor O'Reilly, sir, I don't know if you've been paying attention, but a lot of the lads would like for you to take charge."

O'Reilly smiled and bowed his head to Bertie. "Honoured to be of service. And thank you, Bertie, for the excellent suggestion of a search. Barry, can you and Nonie cope tomorrow?" O'Reilly said. "I'd like to go. Give Arthur a run."

"Sure."

"Then Arthur and I'll be there at nine."

The room broke into applause and gradually the buzz of individual conversations resumed.

O'Reilly glanced at the clock above the bar. "Plenty of time until dinner," he said. "No need to rush our pints." He sat forward. "Now we've done what I promised I'd do," he said, "Barry, I'd like to ask your advice?"

"Fire away."

"I'm sure you know that today's not the first time Kitty's come home banjaxed from work. I do worry about her."

Barry steepled his fingers, held O'Reilly's gaze, and

said nothing. The classic medical approach to counselling. His next move, according to the protocol, would be a sympathetic, "And how do *you* feel about that?"

O'Reilly chuckled. "Son," he said, "I recognise that expression. And the MO. But look, I'm asking you as my friend, not as a bloody shrink. I'm worried about Kitty. That's hardly a psychiatric symptom."

Barry laughed. "I'm sorry," he said. "It's force of, as Donal might say, force of rabbit. So you think Kitty works too hard?"

O'Reilly nodded. "I do. And now with you and Nonie aboard, and Doctor Fitzpatrick from the Kinnegar going to join the rota in February when he's fully recovered from his surgery, I'll have a lot more leisure time. I'd like my wife to be able to spend some of it with me."

"Why not ask her to retire or go part time? I imagine the pair of you could afford it."

O'Reilly smiled. "Kitty's supported herself all her life. I'm not sure she'd be happy with nothing to do but be the doctor's wife."

Barry stroked his chin. "See what you mean. I can tell how Sue would react. She'd tell me to take a lengthy walk off a tiny pier. She's very proud of the job she does, as she should be." He sipped his pint. "And I suppose Kitty wouldn't be interested in helping out with the practice. We could use some administrative help. Those medical service forms are getting more complicated every year and there are times when a nurse on staff would be invaluable. Still, she's a highly trained neurological nursing sister. She probably wouldn't think much of that kind of work."

"She might find it a relief after days like today."

"I'm no great student of military history, but at school we learned about the Ulstermen at the battle of the

Somme. If there was a lesson, it was try to avoid frontal attacks. Try outflanking the obstacle. She said she's off duty tomorrow, didn't she?"

O'Reilly nodded.

"Do you think she'd enjoy a day out in the country with you?"

"She always has," O'Reilly said.

"Why not bring up the question gently while you're out walking. And make sure she has a good day, so she can see what she's missing."

"It's worth a try," O'Reilly said. "And I'll take her on holiday again once you're safely married off." He chuckled. "A couple of years ago I advised you, 'Softly, softly catchee monkee,' now it's your turn to tell me the same thing, and I think you're bang on. Thanks, pal." O'Reilly looked at the clock above the bar. "Right," he said, finishing his pint, "drink up, and home to Kinky's beef stew with cobbler topping."

8

I Did Search for Thee

Kitty and O'Reilly stood beneath the bare branches of the three-hundred-year-old oak tree at the foot of the Ballybucklebo Hills, Arthur between them. His tail pumped back and forth, hitting their blackthorn walking sticks with a series of *thwack*s.

Kitty inhaled a great lungful of air and clapped her mittened hands together. "I love the way people here pull together when someone needs help." She squeezed his arm. "In fact, I love it here just for being with you."

O'Reilly grinned. Dear Kitty. He thought she looked well today in her olive green three-quarter-length Barbour coat, her animated face peeking out from the false-fur-trimmed hood. She'd been back to her old self at dinner last night, but today there were circles under her eyes, and her sleep had been restless. How he loved her. He'd try to grant her anything she wished for—except perhaps new curtains in the dining room.

He surveyed his assembled troops. "Yes, it's a good turnout," he said with satisfaction. They stood in front of a group of twenty men, each stoutly booted, warmly clad, some smoking, all chatting, joking, clearly in good spirits and looking forward to the day's outing. Eight other dogs of various breeds were darting among the crowd, wagging tails and sniffing noses.

"I didn't know your brother Lars was a horseman," Kitty said.

"Neither did I," O'Reilly said, "and judging by the way he keeps shifting in his saddle, I'm damn sure he's not at home up there. But he phoned last night to say that Bertie had been in touch with the marquis and that he and his sister and Lars were able to take the day off and were coming today. Occasionally Lars works too hard. He needs to take it easier." He glanced at Kitty sideways, but it didn't seem as if the remark had registered.

Lars, looking awkward in riding boots, jodhpurs, and a Donegal tweed hacking jacket, reached up to adjust the velvet-covered peaked riding helmet perched on his head. He sat astride a small chestnut mare who was contentedly cropping the grass where she stood. Beside them, a tall bay gelding bore the twenty-seventh Marquis of Ballybucklebo, Lord John MacNeill. The man looked as if he'd been riding since infancy, which he probably had. Perhaps before. His mother, by all accounts, had been mad for the hunt, and the marquis may have spent his first months in utero jostled up and down, over fences and ditches.

John had sent word last night that he would meet the foot party and bring the ten couples of hounds of the Ballybucklebo Hunt. The marquis's widowed sister, Lady Myrna Ferguson, was here too, and like her brother sat her black mount as if to the manner born. She must have had no classes scheduled at Queen's University today, where she was a lecturer in inorganic chemistry.

O'Reilly knew this might be her and the marquis's last chance to ride to the hounds. "John told me last autumn when he and I were snipe shooting that he was being forced to sell his thoroughbred hunters. The family will keep on a couple of hacks like Lars's mount. John'll continue to provide kennels for the hounds because it's the annual subscriptions of the members of the hunt that pay for them and the hunt servants. It's sad," O'Reilly said. "They both love hunting, but it's a huge expense running the estate."

"I didn't know about the horses," Kitty said. "It is a pity, but I suppose the days of keeping a stableful of hunters is over for the MacNeills. Life is changing for the aristocracy."

The three equestrians were surrounded by the pack of liver, white, and black hounds that milled round the horses' legs, barking and baying, legs stiff, tails erect.

"The dogs are raring to go. I'd better get things moving," O'Reilly said. He raised his voice and called, "Right. Let's get ourselves organised. You all know the hills, and we don't want to be tripping over each other. We need to cover as much ground as possible." He turned to the marquis. "So I propose, my lord, that you, Lady Myrna, and Mister O'Reilly take the centre section, which is about a quarter of a mile wide and mostly heather and bracken. Better going for the horses. But please hang on here until the rest of the search party's in place."

"We'll do that," the marquis said. "Let the hounds quarter it. If the dog's there they'll find him and they won't hurt him. They like other dogs."

"Thank you, sir." O'Reilly turned back to the others. "I need you folks to space out at equal intervals from both sides of the area the hunt will be covering to the far edges of the woods and thickets." The group were all experienced outdoorsmen and needed no further instructions from him. Surely if poor old Jasper were out here he'd be found? He might even remember the culvert he'd taken cover in as a puppy where Sonny had found Jasper sixteen years ago.

"Now," said O'Reilly, "this morning we'll be climbing up to the crest, where Mister Bishop will have lunch laid on beside the old watchtower. Let's hope we've found Jasper by then. If not, we'll take a break and then cover the other side of the hills as far as the Comber Road in the afternoon. At least it will be easier going downhill."

A piped series of *pee-wit, pee-wit* came from overhead and he looked up. "Green plover, also called lapwing," he said to Kitty, who had been a city girl until she'd married him. The birds, with their green-tinted backs, white bellies, and black breasts, throats, crowns, and crests, tumbled across the cold, eggshell-blue sky.

"They really are pretty," she said. "I've never seen them before. I remember how much your father loved birds. How you and Lars set up a feeding table right outside his window in Dublin."

O'Reilly smiled. "Father did love his birds," he said. "Bless him. So does Lars."

Lars's mare whinnied loudly. O'Reilly looked over to see her tossing her head and mane, Lars with eyes wide, clenching his teeth, his hands clutching the reins, and Myrna sidling her horse over and calming the animal.

"I think," O'Reilly called, "it's time to get moving. Any questions?" He waited, but none came. "Let's get started." He produced a referee's whistle. "I'll give us a wheep on this when we're all ready so we can start together."

There were general mutterings of assent. O'Reilly waited as searchers strode past him to take up their positions. Patches of snow were scattered on the lower slopes, and the ridgeline was covered and glistening in the weak morning sunlight. The breath of horses, dogs, and people hung on the crisp, still air.

"So, big brother," O'Reilly said as he moved to stand in front of Lars's mount and stroke the horse's soft cheek, smelling her hay-sweet breath, "since when have you been riding?"

"Since he started coming to Ballybucklebo House to help us give most of our lands to the National Trust," said the marquis.

"Your brother, Fingal, is working like a demon for us," said Myrna. "And we're so grateful. It looks as though we'll still have the rights to live there, farm there, and shoot there. He is remarkably industrious and creative." She looked at him and nodded her head. "But he's shy, and does not get nearly enough exercise. I've taken him in hand."

Lars sighed and smiled. "She insists we go riding twice a week, and talked me into coming today. I've learned how to get on—"

"Mount," Myrna said. "Mount. Let's get the terms right. I'd have thought solicitors were sticklers for exactitude when it comes to language." She shook her head but was still smiling. "You, my dear Lars, may know about tort and *res ipsa loquitur,* and the names and breeding habits of hundreds of orchids, but when we started you couldn't tell a cannon from a pastern or a hock from a gaskin."

"Those are parts of a horse, but I won't tell you which ones," Lars said, glancing at Myrna with a grin.

"I'm sure I hardly know one end of a horse from the other." Kitty smiled and winked at O'Reilly. "But I'm impressed. And you're learning, Lars?"

"So far, Kitty, I can walk and trot and we're working on my cantering . . ." He laughed.

Goodness, O'Reilly thought, my usually reserved brother seems to be coming out of himself.

"And so far—so far, I haven't fallen off."

"There are only two kinds of horsemen," said Myrna. "Those who have fallen off and those who are going to. You will, someday. But not today."

This coming from a woman who not so long ago had been thrown and had fractured her now-healed femur. She'd been very brave throughout the whole thing and O'Reilly had got to know and like Lady Myrna Ferguson better and better.

"You'll be fine, Lars. This is Rubidium, thirty-seventh element in the periodic table. Ruby for short. She's as good a horse as there is. Gentle as a kitten. You'll be perfectly safe with Ruby."

A voice O'Reilly recognised came from the left. Donal Donnelly had been released from work today by his boss, Bertie Bishop, to take part. "All set this side, sir."

"Same here," came from Lenny Brown on O'Reilly's right.

"Right, come on, Kitty. See you all for lunch," O'Reilly said. "And no galloping, Lars. Kitty and I are off duty and don't want to be setting any broken bones."

The marquis saluted by touching his crop to the peak of his hard hat.

O'Reilly took Kitty's hand and together they trudged fifty yards from the open area. Donal stood fifty yards farther out.

O'Reilly put his whistle between his lips, looked to each side, nodded to himself, and blew a long blast. "Hey on out, Arthur," he said, and the big dog obeyed.

The small ploughed field smelt of earth, and mud clung to his boots. He didn't expect to find Jasper here. There seemed to be nowhere to hide, but they wouldn't know until they'd walked it. "Not finding the going too bad, pet?" O'Reilly asked.

"Not one bit," she said, matching him pace for pace. "It feels so good to just walk in the open air. I wish I could take a walk when I'm at the hospital, but it's so darn busy I usually just grab a bite at mealtime and keep working."

Before O'Reilly could follow up on that cue, she'd changed the subject. "Arthur's having fun. Look."

The big Lab was running along the edge of a drainage ditch, nose to the ground, tail in the air.

She pointed at a herd of cows grazing in the next field. "What kind are those?"

"Dexters," he said. "Good for both milk and beef."

A sudden hoarse craking and clattering of pinions accompanied two teal as they sprang into the air and flew away.

"Pretty wee birds," O'Reilly said. "Tasty roasted too. Don't let Lars hear me say that, though."

"As long as you don't expect me to pluck and gut them, I'll cook them for you anytime." She looked him in the eye. "Aren't the eye patches on the lead bird pretty? I think teal blue would be a very good colour for the dining room."

So she wasn't going to drop the quest for new curtains. O'Reilly opened a gate standing in the middle of the open field. There was no flanking wall, fence, nor hedge. The gate closed off the bridge over the drainage ditch that flowed between the two fields. "And I think that today we're looking for a lost dog. We're getting close to culverts where he may be hiding." Cows had wandered over, and he moved closer to Kitty, not wanting her frightened by so many big animals. He needn't have worried.

She clapped her hands, yelling, "Get away to hell out of that," and they lumbered off. "I'm not a complete city girl," she said. "Dad used to take us on picnics in farmers' fields in County Wicklow. They call it the garden of Ireland, so green, and Glendalough is stunning. Mum loved Saint Kevin's Monastery."

O'Reilly sang,

In Glendalough lived an ould saint,
Renowned for learning and piety
His manners were curious and quaint
And he looked upon girls with disparity.

"But I don't. I love you, city girl," said O'Reilly, closing the gate. He took her hand and together they followed Arthur as he crashed through several clumps of yellow-flowered gorse, scattering their almond scent, and rabbits that scuttled off, white tails bobbing. O'Reilly and Kitty spent most of the time avoiding stepping in steaming piles of fresh cow clap.

He clambered atop a low dry stone wall and held out his hand. "Let me help you."

Kitty took his hand and he hauled her up. He was going to jump down when Kitty held her free hand above her eyes and said, "Good Lord, whatever's going on over there? And listen to that."

As they had progressed, O'Reilly had glanced from time to time to the clear area to his right. The pack was spread out across the fields and the three equestrians spaced out across the ground had been following the dogs at a leisurely walk. Things had changed. "Holy

Moses," he said, "I think they've started a fox and the hounds are off in full cry." The air was rent by the belling of twenty foxhounds now racing along in a much tighter pack close on the heels of a low russet animal tearing diagonally to cross in front of where O'Reilly and Kitty stood.

Myrna could be heard yelling, "Tallyho," the traditional cry of a hunter who has the fox in view. She was leading, crouched low in the saddle, her horse's hooves pounding on the turf. O'Reilly could hear the animal snorting. "Stay up there, Kitty," O'Reilly said. "This could get exciting. Usually in a hunt, the huntsman and the whippers-in control the dogs. I can see John. He's trying to get ahead of them to stop them, but Myrna's got her blood up, and . . . oh Lord, look at Lars."

"Heaven help the poor man," Kitty said, then yelled, "Hang on, Lars!"

Lars's mare knew her duty. She might be named for a chemical element, but she was a horse. And she had a rider on her back, and ahead the pack was after a fox. Her job, even if she wasn't thoroughbred, was to join in. The little mare was stretched out in a full gallop, bounding forward, nostrils flaring. Lars clearly neither knew his duty nor was able to carry it out. No yells of "view halloo," no soaring along in rhythm with his mount. O'Reilly's poor brother was crouched forward on the horse's neck and had both arms wrapped round it. One rein had worked loose from his grasp and was flying free. Fear was in his eyes. And unless checked, he'd tear past within yards of where O'Reilly and Kitty stood, heading straight for trees with low branches.

"Stay put," O'Reilly said to Kitty, and before she could protest he'd jumped down, taken a few paces, and now stood directly in the horse's path, hoping to God

he correctly recalled reading that horses had a patho-
logical aversion to trampling on people. If Ruby was as
gentle as Myrna said, surely she'd stop.

He glanced at Kitty, who stood on the wall staring at
him, hands clasped in supplication in front of her face.
She was silent, apparently understanding that the last
thing he needed was to be distracted by cries of "Take
care!" or "Look out!"

Horse and rider were so close he could smell the animal's sweat, was almost deafened by the sounds of
hooves. As they swept by, he yelled, "Whoa," grabbed
the free rein, and hauled, trying to force the animal's
head to the side and down. The stink of the horse's
sweat was overpowering. He was jerked off his feet,
thought both arms had been yanked from their sockets,
avoided the flying nearside front hoof, and to his great
relief realised the animal was slowing down.

He was dragged for several yards before the horse
stopped, looked down at him with huge, apologetic, liquid brown eyes, tried to shake her head, and made a
rubbery sound with her lips.

O'Reilly, feeling bruised, but knowing nothing was
broken, got to his feet. He held on to the rein, and gentled the beast. "Easy, Ruby, easy old girl. Easy."

She nuzzled him as a breathless Lars slipped from the
saddle.

"You all right, brother?" Lars gasped.

"I'll live," O'Reilly said. "How about you?"

"I don't give a damn what Myrna's going to think. I
never want to see one of these blasted creatures again.
What in the name of the wee man was she playing at,
tearing off with the pack after that fox. Someone, and
that someone was me, could have been killed."

"All right, Fingal? Lars?" Kitty had scrambled off the

wall and was standing close to O'Reilly. "I thought you were both going to get marmalized. I think, Fingal Flahertie O'Reilly, that you've seen too many Westerns. You are *not* John Wayne." Her eyes blazed, but O'Reilly knew her anger was that of relief that both men were safe and sound—or in his case relatively sound. He ached in muscles he'd forgotten he had. He was going to be stiff for a few days.

"Come on, Kitty," he said. "I've had worse boxing or playing rugby." And, O'Reilly thought, but would not consider voicing, a few bruises were nothing to what might very well have happened to Lars among the trees if the horse hadn't been stopped.

"Are you sure?"

"Yes, pet. Honestly. I'm like James Bond's martinis, a bit shaken, but not stirred."

She laughed, shook her head, and said, "Do you see why I love your buck eejit of a little brother, Lars? He's not quite right in the head." She pecked his cheek, stepped back, and said, "All right. We're all safe. Now what?"

"Lord knows where John and Myrna have got to, but I'll bet when they get things straightened out they'll come back this way and continue the search. Lars, I seem to remember an adage about immediately remounting if you are thrown—"

"I was not thrown, but I could have been. And I have no intention of getting back on Ruby."

"Someone has to get the horse back to Ballybucklebo House, and it's not going to be me. I think," and he looked his brother right in the eye, "it would put your stock up with Myrna if you carry on." He inclined his head to one side. Something about the way she'd teased Lars about his orchids and calmed his horse for him had set bells ringing for O'Reilly. Could his confirmed bachelor of a big brother have stirred something in Myrna Ferguson?

"Lady Myrna is a force of nature but she's been very good to me." Lars grinned. He cocked his head, frowned at the now docile animal, and blew out his breath through pursed lips. "All right. Give me the reins." He stood on the left side of the horse, held the reins in his left hand, and with it grabbed the front of the saddle. "I could use a boost, Fingal." Lars faced to the animal's rear.

O'Reilly bent, locked his hands into a shallow cup, and said, "Right foot in here." In a moment O'Reilly had straightened and thrust his hands up. Bruised muscles in his arms protested, but he kept a straight face.

Lars, as if he'd been mounting horses for years, landed in the saddle. "Thank you," he said. "I'll wait back in that treeless bit and see you both later for lunch. Keep an eye on him, Kitty, and Finn? Thank you for everything." He bent forward, nudged the horse's flanks with his boots, clicked his tongue, and said, "Walk on."

O'Reilly watched his brother, swaying rhythmically in the saddle, walk the horse back to the open field where farther ahead the pack, with John and Myrna in the lead, were emerging from the woods.

"I hope," said Kitty, "the poor old fox got away." She moved closer to him. "And," she kissed him soundly, "I hope I never ever have to watch you nearly getting yourself killed. That was a very brave thing you did."

"Och," said O'Reilly, always uncomfortable with praise, even if it did come from the woman he loved. "I only did what had to be done." And, not giving her a chance to continue, said, "We'd better try to catch up with the others. Come on, old girl. Jasper's got to be waiting for us somewhere."

9

Flowing Water Near the House

"Okay. Unless I ring you back, Dapper, to say I can't get away, I'll see you here as soon as you're finished with your client. I've just finished my home visits for the morning." Barry put the phone down and went into the dining room. "Busy surgery, Nonie?" he asked.

"Pretty routine for a Tuesday," she said, exhaling cigarette smoke. "Sorry about the cigarette," she said, waving her hands in the air. "I thought I had time for a quick one. Fingal and Kitty are out and Kinky's busy getting your lunch ready." She patted the chair next to hers. "Come and sit down. I was starving and Kinky's such a dear she served me first. Her cream of chicken soup was out of this world and she'll do you a heavenly Welsh rarebit."

"Actually," Barry said, "it's only twelve so I'm going to skip lunch if you'll do me a favour."

"For you, Barry? Anything. I'm so glad I have the afternoon off." Her smile was inviting and there was a hint of huskiness in her voice.

Being used to Sue, who was sparing with her makeup, Barry thought Nonie'd been a bit enthusiastic with the eye shadow. He had belonged to the Queen's University

Film Appreciation Society. Pictures of movie vamps like Theda Bara, Pola Negri, and Rita Hayworth flashed into his mind. He cleared his throat. "That's great," he said, keeping his voice light, "because I need you to cover for emergencies, just for an hour."

"Oh, dear. How thoroughly boring," she said, and crushed out her cigarette in a convenient ashtray. "Fingal's out on some silly search for a dog—"

"Come on, Nonie. Not just a dog. Jasper's a much-loved pet."

She shrugged. "I like dogs as well as the next girl. Arthur and I are old chums, but really, this search seems like a waste of time to me, but each to his own. I just thought, since the boss and Kitty aren't here and Kinky's going shopping once she's given you your lunch, that we could have some fun together." She exhaled with a grunt. "Oh, never mind," she said. "Yes, of course I'll cover for you for an hour. But I don't particularly want to sit in here or in the surgery and I only go upstairs when I'm invited. Could I wait in your quarters? They're much more comfortable than my little room in the attic. Sometimes I feel like the poor cousin up there."

"Sure," Barry had blurted out before the possible consequences dawned on him. He'd be coming home to a house deserted by everyone—everyone but a single, very attractive young woman who would be waiting in the privacy of his rooms.

She lifted one eyebrow, pushed her chair back, uncrossed her legs with a rustling of nylon, and walked past Barry. As she did she let one hand brush against his shoulder. "Thanks, Barry. Are you sure you have to go out?"

Barry swallowed. He felt the hairs on the nape of his neck tingle. Damn it all. Behave. You'll be seeing Sue in

February. He was struggling for a reply to her last remark when the front doorbell rang. "I do," he said, following her through the door, "and I'd appreciate it if
you don't smoke in my place."

"Of course I wouldn't." She managed to look hurt.
"Have a good time."

"Thanks." Barry grabbed his cap and coat from the
coatstand. He met Kinky, who was trotting along from
the kitchen to answer the door. "It's all right, Kinky. It's
for me, and I'm sorry, but I can't stay for lunch."

As he opened the door to Dapper Frew, he heard her
tutting behind him. "It does not be a good thing for a
young man to miss his meals, so."

"How's about ye, Doc?" Dapper asked, leading the
way to his new Mark II Ford Cortina.

"Grand, and yourself?" said Barry, who was having a
distinctly saved-by-the-bell feeling with Dapper's timely
arrival.

"Grand altogether. Now, let's get in quick," Dapper
said, holding the passenger door for Barry. "The road's
narrow here and I'm holding up the traffic."

"Right," said Barry.

As the estate agent nipped round the car, Barry
frowned. Nonie Stevenson might be a first-class physician and appreciated by many of the women patients,
but he was seeing some traits that he could not find
appealing. Smoking? The profession had known about
the link between tobacco and lung cancer for years. He
had to admit she was a damned sexy woman, but he
couldn't quite understand her.

Dapper climbed in, started the engine, and drove off
in the direction of Bangor, followed by a string of cars.
"This road was built before the motorcar was invented,"

Dapper said. "There's talk it should be widened, but och, I like it the way it is . . ." He shrugged. "Anyroad, it's not far to the wee house." Two cars passed him on a wider stretch. "The owners'll be out so you can get a good look, and I want, if I can, to stop them knowing a doctor's looking at the place."

"Whatever for?"

"Doctors are rich—"

Barry burst out laughing. "Not this one. I'm a country GP, Dapper. I make two thousand pounds a year before tax and deductions."

"Doctor, dear," Dapper said, "no harm til ye, but you're young. You don't know how the other half lives. If I can sell about ten or twelve houses a year I make about six hundred on commissions. A bloke like Donal? Maybe three hundred a year. Three hundred and fifty at the most, with his schemes on the side. Julie brings in a few quid more with her hair modelling."

"Gosh," Barry said as the car turned left and headed downhill toward the sea. "You're right, Dapper. I didn't even suspect. As long as I've had enough I've never thought about money much."

"Aye, well, lots of other people do think about it. They budget, work hard, and hope they can make both ends meet. And when it comes to selling a house, everyone's out to get the best possible price. I don't want to see you getting rooked because people think you're warm, so I don't."

"But will that not cut into your commission?"

"I get one and a half percent of the sale price, so if I save you two hundred pounds I only lose three quid. You can buy me a couple of pints."

"You're on," Barry said, and grinned.

Dapper drove under a single spandrel railway bridge just as the one-carriage diesel, known to the locals as "The Covered Wagon," rattled overhead. "The place is only a wee doddle from the Cultra Station, so if you don't want to use your car, you can be in Bangor or Belfast and points between like Ballybucklebo in no time."

Barry nodded.

Dapper turned left just past the bridge and onto a lane that passed between tall laurel hedges, behind which very grand three-storey granite or redbrick houses stood in extensive gardens.

"The real highheejins live here," Dapper said, "but wait til you see your bungalow. It's dead wheeker, so it is."

Dapper Frew, Barry thought, you're a damn fine salesman.

They left the leafy hedges behind and crossed a stretch of moorland. Dapper pulled up outside a low, white-washed wall that surrounded a whitewashed bungalow with a grey slate roof. They were at the rear of the house. To the left was an inlet of Belfast Lough that ended against a seawall some sixty yards inland of the bunga-low and not much farther to his right a similar inlet met the same wall. The property effectively was on its own small peninsula. He glanced behind him. The high boundary fence of one of the mansions blocked his view of the house itself, leaving the property in privacy. He took a lungful of air, tasting the saltiness on the air, smelling and hearing the sea.

"Come on, Doc, and we'll go in."

"Right." Barry followed Dapper through a black-painted wrought-iron gate. It squeaked on its hinges as it was closed.

Dapper headed for a back door painted in a light

brown that matched the window trim and opened it wide. "Come on on in."

Barry wiped his shoes on a coconut-fibre doormat and entered a small but functional kitchen overlooking the back garden, a stretch of heath, and a row of tall leafless elms in the near distance.

Dapper closed the door. "This here bungalow's nine hundred square feet. I'm going til give you the grand tour first and then if you want to see more—" Not waiting for a response, Dapper went through the kitchen door. Barry followed.

In less than ten minutes he had inspected two small bedrooms, a bathroom, and a larger bedroom. All neatly furnished. All, by Ulster standards, of a good size. Clean, warm, and practical but, Barry thought—and he had made a lot of home visits to a lot of houses—pretty much universal. Nothing to qualify for Dapper's description of "dead wheeker."

"Now," said Dapper, heading back past the kitchen door to where the hall made a right-angle turn to the left, "the lounge's in here. It's a lounge/dining room that runs the whole width of the house. There's a fireplace . . ." He grinned and opened the lounge door. "But come and see for yourself."

Barry realised that the estate agent had kept the best until last when Dapper spread his arms wide and said, "What do you think of that?"

Barry entered and his mouth dropped open. He'd look at the room later. Almost the entire front wall to his left was filled with a vast picture window.

And the view.

A trimmed lawn was surrounded by a perimeter path of white and black oval stones. A solitary bed, flower-less in January, stood in the centre of the lawn. Barry barely heard Dapper's, "There's a wee snag with the front garden. I hope you and your missus-to-be aren't keen gardeners. Nothing grows this close til the sea but nasturtiums and snapdragons."

And close they were. The garden was thirty feet from house to whitewashed wall. Beyond the wall fifty yards of coarse marram grass stretched to where jagged rocks tumbled fifteen feet to a rocky shore. From out in Belfast Lough grey combers rolled in, rank after rank, to growl and crash as they dashed themselves into far-flung spray.

Past the shore Barry could look to his left and see a freighter nearing the port of Belfast, or Béal Feirste, meaning the mouth of the sandbanks. Cave Hill was in view on the upper far side of the lough, marching east with the Antrim Hills. On their top, the Knockagh monument, a needle obelisk, pierced grey clouds. At their feet squatted Carrickfergus Castle.

If Barry closed his eyes he could picture John de Courcy's men at arms supervising its building in 1177 and hear the clash of steel on steel and the sibilant hissing of flights of goose-feather-fletched longbow arrows as King John Lackland laid siege to it in 1210. With her love of the past Sue would probably gaze at it for hours.

Nothing interrupted his view along the length of the Antrim coast right to Blackhead where the lough joined the Irish Sea. The far-distant mouth of the lough to his right was interrupted by a nearby green and treed County Down peninsula. What a view and what a private site. He could imagine sitting on deck chairs in the garden with Sue, watching a summer sunset, hearing the piping of oystercatchers, the plaintive cries of curlew, the never-ending siren song of sea on shore. Or sitting with her here in the lounge, a cosy fire burning in the grate, hot chocolate or a hot half-un in hand, watching the fury of an equinoctial gale when Poseidon, god of the sea and earthquakes, tamer of horses, sent his war chariots squadron by squadron to storm the unyielding land. She'd love it. He knew that.

Barry drank it all in as a single ray of sunshine, his dad called them angels' searchlights, streamed down through the battleship-grey skies to highlight a vee of greylag geese heading down lough.

Turning to Dapper, Barry said, his voice hushed, "It is wheeker, Dapper." What a wedding present it would make for Sue. "How much?"

Dapper laughed. "Hold your horses," he said. "Hang about. You've not really had a good look at it and," he winked, "we all know that you and Miss Nolan's going til tie the knot in March. The owners don't want til start me selling it officially until April." He laid a finger beside his nose. "I've been in this business a fair wheen of years. Take my advice. Let Miss Nolan get a skelly at it before you try to buy it. You'd feel a right bollix if you had a twenty-five-year mortgage and she didn't like it."

"Oh," said Barry. "Yes. That does make sense. I will let her see it first, but seriously, what is the asking price?"

"Five thousand."

Barry whistled. "Holy oh."

"But I reckon we'll get it for you for forty-seven hundred."

"That's a lot of money," Barry said.

"It's worth it," Dapper said. "I'll only start showing it once it's on the market, or . . ." he laughed, "not show it at all if you and Miss Nolan want to buy it. The owners are getting on a bit and they'd be happy to avoid all the showin's and such if they could get a good price."

"Thank you," Barry said.

"Now, sir," Dapper looked at his watch, "I've a sales meeting coming up back at the office and then I've til pick up Donal on the Comber Road about four. He'll leave a message at work if he's got home sooner because they've found the dog. I'll give you a lift home now."

"I wonder how Doctor and Mrs. O'Reilly are getting on," Barry said, looking up. "I think we're in for rain."

On the short drive home, he kept picturing the little house on its own private peninsula. It wasn't until Dapper dropped Barry off at Number One that he remembered the seductive Nonie Stevenson would be waiting in his quarters.

He let himself in through the front door, hung up his cap and coat, and headed for the kitchen, hoping that Kinky was home from her shopping, but no such luck. The only sign of life was a drowsy Lady Macbeth curled up in front of the range. The door to his quarters was closed. He took a deep breath, opened it, and leaving it wide open strode in, half expecting to find Nonie lying seductively on his settee. She wasn't.

Nonie Stevenson was in his chair at his worktable, slumped over, head on a bent arm, fast asleep. And, damn it all, half his tools—forceps, tiny scissors, a jeweller's loupe, a tube of glue—were littered all over the carpet. He clenched his teeth. Blue blazes. The woman needed her sleep, but it was a damn silly place to doze off, and if she'd been a bit more to the right she'd have knocked the nearly complete *Rattlesnake* onto the floor.

Now what? He was sorely tempted to leave her there. Serve her right if she woke up with a crick in her neck, but she was lying within inches of the almost completed frigate. If she threw her arms wide when she woke up she could still dash it off the table. He stood beside her, put his hands in her armpits, and slowly pulled her backward. Her arms fell limply to her sides. She really was soundly asleep. For a split second he wondered if she'd fainted and that was why she was asleep at the table. He was damned if he was going to carry out a full neurological examination. He felt a vessel pulsing at his temple, but he bent and listened to her breathing. It was steady and regular. He felt for a pulse. Regular, strong, and eighty beats per minute. Nothing to worry about. He bent, got an arm under her knees, picked her up bodily, carried her to the settee, and none too gently lowered her onto it. Still she did not awaken. He shook his head and, still thoroughly irritated, muttered, "Sweet dreams, princess," then turned his back and started to pick up his scattered equipment.

"Anybody home," Kinky called from the kitchen. Thank God I left the door open, Barry thought. He'd not want to be caught in his quarters behind a closed door with a girl other than Sue.

Kinky had her back to him and was unpacking groceries from her shopping basket.

"I'm in here, Kinky. Doctor Stevenson is having a nap." He hurried on with his explanation. Kinky might wonder what Nonie was doing here in the first place. "She was covering for me while I was out and asked if she could sit in here. I'm just back."

Kinky turned, nodded and grinned. "That Doctor Stevenson. She's a grand one for the naps. I suppose the doctor needs her beauty sleep. Now, Doctor Laverty, sir, it's one o'clock and you must be perishing from hunger. Can I not heat up some soup before you start your afternoon home visits? My ma, God rest her, swore by hot soup for keeping up a body's health, so, and I can't have my doctors getting sick."

"That would be lovely," Barry said. Dear old Kinky was such an open, trusting soul that if she'd suspected anything amiss she'd have been standing arms folded across her ample bosom, frowning to beat Bannagher, and, like the mother she almost was to him and O'Reilly, demanding to know exactly what was going on. "And Doctor Stevenson said you'd made Welsh rarebit."

"I had, and I have the cheese sauce yet, so go you through to the dining room. I'll bring the soup in a shmall-little minute, so."

"Thank you, Kinky," Barry said. He turned to look at Nonie. Still flat out. Barry set his collected instruments down on the table. What was he going to do about this Stevenson woman? He had to try to set aside his irritation about how close she'd come to wrecking almost a full year's work. He glanced at her again. This constant need for sleep, her progressively more flirtatious ways? He'd little doubt about what she had been hinting at before he went out. Barry shook his head. Maybe he should talk to Fingal about letting her go before her three-month trial period was over? But taking a nap was hardly a firing matter. And nothing untoward had actually happened. He knew Fingal trusted him completely, but the man still might be surprised by Barry accusing Nonie of being flirtatious. He tried to remember exactly what she'd said. There was nothing overt that he could remember. And being sacked by such a well-respected physician as Fingal O'Reilly would be a very large blot on her professional copybook. He shook his head and sighed. Twenty-two more days and he'd be in France with Sue.

Och, blether. She was a good doctor and seemed to enjoy working here. She had extra training in women's health. Maybe, just maybe, he should let the hare sit—and make sure he didn't let himself get into any compromising situations with Nonie Stevenson in the future.

10

The Hunter Home from the Hill

They had to cross twenty yards of sere brown bracken that crackled underfoot. "Poor old Jasper could have crawled under this anywhere for warmth." O'Reilly poked randomly with his blackthorn walking stick, but to no avail. "I think we're going to have to depend on Arthur's nose."

But the dog had no luck.

They left the open country and entered a wood of old birch trees. The branches were bare, their slender trunks mossy on their north sides. O'Reilly sent Arthur ahead into a forest floor dappled by light and shade and carpeted with last year's brown soggy leaves. They gave off a musty smell that was half decay and half the aroma of the mushrooms in a fairy ring growing directly in front of his path.

"You'll think I'm a superstitious eejit," he said, "but just to be on the safe side, let's skirt that ring of mushrooms."

"Why?"

"Now, don't laugh, but it's called a fairy ring, a place where the fairies supposedly dance. Celtic legend holds that anyone who enters such a ring will either die young or become invisible to the rest of the human race and never be seen again. And I want to go on seeing you for years to come."

She shook her head. "A few years ago I probably would have thought you were being silly, but since then I've heard Kinky's stories about her encounters with the *sidhe,* the little people."

She did not need to say any more, and anyway, they both needed to save their breath for the business of climbing.

Arthur crashed through the undergrowth, but the going was getting tougher as the incline increased. O'Reilly stopped to disentangle clinging bramble thorns from Kitty's coat. "You walk behind me," he said, and forced a way upward for them both using the stick like a machete.

They were coming to a clearing when directly ahead of the big dog a bird with brown and black plumage, liquid brown eyes on either side of its head, and a long straight bill broke cover and flew jinking away among the tree trunks ahead.

"Woodcock," O'Reilly said, and watched it disappear. He stopped and put a hand on his hip. "Let's take a breather for a minute. I'm not as young as I used to be." He ached all over as his stretched muscles groaned and complained.

"I don't like the look of the sky," Kitty said.

He looked up to where billows of heavy clouds, like murky seafoam driven by a rushing tide, were blowing in from the west. "I don't like the look of it either. Let's hope we find Jasper before it starts to rain."

"Poor old thing," Kitty said.

"And poor old us too if it does. I'd hoped for a decent day out for you on your day off. Get your mind off your work."

"Och, Fingal," she said, "I'm having a lovely time and I'll be damned if a bit of rain's going to spoil it." She looked ahead. "I can see Arthur waiting for us. Let's catch up to him."

Donal Donnelly clutched a steaming mug of tomato soup. "I gotta say I'm disappointed, sir. I'd'a thought somebody would have found the poor ould dog by now. There's a brave wheen of good hidey-holes in the ground we've covered, but not a sausage. Neither hide nor hair of him. He's vanished intil thick air, so he has."

O'Reilly managed to hide his grin. "We've still a fair bit of the hills to cover after lunch, Donal."

"And all the lads is still hopeful," Donal said. "They're a good bunch. I'll nip over til their table now, and I'll see you, sir, on the Comber Road at the end of the day. Get you and the missus a lift back til your motor." He finished his soup and headed off to have a word with the rest of his group.

Lunch had helped to keep up the search party's spirits, O'Reilly thought, but there was a lot more ground to cover. With a bit of luck . . .

"I know you're all disappointed about Jasper," said the marquis, "but I think the ladies of the Women's Union who provided the repast deserve a vote of confidence." He sat on his own folding stool at a temporary table set up with four others in the shallow snow on the hill's crest.

O'Reilly knew Kinky had joined her friends at the Bishops' early that morning to help prepare the lunch. It was a tribute to how this village worked and he was happy to be a part of it.

"And of course Mister Bishop for providing the food and making the arrangements," John MacNeill added. "There he is, doing the rounds of the other tables."

"Ballybucklebo Borough Council elections coming soon," O'Reilly said. "Bertie never misses a chance to look for a few more votes. Laying on this lunch won't hurt his chances."

The meal had been served in a wide, grassy area that had been cleared round the old Martello tower. Fifty of the stout, two-storey, circular fortresses were built at the entrances to Ireland's harbours during the French Revolutionary wars of 1792 to 1802. They had been inspired by a circular tower that was part of a Genoese defence system at Mortella Point in Corsica.

"Do you know I've a distant connection with a tower like this in Dublin?" O'Reilly said.

"Don't tell us you helped build it, Fingal," Kitty said, and grinned at him.

Dear God, but that woman was a tease and he loved it and was quite able to tease right back. He shook his head at her and continued. "And you, I suppose, were the tea girl on the building site? Hardly, my lovely young Kitty. No, James Joyce was said to have written in one in Sandycove near Dun Laoghaire in County Dublin. He was accompanied there for several days by his friend Oliver St. John Gogarty, who was included in *Ulysses* as Buck Mulligan. Gogarty went on to become an ENT surgeon. He'd been a friend of my mother and father in Dublin in the '30s. He advised them that I should specialise." He looked around at the crowd of people all there trying to help a neighbour. "I'm very glad I didn't take that route."

Conversation ebbed and flowed. O'Reilly looked at the old structure again. Ballybucklebo's tower had been in poor repair for as long as he could remember, its second storey crumbling, the stones scattered at its base. Still, it held on to an air of history and romance and O'Reilly imagined a single officer in his cocked hat inspecting his garrison of fifteen redcoats, drilling them on the grass beneath the tower.

O'Reilly and Kitty were sitting with the marquis, and Myrna and Lars were engaged in an animated conversation of their own. O'Reilly's pipe sent up smoke signals like those made by an Indian brave in a Western movie. Great heaps of ham, chicken, and fish-paste sandwiches accompanied by steaming mugs of Kinky's tomato or mushroom soup had vanished and only a few dejected crumbs littered the plates.

"I believe, Fingal, that thanks are in order for stopping Ruby," the marquis said.

O'Reilly shrugged.

"I should have felt dreadfully to blame if Lars had been hurt," Myrna said.

"Fingal was very brave," Kitty said. "I'm proud of him."

O'Reilly muttered in imitation of his hero Captain Horatio Hornblower, "Ha-hmm," and took refuge in tamping the tobacco into his pipe more firmly.

"You know you have my thanks, Finn. I was very lucky you were there," Lars said. "I've been trying to explain to Myrna that I just don't see the point of tearing off after a fox who's simply minding his own business and trying to trot across an open field. It simply doesn't make sense to me. And you all already know how I feel about shooting birds."

Oh-oh, O'Reilly thought. I hope he's not going to get into another wildlife preservation spat with Myrna.

Myrna drew herself up to her full seated height. "There is a long and respected history of fox hunting in this country. Foxes have killed more chickens in our coops at Ballybucklebo House than I can begin to count. And the wretched animals are bloodthirsty little creatures. They'll kill every hen in the coop by slitting their throats with those razor-sharp little teeth of theirs, and then eat only one. They're little demons, I tell you. So if you like birds as much as you say you do, my dear Lars, I should think you'd be quite in favour of the hunt. Now I think," she inhaled deeply, "on that subject we must simply agree to differ." She rose, keeping her back stiff. "I'm going to check Ruby's saddle girth. Can't have you falling off because it's loose." She strode off to where the horses were tethered to a tree, munching oats from their nosebags.

Lars looked at Fingal. The elder brother pursed his lips and raised his shoulders, arms outstretched, palms up.

O'Reilly shook his head and busied himself relighting his pipe.

After some silence John MacNeill said, "It's been a while, Fingal, since we've had the pleasure of your and the lovely Kitty's company. I've a rare week free of meetings, so pick a night next week when you're not on duty and the pair of you come for dinner."

"I will," O'Reilly said. He looked at Lars. "And I'll try to make it on one of the nights you're there." O'Reilly wanted to see how things might or might not develop between his brother and the marquis's sister. At the moment they did not look promising.

"Thank you, John," Kitty said as she glanced at Myrna's retreating back, to Lars and back to Myrna.

"Now," said the marquis, rising, "I must go and thank Bertie and then, I suppose, Fingal, you're going to have us search the downslope. I do hope we have better luck there."

"That I am, John, that I am, but I'll need to send a couple of men to bring the cars round to the Comber Road. Nobody's going to want to trudge all the way back. It's a tough struggle through the undergrowth and"—he nodded up—"I don't like the look of the sky either."

〰️

"I am beginning to lose faith," said Kitty. "I don't think we're going to find the poor old thing."

"I think you're right," he said. The going downhill had been easier, but still no yells of triumph had been passed along the line from either side. "I know this coppice. I shoot woodpigeons here. It's the last cover before the road."

The wind was rising and a few heavy drops had rattled through the branches.

"And while I'm disappointed that we've not found Jasper, I'll be glad to get you back undercover. I think we're in for another gale."

She laughed. "You're very sweet worrying about me, pet, but a bit of rain never hurt anyone. My mother used to say, 'You're not made of sugar. You won't melt.'"

O'Reilly's laugh was cut off by Arthur, who had run ahead with his nose to the ground and stopped in his tracks, legs rigid, tail stuck out behind him as stiff as a wrought-iron poker.

"Hang on." O'Reilly's spirits rose. "Arthur's onto something. Birds or rabbits or hares would have burst from cover. Push him out, boy, push him out," O'Reilly said. "Maybe luck is on our side. Just maybe."

Arthur glanced over his shoulder then made a beeline for the base of an oak where two thick, twisted roots lay half exposed above the ground. O'Reilly saw a dark opening between where the roots left the trunk and patches of freshly dug earth at the burrow's mouth.

"I hope Jasper's found a wild animal's den and holed up in it. You wait here, Kitty."

Arthur was digging frantically with his forepaws, hurling sandy soil out in a continuous stream.

A rank stink assailed O'Reilly's nose. Damn it. No. Jasper wasn't down that hole. Something else was. He grabbed Arthur's collar, hauled, and yelled, "Leave it."

Arthur, obedient as ever, stopped digging, but turned and looked with eyes full of reproach at his master as if to say, "Och, boss, I've almost got it," which was the last thing O'Reilly wanted. "Come on," he said, backing off several paces. As he did, a snout appeared.

Arthur gave a small bark.

A pointed muzzle and blunt ears emerged from the hole. Then the white head and face, save for two black stripes running from behind its ears, past its eyes, and down onto its muzzle. It bared needle-sharp teeth and hissed at the man and the dog before hauling the rest of its short, stocky body covered in grey, bristly fur out of the hole. It darted at Arthur and O'Reilly lifted his stick ready to strike, but at the last minute the badger turned aside and trotted off on stumpy legs and with a rolling gait disappeared more deeply into the wood.

O'Reilly heaved a grateful sigh that he'd been able to act quickly enough. "That's a badger. They usually only come out at night," he said, "and if one's cornered it can give a dog a nasty bite. I reckon that old Brock's making a beeline for a safer sett."

"So that's a real-life version of Kenneth Grahame's Mister Badger. What a comical creature."

"If you remember your *Wind in the Willows,* Badger

lived in the Wild Wood and was indeed a shy, retiring animal—until one of his friends was attacked."

"Mister Toad," said Kitty. "When Toad Hall was invaded by the weasels."

"Then Badger became a warrior. It's the same in real life. If one's threatened he'll fight like bejasus."

"Dear old Arthur. He still looks disappointed." The big dog had flopped down on the ground and laid his head on his paws. "I believe he would have taken on the badger to protect us." She stooped and with both hands began petting the dog, who thumped his tail.

"Now, don't forget. Arthur Guinness is a working dog, and he's still working. You'll spoil him." O'Reilly had tried to sound serious but Kitty looked up and smiled her brilliant smile.

"Away off and chase yourself, Fingal O'Reilly. We all deserve some time off, and thank you for arranging mine today. I know we didn't find Jasper and I'm sorry for it, but I enjoyed every exciting minute. Woodcocks and badgers, fairy rings and a fox hunt. And of course your company. I've had a lovely day. It certainly made up for all yesterday's aggro on the ward."

"It was a pleasure, pet," he said, and it was. He'd make damn sure she had more lovely days until the time was ripe to suggest they both slow down at work. That would be then, but now it was time to go. The few earlier drops had turned into a steady rain that pattered through the branches and was beginning to soak his tweed jacket. Good thing Kitty had her Barbour.

She put its hood up and held his hand as they trudged the last few hundred yards to reach the grassy verge onto the tarmac of the Comber Road where the marquis waited and the foxhounds milled about. Only one car was in evidence, a Ford Cortina, with Donal Donnelly in front and Dapper Frew waiting behind the wheel.

"No luck, Fingal?" John MacNeill asked.

O'Reilly shook his head and drops of water sprayed from the soft brim of his paddy hat. "None. We thought we might have found him, but it was just a bad-tempered badger." The wind had an edge. The sooner he and Kitty got home the better.

"Nor did anyone here," the marquis said. "I've sent Myrna ahead to guide poor Lars home. He was more shaken up by his adventure than he'd admitted at lunch."

"But he's all right?" O'Reilly asked.

"Nothing that a hot bath and a stiff brandy won't cure," the marquis said. "Myrna's very good at looking after lame ducks. I think she's feeling contrite. She knows she shouldn't have brought a novice along and then taken off after that fox. Damn fool thing to do and I don't blame your brother one bit for objecting to fox hunting after what he's been through today."

O'Reilly knew that Lars's objection was less because he'd had a scare and more based on his ideas of animal conservation, but he reckoned this was neither the time nor the place to prolong that discussion. He said, "I'm glad to hear that." He looked around. "Have all the rest gone home already?"

"'Fraid so, and I mean home. The men were too tired, wet, and disappointed even to agree to popping into the Duck for a hot half."

"I know how they feel," Kitty said. "All that effort and no good news for the Houstons. And Jasper out in the elements for another night, if he's still—"

"Ah, now, Mrs. O'Reilly, never say die. And to quote

Sir Winston, 'Never, never, never give up.'" The marquis touched his crop to the peak of his hard hat in salute. "It's home for me and the hounds now. Don't forget about next week." Then, followed by the pack, he cantered off into the sheeting rain.

11

Examine Well Your Blood

January brings the snow—"

The voices of Flanders and Swann came from the radio in Barry's Volkswagen as he parked outside the Houstons' garden gate.

"—makes your feet and fingers glow."

He switched off. The month might bring snow in comic verse, but here in County Down on the morning of Thursday the 19th there was none. Instead a north-easter was howling, rocking the car on its springs and driving rattling rain against the roof and windows as if a regiment of vindictive children armed with peashooters was firing a continuous barrage against the metal and glass. Across the road, tall trees bowed and thrashed, whirling their bare branches. Even the Houstons' neatly clipped evergreen privet hedge swayed and rustled. What a day, and this was only the first of seven home visits Barry had to make. More than usual, but the number always went up when the weather was foul and folks would rather be seen at home than brave the elements. All part of the job.

He grabbed his bag, turned up his raincoat collar, and forced the door to open against the blast. As soon as he was outside, a gust ripped his cap off and tossed it whirling over the trees. "Blue bloody . . ." he snapped, and thought, Careful, boy, you may admire Fingal Flahertie O'Reilly, but you don't have to ape everything he does or says. Barry didn't even wait to watch the duncher go, but hurried through the gate and along the path to ring the front doorbell and wait for the now-familiar routine of a voice, this time a woman's calling, "Hang on," and barking dogs. Maggie would be herding their unruly mob, minus Jasper, of course, into the kitchen.

A trickle of water found its way past his collars and ran an icy finger down his back. Barry shuddered and muttered, "Get a move on, Maggie."

"Come in, Doctor, dear," she said as she opened the door.

Barry hurried inside.

"Boys-a-boys," she said, closing it behind him, "no harm til you, but you look like a drowned rat."

Barry ran a hand over his sodden hair, which was plastered to his head. "It's blowing a gale out there," he said. As if, he thought, that wasn't pretty obvious.

"Get you out of that coat and I'll dry it by the kitchen range and bring you a towel. Go on on into the living room. Sonny's expecting you, so he is. We're both anxious to hear about his tests."

"I have his results here." Barry held up his bag before taking off his coat.

She took his coat and gave it a violent shake. She hesitated then asked, "I don't suppose there's any word of Jasper? All kinds of folks have been phoning to say they'd keep an eye out, and they're sorry for our troubles. Jeannie Jingles's cousin Brian Weir works as a printer's apprentice up in Belfast and he made up some posters and they're everywhere. He come to the house two days ago and got a picture of Jasper. Nice young man. Said he lost a dog when he was a young lad and wanted to help. We was so sorry the search party didn't find ours."

"I'm sorry too," he said, "but we mustn't give up hope." God help the creature, Barry thought, if he's still alive and out in that lot. I hope he's found somewhere dry.

"Poor ould thing," she said. "It's all my fault. I shouldn't have let him out of the car, and when he bolted, I should have gone after him."

Barry squeezed her arm. "Maggie, Jasper was bound and determined to get out of that car, you couldn't have stopped him. And we could barely see the noses on our faces that morning. There's no way you could have found Jasper. We'd have more likely lost you too, and then where would Sonny be?"

"You're right. I know you are, but I still feel bad. Mind you, I've heard of dogs missing for weeks and still turning up."

"That's the spirit, Maggie. Now I'd better go and see my patient. Come back soon so I can explain to both of you what's going on."

"I will," she said. "I'll get you that towel and I'll get the kettle on too. I've a wheen of buttermilk scones. I had a half notion Doctor O'Reilly was trying to avoid my plum cake last time he was here so I've made something else."

Barry sighed at the prospect. In his experience, Maggie's scones were only marginally less rock-like than her plum cake. He let himself into the lounge, where in the grate a welcoming coal fire burned, giving off a pleasing warmth as if to cock a snook at the sounds of the windowpanes rattling and the wind howling over the chimney pots. A polished brass coal scuttle reflected the light from a small chandelier.

Sonny, wearing a tartan dressing gown, was teed up in front of the hearth on a sofa that was flanked by two armchairs. General Montgomery was curled up asleep at his feet. Sonny's hair was neatly brushed and he managed a small smile. He was very pale. "Please forgive me for receiving you lying down, Doctor Laverty," he said. "I'm still so weak." He gasped.

And short of breath. "Perfectly all right, Sonny. I understand," Barry said. "Have you noticed anything new since we were here last Friday?" He stood beside Sonny and took his pulse.

Sonny shook his head. "Only that now I understand a bit about what ails me I've been able to keep my temper under control. For that I am very grateful." He motioned to an armchair. "Unless you need to examine me?"

Barry shook his head. "Your pulse is one hundred and I don't expect much else will have changed." One hundred wasn't bad considering what Barry knew from the lab results. He took the armchair beside Sonny's head. "I have your results and I'll explain in more detail as soon as Maggie comes in, but they look promising."

"Thank you, Doctor. That's one less concern, I hope." Sonny looked at a framed photo of a group of dogs on a table beside the sofa. He sighed. "I worry about Jasper. Please thank Doctor O'Reilly for leading that search party. I've phoned Mister Bishop to thank him too."

"I'm sorry they didn't find Jasper," Barry said, knowing full well there was no point mouthing trite platitudes about "not giving up hope" to Sonny. "Some of my patients have told me in the last couple of days that they're looking for him round where they live and neighbour is asking neighbour to join in and do the same. I've even had a couple of calls from folks in Helen's Bay and Holywood asking how they could help, so I've told them to do the same thing. We'll soon have half of North Down keeping an eye out."

Sonny sighed. "We do live in a wonderful place," he said. "People still care." He smiled.

"And we care about you, Doctor Laverty," Maggie said as she came in and handed him a dry towel. "It's been in the hot press," she said, "and that's over the hot water boiler so the towel's nice and warm, so it is."

"Thank you, Maggie," Barry said, accepting the towel and drying his face, neck, and hair.

Maggie laughed. "I thought that would happen," she said. "Your mop looks like a hay rick after a windy day."

Barry, conscious of a tuft that always refused to lie down, rubbed his hand over his crown to try to flatten his hair.

"Here," Maggie said. "Here's a new comb, and don't be shy using it in front of other people . . ."

Barry was. Public personal grooming had been distinctly frowned upon at Campbell College when he was a boy, and old habits died hard.

"All the youngsters do ever since Kookie on *Seventy-Seven Sunset Strip* on the telly did it." She sat in the other armchair.

"Thank you," Barry said, and combed his hair. "Now." He opened his bag and pulled out several pink sheets of paper. "I've got all your tests so I'll explain what they mean and what we'll do next."

"We'd be grateful, Doctor," Sonny said.

Barry read from the first form. "The lab measured your haemoglobin level. That's stuff in the red blood cells. Its job is to carry oxygen. Normally it's fourteen point eight grams per hundred millilitres. Yours is six."

"Six?" Sonny whistled. "That's very low."

Barry had wanted to make that point clearly so he'd used exact numbers, but the rest of the blood indices were difficult to explain in detail so he had determined to avoid using confusing figures and ratios. "It is, and so is your total red cell count. The technical term for red cells is corpuscles. Your body, and it's mostly the bone marrow that does it, isn't producing enough red cells."

"I see."

"And there's another thing. Immature red cells are much bigger than healthy mature ones. And each young one carries more haemoglobin than an older one. The pathologists have defined certain ratios about haemoglobin content and size of the immature and mature cells, and yours meet all the criteria for immaturity. It's like a factory that is short of raw materials and turning out half-finished products. Your bone marrow's trying to cope in the same way by releasing immature cells too soon."

Sonny managed a weak smile. "Immature cells? And it's those cells, or rather the lack of mature ones, that are making me feel as old as Methuselah. I understand."

Barry chuckled, admiring the man's resilience. "Do you know, Mister Houston," Barry said, "when I first met you, you were living in your car and—I hope you'll forgive me—I thought you were—"

"Astray in the head?" Sonny chuckled. "So did everybody else except your senior colleague, Doctor O'Reilly. He is a very sage man." Sonny became more serious. "Fact is I've never much worried about what other people think of me."

"I think you are a very self-sufficient person who knows his own mind and has a very dry sense of humour."

"Oh, he knows his own mind, all right," said Maggie with a sharp cackle. "You might call it self-sufficiency. There's some might call it stubbornness. But I love the old eejit anyway."

"Thank you, Maggie, dear, and thank you, Doctor. If you don't mind me saying, for a young man you are beginning to show a little of the sagacity of Doctor O'Reilly himself."

Barry smiled. "Thank you."

"So your ratios," Sonny said, "have given you a diagnosis?"

"Not entirely," Barry said. "The ratios allow us to make intelligent inferences about the nature of the anaemia and possible causes, but the lab people also spread blood on microscope slides and use special dyes, it's called making a smear, so they can actually examine the individual cells and identify them for exactly what they are."

"I'd like to see one of those smears," Sonny said. "The whole thing sounds a bit like my old trade of archaeology. You suspect something by inference then you dig down layer by layer until you find what you're looking for . . ." he smiled again, "or as is often the case, you don't find it."

"In your situation I think we're getting close," Barry said.

"You just let Doctor Laverty get you all better, you ould goat," Maggie said, and the fondness in her voice was palpable. "Go on, Doctor, dear."

"The report says that among the red cells are ones called normoblasts and others called megaloblasts. 'Blast' means an early cell that's starting to develop and 'meg-alo' means—"

"Of exaggerated size, like in *megalodon,* a giant pre-historic shark," Sonny said. "And that's a big immature red cell. I understand, and please forgive me for inter-rupting."

"And as far as I know there are only two possible causes." He laughed. "Well, there is a third, but unless you are a miracle of science, Sonny Houston, I don't think it applies."

"Anything's possible with Sonny," she said. "What's the third cause, Doctor, dear?"

"Macrocytic—which is a fancy way of saying overly large-celled—anaemia due to . . . pregnancy."

Maggie exploded into her cackly laughter and Sonny smiled. "I am not that self-sufficient, Doctor Laverty."

"Away on, Doctor. You're the quare one for a gag, so you are. And you're too soft a man to be making jokes if you didn't think you could fix my Sonny, and that's a great relief, so it is. I'll leave you and him to collogue away and I'll go and get a cup of tea for til have in our hands and some of them fresh-baked scones."

Barry's pleasure at being described a "soft" man, which he knew meant gentle, wrestled with his horror at the thought of tackling her tea and baking. And it was too late to refuse. He said to Sonny, "My best guess, and it's not really a guess, is that yours is due to, as I told you before, pernicious anaemia, because a chemical is missing from your stomach's gastric juices. The chemi-cal is called 'intrinsic factor.' We believe the body needs the intrinsic factor to combine with the vitamin B_{12} before they can both be absorbed. The only other pos-sible cause is that your lower gut is inherently unable to absorb the vitamin, even if the B_{12} is combined with intrinsic factor."

"Most interesting," Sonny asked. "If it is pernicious anaemia, how would I have got it?"

"We don't know what triggers it, but for some reason your body starts producing antibodies. Do you know what antibodies are?"

"I've read a bit about the immune system," Sonny said. "They're manufactured to attack foreign proteins like bacteria."

"Correct, but in this case they attack the cells in your stomach that produce the very necessary intrinsic factor. None of it, no B_{12} absorption."

Sonny nodded. "In military terms," he said, "I'm producing a fifth column, a bunch of traitors attacking their own from within."

"Very good analogy."

"So how do we counterattack?"

"We may need a bit more . . ." Barry decided to stay with the military model, "intelligence." He hesitated. He knew the textbooks recommended doing a bone marrow biopsy and a gastric juice analysis to see exactly what was happening at the site of production of blood cells. The biopsy was a painful procedure, and while the gastric juice analysis was not painful, it was thoroughly unpleasant. Much as he disliked it, Barry knew he must seek specialist advice. "I'm going to ask Doctor Nelson at the Royal to see you. He specialises in blood disorders. He may need to bring you in for a couple of days for some more tests that I can't do here."

Sonny stretched out a skinny hand and grabbed Barry's arm. "Please, Doctor Laverty," he said, and there was pleading in his eyes, "not a hospital. They terrify me. Stubborn I may be, but in this case, it comes from fear, plain and simple." He firmly clutched Barry's arm. It was the grasp of a terrified man.

"Please, Doctor." Sonny's voice was level as he tried to retain his dignity.

"All right," Barry said, "I have to go to Belfast tomorrow. Doctor Nelson was one of my teachers. I'll go and see him, take the results we already have, and see what he says."

"Would you? I'd be eternally grateful."

"A few more days before we move ahead is neither here nor there," Barry said. "I am sure that once treatment is started we'll have your blood better in no time." Barry nodded as Maggie came in and set a tray on the table.

"You'll take tea, Doctor. Milk and sugar?" she said. "And please excuse my fingers, but I'll butter you a scone too."

"Please," Barry said, regarding the coming cup with the enthusiasm he was sure Socrates had had for the flask of lethal hemlock. Maggie was a firm believer in strong tea. As if to mark his discomfort, a mighty gust outside rattled the panes and blew a puff of coal smoke into the room.

"Tut," said Maggie, "see that oul chimney? We always get blow-downs when the wind's in the northeast." She gave Barry his cup, with a buttered scone balanced on the saucer. "Get that into you, sir, and there's more of everything, so there is, if you'd like seconds before you go out again into that lot."

Barry, with memories still fresh of Maggie's petrified plum cakes, said to himself, Go on, it won't kill you, and took a bite from the warm-from-the-oven scone. His eyes widened. No. Couldn't be. The thing dissolved in his mouth, the delicious melted butter heavier by far than the fluffy confection. He swallowed. "That's delicious, Maggie," he said, working hard to keep the surprise from his voice.

"Aye, well," she said, "I'd like to take credit, but it's not my recipe. Kinky taught me how to make ones like that. My own have more body."

Barry could believe that, but said nothing.

Sonny, accepting his tea and scone, said, "Doctor Laverty's going to consult with a colleague in Belfast and he's sure between them they can put me right."

Maggie bent and kissed the top of his head. "And I'll be dead pleased til have my ould Sonny back. Now if we could just get Jasper too."

Sonny said, "I agree, but to be fair to our doctors, fixing patients is their job. They've already done their very best for us. Thank you, Doctor."

Barry smiled. He glowed inwardly from the satisfaction of having nearly made a difficult diagnosis without having to involve a specialist until the very end, and for being as comfortable as was O'Reilly in turning his efforts to trying to solve other problems for the villagers. He took a deep swallow from his teacup. Despite a spoonful of sugar it was bitter as gall. Socrates, Barry thought, if given the choice between Maggie's stewed tea and poison, would probably have chosen the hemlock.

12

The Fool of Love

L*es sanglots longs des violons d'automne blessent mon coeur d'une langueur monotone.*" Barry was sitting at his usual table near the door in a little upstairs restaurant on Belfast's Arthur Street, rereading Sue's letter. The airmail had arrived two days ago, and Barry had decided that reading it again, here in the Causerie, was a most pleasurable way of killing time until Jack Mills and Helen Hewitt arrived.

The lines on the thin blue airmail paper, bearing the slightest whiff of her favourite perfume, continued, "*You may remember reading* Chanson d'automne *by Paul Verlaine at school . . .*" He did indeed. In his last year at school, back in 1957, every pupil in the upper fifth form in Northern Ireland had to read, among other required French material, a slim tome entitled *French Verse: From Villon to Verlaine.* French Literature was one part of the national exams that had to be passed to qualify him to attend medical school.

He read on, knowing what was coming next and wriggling in anticipation. "*I'm being grounded in French poetry as part of my exchange training,*" she'd written, "*except in my case while there are no long sobs* of violins, and it's winter not autumn today, my heart is wounded. Truly wounded. I'm missing you so very much, my dear darling. Seeing you during the holidays was wonderful."

Barry smiled. It was a warm feeling to be missed by someone you loved and to be told so poetically too. She went on with happy chitchat about what she was up to, that she'd bought an antique *plat à barbe*, an ornate dish like a soup plate but with a notch taken out of the rim so the thing could be fitted round the customer's neck while the Provençal barber shaved him. Apparently her father collected them. She went on, "*You said in your last letter that Fingal will give you a week off in February. Any idea which one yet? If you can let me know I'll ask for time off, say, Thursday, Friday, and Monday. That would give us five whole wonderful days together and leave you two to travel.*" Barry had asked Fingal last night and he'd agreed to let Barry have Wednesday the 8th until Tuesday the 15th, provided Fitzpatrick was fully back in harness and Nonie was available. Five whole days with Sue.

Barry knew what was coming in the next paragraph, but like a small boy saving a favourite Bassett's Liquorice Allsort to be savoured last, he set the letter down and looked round the familiar room. It was well lit at this hour by two large high windows in the far wall. Of the fourteen tables with crisp white napery, shining cutlery and glasses, eight others were occupied—mostly, he assumed, by the staff of local businesses on nearby Anne Street and the Cornmarket. The hum of conversation was muted, but a man's voice could be heard for a moment. "—and we've been having hell's delight getting ten-bore cartridges from Eley-Kynoch." He probably worked at Braddell's, the gunsmith's.

Barry returned to the letter.

"*I know it's naughty,*" she had written, and his breath caught in his throat, "*but I've found a delightful pension on the Rue Saint-Saëns no distance from Le Vieux Port . . .*" The first time Barry had read as far as this he'd assumed she'd found the hotel room for him. He'd forgotten what a right-to-the-point young woman Sue Nolan was. "*We are practically man and wife, will be within a few weeks, my GP put me on the pill four months ago, and anyway who do we know in Marseille? Let me know the dates and I'll book us in. The French understand these things.*" He swallowed. In just thirteen days he'd be holding her, kissing her—and more. He squeezed his elbows into his sides. Much more.

"Here y'are, Doctor Laverty." The waitress, a motherly woman who treated her regulars like family, had greeted him like a long-lost friend when he'd arrived. He and Jack had been coming here even before they had qualified. Now she set a pint of Guinness on the tabletop. Barry knew Peggy McCarthy well. He knew she lived up in Turf Lodge with her husband, Aidan, and a Siamese cat named Maeve. Their four kids were grown now and gone south, scattered all over the Republic, but she had eight grandchildren she doted on. "And I brung some wee menus."

"I'll come back when your friends arrive, and see you, sir? When it comes til your grub, order something strengthening. You've no more meat on you than a wren's shin." She went away, shaking her head, to attend to another table.

Barry smiled at Peggy's retreating back as he reread the last few lines and the signoff, "*With all my dearest love, and longing, now and forever, Sue.*" He inhaled deeply, and took a soothing pull of his pint.

A haze of cigarette smoke hung beneath the ceiling, and a short bar at one side had a mirror on the back wall with glass shelves holding bottles of spirits. One of them was a half-empty bottle of blue Curaçao. Barry could swear the same bottle had been there in 1962 when he had first started coming here. Ulster folks tended to be conservative in what they drank.

He picked up one menu and had just decided to have a steak and Guinness pie and chips when the door was opened and Jack Mills ushered Helen Hewitt in.

"You, Mills, are late," Barry said, rising and grinning. "Hello, Helen."

"Sorry about that, lad," Jack said. "Bit of a B getting parked, hey." His County Antrim accent was still thick as champ. It suited the man, who looked like a ruddy-cheeked farmer. He was from a dairy farm near Cullybackey. He pulled out a chair, seated Helen, then himself.

"My fault we're late," she said. "Hilary term's in full swing and I was in the physiology lab and really wanted to finish an experiment. It's the big professional exam in March. Second MB."

"Second MB," Jack repeated, and shuddered. "It's one of the big hurdles, right, Barry? You're crossing that great divide between basic sciences and starting clinical work." He nodded to Barry. "We both know how important this is."

"I certainly do," said Barry. "You have my sympathy— and my support, Helen. And I know how proud your dad is."

A cough.

"I know it's too soon for til take your orders, Doctor Mills, but would yiz and your young lady like a drink?"

"Hello, Peggy. How are you? And Mister McCarthy?"

"We're well, sir. Thank you."

"Helen? A drink?"

"Have you a nice white by the glass?"

"Aye. There's an Entre Deux Mers open."

"That would be lovely," Helen said.

"And mine's a pint."

"I'll only be a wee minute, dears." Peggy left.

"Second MB," Barry said. "I don't know about you, Jack, but I'll never forget it."

"Me neither," said Jack. "I was scared skinny of that exam." He beamed at Helen. "But I'm sure you'll ace it, love." His smile faded. "At least you should if the amount of time you spend studying is any indication." He shrugged and looked at Barry. "I think, mate, you and I should arrange to see much more of each other while your Sue's away. Trying to drag this one from her studies?" Jack pursed his lips and shook his head. "Like pulling teeth without an anaesthetic. I'm thinking of taking religious orders and a vow of celibacy." His laugh was forced.

"I'd better ace it," she said, and there was an edge in her voice. "Don't forget I'm on a scholarship, thanks to his lordship. I'll lose it if I fail one exam. You know that bloody well, Jack Mills." She didn't quite stamp her foot, but there was fire in her green eyes. "Until the damn thing's over, it's business before pleasure. You'll wait. I know you will."

Jack sighed. "I'm surprised you could make time to have lunch today." He sounded thoroughly dejected, and a little peevish.

Barry sat back. This would bear watching. Had they been having a row? Jack had always been a Lothario. The second a girl seemed to be losing interest, or refused to fall in with his plans, she was replaced. But here was Jack, seemingly willing to put up with being neglected by a green-eyed, red-haired local lass from Ballybucklebo named Helen Hewitt. Not without protest, however. And ineffective protest it appeared. Helen clearly knew what she needed and wanted at this stage in her life. This would be a first for Jack, dating a young woman like her. Barry remembered how she'd dealt with an unpleasant employer by crushing the dressmaker's entire supply of hats and then giving notice.

"All right," Jack said. "All right. I'm sorry." He picked up her hand and tried to kiss it, but she pulled it away and said, "The dean told us last year, 'Pass this one, leave the study of the basic sciences behind and move on to the teaching hospital, and it's practically certain you'll qualify as a doctor. Fail it and—'" Helen inhaled deeply. "I've wanted this for a long time. I-will-not-fail." Each word was stressed.

Barry remembered some strange notions that his earlier, now long-gone love Patricia Spence had got from the writings of two leading "feminist" writers, as they were being called, Gloria Steinem and Betty Friedan. At least they had seemed odd to a boy like him, raised in the '50s to regard the traditional roles of the sexes as the norm. Bob Dylan had sung it in 1964, "Times they are a changin'." And the more time he spent around Sue Nolan, who very much had her own ideas, the more Barry had come to recognise the sound sense and inherent fairness of those changes.

He wondered if Jack, with his ingrained country notions, was going to be able to change with the times. Barry glanced at his oldest friend, saw concern in those honest eyes, and felt for him. Real love was not always easy. Perhaps this once Barry would be the one to offer a shoulder to cry on. Jack had done it often enough for Barry in the past. He was about to try to change the subject, get the tenseness out of the air, when Peggy appeared. "Here's your drinks." She set the two glasses down. "And are youse ready til order yet?"

Helen scanned the menu. "Grilled Dover sole, please."

"T-bone steak. Rare," Jack said. "Thank you."

Barry placed his order.

"They all come with chips and veg," Peggy said, and left.

Barry raised his glass. "Pick yours up, Jack. A toast. To Helen's coming success in Second MB."

At least he was rewarded by one of Helen's bigger smiles.

"By God," said Jack, "I'll drink to that," and this time when he tried to cover her hand with his, she smiled at him and made no demur.

"No need to bother walking me to the bus stop," Helen said as the three stood outside the restaurant. "Thanks for lunch, Jack. Embryology this afternoon with 'Daddy' Morton." She screwed up her face. "I hate embryology." She pursed a mock kiss and was already walking away as Jack called, "When will I see . . ." His shoulders sagged. "Oh, never mind." He turned to Barry. "Women."

Barry let the remark pass. "You going back to the Royal?"

"Aye."

"I need a lift. I came on the train. Brunhilde's at McGimpseys's Garage in Bangor for her six-month service. The poor old thing's getting on."

"Come on, then. Car's not far, hey. You've probably told me before, but why the hell do you call your VW Brunhilde?"

"Mum's a fan of Wagner's *Der Ring des Nibelungen*. She thought it was the perfect name for a German car."

Jack laughed as side by side the two friends threaded their way through the afternoon crowd. Women, shopping bags on their arms, their heads covered in plastic rollers and secured with headscarves, getting their "do" ready for Saturday night. Office-boy messengers, most with cigarettes stuck to their lips. Under the Gaumont cinema's marquee announcing, "*Fantastic Voyage* with Raquel Welch and Stephen Boyd," a queue was forming. School kids in their uniforms skipping afternoon classes. One boy in a Methodist College blazer held hands with a girl wearing the uniform of Princess Gardens Grammar School. Unemployed men in dunchers had their coat collars turned to the wind. Two Queen's students were recognisable by their long black, green, and blue scarves.

One man in laceless boots, pants patched at the knee, and a ragged pullover under a collarless sports jacket walked slowly along the double line of moviegoers. He held his duncher extended in his right hand and was singing, "Saint Theresa of the roses." A coin clinked into the cap. "Thank you, sir. 'I will come til you each night. Near the altar . . .'" Clink. "Thank you, madam. 'In the chapel . . .'"

Across the Cornmarket, a Guinness lorry was unloading barrels for Mooney's pub to the accompaniment of hoarse cries of "Steady there. Hang on til that rope. You're making a right hames of it." Cars jostled through narrow streets, their exhaust fumes mingling with the smoke from the city's few remaining linen mills and the coal fires from row after row of workers' houses. A car horn blared and shoe leather clacked on the paving stones. It was a typical Belfast street scene, Barry thought, and a far cry from driving in Ballybucklebo and the townland. There the scents were of the sea or new-mown hay, and on a Thursday, market day, one was more apt to be driving behind cattle than exhaust-belching lorries. He had no doubt which scene he preferred.

"Hop in," Jack said, opening the driver-side door of a blue Austin A35.

Barry climbed into the passenger's seat.

"What's on at the hospital?" Jack started the engine and pulled out into the traffic.

"I've an appointment with Doctor Nelson."

"Haematologist?"

"Yes. So I thought rather than phone I'd come up in person, which also gives me the chance to see our old mate Harry Sloan and have lunch with you and Helen." Barry hesitated. "You won't mind me asking, but is everything all right there?"

"Women. Jasus, Barry, but I'm utterly confounded. Bewitched, buggered, and bewildered. I never thought it would happen to me." He turned onto High Street.

"It was bound to one day." Hadn't he and Fingal just been saying that perhaps it was time for Jack to settle down? He turned to stare at his friend. "And when you get used to it, love is grand, Jack. Honest."

Jack stopped at the traffic light where Donegal Place crossed High Street to become Royal Avenue. "Hmmm. Well, you'd know," Jack said. "The Mam'selle at school, a certain green-eyed nurse . . ."

The light changed and Jack drove across the intersection onto what was now Divis Street, one boundary of the Catholic Falls District.

Barry waited to see if his friend would mention Patricia

and was pleased when he did not. Although Sue filled Patricia's place to overflowing now, Barry had hurt when she'd dumped him for a fellow Cambridge student. And Jack, knowing that only too well, had comforted Barry at the time and was being tactful now. "I know. I'm a big softie, but I'll tell you what, my rugby-playing friend. The right woman can make big softies of us all inside. Even you."

Jack nodded, braking to allow a lorry to make a right turn across the traffic. "I think she has, Barry," he drove ahead, "but, Lord, it's hard to take this having to play second fiddle to Helen's studying." He indicated for a left turn where the Royal Victoria's redbrick three-storey King Edward Building stood on the corner of the Grosvenor and Falls Road. "I'm daft about her, Barry, but I worry. She's such a corker. I see the way other fellows look at her."

"She's a lovely girl," Barry said, "and I know what you mean. A lad looks sideways at her and you get tachycardia."

Jack grunted. "Spot on, mate." He turned the Austin onto the Grosvenor Road, past the hospital's West Wing, the gatehouse, and the East Wing before stopping to turn right into the grounds at the Clinical Sciences Building. They passed through the tall open gates and headed for the car park.

"It is tough having to stay in the background," said Barry, "but both of us know what it takes to get through. Give her her head. Let her study. She'll thank you for it when she passes—and hate you if she spends what she sees as too much time with you—and fails."

Jack shook his head. "She'll not fail, Barry. She's smart. Really smart. But I'll try. She's worth it." He found a spot and brought the car to an abrupt halt.

"Hey." Barry braced himself against the dashboard.

"Sorry, Barry. Mind's on other things."

They got out to walk through the park and along the narrow lane between the mortuary and the old plywood hutment that still served as bedrooms for housemen and students.

"One thing, Jack," Barry said. "If things do progress—"

"You mean if I propose and she accepts?" Jack stopped in his tracks. "I hadn't quite got that far in my thinking. And there's another thing . . ." Jack bit his lower lip. "I'm a Protestant and . . ."

"Good Lord," said Barry.

"Right."

"How could I forget? She's Roman Catholic. Digs with the other foot." Barry pursed his lips. "I know the old sectarian thing's easing up. There have been cross-border talks between the Ulster and Republic of Ireland governments, but remember September '64 and those nights of rioting on Divis Street? The undercurrents are still there." And, he thought, once back from France, Sue would be getting on with her work for the Campaign for Social Justice, aimed at bettering the lot of Ulster's Catholics. Things might be quiet between them today, but the Orange and the Green hadn't buried the hatchet yet.

Jack shook his head. "We'd be fools here in Ulster if she and I didn't at least talk about it, but I'm sure we could get round it somehow. I know a couple of mixed-marriage folks from Cullybackey who went to Canada. Say it's a great country. And remember the riots were on the Falls Road, not the Upper Malone where the swells live. Religion doesn't matter to me, but then I've never bothered asking girls before about their religion." His grin was wry. "Come to think of it, I've never bothered feeling like this before neither."

"I said 'if,' Jack. If that should happen, you'll have a wife who understands completely what being a doctor is all about. And your religious differences? You will have to talk about them, even though there's not quite the same degree of constraint as in our parents' days."

"We'll sort it out," Jack said. "I hope."

"I'm sure you will," Barry said.

"We will, and you're right on both counts. We will have to talk and I will have a wife who understands being a doctor, won't I, hey?" Jack visibly brightened before taking refuge in a quiet, "If I propose."

They went into the passageway leading past the out-patient clinics on their right and the cafeteria on the left and on to the staircase up to the hospital's main corridor. As they climbed, Jack put his hand on Barry's arm and said, "Thanks for the advice, chum. I'll do my best to take it." He glanced at his watch. "Gotta run now. Sir Donald Cromie gets a bit shirty if I'm late for his rounds."

Barry stood at the head of the stairs in the bustle of the main corridor and watched his friend hurry to wards 17 and 18, the orthopaedic units, before he, Barry, set off to find Doctor Nelson and get advice about Sonny Houston.

13

To Please Thee with My Answer

"Come in, young Laverty." Doctor Nelson spoke from behind his cluttered desk where untidy heaps of journal reprints jostled with in and out trays, an unsteady cairn of textbooks, and an antique single-barrelled brass microscope that needed a polishing. "Have a pew." He indicated a comfortable chair. "Can I get you a cup of tea? Biscuits?"

"No, thank you, sir." Barry sat stiffly. Doctor Gerald Nelson, head of the department of haematology, offering him tea and biscuits? He almost laughed out loud. Barry remembered the man giving his lectures, always lightened with a joke or two. A man who could make a dry subject interesting yet still expected high levels of performance from his students. Even though Barry was now a physician in his own right, he was still a little in awe of the senior man, a hangover from student days when senior consulting staff of the teaching hospital had been regarded as godlike figures. "And thank you for seeing me at short notice."

The haematologist laughed. It was a full, deep-throated, comfortable laugh coming from a man with an open face under a full head of neatly cut auburn hair.

"Why wouldn't I? We're colleagues, Doctor. And you have a patient who needs our care." He sat forward in his chair and stretched out a hand, which Barry reflexively shook. "And the name's Gerry, not sir."

Barry swallowed. If there was any symbol of being accepted as an equal it was permission to use someone's Christian name. "Barry," he said, and released the hand.

"Good. That's settled. Now, what can I do for you, Barry?"

Barry felt himself relax and leant back into the chair. "I need advice . . . Gerry," he said, and fished in his inside pocket to produce Sonny's results. "My patient is a sixty-one-year-old man." Barry summarised Sonny's symptoms and physical findings. "I suspected pernicious anaemia with subacute combined degeneration of the cord, so I had these tests done." He handed over the forms and waited.

"I'd agree with your diagnosis," Doctor Nelson said, "but we should confirm it with a bone-marrow biopsy to exclude any of the blood cancers and a histamine-stimulated gastric aspiration to confirm that lack of intrinsic factor is indeed at the root of the situation. The same gastric cells that produce it also produce hydrochloric acid and will do so in response to histamine stimulation. If HCl's present in the aspirate, the patient doesn't have pernicious anaemia. I'll arrange to have him admitted if you like."

It was of course the answer Barry had anticipated, but he said, "Mister Houston is terrified of hospitals. That's why I came to see you, Gerry." It felt strange, but very satisfying for Barry to know he was accepted as a peer.

Doctor Nelson frowned.

Barry ploughed on. "I wanted to ask if we could

perhaps keep him at home and confirm the diagnosis by doing a therapeutic trial instead of tests?"

Doctor Nelson inclined his head. "A trial?"

"Yes. If he has got PA then it should respond to injections of B_{12} pretty quickly, shouldn't it?"

The haematologist frowned, then nodded and smiled. "It should," he said. "Of course, if his condition doesn't improve . . ."

Barry inhaled.

"If you're wrong and it's a blood cancer . . . You said he's sixty-one?"

"Yes."

"The leukaemias tend to be slow to progress at that age, but you'd be risking delaying the diagnosis and treatment." He steepled his fingers. "Willing to accept that on behalf of your patient?"

Barry barely hesitated. "I haven't discussed it with him. I'm trying not to worry him unless it's absolutely necessary. If I'm right, we'd be sparing him painful and unpleasant tests, wouldn't we? And a lot of anguish if we can keep him out of hospital. I hope a week, ten days wouldn't be critical if I'm wrong."

Doctor Nelson drummed his fingers on the desktop, then smiled. "You care about your patients, don't you, Barry, not just their diseases?"

Barry knew he was reddening.

"I suppose if you've been working with Fingal O'Reilly it was bound to rub off. We know all about him through his classmates Charlie Greer and Donald Cromie. They say he was always an old marshmallow hiding under a fake crusty exterior. You could be emulating a much worse model." He leant forward and looked into Barry's face. "Mind you, I seem to remember the way you looked after a patient with polycythaemia. As a student you went the extra mile for that man. Good for you."

Barry recalled the man, a Mister Steele from Ballybogey in County Antrim.

Gerry Nelson pointed a finger and for a moment Barry felt like a student again. "And don't ever stop caring. In our trade it can be very easy to focus on the disease and ignore the patient. Don't." He returned the lab forms. "I'll support your idea. I couldn't get him admitted until next week anyway. It would take a day or two to get the tests done. If you don't mind dropping in on him on your way home tonight you could get treatment of his suspected PA started straightaway. He'll need daily intramuscular injections of one hundred micrograms of B_{12}."

"I'll see him this evening."

"His current tests show an absence of reticulocytes."

Barry struggled to remember his pathology classes, when they had been taught how to examine blood smears. Reticulocytes were immature red blood cells that left the bone marrow where blood was produced. They were easy to see under the microscope because, when stained, a network of intracellular protein became identifiable. They appeared in the blood stream, where they then matured in one day and the network disappeared. Ordinarily they were about 1 percent of all red cells. The percentage of reticulocytes could be used to assess bone marrow activity. A low count or their absence was consistent with pernicious anemia, but could be due to other blood disorders, including the leukaemias.

"Re-measure them in ten days. If the count is very high, say forty to fifty percent, then the marrow is working at top speed to make red cells because at last it's getting B_{12} and you'll have been proven right."

"And more, Mister Houston will be on the mend," said Barry.

"He will, but he'll still need daily injections until his complete blood count is normal, then one every four weeks for life." Doctor Nelson nodded. "But if the count's not up, then it's not PA, so phone my secretary and get him admitted at once. I'll arrange it in advance and we'll do whatever is necessary to make a diagnosis."

"I will, Gerry." Barry rose. Using the senior man's name got easier with each repetition. "Thank you for your time and advice."

"It's been a pleasure. Always is to see our old students doing well. Consult me any time." He rose, went to a small fridge, and took out a glass bottle containing pink liquid. "You'll need this. Cyanocobalamin. Vitamin B_{12}. I presume you have hypodermics with you?"

"I have."

Gerry Nelson stretched out his hand, which Barry shook. "Good luck and do let me know how it turns out."

"I will, and thanks again." Barry let himself out, closed the office door, and let out a sigh. That had gone even better than he'd hoped for, in more ways than one. Not only had he achieved the outcome he'd wanted for Sonny, it was very gratifying to be accepted as an equal within the medical hierarchy. He glanced at his watch. There was just time to nip over to the pathology department and see his old classmate Harry Sloan, then stop off at Erskine Mayne's bookstore to get a book for Kitty's imminent birthday. And if he caught the four o'clock train to Bangor, picked up Brunhilde and drove to the

Houstons', he could still be back at Number One in time for a predinner drink.

◌◌◌

"It's quare and decent of you to come out again the day," Maggie said as she took Barry's coat and ushered him into the living room. "At least the gale's blown over." She spoke to Sonny, who was sitting, fully dressed, in an armchair before the fire reading a book. "Doctor Laverty's come til see us, dear."

Sonny put down the book. "How very kind. Please have a seat." He indicated a vacant armchair.

Barry sat and glanced at the book's cover. Nancy Mitford's *The Sun King*. "I've never read her. Are you enjoying Louis the Fourteenth's biography?"

"Enormously," Sonny said. "Mitford writes very well. You should try her. Her *Madame de Pompadour*'s great fun." He gasped a short breath and then said, "But I don't think, Doctor, you came out here to get my recommendations on what to read, did you?"

"No, I haven't," Barry said, "but I will take your advice about the book. Sorry I hadn't had it earlier. I was in a bookstore this afternoon on my way back from the Royal Victoria Hospital where I'd consulted with a specialist about you. He says he agrees that we can assume you do have the kind of anaemia I think you do."

"Thon pernicious thing?" Maggie said.

"That's right, anaemia due to B_{12} lack, so we can start your treatment today and see what happens. We'll do another blood test in ten days. If the test shows what we expect it to, and that would be the return of red blood cell production, then the diagnosis is correct and you'll be on the road to recovery."

Sonny nodded. "So," he said, "I am to be an experiment with a sample size of one—me? Is that correct?"

"It is."

Sonny smiled. "I'll be delighted to participate. What must I do?"

Barry rummaged in his bag and fished out the cyanocobalamin, a prepacked hypodermic, a bottle of methylated spirits, and a cotton wool ball. "If you'd roll up your sleeve to above your shoulder, please." He soaked the cotton wool in the methylated spirits. The fumes stung his nostrils. In moments he had swabbed the rubber cap of the little bottle and filled the small syringe. "It'll only sting a bit," he said, swabbing Sonny's exposed shoulder over the large muscle, the deltoid, at its point. The injection took seconds.

Sonny sucked in his breath.

"There," Barry said. "All done."

"Thank you, Doctor," Sonny said. "Not bad at all."

"I'm afraid you're going to start feeling a bit like a pincushion," Barry said. "You're going to need daily injections until your blood count is entirely normal. Each one of us will put you on our home visit list so you'll not need to come to the surgery."

"Thank you, sir," Maggie said.

"And assuming you are right in your diagnosis, how long will it take to get my counts to become normal again?" Sonny asked.

"About a month," Barry said, "and then it's once-a-month injections for life."

"That's not too bad, dear," Maggie said. She tugged at her nose. "I've a cousin with diabetes. She has to give herself injections twice a day every day." She cocked her head to one side. "Doctor Laverty, could you mebbe teach Sonny how to do it himself or me to do it for him? Save youse doctors an awful lot of trips?"

"There's an idea," Barry said, and wondered why if, as he well knew, diabetics could be taught to self-administer their insulin, other patients needing regular jags could not? "It's not usual for PA patients," he said. "Let me think about that in a couple of weeks. We'll be doing a blood test in ten days and if it's showing the right response we'll mebbe teach Sonny or you, Maggie, to do the injections."

"That would be grand," she said, and grinned her toothless grin at Sonny. "And there'll be no *craic* to our friends that I'm always needling you neither."

Sonny and Barry laughed. That Maggie could joke was a measure of her relief. Barry handed her the bottle of B$_{12}$. "Pop that in your fridge, but take it out in the morning."

"I will," she said.

"I'm sorry," Barry said, "that we can't fix your nerve damage."

Sonny nodded. "You did tell me earlier. Pity, but it's not so bad. Bit of pins and needles. Not always being sure where my feet are. I'm not in pain. I can live with it." He smiled at Maggie. "And don't you be worrying your head either."

Typical of the man, Barry thought. "That's it then," he said. "I'll write out your lab forms for Monday week, and then I'll be off." Barry sat at a table and started filling in the forms. "I suppose there's no word about Jasper?"

Sonny shook his head. "I'm afraid not." He took a deep breath. "But we keep hoping."

Maggie stood behind her husband and squeezed his shoulder. "We do, and thanks for asking, Doctor."

"I'm sorry," Barry said, and completed the requisition for the blood work, including a reticulocyte count. "Here," he said, "and I'll arrange for the ambulance again too." He stood.

"I'll see you out, sir," Maggie said, and after Sonny and Barry had said their good-byes he followed her into the hall. It was going to be very satisfying if he were proven right in about ten days' time. If he wasn't, and he'd deliberately avoided talking about the implications so as not to worry the Houstons, it was going to be difficult having to tell them. But, damn it all, it was a risk worth taking.

14

He Has a Fever

O'Reilly watched Kitty examine several grapefruit before selecting three and putting them in his shopping basket to keep half a dozen carrots and a fresh cauliflower company. He felt the increased weight on his left arm.

"Morning, Doctor and Mrs. O'Reilly," Aggie Arbuthnot said. "Helping out with the shopping, sir?"

"That I am," he said. "Mrs. O'Reilly calls me Bob. It's short for 'beast of burden.'"

Aggie laughed. "You're a quare gag, sir, so you are, but it is about time men started giving their missusses a hand. Fair play til you. When my Henry, God love him, was alive he was a great one for helping round the place." She wandered off in the direction of a table where ranks of onions rubbed shoulders with paper bags of mushrooms lying beside rows of cucumbers. Lennon's greengrocers was well stocked and O'Reilly marvelled at the out-of-season fresh fruit and vegetables. They would have been flown in from places like Israel and the U.S.A. This shopping for grub was all foreign to him. Kinky had taken care of all that before he'd married. Now Kitty liked to do some herself if she was off duty.

As part of his plan to get her to slow down from her nursing, O'Reilly had come along to keep her company. He intended to turn the routine Saturday morning chore into an outing by surprising her with a trip to Culloden for lunch, which was why they'd come in the Rover rather than enjoying the short walk from Number One. The treat would also be a diversionary tactic. Kitty had been muttering about popping into Alice Moloney's shop to look at some new bolts of material and he was damn sure she did not intend having a dress made.

"That's about it unless you fancy some artichokes."

"No, thanks. I've never quite understood the appeal of the artichoke. There seems to be so much work to eat them for so little reward. " He joined her at the back of a short queue.

Connie Brown had son Colin by the hand and was waiting in line behind Cissie Sloan. Colin's best friend Murphy the mongrel was on a leash, sitting obediently at his feet. Colin and Donal Donnelly had trained the pup well.

On the far side of the scrubbed wooden counter, Mister Lennon, the owner, was totting up Cissie's bill, licking the end of a pencil as he did the addition on a small slip of paper. Like all workers in village specialist shops—grocers, butchers, fishmongers, bakers, greengrocers, newsagents—he wore a long, lightweight linen coat. He also had a barely controlled look of irritation on his face as he tried to tot up the bill while Cissie rambled on—and on.

"... anyroad, I says til her, says I, 'Is that a fact?' Says she til me, 'In soul it is. I would not of had've believed it if I had not of would've been there and seen it for myself—'"

"That's be seven shillings and ninepence ha'penny, Mrs. Sloan." The grocer let out a sigh, and sticking the pencil behind his ear, opened the cash register with a loud *ting*.

O'Reilly watched a look close to surprise cross Cissie's face as if only now had it dawned on her that she'd be expected to pay. Then the ritual, strange to O'Reilly, began. She rummaged in her handbag like an archaeologist sifting through mounds of pot shards in a midden and muttering to herself until finally she found her change purse. "Seven and ninepence ha'penny?"

"Correct," said Mister Lennon, his eyes behind thick-lensed spectacles raised in supplication.

"There's a two-bob bit, and another one, that's four shillings." Methodically and ponderously she counted out coin after coin. O'Reilly chuckled. It's a good thing they weren't in a rush.

Kitty was hunkered down beside Colin, looking at his face. "Fingal? I don't think young Colin's very well. I just patted his head and he's on fire."

"I didn't think he was at himself yesterday. He was restless and a bit drowsy, and had a wee cough and a runny nose," Connie said. "I kept him home from school."

To emphasise her words, Colin hacked.

"But I give him baby aspirin and it seemed til help. The shipyard's on overtime this weekend so Lenny's at work and we needed milk and eggs so I thought I'd just pop out with him for a few minutes."

Colin sniffed and said, "My mammy always buys me sweeties when we go shopping, and then me and Murphy was going til go looking for Jasper. Murphy's mammy is Missy, one of Mister Sonny Houston's dogs, so I thought mebbe he might remember Jasper's smell. But

I'm feeling funny. I've a sore head and the light's hurting my eyes, so it is."

O'Reilly glanced at Kitty. He guessed she was probably thinking what he was. Colin might be in the early stages of one of the many "inevitable" childhood fevers. Until very recently, as vaccines were being developed and introduced, very few people reached adulthood without having had bouts of measles, German measles, chicken pox, mumps, whooping cough, and scarlet fever. The scourge of poliomyelitis was being defeated with the Sabin vaccine, introduced in 1962.

"I rubbed some Vicks vapour ointment on his chest this morning to help his wee cough and brung him along. I needed to go and it's just a wee treat for him, so it is." Connie looked anxiously down at her son.

O'Reilly squatted beside Kitty. The heat from Colin's body was releasing the unguent's decongestant vapours. Their scent was heavy on the air. "Not feeling so hot, Colin?" O'Reilly put the back of his hand to Colin's forehead. The boy was febrile, all right.

"—and there's three more ha'pennies." There was triumph in Cissy Sloan's voice. "Now you've made me late for me hair appointment, Mister Lennon. I've got to be getting along." She smiled and nodded to the O'Reillys, and left.

"Ahem," said Mister Lennon. "You're next, Mrs. Brown."

"Go ahead, Connie," O'Reilly said. "We'll keep an eye to Colin."

Kitty put her head close to O'Reilly's and whispered so Colin wouldn't hear. "Bet you it's measles. It's that time of the year."

O'Reilly nodded. Colin needed to be examined, but not here in the shop, and in the early four-day overt period of the disease it was highly contagious. If that was indeed what Colin had. O'Reilly handed Kitty the shopping basket and she stood up.

Ting.

"Thank you, Mrs. Brown. Mrs. O'Reilly. Nice to see you."

"Connie," O'Reilly said, "I'd like to take a proper look at Colin." No matter that Barry was on call. O'Reilly wanted to drive the Browns home in a kind of quarantine. Keep the little tyke out of contact with other children they might meet on the street. He may as well examine the boy while he was at it. "We'll run you home. I've got my medical bag in the car."

"If you say so, Doctor, thank you. And I'm sorry, I never should have brung him to the store today. I knew he wasn't well but I didn't want to leave him alone. Come along, Colin. We're going for a ride in Doctor O'Reilly's Rover."

<hr />

"Come in. Come in." Connie ushered them into the small thatched cottage on Station Road beside the tobacconist's and round the corner from the Mucky Duck. "I'm going to take him upstairs and put him to bed. Will youse go into the lounge until I'm ready?"

"We will," O'Reilly said. "And take your time. We're not in a rush." Still lots of time to go to Culloden once Colin was sorted out. He followed Kitty into the small, tidy lounge.

"I will bet you it's measles," she said.

"It could be lots of other things."

She inclined her head to one side. "I've been a nurse as long as you've been a doctor and I worked for four years in an orphanage in Tenerife. I'll bet you right now it's measles. And just because I'm willing to bet doesn't mean I'm taking Colin's illness lightly."

There was a light in her eyes that made him uneasy, but he couldn't resist the bet. "You're on," he said, and offered his hand for a shake. She took it. "And what are the stakes?"

"New curtains," she said, and had to stifle her laughter.

"You witch," he said. "Oh, you sorceress. All right." His own chuckles had subsided by the time Connie came back. He really could never get cross with Kitty. And it was time to stop trying to avoid the inevitable. Why not be gracious? "I have him tucked up in his wee bed, upstairs. Will you come and see him, sir? And Mrs. O'Reilly too?" She led the way up a steep, narrow staircase.

O'Reilly and Kitty followed. He noticed how the brass stair rods that held a worn carpet in place had been polished until they glowed. Connie Brown was a house-proud woman. The bannister wobbled under his grasp.

She tutted and said, "Sorry it's a bit loose. Lenny's going til fix it—one day." She shook her head. "He just keeps forgetting, that's all. It's not just the overtime. He's working two jobs now. He wants to put some aside—for Colin, for his education," she said. "Mister Bishop'll be giving money when Colin goes to Queen's, but there's bound to be extras."

O'Reilly could hear the pride in her voice. Colin Brown was a typical twelve-year-old boy. He loved his dog and his white mouse, Snowball. And he was mad about soccer and aeroplanes and ice cream and playing practical jokes and getting into mischief. And good God, he thought. At his age he might even be getting interested in girls. But, with Sue Nolan's help, he was also a diligent and highly intelligent pupil.

His mother opened a door to a small bedroom.

The plaid curtains were closed and it was dim in the room. Only a single sixty-watt bulb surrounded by an elderly pink tasseled light hung from the ceiling, and flanking it were balsa and doped-paper models of a Spitfire, a Lancaster bomber, and an SE5a World War I biplane, all suspended by threads. A poster for the Disney hit *Lady and the Tramp* was tacked to the wall beside a small single bed.

An aquarium, empty save for a layer of sand at the bottom, on which were arranged stones and logs, sat on a small table close to the bed. Lord alone knew what was or had been in there. In a cage beside it, Snowball the white mouse sat up and whiffled his whiskers. Animal mad, that was Colin Brown.

He lay curled up in the middle of the bed. He sniffled and then sneezed.

Kitty went to one side of the bed and stood there.

"Mrs. O'Reilly's a nurse, Colin. She's come to help me." O'Reilly hitched his own backside onto the edge of the bed. "Getting worse, is it, son?"

"Aye." Colin rolled onto his back. "I'm dead sick now, so I am. I thought I was okay this morning, but now I feel all hot," Colin said. "And the light's hurting my eyes worser and my head's sore." He coughed, a dry, sharp hack.

"We'll have to see about making you better," O'Reilly said. He rummaged in his bag. "Here, let's pop this under your tongue." Photophobia and headache could be due to meningitis, inflammation of the membranes that surrounded the brain, or a brain tumour, but were more likely to be associated with one of the fevers of childhood. O'Reilly took Colin's pulse. It was one hundred and his skin was hot to the touch.

"You said he started feeling off-colour yesterday, Mammy?"

"Aye. I thought it was just a cold, but I kept him out of school."

Colin might be sick, but it didn't prevent him saying, "That was wheeker 'cause school's no good if that wee corker Miss Nolan's not there. She makes the lessons great *craic* too."

O'Reilly secretly had to agree with Colin. Sue was an extremely attractive young woman and he had no doubt that she made learning fun.

"Once I gave him the aspirin, he seemed to get a wee bit better so I let him come til the shops."

Which was a pity. How many people had Colin come into contact with? Many infections were known as "notifiable," which meant the Department of Health would have to be. More bloody paperwork, an aspect of his work he detested. But it couldn't be helped. He'd fill out the forms after lunch.

O'Reilly removed the thermometer. "Hundred and one," he said. "Bit high." He moved up the bed. "I'm going to have a look at you, Colin, so can you sit up?"

"I'll help you," Kitty said.

Once Kitty had Colin settled, O'Reilly put a hand behind the boy's head and gently pushed forward until the boy's chin touched his chest. "That hurt?"

"No, Doctor."

Good. That and the fact that the great muscles at the back of the neck had not tightened up was conclusive evidence that there was no meningeal irritation.

O'Reilly took out an ophthalmoscope. "Have to look

in your eyes. Can you stare at . . ." He turned to the poster. "Tramp's nose and try not to blink?"

"Aye, certainly."

He looked at Kitty. "And Mrs. O'Reilly will help by holding your head still."

O'Reilly, knowing that the instrument's brighter light would be uncomfortable, managed to examine both eyes quickly. "Good," he said. "Normal." He'd been looking for papilloedema, distortion and swelling of the optic nerve, a sure sign that intracranial pressure was increased, a finding associated with brain tumours. In its absence he was pretty sure Colin had one of the fevers of childhood. Which one? Most were characterised by rashes, and certainly there wasn't one on Colin's face. "Can we take off your pajama jacket, please?"

Kitty unbuttoned his faded red-and-white-striped pyjamas. In a household like the Browns', clothes had to be made to last. No rash. Too early probably. It took minutes to listen with the stethoscope. The boy's lungs were clear. Most fevers could be complicated by secondary infections like pneumonia. Not this one. He fished in his inside jacket pocket and produced a pencil torch. His bag yielded a wooden tongue depressor. "Open wide, please, and stick out your tongue." As Colin did, O'Reilly used the spatula to push Colin's cheek away from his back teeth. There, plain to see, were tiny bluish-white dots studding an inflamed and reddened mucous membrane. O'Reilly removed the speculum. Koplik's spots, named for the American doctor who described them in 1896, meant one thing only. Colin Brown had measles in the early or catarrhal stage, which would last for the rest of today, tomorrow, and the day after, when the typical morbilliform rash would start to appear.

O'Reilly helped Colin button up his jacket. "You, young man," O'Reilly said, "have the red measles. *Rubeola,* if you want to know the scientific name." And I, he thought, I am going to have new curtains. He deliberately avoided catching Kitty's eye.

"Rub-e-ola," Colin sounded out slowly. "Like ruby, right? Meaning red? So does that mean I'll live forever?"

Kitty frowned.

O'Reilly sang the first lines of an old playground song,

Wallflower, wallflower growing up so high,
He's got the measles. He'll never, never die.

He chuckled. "Probably not, but, Mummy, your Colin's going to get a rash soon. It'll start on his ears and forehead. Wee red points that get bigger and run into each other making shapes like half-moons and blotches—"

"I don't mean til interrupt, sir, but we've all seen kiddies with the measles." Connie rubbed her brow and looked at her son. For the first time, O'Reilly noticed the circles under Connie Brown's eyes. She looked weary.

"You're quite right, Connie," he said gently. "We've all seen measles or had them. The rash will last for about four days, then fade. About that time his temperature will be normal again."

"And do I get to stay off school?"

"Good question," O'Reilly said. "And the answer is, yes. For ten days after the rash is gone."

Despite his illness, Colin Brown grinned and grinned. "Can I go outside?"

"If the weather's good. We'll tell you when. Why?"

"I told you, me and Murphy was going to look for Jasper the day. I want to be the one to find him and solve the mystery."

"You're going nowhere today, young Sherlock. I know you're worried about Jasper, but the search will have to wait for later, Colin. Get some rest, and you'll have to take some medicine."

"Yeugh."

"Connie," O'Reilly said, "I'll write you a scrip for penicillin V. I want Colin to take one tablet every six hours for a week starting when the rash appears, but I or one of the other doctors will be in to see him when it does. Let Kinky know."

"And will the penicillin cure the measles? Mean he won't be off school so long."

He shook his head. "No. It's a precaution." And he saw no reason to worry Connie by telling her that secondary bacterial infection could cause pneumonia, middle ear infection, and ulcers of the cornea that could lead to blindness.

"I'm very glad it's just one of them children's diseases. Not serious, like," she said, smoothing the hair from Colin's forehead. "Poor little mite."

O'Reilly nodded, but in his opinion the sooner every child was immunised in infancy the better. A measles jag had been available since 1963, one for mumps would be introduced later this year, and work was advancing on rubella prevention. They would protect each individual from three diseases, any of which could have serious complications, and it would protect the other kids too.

"Right," he said, "we'll be off."

The empty aquarium must have caught Kitty's eye. "Colin," she said, "what did you keep in there?"

Colin smiled sleepily. "Great crested newts. They're still in there, hibernating under the rocks. My daddy took me to the lead mines at Conlig last summer and we caught them in a wee pond."

"Mmmm," said O'Reilly, "any idea . . ." But he cut himself off short. There'd be plenty of time to ask Colin what he wanted to be when he grew up. The lad was drowsy, not well. "I'll see you soon," O'Reilly said.

Connie bade them farewell at the doorstep and he held open the door of the Rover and shut it behind Kitty. Together inside they both spoke at once.

"Kinky says Miss Moloney's got some lovely teal blue—"

"Have you had the measles, Kitty?"

"Yes."

"So have I. Which makes us both unsusceptible contacts, so we don't have to be quarantined. And I, dear Mrs. Fingal Flahertie O'Reilly, am going to take the woman I love for lunch at the Culloden—"

She laughed. "Lunch at the Culloden! You old reprobate, you're welshing on the bet. You'll try anything to get out of buying new curtains."

He pulled away from the kerb. "Nonsense. I've been planning this little treat since this morning. Long before I was hoodwinked into agreeing to your bet. And, as I was going to say before I was interrupted, after lunch we'll visit Miss Moloney."

"Lunch and new curtains all on the same day. You are a pet." Kitty leant over and pecked his cheek.

"I know," said O'Reilly with a smug grin, "but don't you tell anybody. I have a reputation to uphold. Now, Culloden," he accelerated, "here we come."

15

That Will Batter the Gateway

Did you enjoy your lunch, Kitty?"

"I think," she said, "that, after Kinky of course, the Culloden does the best steak and kidney pie in Ulster. Thank you. A girl could get used to being spoiled."

That is, of course, the object of the exercise, he thought, but said, "My pleasure." O'Reilly, replete himself following a plate of beer-battered halibut and chips, listened to the rain bouncing off the Rover's roof as the old car neared the corner at Number One Main on the Bangor to Belfast Road. "I've not forgotten we're going to Miss Moloney's, but I want to pop in home first, pick up a pair of boots that need resoling so I can drop them off at the cobblers."

"Fair enough."

"Then home for a leisurely afternoon. There's a rugby game on the telly. Ireland are playing Australia in Dublin." As he braked he indicated and turned left onto the lane leading to his garage behind his house and the gate to his back garden.

Looking back, Kitty said, "Fingal, there's a lorry's coming down the road at a ferocious tilt."

O'Reilly stopped the car beside the gate. "Sit you here, girl, and keep dry. I'll just be a tick," and, ignoring the downpour, he got out to head for the house to get his boots. He heard the sudden explosive hiss of air brakes, turned, and looked back up the road. Begob, Kitty was right. The lorry in question was taking the downhill, nearly ninety-degree, right-hand bend where his house faced the Presbyterian church.

It was a dangerous corner, and for years the council had been threatening halfheartedly to straighten it, but to do so they'd have to expropriate either the church or Number One Main. The Presbyterians had objected with sanctified fervour. Their churchyard with its two-hundred-year-old occupants would have to be disturbed, and the bureaucrats would take away O'Reilly's house over his dead body.

The lorry was going too fast—much too fast—and in this rain the road would be slick. A quick glance reassured him that there were no other vehicles coming this way. The big, articulated vehicle was swaying from side to side. Tyres squealed. Black rubber skid marks appeared on the asphalt. The lorry was halfway into the turn.

"Go on," O'Reilly begged. "Get round the bloody corner. Please."

But the cab missed the crown of the bend and, shuddering and clattering, mounted the footpath.

"Bugger it," O'Reilly yelled as the front wheels destroyed the rosebushes into which he had chucked the hapless Seamus Galvin the day Barry had come to be interviewed in 1964. The cab, to the accompaniment of tearing metal and splintering glass, smashed through the dining room window. The vehicle came to a stop with the bonnet, steam jetting from its radiator, and the front of the cab right through the front wall of Number One Main Street.

O'Reilly ran round the lorry, climbed up on the step, and wrenched the driver's door open.

A man wearing a duncher and dungarees was sitting rigidly, arms braced as his hands clutched the steering wheel. His eyes stared straight ahead, he was trembling all over, and kept repeating, "Oh shite, oh shite, oh shite."

At least he was conscious and did not appear to be in pain, so it was unlikely that any bones were broken. And as far as O'Reilly could see, the man was not bleeding.

Kitty appeared at O'Reilly's shoulder. "Is he okay?"

"Seems to be," he said as he took the man's pulse. "Nip inside and call nine-nine-nine. Then go into the dining room and make sure nobody was hurt in the house. I'll see what I can do here, and when you come back bring some hot sweet tea." It was useful in shock cases, and with a pulse rate of 110 per minute and the pulse itself feeble the man definitely was in shock.

"Right," she said, and headed off.

O'Reilly said, "Can you hear me? I'm a doctor."

The driver said, "I can, sir."

"Have you hurt yourself?"

"I don't think so. I'm just all shook up, so I am."

"What's your name?"

"Sid. Sid Coulter. From Lisburn."

A few more questions told him that the man knew where he was and what day it was. Probably no head injury either. "I think," O'Reilly said, "that apart from banjaxing your lorry you've got away with it. We'll know for certain when the ambulance gets here."

Barry appeared. "Fingal, what the hell happened? From the kitchen it felt like an earthquake."

"Lorry skidded," O'Reilly said.

"Is the driver okay?"

"Seems to be. Is anybody else in there?"

"No. It's Saturday. Nonie's off and Kinky doesn't usually come in at weekends."

"Good. Now go on back into the house. You're getting soaked. There's nothing you can do here and you're on call. Kitty's phoning nine-nine-nine."

"I passed her in the hall."

Kitty appeared. "I've rung for the emergency services. They're on their way."

"'Bout time. The traffic's starting to pile up."

"And here." She handed him a steaming mug. "Hot tea, lots of sugar. Barry was making himself a cuppa."

"Thanks." O'Reilly handed the mug to the driver. "Get that into you." He heard a rapidly approaching *nee-naw, nee-naw.*

"Good. Now go on, the pair of you, in out of the rain. There's not much to do here until the police arrive. Kitty, phone Bertie Bishop, would you? Ask him to come round if he can. We're going to need his help to plug that ruddy great hole in our dining room once the lorry's hauled out."

O'Reilly, together with Kitty and Bertie Bishop, stood in the dining room doorway surveying the damage. Barry had been called out to a case of croup up in the housing estate. The ambulance men had fitted Sid Coulter with a protective neck brace before carrying him to the ambulance, where O'Reilly had made sure the lorry driver had not sustained any serious injuries.

Constable Mulligan and two officers in a police car

from Holywood had between them taken the details of the accident and directed traffic until a tow truck had arrived and dragged the battered lorry away. The fire brigade had stood by until the firemen were satisfied there was no risk of fire.

"What a mess," Kitty said. She gave O'Reilly a sympathetic look as if to say, I know I wanted to get rid of them, but . . . "New curtains are the least of our worries now," she said. O'Reilly flashed her a grateful smile.

"Right," said Bertie. "The first thing is to get onto your insurers. Get permission to protect the house from further spoilage. Have them send an assessor round too."

"The policy's in my desk. Top right-hand drawer," O'Reilly said. "Kitty, could you get it and phone?"

"At once." She went into the surgery.

"Boys-a-boys," Bertie said. "You're lucky nobody was in here sitting with their back to the window."

The lorry had shoved one of the dining room chairs underneath the table. Between it and the jagged hole in the outside wall, broken pieces of window frame were jumbled up with pieces of glass, plaster, laths, and bricks.

"Leave it til me, Doctor." Bertie strode into the room, followed by O'Reilly. They picked their way past the debris to the broken wall. Bertie examined the place where the window had stood. "Right," he said. "Once we get permission, a wooden frame and canvas'll do the trick. Keep the rain out until Monday. Then I'll get a crew with a skip straight round. Clean out the rubbish."

"I'd be grateful, Bertie." O'Reilly could vaguely hear Kitty on the hall phone.

"Och, sure, isn't it what I do, Doctor? Meantime,

you'll need til follow up with your insurance people and have them talk to the lorry driver's insurers. It'll cost a penny or two to rebuild, so it will."

"I thought so," O'Reilly said. "Can't be helped."

"The driver's insurance should take care of it," Bertie said. "It shouldn't need to go to court. That corner's been a known hazard for years."

Kitty came back. "The Cornhill Insurance people have been most helpful. Disturb as little as possible, they say, but we have permission to put up a bit of weather proofing. It's to their advantage that the less extra damage done the better."

"Great," said Bertie. "If I can use your phone I'll get Donal and a couple of other lads round right away to get the hole plugged."

"In the hall," O'Reilly said. "Meanwhile, we'll cover up the rest of the furniture in here with dust sheets, and when we've done, Bertie, will you join Mrs. O'Reilly and me upstairs for a cup of tea?"

O'Reilly, Kitty, and Bertie sat round the fire in the cosy upstairs lounge. Distant sounds of sawing and hammering came from below where Donal Donnelly and two other workmen were building the patch for the dining room wall. For some time to come the folks at Number One would have to take their meals up here while reconstruction went ahead. At least the surgery was intact.

"Here, Bertie," said Kitty, offering a three-tiered cake stand. "Jacob's Afternoon Tea biscuits, Kinky's jam tarts, or McVitie's digestive biscuits."

"Thanks very much, Mrs. O'Reilly." He took a jam tart. "My Flo makes these with Kinky's recipe, but, no harm til Flo, hers are never quite the same, so they're not."

Kitty laughed. "Kinky really is one of a kind."

O'Reilly said, "And so are you, Bertie. It's very decent of you coming out on a pouring Saturday afternoon to arrange for temporary repairs."

Bertie swallowed a bite of jam tart. "It's no different to yourself. You don't say, 'Sorry it's Saturday' if there's an emergency, do you?"

" 'Course not," O'Reilly said, then, "Pass me a digestive, please, love." He took a bite. "Tell me, Bertie, how long will it take to get the dining room fixed?"

Bertie Bishop pursed his lips. "There may be a wee snag."

"Oh?" O'Reilly sat forward. "Snag?"

"You see, as long as I've been on council they've been chuntering on about straightening the road at this corner. An accident like today's was bound til happen sooner or later. It's a mercy no one was hurt."

O'Reilly frowned. "I don't see what that has to do with the price of corn."

"You see, Doctor, everybody on council knows yourself. They haven't wanted to upset you. We've spoken to the ministry to see if we could go through the churchyard, but there's laws hundreds of years old, so there are. You can't dig up graves without enough paperwork to run the *Belfast Telegraph* for a month."

What was Bertie hinting at? Had this accident opened some doors to official action on straightening the road through his property? O'Reilly looked around the room in the house that had been a central part of his life since 1946. It held his furniture, his books, his records, his memories. And he could lose it? He gritted his teeth and clenched his fists. Not without a fight he'd not.

Bertie said, "Your house was built for the Presbyterians too."

"I know," said O'Reilly. "Old Doctor Flanagan told me about it. When Flanagan's grandfather, Michael, was minister here, a donor put up two hundred and fifty pounds in 1817 and took a two-hundred-year lease from the MacNeills. He built a manse to give to the church, and finished the building in 1818. Michael's son Ethan succeeded him as pastor to the Presbyterian flock. None of Ethan's sons went into the church, but his oldest boy, my old boss Doctor Flanagan, studied medicine. By the time he was ready to set up his medical practice in 1897 the new minister was a bachelor and needed something smaller. The church allowed Doctor Flanagan to buy the old manse from them and his estate eventually sold it to me after the war."

"I didn't know that," Bertie said. "But if that's when it was built it's Georgian. I'll have to apply for planning permission to do any renovations and major repairs on a house of that period. There's a group on council wants that there road straightened . . ."

"I don't believe it," O'Reilly growled. "Through my house?" He looked at Kitty. Her hands were clasped tightly in her lap, her gaze intent on Bertie.

"I'm sorry, Doctor, Mrs. O'Reilly, but it'll have til be debated at the next meeting."

"And when's that?" Kitty said quietly.

"Two weeks."

"So we'll have to live under canvas for two weeks before you can even get started on the repairs?" O'Reilly'd lost interest in his tea and biscuit.

"I'm afraid so, but . . ." Bertie brightened, "there's another party would like til see a bypass round the south side of Ballybucklebo. There's far too much traffic go-

ing through the village now and it's going til get worse."
His smile was self-deprecatory. "I'm the chairman of
that group and we've been consulting with contrac-
tors in Belfast too. My company could handle the,"
Bertie paused, "the demolition—sorry, sir—of Number
One . . ."

O'Reilly flinched.

". . . and a bit of road straightening here. But a road
round the village is a bigger job than my company can
handle by itself."

"Do you think you'll have a chance? I mean to get the
bypass round the village," Kitty asked.

"If it comes to a vote, it'll be close," Bertie said, "but
I didn't come down the Lagan on a soap bubble yesterday."

"Indeed you didn't." Bertie Bishop was one of the
most politically astute men in the village. Particularly,
the thought struck O'Reilly, if there was likely to be a
profit in it for Councillor Bishop.

"I wish I could tell youse different, but that's the way
it is." Bertie stood. "And there's one other snag. You
know there were two vacancies filled on council just before Christmas?"

"Yes, I know," O'Reilly said, "Alice Moloney was
elected to one of them. She was telling me all about it
when I bumped into her the other day. And the other
one is . . . damn it to hell . . ."

"Hubert Doran."

"Hubert Doran. Hubert bloody Doran. I remembered
thinking at the time that it might be a problem. He and
I have been at daggers drawn for years. I certainly did not
vote for that man, but he got in, bugger it," said O'Reilly.
"Sorry, Kitty, but Hubert Doran, pardon my French, is
a turd of the first magnitude."

"Fingal," Kitty said, "in my job, I'm no stranger to language. I understand that you're upset, but I'll not 'pardon your French' in our own home."

"Look. I'm sorry, but this is all such a bloo—I mean a ruddy shock. I had no idea council has been quietly plotting to demolish my house."

Kitty softened. "All right. This once, but please, Fingal, don't make a habit of it."

O'Reilly saw Bertie try to hide a smile and fail. "There's been no plotting going on, Doctor, just civic due diligence is all. I guessed something like that was going on with you and Doran," Bertie said. "He's definitely in favour of, and I'm sorry, demolishing Number One."

"Blue—" O'Reilly glanced at Kitty and cut himself off. "And I don't suppose there's anything we can do to stop him, or start our own campaign?"

"Yes," said Kitty. "We can fight this, surely?"

"Leave it til me. I'll not ask what the feud is about. It's none of my business, so it isn't. I'll just do everything I can."

"Thank you, Bertie. I appreciate that. Will the council meeting be open to the public?" O'Reilly asked.

"As far as I know," Bertie said, "but I'll be in touch the minute I hear anything about what might happen at council. And I promise I'll do all I can."

"Thanks, Bertie," Kitty said.

"Thank you for the tea, Mrs. O'Reilly. I promised Flo I'd take her to the Grand Opera House the night. It's the last performance of this year's pantomime, *Aladdin and His Wonderful Lamp,* so I'll have to be checking on Donal and his men, then be running along. I'll see myself out."

O'Reilly stood. Two bloody weeks to wait. Bureaucracy, blast and damnation, O'Reilly thought. And the reams of paperwork for this would make Colin Brown's measles notification form look like a page from a kiddy's copybook. "Thanks for everything, Bertie," O'Reilly said.

"Say hello to Flo," Kitty said as the portly councillor left. "Now sit down, Fingal, and tell me about this Doran man. Why are you and he feuding?"

O'Reilly collapsed into the chair beside Kitty's and gripped its upholstered arms. "He's a very well-off farmer. Has about sixty acres that marches with the Houstons' place. Thinks he's no goat's toe. He rarely comes into the village, thank God, so I don't see much of him, but six or seven years ago I was out there giving Arthur his constitutional. There's a warren up there at the back of Sonny and Maggie's and you know how Arthur loves to push the bunnies out.

"I heard a ferocious howling and there was the bastard holding a golden retriever bitch by her ear—her ear—and beating the tar out of her with her own leash. He was screaming at her and he punched her. I made Arthur stay, ran over and—damn it all I was furious. He set up to hit her again so I grabbed his arm and I decked him. He was out for about two minutes. When he came to, I told him if he ever, *ever* laid hands on a dog like that again I'd thrash the bejasus out of him. Then I walked away. As I went back to Arthur, I heard him yell, 'I'll get you, O'Reilly, you shite, and you know what long memories Ulstermen have.'"

"That's horrible, Fingal. Horrible. All of it, the dog beating, the threat to you," Kitty said. "It does sound like you've made a bad enemy." She frowned. "But Bertie's on your side. So is John MacNeill. With luck, Doran won't be able to influence too many councillors. Try not to worry too much, love. We'll have to wait and see, that's all," she said, "and I have great faith in Bertie."

"So do I," O'Reilly said, "especially if there's likely to be money for him in any dealings."

"And I'm sure your brother, Lars, will have an opinion. You can ask him next Tuesday when we have dinner at Ballybucklebo House."

"I can, can't I?" O'Reilly said, brightening.

"And," said Kitty with a twinkle in those grey eyes flecked with amber, "it's an ill wind or in this case an ill rain that blows nobody any good."

"What are you on about?"

"It'll be months now until you have to get new dining room curtains. And, I did ask, the insurance will pay for them."

"Kitty O'Hallorhan," he said, "I do love you."

16

Taxes upon Every Article

T hank you, Thompson," John MacNeill said.
"Will that be all, my lord?" The marquis's valet/
butler, who had served in the war with O'Reilly on
HMS *Warspite,* stood at attention, a silver tray tucked
under one arm. He had given whiskeys to the men while
Myrna sipped a small glass of Harvey's Shooting Sherry
and Kitty her usual gin and tonic.

"Yes, thank you. I'll ring if we need anything else.
Please tell Cook we'll dine at seven forty-five."

"My lord." Thompson left.

Logs blazed in the grate and Finn MacCool, one of
the marquis's red setters, lay on the rug.

The lord of the manor stood leaning against the corner of the drawing room mantelpiece with one leg
crossed over the other at the ankle. He wore a blazer
with the eight-pointed star crest of the Irish Guards embroidered in silver wire on the left breast pocket. A ma-
roon silk cravat filled the open neck of a white shirt and
there were knife-edge creases in his grey flannels.
O'Reilly glanced above the fireplace at an enormous oil
painting in the style of Sir Joshua Reynolds of a man in
the ermine-trimmed robes of an eighteenth-century peer

of the realm. Then he looked at the semicircle of seated guests surrounding the present peer. It was a tableau from a way of life that was passing. That, of course, was why Lars was here. To help with the transition.

"Glad you could make it, Fingal, Kitty. And for a change on an evening when it's not lashing down. The forecast says we should have sunny skies for the next few days."

"Thank you for inviting us, John," Kitty said.

O'Reilly thought she looked lovely tonight in a simple knee-length black satin sheath dress. "By five thirty it's still as dark as old Nick's hatband," he said, "but at least it's warmer." O'Reilly noted that while John Mac-Neill was an Ulsterman through and through, he had adopted the very English custom of using the weather as a neutral kickoff for any conversation.

"Which I imagine will make things a bit less draughty at Number One, Kitty," Myrna said. "I can't imagine what it must have been like having a dirty great lorry come through your window. I drove past your place yesterday. Usual Monday-morning departmental meeting at Queen's. Your rosebushes have had it and that's quite a hole patched up in your wall."

"The driver made a right bollocks of that turn," O'Reilly said. "Kitty and I had just driven into our lane and she could tell he was going too fast. Next thing we knew air brakes were hissing, tyres were squealing, and then a bloody great bang when the cab hit the wall. Bricks and broken glass everywhere. Luckily no one was hurt. Kinky and Archie came straight round on Saturday evening to see if they could help. Decent of them. An insurance assessor came, but unfortunately we can't start work on the repairs yet."

"Why on earth not?" Lars asked.

O'Reilly sighed. "Apparently council has for years been arguing about whether to widen that road. Now they're seriously looking at their options. Trying to decide whether to give me planning permission to do the repairs or expropriate my property."

"Expropriate Number One Main? Really?" said Lars.

"Afraid so, brother."

"Well, they'll have to give you fair market price and a decent settlement to cover the costs of inconvenience. You can be sure I'll see to that for you."

Having a solicitor for a brother did come in handy at times, O'Reilly thought.

"Fingal and I don't want money from the council," Kitty said. "We want to stay put. It's our home."

"I've been in that house since 1938 when I joined old Doctor Flanagan. When I came back after the war and bought the practice I kept the place exactly as it had been."

"Right down to the dining room curtains," Kitty said.

O'Reilly laughed. "We'll be getting new ones." He grew more serious. "I've a lot of memories wrapped up in that old place and we're not going to give it up without a fight."

"Good for you, Fingal," Myrna said.

"I wonder," Lars said, "if the lorry owners or their insurers might try to sue the borough council?"

"Whatever for? If the man was driving too fast," Myrna asked.

"For having a known dangerous corner and not doing anything about it. If Kitty could testify that the lorry was being driven recklessly, then the case would probably collapse."

"We'll keep our fingers crossed that it doesn't come

to that, Lars," O'Reilly said. "Kitty and I can do without court appearances. We've enough to worry about wondering whether the house might be expropriated."

"There'd be no question of that," the marquis said, "if our family still owned the land where your house is, but . . ." He shrugged.

Myrna snorted and said with an edge to her voice, "We can thank Sir William Harcourt and Gladstone's Liberals for that. The nineteenth-century Liberals were socialists at heart, bunch of sociological Robin Hoods, rob the rich and give to the poor," Myrna said. "Although I suppose the conditions of the working poor after the Industrial Revolution were pretty grim."

"You just have to read Dickens," O'Reilly said. "Oliver Twist in the workhouse."

"And," John said, "in fairness, Myrna, there was an enormous gap between the very rich and the very poor. On the other hand, the peerage and landed gentry provided a great deal of employment, cheap housing, board, keep, got doctors for their servants if they fell ill."

"A way of life I've only read about in books," said O'Reilly. "Wodehouse, Galsworthy. Although even when I was growing up in Dublin, we had a live-in cook and maid."

"Ah, well, in our father's day, before the first war, the big house here had butlers, footmen, a housekeeper, cooks, all kinds of maids, nannies, and that was just the indoor staff. The Liberals did not approve of people who lived as we did. I suppose they saw it as a kind of feudalism. And it was, I dare say," Myrna said with a sigh. "They were all for taking from the wealthy to fund what we'd call social services today. Their government had a four-million-pound deficit, so in 1894 the chancellor of the exchequer, Harcourt, introduced an eight percent death duty and it's been a source of revenue for successive governments ever since. Huh. Has anyone ever heard of a government that lowered taxes?"

"At least," John said, "until 1911, the year after I was born, the House of Lords could veto bills from the House of Commons, keep rates at a reasonable level. Then, when Dad was still Marquis of Ballybucklebo, H. H. Asquith, another Liberal prime minister, removed the peers' power of veto with the Parliament Act. Then he introduced increased estate duties in 1914. I can still remember Father coming home from taking his seat in Westminster."

"He must have been spitting teeth," said O'Reilly.

"Oh, he was. He knew it was the end, and he was right too, as far as the MacNeill family was concerned."

"It was a very bad time for us MacNeills," Myrna added. "Our father's younger brother, Uncle Albert—"

John MacNeill laughed. "Myrna, must we tell all our secrets?" His laugh was light, but there was a warning sound in his voice.

"Come on, John, you don't mind if I tell our friends about our black sheep?"

The marquis picked up his drink from the mantel, walked to a wingback chair a few steps away, and settled into it. "No, not really. Not at all, in fact. I suppose most aristocratic families have one. Often the younger brother of the title holder. It's been part of our family lore for years. Go ahead, Myrna."

O'Reilly saw Kitty and Lars both lean forward. He'd heard bits and pieces of the story over the years but never from the family themselves.

"Uncle Albert had what might have been called a chequered career. He was expelled from Eton, so grandfather got him into Portora Royal School in County

Fermanagh. Then another year at Gonville and Caius College in Cambridge, where he was sent down for embezzling undergraduate society funds, which of course Grampa had to repay. Albert then said he wanted to write, so he took over the townhouse in Belgravia and as far as we know produced nothing much—"

"Except," John said, "a massive gambling debt—"

"And a standing order for Veuve Clicquot?" said Kitty with a wicked smile.

"Kitty," O'Reilly said.

Myrna exploded into laughter and had to put her drink on the table before she spilled it. She nodded vigorously to Kitty. "And quite possibly a few illegitimate children."

"Myrna." John MacNeill was shaking his head, but he was also smiling and looking at his sister with a fondness O'Reilly found touching. "Anyway, the family connection had given him membership at White's gentlemen's club. It always had that reputation. As for the champagne, I'm sure you're right, Kitty. The house on Wilton Crescent became the site of some quite wild parties."

"So, to cut a very long story short," Myrna said, "two town houses in London had to go on the auction block and father had to sell off everything we owned from the Black Swan north to the tide line to get Uncle Albert out of debt. There was some talk of making him a remittance man."

"I know what those were," said Kitty, smiling. "I've read my Somerset Maugham. They were wastrel sons of wealthy families who were shipped off to the South Sea Islands or remote corners of the empire like Canada and sent money, a remittance, every month on the condition that they never returned to England. I have the feeling your uncle Albert would still have found a way to get into mischief."

Myrna took a sip from her glass. "I agree, Kitty. And by all accounts he was charming and very funny. Our aunt Dahlia always said her brother was just misunderstood. That he was actually a creative genius."

"A creative genius he might have been, but he was also a notorious gambler, and the only thing he ever created as far as I know were a few poems I could never understand."

"They were very . . . um . . . very modern," said Myrna.

"He did redeem himself," John said. "He volunteered in 1914, was one of Kitchener's New Army, won the Military Cross at Thiepval Wood in 1916, and was killed at Pilckem Ridge in 1917."

O'Reilly cocked his head and peered at Lars. "Well, big brother," he said, "no skeletons in the O'Reilly closet?"

Lars chuckled. "Not as far as I know." He looked at Myrna. "I think your aunt Dahlia might have been right, though. Your uncle was a creative genius, but with his life. What a marvellous story of dissolution and ultimate heroic redemption. Someone should write it down."

"I think one of his writer friends might have at the time. But as if our uncle's squandering a fortune wasn't enough, between 1911 and his death in 1917, income taxes went from six to thirty percent, and estate duties increased."

"I don't mean to sound callous, John, but it sounds like it's a very good thing your father wasn't killed in the Great War," said O'Reilly. "I know he served."

"I seem to remember a case where a wealthy father

and his two successors were all killed in sequence, and each time the taxes were levied. It ruined the family," Lars said.

"That's iniquitous," O'Reilly said.

"I remember that family, Lars. It *was* iniquitous, Fingal, particularly when the last one to go had been awarded a posthumous VC. But that nasty little Welshman, Lloyd George, the PM, was determined to smash the upper class," John said.

"Just to set the record straight," Lars said, "from the purely fiscal point of view, if John's father had been killed in the war, John would have inherited the title but would have had to pay a lot less in death duties than he eventually did."

John MacNeill nodded. "Lars is right. They really started to bite in 1927 when the rate went up to forty percent. Great estates all over the United Kingdom were being broken up to raise the money to pay the taxes. When our father did die in '54, the rate had risen to seventy-five percent on estates worth more than two million pounds. It was worth that then, and, for our sins, it currently still is. But lands in Ayrshire, a cotton mill in Belfast, and much of our property to the west of the big house, from the Duck south to the foot of the Ballybucklebo Hills, had to go to pay the death duties."

"And of course," Kitty said, "that includes the land under Number One, Fingal. You pay your ground rent to the new owners. The holding company that bought all that property after the marquis's father died got title to your parcel too."

O'Reilly said, "I pay the ground rent to a numbered account at the Bank of Ireland every year. I've no idea who the account holder is."

"I'm afraid I can't help you there," Myrna said.

"Doesn't matter," O'Reilly said. "Tell us more about John's present problem. I didn't realise how brutal the taxation was. I can understand why so much had to go."

"And as you know, Fingal," Myrna said, "that's why your clever brother is showing us a way to avoid having to break up more of the estate, aren't you, Lars?"

O'Reilly heard something in her voice—admiration? affection?—and noticed a smile flickering on Lars's lips.

"I'm trying." Lars, true to form, had had little to say for several minutes. "With Myrna's help."

"I hate to interrupt," the marquis said, "but your glass is empty, Fingal. The drinks are on the sideboard. Please help yourself. Anyone else?"

"Not for me, thanks," Kitty said, holding up a half-full Waterford glass.

"Please," Myrna said, and as he rose handed O'Reilly her glass. He walked across a deep-pile Axminster carpet to a mahogany sideboard with fretwork legs, and Gothic arches above the flat top.

As O'Reilly poured, he heard Kitty say, "I have to confess I tend to lean a bit to the left. I can see the fundamental injustice of inherited wealth—sorry, John, Myrna. Of some people living in great wealth and others living in terrible poverty. It's not something that can be fixed in one generation or even two I suppose, and yet I find I can't completely condemn the British Parliament for trying." A log fell in the grate and a spray of embers crackled and hissed. John rose, picked up a fresh log from a large brass log holder, and placed it gently on the embers, which licked at it greedily and then burst into new flames.

17

Death and Taxes

The silence stretched out and Fingal wondered if he and Kitty might be looking elsewhere for their evening meal. He inclined his head and looked at her. She made a tight O with her lips and closed her grey eyes. He hoped to God she'd not dropped a clanger.

"You have a point, Kitty," John said, staring into the flames, "and, philosophically, I have to agree with you about inherited money."

O'Reilly's frown vanished. Kitty sighed and opened her eyes.

"Our dear old uncle Albert was a pretty good example of abuse of privilege. Never did a hand's turn of work in his life until he joined up." The marquis waved an arm to encompass the room. "Myrna and I bounce around in this massive mansion like peas on a drum. It's far too big for just the two of us—"

"But we do work," said Myrna quickly. "I'm at the university almost every day during the week and John is very hands-on with the estate and sits on half a dozen committees at least."

"Yes, but you need go no farther than the Falls Road or Sandy Row in Belfast to see the other end of the housing spectrum. That's all at an intellectual level, though. There are feelings . . ." He tapped the left side of his chest. "In here." The graciousness of John MacNeill, even when he had been challenged, was something no one could take away, O'Reilly thought. The room fell still again and O'Reilly stared into the fire, watching it consume the new log.

"I'm from Tallaght," Kitty said, "which is not by any means Dublin 4 where the toffs live."

A polite way, O'Reilly thought, of saying her part of Dublin was predominately working class.

"My grandfather was a cooper at Guinness's. If Dad hadn't been a scholarship boy funded by the taxpayer he'd have been a cooper too. Not that there's anything wrong with being a cooper, but he wasn't good with his hands, he was good with numbers. He understood them, and he wanted to move up in the world. And yet, even though he had, he loved his part of Dublin, refused to leave it, and I imagine, given the history surrounding this place, you and Myrna love your estate too."

"Exactly," John said. "We do. As a reasonably wealthy man I don't mind paying my fair share. Everybody should have a chance in life, like your father. Even though my dad was a member of the Conservative and Unionist Party, he supported Asquith's Liberal old-age pension acts, free school meals, and other social reforms, all to be paid for by taxpayers."

"Which is fair," said Myrna, "but seventy-five percent of everything we own when you go, John?"

"And," said Lars, "for Finn and Kitty's benefit so you'll understand, I'm afraid it does mean everything. All of the assets, and that includes land, houses, businesses, investments . . ." He pointed to the painting over the fireplace. "Art. I could go on . . ."

"I get the drift," Kitty said. "I'm all for reducing the gaps between the classes, but things have gone too far too fast. I really am sorry for you both, and I do hope Lars is going to be able to help."

"He is," Myrna said, and bestowed a beaming smile on the older O'Reilly, "and a damn good thing too. For a start, I'm going to be able to live on here after . . ." she left the "John goes" to be understood, "and I'd hate to have to leave. I love this land. I love the things that the family finances let us have, like the hunting and shooting . . . and I know bloody well you don't approve, Lars Porsena O'Reilly." But she smiled at him, and O'Reilly wondered since when had she been privy to his middle name, something Lars rarely if ever told even his friends? He glanced at his brother. There was definitely fondness in the look he was giving Myrna.

"And I love our history." She smiled. "The family's been in Ireland since just about after the Ark landed on Ararat. One of our early progenitors who came over with William the Conqueror in 1066 was granted a Welsh barony. One of *his* descendants came to Ireland in 1170 with Strongbow, the Earl of Pembroke, and he came here because he'd fallen out with Henry II, who took back the Welsh lands."

"I'm no genealogy expert but 'MacNeill' is hardly an Anglo-Norman name," Kitty said.

"It's not. We were originally de Blanchevilles," John said. "But Myrna's the family archivist. I'll let her explain."

"By the fourteenth century, the Normans had settled and intermarried with the native Irish and were *Hiberniores Ipsis Hibernis,* more Irish than the Irish. They even spoke Irish. They controlled a great part of the island and the de Blanchevilles had settled in what is now

North Down in the Province of Ulaidstir, Ulster. Henri de Blancheville married Aoife MacNeill, a direct descendant of Niall Noigiallach, Niall of the Nine Hostages, an ancient high king of Ireland. When a son was born, to keep the noble lineage alive, he took his mother's surname and we've been MacNeills ever since."

"So," said O'Reilly, "you must be one of the very last basically native peerages."

"We are," said John. "One of our ancestors, right round the time Henry VIII was leaving the Catholic church, had the political wit to become an Anglican. As a reward he was made Lord Ballybucklebo and given a large chunk of North Down. And we were lucky to hang on to it, at least until Dad died.

"Most of the other native Irish Catholic lords took what turned out to be the wrong sides in the rebellions of 1595 and 1641—and in the war between James and William in 1690. Their estates were broken up and given to Anglican English. The MacNeills were on William's side."

Kitty blew out her lips. "'God save Ireland, said the heroes,'" she said, quoting the chorus of a rebel song. "How much hurt has been caused here in this small island in the name of 'Gentle Jesus, meek and mild'?"

O'Reilly looked around the room to see four heads nodding in agreement.

"And still is being caused," said Lars.

And O'Reilly knew his brother was thinking of "Operation Harvest," a campaign that remnants of the Irish Republican Army, who wanted Protestant Northern Ireland united with the Catholic Republic of Ireland, had run from 1956 until 1962. The IRA had taken aim primarily against the Royal Ulster Constabulary barracks and their occupants and lost eleven of their own men in the effort. The RUC had lost six officers with thirty-two wounded.

Lars, perhaps to give everyone a breather from the Irish history lesson, pointed to his empty glass and said, "If I may, John?"

"Please help yourself."

"Anyone else?"

Kitty and O'Reilly both shook their heads. Myrna held out her glass, Lars rose and took it. He held her gaze for a while before crossing to the sideboard.

"Correct me if I'm wrong," said O'Reilly, "but wasn't it the giving of Irish properties to Anglicans that was the start of what came to be known as the Ascendancy? A wealthy Protestant minority owning the land with the Catholic majority cast as labourers or tenant farmers?"

"Yes, the MacNeills were a part of the Ascendancy. With one difference. Many of the estates were run by managers while the owners were absentee landlords. This was a cause of great bitterness among the tenant farmers. Our family stayed, worked the estates, took care of our employees. My great-grandfather set up soup kitchens and forgave rents during An Gorta Mor, the great famine from 1845 to '52. Not one of his tenants was evicted."

"Noblesse oblige used to mean something," Myrna said, looking into her glass.

"I believe," Kitty said, "from what I've seen since I came north, it still does. Helen Hewitt wouldn't be going to medical school but for the MacNeill bursary."

John MacNeill inclined his head. "It was set up before my time. But I do think my philanthropic forebears, at least locally, had earned the respect of their neighbours. Have you any idea how many stately homes were burned down during the 1919 to 1921 Anglo-Irish War?"

"I was just eleven," said O'Reilly, "and . . ." It was impolite to discuss a lady's age, "Kitty was even younger."

He was rewarded with a smile.

"More than three hundred."

"Holy O," O'Reilly said.

"Holy O's right," the marquis said, "but ours was left alone. I certainly don't want to give up all our money, but I find the irony hard to take. The MacNeills have held on to most of what they fought for during all of Ireland's many upheavals, but now we're in danger of losing the lot by—"

"Legal government robbery," Kitty said, her face flushed. "I'm sorry to interrupt, John, but yes, I do see now that it simply isn't fair."

"Thank you," he said, "and Lars is being very helpful."

Lars nodded. "It's all coming together rather well. Myrna and I have worked with Simon O'Hally, the family's solicitor, to sort out all the deeds and titles we need. I've had some help from the legal department at Queen's University. We all know about the concept of 'gifts with reservations of benefit,' where essentially you can give away your house, but reserve the benefit to go on living in an apartment, give away your estate and grouse moor, but keep some of the fishing rights on the Bucklebo River and the shooting rights."

"It's what we've decided to do," John said. "The physical estate must go to the National Trust after I'm gone."

"I'm sorry that it's the best we can do," said Lars. "At least it brings the value of the estate to just that of your stocks, shares, and cash. It's a level at which we can make certain it'll be able to hang on to a goodly chunk. We'll be meeting with the trust in the next couple of weeks."

"I truly appreciate all that you have done, Lars, and you, Fingal, for suggesting your brother might be able to help," John MacNeill said. "I've not been entirely idle while you've been beavering away. I've looked into the situation at Castleward on the Strangford Town side of Strangford Lough. When the sixth Viscount Bangor died in 1950 the house and estate, all eight hundred and twenty acres of it, were given to the Government of Northern Ireland in lieu of death duties and then passed on to the National Trust in 1952. It's open to the public now. A Mister McCoubrey from Ballynahinch and his syndicate rent the shooting rights. Myrna and I know McCoubrey. We've had him at our grouse moor and he's had us at Castleward. Typical upstanding country merchant. Straw on the soles of his boots, taciturn. Slow of speech. Looks a bit dim, but it's all an act. Inside he's sharp as a tack, not a man to underestimate, as some of his business competitors have come to rue. And he's a bloody good shot. Do you know him, Fingal?"

"I'm afraid not." O'Reilly shook his head. "I shoot on the other side of the lough."

The marquis walked to the sideboard. "I'm greatly relieved to hear that Myrna and my son, Sean, are almost certainly going to be able to live here and farm here and, I believe, so will his descendants, if, of course, he has any, and at the moment he doesn't seem to have any inclination." He lifted the whiskey bottle. "My goodness. All this unburdening of the family skeletons has left me feeling like a celebratory tot. Anybody else?"

Before his marriage to Kitty, O'Reilly would not have hesitated to have a third before dinner, but the city girl from Tallaght was working her influence on him in subtle ways—and he was looking forward to dinner. "I'll pass," he said, "but I trust, John, you'll be having one of your fine clarets with our feast."

"Actually I do. It's a Rothschild '61, but we'll be starting with a Bâtard Montrachet."

"Yum," said O'Reilly. "Sounds perfect. Your cook's a patient of mine and a bosom pal of Kinky's. A little bird told me, John, that you're kicking off with mulligatawny, then smoked trout, plaice, squab, beef Bourguignon, a baked Alaska, and finishing with fruit and nuts."

"Well, yes," said the marquis, somewhat apologetically. "One does still like to entertain properly."

"And here," said O'Reilly, "was me thinking, seeing you're going to be such a poor man, it would be gruel, bangers, and mash."

And John MacNeill, Marquis of Ballybucklebo, slapped his knee, nearly choked on his whiskey, and laughed like a drain.

18

Hunting and Shooting

O'Reilly opened the front door of Number One. "Jack Sinton. What in the blue blazes are you doing on my doorstep? Come in. Come in." O'Reilly had finished the Friday-morning surgery and was on his way upstairs for lunch in the lounge, which now doubled as a dining room. "Good to see you, Jack."

"And you, Fingal." Jack Sinton took off his cap with a flourish and stepped over the wide wood threshold. "I was down in Bangor doing a favour for a pal of mine, Jamsey Bowman. He has the flu and because he has, now I need a favour and thought you might be able to help. So I nipped in to ask."

Doctor Jack Sinton, a Trinity graduate though not a classmate, was an old shooting friend who had a general practice on the Stranmillis Road. It was the one Jenny Bradley had thought of working at when she was considering moving back to Belfast last year. Jack, his brother Victor, and two Bangor men, all doctors, owned the Long and Round Islands on Strangford Lough, about a mile southwest of the Blackstaff where O'Reilly usually shot. O'Reilly had several times been Jack's guest gun on the islands. "Come into the surgery," O'Reilly said. "I'm afraid a lorry remodelled my dining room." His grin was rueful. "But don't worry about it. No one got hurt."

"I'm very glad to hear it. I hope you get it fixed soon, but let's chat here. I'm in a bit of a rush. Maybe I can cheer you up. Fancy a day with me on the Long Island tomorrow?"

O'Reilly frowned. A day on Long Island. The shooting was good out there. Very good. But he was on call.

"The greylag geese are in," Jack said.

"The geese, by God?" O'Reilly knew that the greylag, which bred in Norway and Spitzbergen in the summer, was one of the last species of waterfowl to migrate south for the winter. When they arrived, they preferred the grassy islands of Strangford to the shore. He'd never shot one.

"Victor and Jimmy Taylor aren't free tomorrow and like I said, Jamsey Bowman's got flu, poor divil, and he's the only one of us with a retriever now. If I have to make a water retrieve without a dog . . ." He grimaced. "How would you like to join me and bring your Arthur Guinness? I'll need a hand to launch the inflatable too, and I'd enjoy the *craic*."

"Arthur and I'd love to come," O'Reilly said, "but I am on call." Surely either Barry or Nonie would be willing to swap. How often did O'Reilly get an invitation like this? "I've two juniors in the practice, so hang on. I'll nip up and ask."

"Can't wait," Jack said. "I've a woman in labour on Riverview Street. She's in the first stage, the midwife says, but it's her second. Ring me later or leave a message with my wife, and if you can make it tomorrow, I'll meet you and Arthur in Greyabbey an hour before dawn. Say quarter past seven?"

"You're on, Jack," said O'Reilly with a massive grin. He opened the door. "I'll ring," he said, and waved as Jack Sinton headed for a slate blue Morris Minor parked in front of the house. What a great invitation, O'Reilly thought as he closed the door. He took the stairs two at a time. The wildfowling season ended next Tuesday. This Saturday would be his last chance until September. And he might get his first goose.

Nonie was speaking as O'Reilly entered the lounge. She and Barry were sitting round a collapsible card table.

"I'm off this weekend, thank the Lord. I'm knackered."

"Come on, Nonie," Barry said. "One in three's not bad, and Doctor Fitzpatrick'll be in the rota in a week. Then it'll be one in four."

"Roll on with the change in the rota," she said. "I really don't like night work." She pursed her lips. "But I'm looking forward to the weekend. My boyfriend and I are going to a theatre matinée tomorrow. A revival of Sam Thompson's play *Over the Bridge* at the Empire."

That's one possible cover gone west, O'Reilly thought, reluctant to barge into the conversation.

She looked up. "Hello, Fingal. Surgery over?"

"It is," he said, sitting. "*Over the Bridge*? I seem to remember some fuss in 1959 when the Group Theatre agreed to stage it."

"Their board of directors refused to produce it," said Nonie, picking up her napkin and spreading it on her lap. "They wanted to avoid the controversy. There were mass resignations by the director, James Ellis, and the cast and it was eventually put on at the Empire."

"Not my cup of tea," said Barry, "a play about sectarianism in the Belfast shipyards. To each his own, I suppose, but there's enough of that rubbish under the surface of real life in the Wee North."

"I hear you, Barry. Still, it's a part of life here. I saw the play then and I thought Thompson was right on about bigotry," said Fingal, "and Ellis and company were gutsy to stage it. As I recall, it was pretty good stuff."

"And there does be good stuff for your lunches, Doctors," Kinky said as she came in accompanied by clouds of fragrant steam escaping through the lids covering three hefty casseroles. "Stuffed beef olives, champ, and Yorkshire puddings." She set the tray on the sideboard and whipped off the lids. "Nice and hot."

"Smells heavenly, Kinky. Thank you," said Nonie. "I'm famished."

"You're welcome. And there's some of my coffee cake for dessert, and a pot of coffee to go with it." The plate and pot went onto the sideboard. "I know you're partial to that, Doctor Stevenson." Kinky put a hand to the small of her back. "I think you've added an extension to the stairs, sir. They do seem to get higher every day," she said, and puffed before serving. "I was wondering, and there's lots of room, so, I was wondering, until the dining room's fixed if you'd all like to take your meals in my kitchen?"

Kitty came in. She had a half day today. "Hello, everybody. Don't mind me. I'll just get some coffee. They gave us sandwiches at the committee meeting before I left the Royal." She helped herself. There was a chorus of "Hi, Kitty" as she sat at the last empty chair opposite O'Reilly and said, "I heard that, Kinky, and I think that would be a great idea, at least for breakfast and lunch. Doctor O'Reilly and I can worry about dinner. It's been thoughtless of us not considering all the traipsing up and downstairs you've had to do since the crash."

"Thank you, Kitty. It would be greatly appreciated. I'll leave the tray now."

"And don't worry about the dirty dishes," Barry said as Kinky left. "One of us will bring them down."

◧

O'Reilly took his last mouthful. Delicious. Conversation had been desultory during the meal and he'd been in no rush to make his request. Now that everyone was silent, it seemed like an opportunity. "Actually, there's something I really want to do tomorrow, Kitty. Jack Sinton's invited me down to shoot on the Long Island. I'd love to go."

He saw Nonie frown and open her mouth, but before she could speak, Kitty said, "Go right ahead. I'd planned to go shopping in Belfast, because I thought you were on call this weekend and I know how much you love shopping." She smiled. "I'm meeting Jane Hoey for lunch."

"I'm supposed to be on call, but I was wondering if someone . . ." and he meant Barry, "could cover—"

"You can count me out," Nonie said with emphasis. "I'm off duty as of right now."

"I shouldn't have put it that way," O'Reilly said. "I'm sorry. I know you have plans."

"I certainly do," she said. "I often have. Medicine's not all of my life. I like the theatre and the cinema and I always need two nights' sleep in a row to get over my last on call. I'd be grateful if you'd both remember that." She rose, lit a cigarette, and grabbed her handbag from a nearby armchair. "I think I'll have to take a miss on

Kinky's dessert. Have a lovely time. I'll see you on Monday." And with that she swept out of the room.

O'Reilly glanced at Kitty, who was frowning and raising an eyebrow.

O'Reilly shook his shaggy head. He pursed his lips. "I've not seen that side of her before, Barry. She seemed to be fitting in well, but of course it's only been four weeks."

Barry shrugged. "I did mention before we hired her that as a student she could be a bit tricky when it came to swapping call."

"I remember."

"But we agreed that with three of us, four when Fitzpatrick joins the evening and weekend rota next week, it shouldn't be a problem."

O'Reilly nodded. "True, but I thought she was a bit . . ." He looked for the right word. "Bloody rude" came to mind, but, least said, soonest mended. ". . . brusque in the way she left."

"She was," Kitty said.

O'Reilly, who was considering what should be done, guessed that by the way Barry was frowning and repeatedly using his hand to smooth the tuft of hair at his crown that always refused to lie down, the lad was trying to decide what he should do too.

"Some of the girls in my year did get a bit, as you said, brusque after six years of having to fight their corners. It's not so long ago that the Debating Society entertained a motion—I remember the words clearly: 'This house does not consider that women possess the necessary emotional stamina to study medicine.' Quite a few of the lads felt that way."

"It was the same in my day, but not all the girls were so prickly. I'll never forget wee Hilda Manwell.

And Jenny Bradley, your contemporary, certainly wasn't." He exhaled through his nose. "We can't just let it pass."

"No, you can't, Fingal," Kitty said. "I know she's perfectly within her rights, but I'd not have said brusque. I'd have called her downright rude." She cocked her head. "You're a doctor, Barry, and a friend, so you'll not be embarrassed by what I'm going to say. I'm well past it, but there is a time of the month for younger women . . ." She let it hang.

Barry smiled and said, "Fortunes were made in Victorian times selling patent medicines, and I quote, 'to control the tyrannous processes of the menstrual cycle.'"

O'Reilly paused and considered before he said, "Women were told to ignore their physiology when they were needed to do men's work during the war, and then told their cycles made them unfit for work when the men came home and needed their jobs back and there was a move to get women out of the workforce." He shrugged. "I'll take that into consideration, Kitty, but you're right about one thing. She was rude and I don't want any repetitions. Something's got to be done." He paused before saying, "It was a custom in the navy that the most junior officer at a court-martial gave his verdict first so he could not be intimidated by the opinions of his seniors. I'm not suggesting this is anything like as serious as a trial, but we may have to work with her for a lot of years. What do you make of our Doctor Nonie Stevenson so far, Barry?"

Barry gave his cowlick a pat before saying, "She's a good doctor and she has extra obstetrics and gynaecology training and the skills we need for the well-woman clinic. The patients like her. I had one leave a couple of weeks ago because 'The lady doctor wasn't going to be there.' I think we're going to see more of that. There aren't that many female physicians to choose from in Ulster. There were only half a dozen in my year."

Barry Laverty has a well-honed sense of justice, O'Reilly thought, starting by giving her credit for her good points. And a sense of the practical. A female physician was a plus for the practice.

"If anything," Barry said, "I'd be more worried about her habit of needing so many naps, but she hasn't let it interfere with her work. Not yet, anyhow."

"So you're saying we should keep her?"

Barry nodded. "But you're the senior partner. One of my surgical teachers used to say when he put a double suture round an important artery before he divided it, 'A stitch in time can save *more* than nine.' A word in her ear from you on Monday's probably all that it'll take to get her to understand."

"I think Barry's right, Fingal," Kitty said.

"Fair enough," O'Reilly said. "I'll see to it."

"And, oh wise and learnèd senior partner," Barry said with a grin, "I'd hate to deprive you of an opportunity tomorrow to commit murder and mayhem among multitudes of misfortunate mallard, so I'll take call."

Kitty laughed. "You're quite the alliterationist . . . if there is such a word."

"More to the point," O'Reilly said, "you, Doctor Barry Laverty, are a gentleman and a scholar."

Barry laughed. "You may change your tune when I tell you what it's going to cost."

"Go ahead."

"You take my call next Saturday and a pint in the Duck when my afternoon's work is done today—if Kitty doesn't mind."

"You run along and play, boys," Kitty said, and

chuckled. "And if you've no plans tonight, Barry, have dinner with us."

"Dead on," said O'Reilly, and he thought, even if Nonie Stevenson may not be the absolutely ideal colleague, he'd have a long road to travel before he'd get a better one than the son of Tom Laverty, his old shipmate.

19

Wild Geese Spread the Grey Wing

O ne more heave."
    Jack Sinton stood beside the inflatable boat's
starboard bow up to the knees of his hip-waders in the
tide. O'Reilly and Arthur had met the middle-aged doctor in Greyabbey an hour before dawn. They'd left the
Rover there, driving down in Jack's Morris Minor, a
Humber inflatable held with straps and bungee cords to
the roof rack. Together they'd launched the craft in the
still waters of the Dorn, a sheltered inlet of the lough
south of the Castle Hill, as Arthur Guinness danced his
excitement at being on the water.

"All right," said O'Reilly from the port side, "but give
me a minute to catch my breath." He hauled in a couple
of lungfuls and took a tight hold of a rope running
round the pontoon. "Go." He put his back into hauling.
The shingle crunched under the soles of boots and the
boat's bottom. His nose was filled with the tang of seaweed and salt, and the distinctive petrol/oil niff of the
Johnson Seahorse outboard clamped to the dinghy's
stern.

On the run out to the Long Island minutes before,
only the puttering of the engine, the *slap, slap* of the

boat's flat bottom on small waves, and occasional throaty mumblings from Arthur had broken the deep silence. There had been no need for chatter. Although they were not close friends, O'Reilly had got to know Jack Sinton well enough since they'd met at an Ulster Medical Association dinner years ago to discover a mutual interest in "fowling" and the works of Mozart, especially *The Magic Flute*. Instead of shouting over the engine's noise, O'Reilly had stared up, savouring the high anthracite canopy, where a waxing gibbous moon looked down and myriad icy stars shone and sparkled, waiting for the first fingers of the dawn to dim them one by one. One heavenly body, more impatient than the rest, had flashed its meteor's silver tail as it streaked to a fiery death.

"That'll do," Jack said now. "Give me a minute to set the anchor well above the tide line, then we'll head for the hide. Bring Arthur and we'll get settled in." He strode off.

O'Reilly reached into the boat and picked up his twelve bore and game bag. He slung the bag over his shoulder and cradled the unloaded gun in the crook of his left arm. The wind from the south that ruffled the sea and cut through his waterproof coat was chilling, but God, it was good to be back on the lough, and with a prospect of even better sport than he might anticipate in his usual spot on the banks of the Blackstaff Stream. He turned up his coat collar, pulled his paddy hat well down.

"That's done," Jack said. "Come on."

"Heel." Arthur tucked in and the two men strode along the springy turf at the shingle's edge. O'Reilly glanced inshore and saw that the lights of Davy McMaster's farmhouse were lit. It would be cosy there with the great kitchen range burning and hot tea for everyone.

The sky was beginning to lighten and O'Reilly could make out a solid object ahead, bulking more darkly at the grass's edge about the height of a man's shoulders and perhaps twelve feet long.

"You know we call this the 'house,'" Jack said as they passed a corner of the structure.

"Aye. The old farmer who owned the island before your syndicate bought it dried seaweed for fertiliser in here. It still smells salty." O'Reilly passed through the gap in the dry stone wall. "It's not as draughty in here and it makes a great hide."

The wind made lonely sighing noises as it found its way through chinks between the stones. He unslung his game bag and set it against a wall, pulling two cartridges from his pocket. Then he loaded his shotgun, set the safety catch, and propped it beside the game bag. O'Reilly pointed to a sheltered corner and said, "Lie down."

Arthur, well used to conditions on the lough, tucked in, curled up, sighed, and put his nose on his forepaws.

"Not long to dawn now," Jack Sinton said. "Sunrise is at eight nineteen." He hauled a thermos from his game bag. "Fancy a cup of coffee?"

"Please." O'Reilly accepted the mug. "Hits the spot," he said as he took his first sip of the hot, sweet liquid. "And thanks for asking me along, Jack. I've had some great days out here with you and your friends."

"It's always been a pleasure having you, Fingal, and old Arthur. He's a good-natured animal. He really got on well with Jamsey Bowman's Rex and my old spaniel, Tara, God rest her. Gone two years now and I haven't had the heart to replace her."

O'Reilly looked over at Arthur Guinness. He knew how Jack felt. Old Arthur would be hard to replace too. "I hope Jamsey's flu isn't too bad," he said.

"He was feeling rotten yesterday. He should be on the mend today, but it'll be harder for him to throw it off. None of us are getting any younger." He rubbed his hands. "Och," he said, "it's been a brave wheen of years since four fellahs got together after the war to buy the islands."

"The war does seem long ago now," O'Reilly said, not wanting to dwell on that subject and happy to be warmed by the hot coffee.

"D'you know years ago Jimmy Taylor was here by himself? He had no dog, and he shot a goose that fell in the sea. Jimmy used to be a champion swimmer. Didn't he strip off, swim out, and get the bird?"

"Aye," said O'Reilly, inwardly shuddering at the thought of how cold the winter sea was. "The joys of youth."

"When we were young, we used to row out from the Blackstaff in a punt," Jack said.

O'Reilly whistled. "That's some row."

Jack laughed. "At least a mile, and heavy going in a sea. I really like outboard motors, and," he said, a serious tone creeping into his voice, "I love Strangford."

"Me too," said O'Reilly. "Just look at that."

The sky was lighter now. Little whitecaps punctuated a sea that earlier had been a monochromatic darkness, at one with the sky and the land. Low seaweed-covered reefs called pladdies between the island and the mainland shore started to turn from grey to brown. Above the spiny ridge of the Ards—Irish for "high"—Peninsula, the undersurfaces of dove-grey clouds were being dyed a delicate cerise that, as he watched, turned deeper red shot through by yellows and scarlets. And over the left shoulder of the Castle Hill the upper limb of the sun's circle crept slowly up, bathing everything in soft greens and grey—the hill, the ruins of Saint Mary's Church, and the remains of the castle built in the thirteenth century by the Norman Baron Le Sauvage.

"It is a very special place for me," Jack Sinton said.

In the daylight, O'Reilly could see the man who before the dawn had been but an indistinct blur. Five foot nine, slight build, greying hair peeping out from under a duncher. A neatly clipped grey moustache under a sharp nose set between pale eyes with deep laugh lines at the corners.

"I know what you mean," O'Reilly said, not a bit concerned about letting his feelings about the place show. "I love it here too, and when everyday life intrudes, it's a very safe haven. No phones, no tough clinical decisions, no forms to fill in." And no bloody great hole in my house that may not be mine much longer. No tetchy juniors to reprimand. He glanced at Arthur and felt the familiar worry about Sonny Houston's lost Jasper creep into his mind.

"Get down," Jack said.

O'Reilly watched as Jack put two fat cartridges into the twin breeches of his ten bore. It would be the man's goose gun, firing a heavier load than O'Reilly's twelve. Jack's brother, Victor, had for several years used an eight bore, a veritable shoulder cannon that fired black powder, not smokeless powder shells. Jack cocked two hammers and whispered, "Ball of five birds coming down from Gransha Point direction in the north. Low. Out there." He moved to the far wall and crouched, eyes barely over the coping stones, gun held across his body, muzzles up.

O'Reilly, feeling the adrenaline run, grabbed his gun and crouched to Jack Sinton's left. The man was an experienced wildfowler. He'd track the birds' progress, call when they were in range, then take birds to the right and leave those on the left for O'Reilly. He heard a faint repeated whistling, a *psweeoo, psweewoo,* then the sound of wind on pinions, and Jack's curt "Now."

O'Reilly stood but did not raise his gun.

Ahead, beating into the wind, was a line of five widgeon, the chestnut heads of two drakes with creamy crowns and white bellies in contrast to the grey heads of the females.

To O'Reilly's surprise, Jack Sinton hadn't fired a shot either.

The five ducks flared, turned, and sped off downwind.

Both men turned, looked at each other, and started to laugh. Each made his gun safe and propped it up.

"I think," said O'Reilly, "I must be getting old. But if you want to know why I didn't fire, it's because I don't really like the taste of widgeon. Too fishy for me. They feed off eel grass on the mud flats."

"And I didn't because I simply have a soft spot for the breed. *Anas penelope.* Linnaeus called them that in 1758," Jack said. "I started fowling, like you, because I really loved the thrill of the hunt and being here on the lough, but several years ago I began reading up on wildfowl and I keep a sighting diary. Birds really are interesting. Sometimes," he said, "I bring an eight-millimetre ciné camera and shoot them on film instead of with a gun. It's just as tricky. I haven't given up shooting. I still love a day out here and I enjoy roast mallard or goose. I just don't need to shoot everything in sight anymore."

"Jack, you know my brother, Lars."

Jack said, "From Portaferry. The solicitor. We both do work for the Royal Society for the Protection of Birds."

"I know."

"Sound man, your brother. I saw him in Belfast on Thursday. He was having lunch in The Buttery near the law courts. It's a favourite pub restaurant among the legal fraternity. I'd popped in for a quick one, passed his table. He introduced me to his guest. Handsome woman, Lady Myrna Ferguson. They seemed to be enjoying themselves."

"I'm sure they were," said O'Reilly, and smiled. That would be something to tell Kitty tonight. Good for you, Lars. O'Reilly was delighted.

The morning passed with the sun's ascent bringing a weak warmth to the day. Several mallard and teal skirted the island, raising hopes, but none came within range.

"Not much sport today," O'Reilly said, "but it's all right. Simply being here is enough—"

"Der Vogelfänger bin ich ja," sang Jack softly in a slightly off-key baritone.

"I am the merry bird-catcher," sang O'Reilly in response. "Papageno, Act 1 of *Die Zauberflöte, The Magic Flute*. One of my favourite arias." He smiled at Jack. "But we're not catching much today." O'Reilly glanced down. Arthur was sitting bolt upright, head thrown back, staring into the sky. He made a tiny whimper and then O'Reilly heard, from upwind, a faint series of harsh cackling *ho-oh-onk*s. Geese.

And they were coming this way.

He crouched and turned slowly. "Jack. Geese." O'Reilly kept his voice low. The birds had acute hearing and eyesight. He lifted his gun, crept under the shelter of the wall, keeping his head only high enough to keep the birds in view. As he counted, ten, twelve, fifteen grey-lag came at him in a ragged vee limned against the bulk of the Castle Hill. They were flying low and could pass in range. He felt his pulse quicken.

And all the while the big birds scolded and cackled and drew closer.

Jack slipped in close by as O'Reilly took off his safety catch and heard the double click of the hammers as Jack's ten bore was cocked.

The geese were sixty yards out, coming straight for the "house," flying at an altitude of about thirty yards. The lethal range of a shotgun was forty. As they neared, he saw in detail the leading bird's yellow bill on an oval head thrust forward on a long, stiff neck. The words of Uncle Hedley to a thirteen-year-old Fingal came rushing back: "If you ever get a chance for a goose, aim for the head. It's nearly as big as a teal and you'll get a clean kill, not a wounded goose." O'Reilly's breath came in short gasps. After all these years he was going to get that chance.

Now he could make out more details. As great wings slowly, powerfully beat he could hear the air being displaced by hundreds of primary flight feathers. Each bird flew en echelon, riding on the slipstream of the goose ahead. He saw their grey brow plumage, their heads darker than their bodies and, on the mature adults, black spots scattered at random on their pale bellies, yellow paddles tucked in under white tails.

The cackling was louder now, and in seconds the birds would be directly overhead. "Now," O'Reilly said, and stood upright. The honking went up an octave as the birds scattered.

In a fluid movement, he slammed the butt into his

right shoulder, the gun's metal barrels cold on his left hand. With both eyes open, he sighted along the rib between the double barrels, swung the bead foresight through the body of a goose that was clawing for height and trying to break to its left. More swing, past the head for sufficient lead-off, then he squeezed the trigger of the left barrel. Its bore was full choke, deliberately made narrower so the shot pattern would be denser than that from the unchoked right barrel. His aim must be more accurate, but if it were, more pellets would be delivered on target.

The gun roared and the butt slammed into his shoulder.

Simultaneously, he heard the deeper boom of Jack's heavier weapon.

O'Reilly watched as the remaining geese each sought their own salvation. His bird's head had snapped back across its body as the great wings folded in death. On the left side of the flock, a second bird was tumbling down. They were still in range of the right barrel, but O'Reilly shook his head as his goose hit the ground with an audible *thump*. He watched as Jack's bird splashed into the sea ten yards off shore. "Good shot," O'Reilly said, and grinned.

"You too." Jack smiled back.

"I'll send Arthur for your bird." He put the safety catch on and propped his gun against the wall.

"And I'll pick up yours."

"Come on, pup."

Arthur needed no more bidding. He trotted at O'Reilly's heel as he walked down to the edge of the tide, pointed at the goose, which was bobbing up and down on the small waves, and said, "Hi lost."

Arthur hurled himself in, front and hind legs stretched out fore and aft, landing with a crashing splash, spray flying. Powerful strokes carried him, head high, out to the bird. This was going to be the biggest object Arthur had ever retrieved. The dog sniffed at the goose, then took its neck in his jaws and, snuffling and snorting through his nose, swam ashore with the goose's body bobbing alongside his.

Once ashore, he ran straight to O'Reilly, sat, and presented the bird. O'Reilly took it, guessing it probably weighed six to eight pounds. "Good boy," he said, and patted Arthur's head. Arthur grinned and shook himself. Together they went back to the hide where Jack was waiting with O'Reilly's bird.

"Thanks," they both said at the same time, exchanging their trophies.

O'Reilly towelled Arthur off. That water was bloody cold. Jimmy Taylor must have had the constitution of an ox to go swimming in it. O'Reilly pointed to the sheltered corner. "Lie down."

The dog obeyed and O'Reilly gave him a Bonio dog biscuit. Good behaviour must always be rewarded.

"Well," said Jack, "you've shot your first goose. How does it feel?"

O'Reilly looked at the bird. He smiled. "It was the biggest thrill I've ever had wildfowling," he said. Then his smile fled. He inhaled. "This big boy's going to be tasty when Kinky has stuffed and roasted him." He smiled at the thought of the potato stuffing the Corkwoman made for goose. "But at the heels of the hunt, although I had a great thrill, the goose didn't." And there was a sadness in the heart of the big man.

"I didn't take a second bird either," Jack said, and left it at that. He had no need to explain. He looked at his watch. "The day's half over. Not much is likely to come on a dropping tide until the four o'clock flight from the Quoile River. What would you like to do?"

O'Reilly thought for a moment. "Let's have lunch here. Enjoy the day for a bit longer. You'll not get back until next year."

"And I'll get you and Arthur down for a day or two. We're permitted to bring three guests each a season."

"That's very civil. I might take you up on it, but I can see how much fun Lars is having working in conservation. I might just put the musket away. Either way, let's keep in touch."

"Fair enough," Jack said. "Leisurely lunch now, then we'll head ashore."

"And let's stop in the Mermaid in Kircubbin on our way home," O'Reilly said, rubbing his cold hands together. "I owe you a hot half-un and Arthur never turns down a Smithwick's, do you, lummox?"

And the big dog, content to be doing what he'd been bred for, thrashed his tail and grinned at O'Reilly.

20

He Was Lost and Is Found

Have you seen my stethoscope, Fingal?" Barry said,
letting himself into the otherwise empty surgery.
O'Reilly, muttering profanities under his breath, was
sitting at the rolltop desk, half-moon spectacles perched
on his nose, filling in a form.

"What?" O'Reilly turned. "Stethoscope? Yes. It's
hanging up near the couch."

"Oh, right. Thanks." Barry stuffed it into his jacket
pocket and turned to go.

"Had a word with Nonie this morning when she
popped in to get her list of home visits," O'Reilly said.

Barry stopped. "And?"

"I'll not go into details, I've got patients waiting, but
between the jigs and reels of it she now understands
that it is expected that we all, including her, will collab-
orate on granting requests for cover, and that there will
be a generally more collegial atmosphere." O'Reilly
smiled. "I must say I'd been expecting some resistance,
but she agreed, apologised, and promised to do better
in future."

"I'm delighted to hear it," Barry said. "She's not a
bad head." He was relieved that O'Reilly had done as

he'd promised last week. Barry'd not have expected otherwise of the big man. No doubt O'Reilly handled matters tactfully, but being pulled up short by a senior colleague first thing on a Monday morning was never easy for any young doctor. Barry could find it in his own heart to feel sympathy for Doctor Nonie Stevenson.

"As far as I'm concerned, Barry, the slate's wiped clean and the girl gets a fresh start. Fair enough?"

"Fair enough," Barry said, and yawned. "Sorry, but it was a long weekend. Flu galore, two cases of croup, and a buck eejit at five A.M. on Sunday claiming his pounding headache must be because he got a bad bottle on Saturday night. Hangover is a self-inflicted injury." He yawned again.

"Lord," said O'Reilly, "don't tell me the ever-nap-needing Nonie's starting an epidemic?"

Barry laughed. "Not at all. I'm short of oxygen. Isn't that why people yawn? That's what I learned at—" He stopped, listening. "Sounds like there's ructions going on in the waiting room."

O'Reilly cocked his head. "God only knows. Come on." He rose and headed down the hall with Barry in hot pursuit. They met Kinky coming the other way from her kitchen, drying her hands on her apron and frowning.

Barry took in the scene at once. Shooey Gamble was applauding—applauding, of all things. Cissie Sloan was in floods of joyful tears. Melanie Finnegan had brought her husband Dermot and he was waving clasped hands above his head like a prizefighter.

Everyone was talking at once.

And in the middle of the room stood a grinning Colin Brown, one sock round his ankle, his mongrel Murphy at his feet, and a bedraggled, skeletal, shuddering poodle-Labrador cross with droopy ears looking as gormless as ever.

"Holy thundering Mother of—" O'Reilly said. "Colin Brown, now you're better you've found Jasper."

"Murphy did," Colin said, "so he did, and—"

"Well, what are you doing standing there with both legs the same length. We've got to get this dog back to the Houstons. Doctor Laverty, I—"

"No, Doctors, please, I don't want them to see him like this. Can we not clean him up a bit first? And Jasper needs til get warm and dry right now, and something til eat. And he should see a vet, so he should, but Mister Porter has his surgery away far away in Conlig. My daddy's at work and Mammy's gone shopping and so, sure, where else could I come but here?"

"Where indeed," said Kinky, smiling.

"Poor oul Jasper was having trouble walking the last wee ways round the sea path and I was trying til carry him. I was dead lucky because when I got onto the Shore Road, Mister Auchinleck was doing his milk rounds. He brung me and the dogs here on his electric float. He said til say 'Hello,' Mrs. Auchinleck, and he'll see you at teatime. He couldn't wait, for he'd his rounds to finish."

Kinky smiled and nodded.

"You're a very clever boy, Colin," Cissie said, mopping her eyes with a spotted handkerchief. "I was just saying til Mister Gamble—wasn't I, Shooey?—that it's a powerful shame about the front of your house, Doctor O'Reilly, when in comes the wee lad and the doggies and he says, says he, 'I have for til see Doctor O'Reilly at once. It's an emergency.' I was for telling him it wasn't a vet's and to run away off and chase himself, that the doctor had patients he needed to see, but the look on his face would have melted a stone and—"

"I'm sure it would have, Cissie." O'Reilly's tones were kind, but firm.

Barry smiled. Cissie Sloan was, in local parlance, a woman who could talk the hind leg off a donkey. O'Reilly was one of the few people who could shut her up.

"I'll ask you all to bide for a minute or two," O'Reilly said. "We'll see to Colin, then I'll be back to take who-ever's first."

"You see to the little boy, *Docteur*," said Melanie Ferguson. "It is all right. We wait." Even after all the years since she'd come from France as Dermot's war bride, her English was still accented.

Barry looked round. Everyone was smiling. He felt a sharp pang of regret that Sue was in France and he wouldn't be able to call her this evening and describe the scene. She had a particular soft spot for the impish Colin and had been instrumental in proposing he write the exam that would ensure a grammar school educa-tion for the lad. Colin's rescue of Jasper and the bunga-low he'd found and wanted to buy would be high on his list to chat about over a glass of *vin blanc* in some picturesque little café in Marseille.

"You done very good, so you did, Colin Brown," said Dermot. "We're all very proud of you."

Everyone muttered assent.

"Come on," said O'Reilly, leading the way. "I'll be back very soon."

"You go first, Cissie, when the doctor comes back," Shooey said. "I'm in no rush."

"But you was here first . . ."

Barry could hear them still arguing over who should

have the privilege of stepping aside as O'Reilly ushered him, Kinky, Colin, and the dogs into the kitchen and closed the door. "It's a lot warmer in here than in the surgery and that poor beast needs the heat."

Barry was happy enough to let O'Reilly take command.

The big man knelt beside Jasper and began to run his hands from the dog's shoulders to the base of his tail. As he worked, he said, "Kinky, Colin looks foundered. Can you . . . ?"

"I'll have hot chocolate and some of my ginger biscuits ready in no time, so. Sit you there on that chair, son."

Colin sat, legs dangling, and without bidding, Murphy headed for the warmth of the range and curled up on the floor.

O'Reilly examined each leg in turn as Jasper's milky gaze followed every move. "I can't find any cuts or broken bones, but his fur's matted and full of burrs and there's more meat on a hammer than on this poor pup."

"Mrs. Auchinleck," Colin said, "could you borrow me one of Arthur's brushes?"

"Certainly." She went to a cupboard and returned with a dog brush.

"Thanks." Colin stood beside Jasper and began to brush his coat. "Poor ould fellah, I don't think you've had anything much to eat since you ran away," Colin said, "but last year a Labrador was lost for three weeks from Holywood and when he was found he was nothing but skin and bone, but he was still alive. It's water they need. Just like us. We learned in school how, during the Irish War of Independence, Terence MacSwiney, Lord Mayor of Cork City, had gone on a hunger strike in 1920 and lived for seventy-four days."

"I was a girl a little younger than you when that happened," said Kinky. "I remember it well. I'll see to the poor crayture. Bread and warm milk and a drink of water will do. His poor wee tummy will be all shrunk, so. We'll have to take it easy to start with."

O'Reilly straightened, went to the sink, and washed his hands. "I want to hear all about the rescue, but I've customers to see." He grabbed a towel. "Let's get Colin and Jasper fed and warmed up and by then I'll be done and we'll run Colin and the dogs out to the Houstons'. They'll be delighted." He left.

"Here's your hot chocolate and ginger bickies, bye," Kinky said.

"Thank you, Mrs. Auchinleck." Colin set the brush aside.

She fussed at the stove and returned carrying a soup plate and one of Arthur's bowls. "Bread and warm milk, and water for you, Jasper." She set the bowls on the floor close to the range. Murphy looked up as Jasper crossed the floor.

"Leave it, Murphy," Colin said, and with a sigh the mongrel laid his head back on his paws.

"So, Colin," said Barry, parking himself on a wooden chair. "I'm dying to know. How did you find him?"

Colin pointed at his mouth and kept chewing his second biscuit. He swallowed and said, "Mammy says I'm not to talk with my mouth full."

Kinky tousled his hair. "You're a good boy for minding your manners."

"Anyroad," Colin said, picking up the brush and beginning to tease out the burrs in Jasper's coat. The dog, still intent on his bowl, paid no attention. "I was worried a couple of weeks back when I heard he'd run away in that blizzard, but my daddy told me Jasper'd probably come home. But he never. And the hunt for him didn't work neither." Colin looked longingly at the plate of biscuits.

"Go ahead," Kinky said. "Help yourself."

Colin did, but before he took a bite, said, "I told my daddy maybe Jasper had gone til the shore, but Daddy had til work and I had til go til school. It was dark by the time Daddy got home so we never went looking. I was going til go on the Saturday, but then I took sick with measles and I didn't think much of it after that. When I was getting better, I asked Daddy again, but he said to let the hare sit." Colin looked sad. "I think they'd all given up hope." He bit into his biscuit.

Barry waited as Jasper's chewing kept pace with Colin's, and Kinky went about skinning Cookstown sausages. "Toad in the hole for lunch," she said.

"I never gave up. Doctor O'Reilly said I had til stay in the house for ten days after my measles went away, but I could start going out last Saturday. So I did. I went to the shore, but no luck. On Sunday," he grinned, "I wasn't allowed to go til Sunday school neither, so me and Murphy went and hunted along the shore toward Bangor. We went a bit farther each day. No luck. But this morning I met Art O'Callaghan on his way to class. Him and me was down last summer on the beach at Smelt Mill Bay."

"Near Strickland's Glen?" Barry said.

"That's right, Doctor, and do you know what? Art reminded me of a great hidey-hole there that not many people know about."

Jasper lifted his head from the bowl.

Colin scratched the dog's head and said, "Feeling better now?"

Jasper made a strangled "aarghaargh" noise and looked at Colin with adoration.

Colin kept on brushing.

"Tell us more," Barry said.

"It's a wee cave and you can only get at the mouth of it when the tide's out. The cave doesn't flood when the tide's in and the sand in it is dead dry, and it's no distance from Bryan's Burn that runs down through the glen. So today me and Murphy made a beeline for Smelt Mill Bay. As soon as we got there, Murphy couldn't wait for til go in the cave and, hey, presto, nothing but barking in the cave and then out he comes with Jasper in tow. I told Doctor O'Reilly that the two dogs knew each other."

"You do be a very clever young man, Colin Brown, bye," Kinky said. "Here. Have another ginger bickie."

"Wheeker," said Colin.

"And," Barry asked, "you brought him here?"

"I did in soul. He was very weak but able to walk quite a ways back round the sea path. I thought I was going til have til carry him the last quarter of a mile so I could get him here, but I told youse about Mister Auchinleck."

"But why here?" Barry asked.

"The poor ol' thing needed seeing to—and sure isn't a doctor the next best thing to a vet?"

So much, Barry thought with a smile, for the elevated status of physicians. He heard Kinky chortling.

"And didn't Doctor O'Reilly himself do as well as a vet," she said, "and say Jasper was hungry, but fine?"

"I did," said O'Reilly, sticking his head round the door. "Everyone was very cooperative and surgery's all done, so I'll run Colin and the dogs out. Want to come, Barry?"

"Try to stop me," Barry said.

"Nonie's still out. I'm on call, but you'll know where to find us, Kinky," O'Reilly said.

"I will, so." She moved over to a cupboard and brought out a paper bag. "That is for you, Colin, for being such a clever boy. It's my own homemade fudge."

"Sticking out a mile," Colin said with a grin, accepting the bag. "Thanks very much, Mrs. Auchinleck."

Barry knew that this was the boy's big moment. The door opened. Sonny was a tall man and, distracted by the sight of the two doctors, he must not have noticed the boy on his doorstep. "I went for my tests this morning. I wasn't expecting one of you until my results—"

Jasper let go a loud "Woof."

Sonny took a step back, then knelt, threw his arms round Jasper's neck, and paid no attention to the dog licking his face and drinking Sonny's tears. "Jasper. Jasper. Jasper."

Maggie appeared, standing behind Sonny. "I don't believe it," she said. "You've found him." Her toothless grin was vast.

"I don't know who to thank," he said, "but please come in, everybody. I'll have to get Jasper water and something to eat. He looked at the dog. "You must be starving, boy."

"Don't worry, Sonny," O'Reilly said, helping the man to his feet. "I've given him the once-over, Kinky's fed and watered him, and Colin's got the worst of the burrs out. He'll want more food soon, I'm sure, but best to start him off slowly."

"In that case," Sonny said, "let's all go through into the sitting room. Please, everybody take a seat."

Barry took an armchair beside the fire next to O'Reilly's, Colin perched on a leather pouffe, Maggie stood beaming down at them, and Sonny, with Jasper lying beside him, took the sofa.

"Now," said Sonny, "who did find him?"

"Murphy, sir," Colin said, "but I helped him."

Sonny said, "Well done, both of you."

Barry listened while Colin, without interruption and, Barry thought, with considerable succinctness for a boy who could have revelled in his glory, told Sonny what had happened.

"Remarkable," Sonny said. "I simply cannot thank you enough, young Master Brown." He rose and brought back something from a china cabinet. "Colin, I want you to have this as a symbol of my gratitude. It's a fossilised ammonite."

Colin looked at it, his eyes wide, mouth open.

"It's from the Jurassic period," Sonny said. "So it's about one hundred and fifty million years old."

"Crikey. There was dinosaurs then," Colin said. "Miss Nolan taught us about them. Thon *Tyrannosaurus rex* had a power of architecture about him. Big teeth too." He looked at the fossil again and stretched out his hand, holding it toward Sonny. "Mister Houston, no harm til ye, but this is far too precious like. I can't take this off you, so I can't."

Barry felt a lump in his throat grow larger when Sonny said, "No, Colin. Jasper is precious. All our dogs are. You returned Jasper to me. I want to give you something to show how much I appreciate that. Please keep it."

And, eyes still shining with wonder, Colin said, "Thank you, sir."

"I know Colin and Murphy found Jasper," Sonny said, "but thank you, Doctors, for examining Jasper and bringing him home. It feels as if our family is complete again."

"And that's just how it should be," O'Reilly said. He rose. "Now we'd better get Colin home, and back to work for us doctors."

Barry stood and as he followed O'Reilly he mulled over Sonny's last remark, "Our family is complete." And wasn't that what Ballybucklebo was? A great big scattered family where in a crisis ranks closed and everyone pitched in. By God, he thought as he closed the front door, there's nowhere else I'd rather live.

21

A Little Sleep, a Little Slumber

For God's sake, Kinky, get a doctor," a man shouted from, it seemed, somewhere in outer space. Barry crawled up from the depths of slumber. After delivering Emer O'Loughlin's second baby, a girl, he'd tumbled into his bed at five thirty this morning and had been glad to be off duty after nine o'clock so he could sleep on. He was barely aware of the door to his quarters opening and Kinky standing in the doorway.

"Please, sir, wake up," she said.

Barry forced his eyes open fully and sat up. He was fully compos mentis now. He fisted his eyes. "What time is it?"

"Eleven thirty, but we need you at once, so. Willie Dunleavy says Doctor Stevenson's taking a fit or something."

"What? Where is she?"

"In the surgery. Please come, sir." Kinky stood wringing her hands.

Many years of learning to respond at once had Barry leaping out of bed, grabbing and donning a plaid dressing gown over his pyjamas, struggling into carpet slippers, and regardless of his appearance—his hair must look like a ruined haystack—heading into the kitchen where big, round Willie Dunleavy was shifting from foot to foot. "Come on, Doc," he said, starting to trot to the hall.

Barry and Kinky hurried after.

"I was so scared I near took the rickets. Doctor Stevenson just, well, had a bit of a fit like and then fell dead asleep, so she did. Right while she was filling out my form."

Oh Lord, Nonie. Not again. And in front of a patient this time. Barry sighed. "Tell me exactly what happened."

"I'm the last patient. There's her sitting at her desk. 'Excuse me,' says she, and chucks the pen at me—like her arm had a spasm. Then she puts her head down on the desk and falls asleep. I didn't dare try til wake her up. I read in *Reader's Digest* not to do that for sleepwalkers. I just left and come running to get help. I was scared skinny." He stood aside to let Barry and Kinky precede him into the surgery.

Nonie was sprawled in the swivel chair, head turned to one side lying on the desk blotter, eyes tightly closed, mouth agape. Laboratory requisition forms lay in disarray on the floor.

Taking naps all over the house while she was off duty was one thing, but falling asleep in front of a patient? There had to be more to this than simple tiredness.

She sat bolt upright, still, it seemed, asleep. "No. No. Take it away. No. Please. No." She screamed, a high-pitched, eldritch sound.

Willie muttered, "Jaysus Murphy," and took a step back.

Kinky looked at Barry, her eyes wide. "What's wrong with her, sir?"

"I'm not sure yet, but I'll need to examine her." She

must be dreaming, he thought, and whatever she was dreaming about wasn't pleasant. He frowned. Took her pulse. One hundred. A bit fast. Now what? Should he wake her up? He tried to remember a lecture about certain neurological disorders and was racking his brain when Nonie shook her head and said in a perfectly reasonable voice, "Hello, Barry."

"Are you all right, Doctor Stevenson?" Barry said, glancing at Kinky and Willie Dunleavy.

She shook her head. "Not entirely. I must have nodded off . . ."

"Take your time." Barry put a hand on her shoulder. "Kinky, would you please take Willie to your kitchen. Give him a cup of tea? He's had a bit of a shock. I'll see to him when I've finished here."

"I will, so. Come along now, Willie, like the good man that you are and let the doctors get on with it. I'll toast some barmbrack." She took his elbow and guided him from the room, closing the door behind them.

Kinky Auchinleck, Barry thought, Ballybucklebo's rock of ages, and in a crisis as reliable as Big Ben chiming the hour.

"I'm sorry about that," Nonie said, and forced a smile, "and in front of a patient too. But I must have nodded off and just there, now, I think I was hallucinating or having a God-awful nightmare. I could see something, I don't know what, with huge teeth coming for me. And I was hearing a train whistle."

"I was here," Barry said. "You screamed, then you woke up." As he spoke, his mind raced. Constant need to nap, possibly a scary, he remembered the term, hypnopompic hallucination, seeing or hearing things as you woke up, pointed in one direction. Had his knowledge of her unwillingness to trade call, his irritation when two weeks ago he'd found her slumped on his table within inches of his precious model, had they blinded him? Was there more to her drowsiness than simply being a sleepyhead and possibly lazy? Could Nonie have—?

She stood up and her voice was slurred. "Oh dear me. Now I'm seeing double," and as she spoke her knees started to buckle.

Barry stepped forward, grabbed her, and got her back into the chair. Loss of muscle function marked by slurred speech, double vision, and going weak at the knees all brought on by strong emotions like anger or fear—and she'd been terrified moments ago—was called cataplexy. Add that to napping and waking hallucinations and, good Lord. Did Nonie Stevenson have narcolepsy?

He stepped back, relieved to note she was having no difficulty breathing, no muscle spasms. Were there any physical findings he should be looking for to help him make a diagnosis? Any intervention he should make like putting a spatula in her mouth to stop her biting her tongue as one did with epileptics? He shook his head. He realised he and, he suspected the rest of his profession, knew precious little about the condition other than that the victim had uncontrollable urges to nap, and displayed the symptoms and signs he'd already noticed.

Nonie looked up at him, blinking and rubbing her eyes. "Thanks, Barry. I don't know what came over me." Her voice was normal, but shaky. "It's a damn good thing I wasn't in the middle of giving an injection or lancing an abscess."

"You had a wee turn," he said, trying to sound reassuring, but the same image of Nonie falling asleep with a scalpel or a needle in her hand had flashed through his mind more than once since he'd come into the surgery. "But I think you're coming out of it." Guilt like a cold stone lodged in the pit of his stomach. All along he'd been, if not actively disliking Nonie Stevenson, not able to warm to her. But what if much of her behaviour was due to an illness?

So far he hadn't done much about making a firm diagnosis. Things had been happening too fast, and while they were, he'd been concentrating on making sure no life-saving measures would be necessary. Now the sudden event was over, he should treat her as he would anyone who was sick, although as colleague to colleague it would be necessary to be perhaps a little more circumspect. "Nonie," he said, "I'd like to ask you some questions."

"Go right ahead."

He sat on one of the patients' chairs. "Have you always had this need to nap?"

She frowned. "No. Not until about . . . about four years ago when we were housemen. I thought it was because of the terrible hours we kept."

Narcolepsy usually started in the late teens or early twenties.

"I thought the same when I was training in obstetrics. I couldn't seem to get enough sleep at night." She forced a smile. "Even now I don't. I keep waking up, never get a whole night right through, and, boy, do I have dreams! I'm always tired."

All of which, Barry thought, was also typical of narcolepsy. Now what should he do? Was he completely sure of his diagnosis? To his knowledge there were no special tests that would confirm or refute his idea, nor any cut-and-dried physical findings, so really no point in doing a thorough physical examination, because he'd have no idea what he was looking for. It was a job for a specialist and one he had no qualms about turning over. And Nonie wasn't an ordinary patient. How would she as a doctor respond if he told her what he was thinking? Had she not suspected something like this herself, or was she like so many physicians who believed that disease was what happened to other people and that doctors were somehow immune? He pursed his lips. What would he want if the positions were reversed? No question. He'd want to know. "Nonie," he said, keeping his voice level, "do you know what I think about what just happened, your broken nights, your always being sleepy?"

"Tell me."

He inhaled, then said, "I've never seen a case, but I think you may have narcolepsy."

"Narcolepsy?" She frowned. "Narcolepsy? Do you really think so?" She took a deep breath and shook her head. "I suppose I've always wondered about it myself. The sleepiness, the vivid dreams." Her laugh was brittle. "But narcolepsy?" She frowned. "I've always thought that was kind of a joke. Like something you see in slapstick comedies. People falling asleep in the middle of conversations. But this is no joke. Barry, I think I've been avoiding the whole thing, hoping it would go away. Do you really think that's what I've got?"

He nodded, grateful for her willingness to consider the diagnosis. Many people—and doctors, contrary to the beliefs of many members of the profession, were just that, people—denied bad news. Refused even to consider it. Now she clearly recognised that. "I do," he said.

"Are you sure?"

"Pretty sure," he said, "but if I were in your shoes I'd

not take the word of a country GP, and that's not false modesty. I'd want to have a word with a specialist neurologist."

"Me too. I've got to get to the bottom of this. I know sweet Fanny Adams about narcolepsy, but I remember that passing out like that might be due to some kind of epilepsy or," she shuddered, "perish the thought, a brain tumour. I think I should see Doctor Millar at the Royal."

"I agree," he said. "But it's not exactly an emergency. You didn't pass out, precisely, according to Willie. You quite deliberately put your head down and fell asleep. But you should be seen as soon as possible. Would you like me to make an appointment for you?"

"Yes, please," she said in a low voice. "I wasn't very good at neurology. Can they do anything about it?"

"I'm not sure. I believe so, but Doctor Millar can advise you better. I have a hazy memory of reading an article several years ago that said small doses of amphetamine are used, but I've never had to prescribe them."

"It's scary," she said. "Unless he can do something, I don't see how I can manage. God, what if I fell asleep behind the wheel while driving?"

Barry hesitated. The answer was obvious, but he was in no rush to blurt it out. Instead he said, "I've seen you in the middle of an episode twice, but never at the very start. How quickly does it happen?"

She shook her head. "Usually I get warning. I know I'm going to have to sleep very soon, but once in a while I go out like a light, just as if I was lying in bed."

He remembered Willie's description. She'd had no warning this morning. "I told you I'm no expert, but I reckon for the time being you shouldn't be driving, until Doctor Millar gives you the go-ahead."

"God, that's awful." She took a deep breath, managed

a weak smile, and said, "But of course I shouldn't." She sat back in her chair. "Barry Laverty, you are a good man. Thank you. I needed someone to make me face up to what was going on. Thank you."

Barry shrugged.

"And," she said, "I'm sorry I came on to you, but you are a most attractive man . . ."

He blushed, looked at his dressing gown and slippers, hardly the attire in which to be discussing these kinds of things. He smoothed his tuft.

"I apologise. I'm sorry I've been a bitch about not swapping call. Fingal was right to tick me off. If I have got narcolepsy, it may explain some of that, but even if it doesn't, I do enjoy my work here. I'll try to improve. I promise."

"I know you will, Nonie," Barry said, "and the first step is for me to ring ward 22, the neurology unit. Get you seen."

"You are a pet, you know," she said, "and a fine physician. Thank you."

He smiled. "You have a rest," he said. "I'll see to Willie. Send him home. Then I'll call the ward." He laughed. "And then I'd better get washed, shaved, and dressed."

"Thank you, Barry. At least Willie was my last patient. He needs forms filled in so we can check his uric acid levels. I'm going upstairs to lie down for a while."

"I'll look after the forms. You stay there until I'm ready, then I'll run you home to Belfast. Will you be okay taking the bus to see the specialist?" he asked, and saw her nod.

"All right, then once you've seen Doctor Millar, we'll have to talk to Fingal about how this will affect your work in the practice."

She took a deep breath. "I understand. Thanks, Barry. Thanks for everything."

He wrote up Willie's lab requisition, then headed for the door, feeling a sense of pride at his diagnostic achievement and a little ashamed for having misjudged her. But now they had a dilemma. Certainly it was a kind of relief to know that Nonie's difficulties probably stemmed from a physical disorder, but if it could not be treated, should she be allowed to work with patients? Or even drive a car? That was certainly something to discuss with Fingal.

The scent of toasted barmbrack was mouth-watering when Barry entered the kitchen, and he realised he hadn't eaten since last night. Kinky said nothing. She'd understand the need for confidentiality.

"Everything okay, Doc?" Willie wanted to know.

"Fine," said Barry. "Doctor Stevenson just had a wee faint. No need to worry."

"Right enough," Willie said, "it could happen to a lady bishop—except there are no lady bishops. I don't mind telling you it scared the living daylights out of me. I hope she'll be all right, so I do. She's a very nice wee lady."

"I'm sure everything will be fine. Here," Barry handed over the requisition, "and do me a favour, Willie. Mum's the word."

Willie chuckled. "Doc, if I told you all the things a barman hears they'd blister the paint off the walls. Of course I'll keep my trap shut."

"You are a sound man, Willie Dunleavy," Kinky said.

"And I'll be running along," Willie said, rising. "I'll see myself out."

"Thanks for seeing to Willie," Barry said. "Things were a bit fraught for a while there."

Kinky tutted. "And did the doctor have a fit?"

"Not exactly," Barry said, "but Doctor Stevenson's not well."

"The poor wee dote."

"I'm a bit worried about her. I think she's got a thing called narcolepsy." Kinky was a trusted member of the practice with a mouth like a steel trap. Anything Barry told Kinky would stay with Kinky.

"I never did hear of that."

"It's pretty rare, but I hope we're going to get it sorted out." He half turned. "And if we are, I've a phone call to make."

"You trot along, Doctor, dear," Kinky said.

Barry went to the hall phone. As he waited during the inevitable delays of getting through to the switchboard and then being connected to Doctor Millar's secretary, he noticed a buff envelope from the laboratory on the hall table. It was addressed to him.

A voice on the other end said, "Doctor Laverty?"

It took only a few moments to arrange an appointment for Nonie, and as a doctor she was paid the professional courtesy of a ten o'clock appointment the following day.

"Thank you very much," Barry said, and replaced the receiver. He opened the envelope and grinned. Sonny's results. And they were what Barry had been hoping for.

Right. He'd take care of his ablutions, get a quick bite to eat, ask Kinky to tell Nonie he'd had to nip out to the Houstons', but that he'd not be too long and then he'd take her to Belfast.

22

Thou Migh's't Him Yet Recover

Once in a while, an early February day in Ulster can feel like spring. Barry parked outside the Houstons' house, grabbed his bag, and left the car. He needed no overcoat as the early afternoon sun beamed down from a blue sky. The roadside elms were still bare, but each twig had the beginnings of a bud. From somewhere high in one of the trees came the loud, clear trilling of a song thrush, each phrase repeated thrice. To Barry's delight he heard an accurate imitation of a telephone's ring. The birds were noted for their mimicry.

I grew up in Bangor, he thought, looking up into the sky. A small place where he'd learned to love sailing and the countryside. I've never been one much for huntin' and shootin', but I do enjoy a day's fishing. He was sure John MacNeill would give permission for a day on the Bucklebo River soon. No matter what cares might bedevil Barry's everyday life, the quiet of the riverbank, broken only by the chuckling of the waters over rocks or the splashing of moorhens in the shallows, was balm for the soul. It was so easy to become lost in the fluid actions of cast and retrieve, cast and retrieve, until satisfied by its position, he let the fly drift onto the water upstream from the rings left by a rising trout. No matter that on that try the fish ignored the bait. Just repeat, cast and retrieve, cast and retrieve in harmony with the rhythm of the rippling river.

But that, of course, was to come.

Sonny Houston was sitting reading at a white wrought-iron table in his garden. As Barry approached the gate, the dogs, Jasper included, came bounding across the lawn, yipping, barking, tails thrashing, jostling each other. "Can I come in, Sonny?"

"Doctor, of course. Give me a minute." Sonny rose and walked to the gate, his steps even and assured. "Come to me, dogs," he said. "To me."

They clustered round him.

Sonny opened the gate. "They'll not bother you."

Barry let himself in. Each dog in turn came to him, sniffed him, and bounded off.

Sonny grabbed Jasper by the collar. "Here's old Jasper. He's put on a bit of beef in the last ten days. We're very grateful to you, and especially to Colin Brown."

"Everyone's delighted," Barry said, running a hand over the dog's soft, sun-warmed head. "Off you trot, Jasper. Go and play with your pals." Sonny let the dog go.

Barry walked with Sonny along the path, noticing that the man's complexion had returned to normal and that he was breathing without difficulty.

"Isn't it a wonderful day?" Sonny said. "I just couldn't bear being cooped up, so the dogs and I came and sat outside." He pointed to one of the chairs. "Please have a seat."

Barry did. The metal of the chair was warm under his backside. He put his bag on the tabletop.

"Maggie'll be sorry she missed you," Sonny said as he sat. "She was so excited by the prospect of spring she decided she had to go into Ballybucklebo and buy a new hat. Alice Moloney will be thrilled. She's been tempting my dear wife with new hats for at least a year now."

"Give Maggie my regards." Sonny had been reading what must be an ancient tome. The fading brown leather covers were scuffed and a lengthy title was picked out in gold leaf.

"It's by Heinrich Schliemann," Sonny said. "He published it in 1881. It's all about his excavation of Troy."

"Have you been there?"

"Oh, yes, many times. The site was in Hisarlik in northwestern Turkey. Schliemann's methods were, shall we say, a tad unorthodox. He used dynamite instead of proper dig methods to excavate the early levels." Sonny shook his head with an indulgent smile. "Some feel the man was little more than a treasure hunter. But it's interesting reading all the same."

"Sue's fascinated by all that," Barry said. Only six more days.

"She would be welcome to borrow it when she's home again," Sonny said.

"Thank you." Barry opened his bag. "I've got some welcome news for you." He produced the forms and smiled. "I've brought your test results and I'll come right to the point. You do have pernicious anaemia, and the treatment is working."

"Thank you, Doctor. I am very relieved. Very relieved," Sonny said. "And I'm not surprised. I've been feeling much better every day since we started the injections."

Jasper wandered over, thrusting his head onto Sonny's knee, demanding Sonny pet him.

"You're forgiven, you know," Sonny said, and stroked the dog's flank.

Jasper head-butted Sonny like a cat demanding attention.

Barry watched the old man and his dog, each happily at home with the other.

He'd been right not to insist on a bone marrow biopsy or a gastric fluid analysis. Sonny's reticulocyte count was now 50 percent and his haemoglobin was on the rise. Barry allowed the feeling of satisfaction at taking a chance and being right to sink in, along with the warmth of the sun. What was even more important, though, was the satisfaction of having been able to spare a delightful and scared old man pain and discomfort. And what's more, in general practice, when you made a diagnosis, you had to follow up, and Barry would have been pretending if he didn't admit it was gratifying when a patient said thanks.

"You remember that your haemoglobin level was very low?"

"I do. When numbers apply to one's self, you don't forget them. It was six and should have been fourteen point eight."

"It's nine point five now. Another couple of weeks and it should be back up to that fourteen point eight mark. Then we'll cut your injections down to once a month."

Sonny laughed. "I'll not mind that," he said, "and do you think you could teach Maggie to give me them? I really have been quite a drain on your resources having a doctor call every day."

Barry smiled and opened his bag. "It's our job, Sonny. We don't mind."

Sonny needed no bidding. He rolled up his shirtsleeve. In moments, today's injection was given.

"Thanks," Sonny said.

"Honestly. It's no bother," Barry said, putting his gear away, "and it'll be Doctor O'Reilly's turn tomorrow. I'll have a word. I'm sure he could teach Maggie."

"Excellent," Sonny said.

Barry rose, and said, "I'll be trotting on now. Please don't get up."

"Thanks again for everything, Doctor," Sonny said.

Barry smiled and wandered off down the path, noting the little clumps of snowdrops and crocuses blooming in the sun. He turned as he closed the gate behind him, looking back at one of the most contented men he had ever known. Sonny Houston sat clearly engrossed in the excavation of Troy, surrounded by all his faithful canine friends, well on the mend from a disease that only forty years ago would have killed him.

He waved and Barry waved back and turned to go, but for a moment was distracted by a bleating from the next field. He glanced across. The lambs that had been born before Christmas were growing and one, in the inexplicable way of its kind, was bouncing on stiff legs like some ovine pogo-stick jumper revelling in the weak sunshine. The green field, bounded by dry stone walls, was mottled with white ewes heavy in their winter fleeces. Several lambs, including two black ones, were nuzzling at their mothers' teats. It wasn't spring yet, but the year was moving along. The promise was there.

Damn it all, the smartest thing Barry Laverty had done in his twenty-six years had been to decide to go to medical school. He paused. That had been the beginning of the journey that found him here, at the edge of this field at the top of the Ballybucklebo Hills. He'd worked bloody hard and qualified, he'd accepted the offer of a crusty old GP named Fingal Flahertie O'Reilly to wo in his rustic village, and now he was about to marry Sue Nolan.

High above him, the thrush's notes soared in a sweet, liquid ode to joy.

23

Cries, and Falls into a Cough

"Thank you, Nonie, for coming down early from Belfast on a Monday morning, especially coming by train," O'Reilly said, wondering whether he should take the last piece of toast.

The kitchen where the three doctors were having breakfast was cosy and filled with the aroma of Kinky's freshly toasted raisin bread. "Barry here told me about your possible narcolepsy. How did things go with Doctor Millar on Friday?"

Nonie sipped her coffee. "He was very understanding," she said. "There's no test that says the diagnosis is certain, but he had me have an electroencephalogram and a skull X-ray. No abnormal brainwaves, no space-occupying lesions, so I don't seem to have epilepsy or a brain tumour, which," she smiled, "I must say is a great relief."

"To all of us," Barry said.

"He told me that we'd have to work with a probable diagnosis of narcolepsy. I'm taking amphetamine ten milligrams every day when I wake up and we can increase the dose by ten more milligrams up to a maximum of sixty until I have the nodding off under control."

"Does that mean," Barry asked, "that you'll be fit to drive, see patients?"

She shook her head. "I mustn't drive until I've been a month free from uncontrollable napping, he said. He reckons if I take my first pill at eight thirty and start the surgery at nine I should be able to cope. And if I don't do any procedures, I'd be no risk to patients."

O'Reilly scratched his chin. "Mmmm," he said. "So you couldn't make home visits for a while except maybe the odd one you could walk to. Most home visits are out in the country, of course. If it's walkable, patients usually come to the surgery. No driving means no night call too."

"Not until Doctor Millar gives me the go-ahead to drive."

"And that could take a couple of months."

"I'm afraid so."

"I'd not mind," Barry said. "Now that Doctor Fitzpatrick's joined the rota, it'll still only be one in three. Although my trip—"

"You'll still get your trip to Marseille, Barry. I'm sure Ronald and I can cope for a while." O'Reilly saw the look of relief on the young man's face. "I suggest, Nonie, that you continue to run your well-woman clinics and take some extra surgeries. Barry and I will handle emergencies and home visits. All right with you, Barry?"

"Fine by me, although that's easy for me to say seeing as I'll be away for a week," Barry said.

O'Reilly thought he saw Nonie's eyes glisten. She sniffed and said, "I believe you are both being very generous."

"Rubbish," said O'Reilly. "You're ill. It could be Barry or me and we'd have to work out a way to carry on."

"I'm still very grateful," she said, "and I'll have to ask your indulgence on something else too."

"Oh?" said O'Reilly.

"I've to stop smoking. I may be a bit tetchy for a few days. It's killing me."

"Good for you," Barry said. "You'll be all the better for it in the long run."

"You two are wonderful," she said.

O'Reilly had to laugh. Before he himself could harrumph, Barry had beaten him to it. "Right," he said. "I'll have a word with Fitzpatrick and we'll see how we get on." He looked at his watch. "All this blethering won't get the baby a new coat today. Nonie, upstairs. If we get an emergency while Barry's making home visits, you can take over the surgery and I'll see to the case."

"Thank you both," she said. "I'll do that and while I am upstairs . . ." She smiled, and it was a wicked little smile. "I'll try not to fall asleep."

"So, Julie, everything seems pretty normal. Blood pressure's up a tad, but nothing to worry about." It was no worse, according to Barry's reading in the antenatal record. "Your blood work has all come back and is satisfactory. Keep on taking the iron and folic acid, drink lots of milk, plenty of fresh vegetables. Hard this time of year, I know. But do your best."

"Yes, sir." Julie adjusted the waist of her tweed skirt and slipped down off the examining couch. "I-I felt the wee one move last week," she said, smoothing down the fabric. "I never felt Tori until I was five months gone. Is that normal?"

"Twenty weeks is the usual for first pregnancies, but

women who have been pregnant before can feel what we call 'quickening' any time after sixteen weeks. You're eighteen weeks now, so it's what we would have expected."

"Great," she said. "Donal's been going round like a bee on a hot brick getting a new crib in Tori's room ready for this one. Do you know Tori's one year and seven months now? Gets intil everything. Wants for til do everything herself. If I hear 'I do it' once more . . ." She shook her head and laughed. "She'll be all grown up before we know it."

"Enjoy her," O'Reilly said, feeling a pang for his never-born child who'd died in 1941 and would have been twenty-six now. A year younger than Barry. At least now, since Christmas when he'd finally laid that ghost, he was comfortable acknowledging his loss.

"He's hung one of them mobiles over the new crib," Julie said. "All soccer players." She slipped into her raincoat and used her right hand to flick her long blond hair in a shining cascade over the coat's collar. She smiled. "He's bound and determined to believe that I'm having a wee boy."

"You might be, but we'll have to wait and see."

"Fair enough, sir." She picked up her shopping basket from where she'd left it on a chair and said, "I'll be trotting on. I've til nip off til the butcher's. Get some nice lamb's liver and rashers for Donal's tea."

She buttoned her coat. "Come back in a month?"

"That's right, and you know to get hold of one of us if you're worried about anything." He walked her to the door. "Off you go, Julie."

She went out the front door and he walked back to the waiting room, pausing only to glance at the shut door to the dining room before heading on. Tonight, February the sixth, at seven o'clock, the borough council would be meeting to discuss the fate of Number One Main Street and, by God, he and Kitty would be there.

O'Reilly stuck his head round the waiting room door, as ever admiring the mural of floribunda roses that Donal Donnelly had painted. Only one patient was left, an older man wearing a duncher, Dexter raincoat, collarless shirt, moleskin trousers, and scuffed boots. He looked up when O'Reilly entered. Even from the doorway, O'Reilly could hear the man's chest wheezing. It was that time of year when the cold and damp exacerbated chest conditions.

The man coughed and said in a hoarse voice, "How's about ye, Doc?"

"I think, Willie John Andrews," O'Reilly said, "the question should be how are you?"

"Not so hot, sir." He wheezed. "I doubt but I have a wee touch of the brownkitees."

O'Reilly smiled. "Just listening to you I'd be inclined to agree. There's a lot of bronchitis about right now. Come on to the surgery. I need to take a look at you."

As they walked along the hall together, O'Reilly asked, "Still working at Mackie's Foundry?"

"Aye. Man and boy forty-nine years. Pay's good, but it's a desperate smoky place. There's a brave wheen of the lads with the chronic brownkitees and a thing the doctors at the Royal call, em . . . Och, bollix, I've forgot."

"Emphysema?"

"That's the fellah. Anyroad, hospital's just down the road from Mackie's, and if our folks is sick they go til casualty there when they come off shift." They paused at the surgery door. "My lungs's been grand until now,"

Willie John Andrews said. "I never smoked a fag in my puff and I was playing Gaelic football until you mind I broke my left arm five years ago?"

"I remember it very well," O'Reilly said. "Wasn't I at the clubhouse at a meeting when you did it, and didn't I splint it for you before you went to hospital to get it set?" He laughed. "You were fit to be tied. Swore once you were better, you'd give the Galwayman who broke it, and I quote, 'A bloody good dig in the gub.'"

He ushered Willie John into the surgery.

"Didn't get the chance," he said. "Seemed like a good time to be giving it up. Not gettin' any younger, Doc." Willie John Andrews coughed, a wet, hacking noise.

"I hear you. Now, Willie," O'Reilly said, "let me give you a hand." He helped the man take off his raincoat and clamber up on the examining couch. "I haven't seen you for a while. Not since you had to have your appendix out last year." And that, apart from the usual childhood diseases, was the extent of the man's previous medical history. "So, tell me about this chest of yours."

"I took a wee head cold last week, and now I've a terrible hirstle in my thrapple. I was up half the night hacking and bringing up phlegm and it's dead sore behind my breastbone, so it is."

O'Reilly smiled at how expressions that had originated in Scotland were firmly entrenched in Ulsterspeak. And wasn't "hirstle" practically onomatopoeic for the wheezing the man made as he breathed? O'Reilly noted that his skin was hot and sweaty, but not burning up. His lips were pink, not the blue associated with cyanosis. His pulse and respiratory rates were both rapid, but not galloping. Although he was having some difficulty breathing, his nostrils did not flare nor did the great strap muscles in his neck stand out. "Hoist up your shirt."

Willie John complied. His skin was flushed and his chest moving rapidly in and out but there was no indrawing of the muscles between the ribs. All the negative findings suggested that he was unlikely to have pneumonia.

O'Reilly laid the inner edge of his palm on Willie John's back. "Say 'ninety-nine.'"

"Why ninety-nine, Doc? Why not seventy-four or a hundred and eight?"

"And you went to which medical school? I'm the bleeding doctor. Now, say 'ninety-nine.'"

"Sorry, Doc. Ninety-nine."

O'Reilly felt a vibration, tactile fremitus, an indication of fluid in the airways. He laid his left hand flat on the lower chest at the back and, using the first two fingers of his right hand, percussed. The sound was resonant, so there was no fluid in or consolidation of the lung bases. "Take as deep a breath as you can, please." O'Reilly listened with his stethoscope. There were rhonchi, coarse rattling sounds, all over the chest. More evidence of fluid in the airways. He removed the earpieces. "You hardly needed me, Willie John. You were spot on. You have got acute bronchitis. How did you come here?"

"On my bike."

"Can you get home on it?" If not, O'Reilly would load man and bike into the Rover.

"Aye. If I take her easy. It's a grand day out there."

"Good," said O'Reilly, "because I want you home in bed. You'll need to go to the chemist's first. Get your shirt tucked in. I'll write you a scrip." Hospital beds were scarce at this time of the year and while there was always a risk that acute bronchitis could be complicated by pneumonia, it was expected of conscientious GPs to look after as many people at home as possible. He sat at his desk and wrote a prescription for linctus codeine, a cough depressant, four millilitres to be taken three times daily, and elixir diphenhydramine, four millilitres to be taken at bedtime as an aid to sleeping.

"Now mind what I said. It's bed for you as soon as you get home. Here's your scrip." O'Reilly explained how the medication should be taken. "And I've asked the chemist to give you some friar's balsam. You know how to use it?"

"Aye, certainly. My ould granny swore by it. It's been around forever."

"Actually since about 1760. A Doctor Ward invented it. Inhale three times a day, light diet, lots of warm fluids."

"Right, sir." He put on his coat and sighed. "My sister's been at me since I came down with the cold. Made me promise to come to see you this morning. She's coming this afternoon to stay for a wee while. Look after me. She's a good woman, but she fusses." His voice cracked. "I've had no one since the missus ran off with that English git twelve years ago."

O'Reilly remembered. It had been the talk of Ballybucklebo, and Willie John had been a hard man to comfort. O'Reilly said, and meant it in more ways than one, "You need fussing over, Willie John. One of us will pop round tomorrow and fuss a bit—if that's okay." O'Reilly smiled at the man.

"Oh, aye, Doctor. That's your job."

O'Reilly walked Willie John to the front door. "Safe home." He closed the front door. All part of a day's work, but tonight at the council meeting wouldn't be routine, that was for sure. He scowled.

Apart from the interruption of the war years, O'Reilly had been seeing patients in this house since he'd joined old Doctor Flanagan in 1938. Old friends like Willie John Andrews; new ones like Julie Donnelly, who had come to Ballybucklebo as a maid of all work for the Bishops only a few years ago. This place had had a doctor in it since 1894, the year Robert Louis Stevenson had died. If O'Reilly had his way, it would still have in the person of Barry Laverty long after O'Reilly was gone.

This was his home. Bedamned if he was going to be pushed out by some bloody road-widening scheme. Something John MacNeill had said surfaced from somewhere in the depths of O'Reilly's mind. The lease to the land under his house had been granted by the Mac-Neills at about the same time they'd done the same for the Mucky Duck—and that lease had strings attached about remodelling. I wonder, he thought. I just wonder. Lunch could wait until he'd phoned John MacNeill.

24

As If I Was a Public Meeting

Ballybucklebo's town hall was a plain building with a grey slate roof, set back from the main Bangor to Belfast Road. When O'Reilly and Kitty arrived at five to seven, at least fifty people were standing in the main hall, surrounded by the sober sepia-tint photos of earlier, unsmiling councillors. Every face in the parquet-floored hall looked familiar, but there was one man with whom O'Reilly very much wanted a word. He grabbed Kitty's hand and made his way across the hall, mouthing greetings as they passed. "Evening, Mister Robinson."

"Good evening, Doctor, Mrs. O'Reilly." Two of the bottom buttons of the man's waistcoat were undone to accommodate the swell of his ample belly. His fair hair had been inexpertly trimmed and was a ragged curtain round his head. O'Reilly knew that Mrs. Robinson was the minister's barber. "I do hope council can be persuaded to choose the southern option."

"So do we," said Kitty, "and let's hope they make that decision soon. We'd like to get a start on repairs and feel we have a future at Number One."

"I hope you and I don't have to disagree, Your Reverence, but if they do decide to straighten, they'll have to put one of us out." O'Reilly sighed. "I'm told trying to move you is going to meet with some pretty stiff obstacles."

"It will, I fear, Doctor. We do have friends in some pretty high places." Mister Robinson took a brief glance up and then lowered his head.

"I understand, but it's just possible you may be able to help me."

"Oh? I'll certainly try, but in fairness I'll not do anything to weaken the church's position."

"We'd not expect otherwise," Kitty said.

"You know my house was originally a Presbyterian manse."

"It was. It was. The Flanagans—the grandfather, Michael, and his son, Ethan, both ministers—lived in it. When Ethan died, his successor, my predecessor, was a bachelor. He needed something smaller, so the church sold the house to Doctor Flanagan, Ethan's elder boy, and built the present manse that Mrs. Robinson and I and our family now occupy."

"Number One was and still is a leasehold," O'Reilly said. "I need to know the terms of the original lease. Would you happen to have a copy in the church records?"

Mister Robinson frowned. "I honestly don't know."

"Could you look?"

"Certainly. May I ask why?"

"The lease was originally held by the MacNeill family. I spoke with his lordship at lunchtime. He's looking into it too, but I want to pursue every possible avenue in case there are any restrictions on use of the land."

"I'll take a look as soon as the meeting's over."

"Thank you. Now," said O'Reilly, "we'd better take

our seats. Here comes council." He took Kitty's hand and led her to the front row. "There's Willie Dunleavy. I wonder what he'd prefer? The Duck's on Main Street too. And there's Donal Donnelly. He's probably just here to rubberneck. And there's Kinky and Archie."

Donal waved and O'Reilly waved back as he and Kitty took their seats. A long committee table dotted with notepads, pencils, and glasses of water was set on a raised dais. Members of council were climbing up short flights of stairs at each side to sit behind the table.

And there was that bastard Doran. He was an unpleasant-looking fellow, a short man with a sallow complexion, oiled black hair parted in the centre, narrow dark eyes, and a mouth that seemed to be set permanently at twenty past eight. O'Reilly ground his teeth. That little dog-beater, and by God, even if striking the man had turned him into an implacable enemy who might cost O'Reilly and Kitty Number One, if he had it all to do over again, even knowing that, O'Reilly'd paste the bollix twice as hard.

The councillors were seated. Robert Baxter, the chairman, sat in the centre, a tall man with thinning grey hair swept across a shining area of bald scalp. To his right was a man in a three-piece charcoal pinstripe suit. They were flanked on the far side by the eight other council members, six men and two women, all seated facing the spectators in the body of the council chamber. The scene on the dais, although short of numbers, put O'Reilly in mind of Da Vinci's mural *The Last Supper*. He certainly hoped he and Kitty would not be having their last supper at Number One Main any time soon.

"Look," said Kitty, "there's the marquis and Bertie Bishop."

The two men sat side by side to the chairman's left.

Lord John MacNeill looked sad and shook his head in O'Reilly's direction.

Oh-oh, O'Reilly thought. That means he's had no luck finding that damn lease. Still, he could pretty well count on votes from Bertie and John MacNeill. "And there's Alice Moloney. She was elected in December to fill a vacancy. I'm not sure how she'd vote." He certainly knew how that gurrier Doran was planning to vote. O'Reilly glanced his way and saw him scowling directly at Kitty and him.

The look was as piercing as the flame of a cutting torch and O'Reilly had to fight to keep his face impassive. He would not give the bloody man the satisfaction of acknowledging his animus and his obvious desire for revenge. O'Reilly said, "The rest of the folks are from the other townlands and villages that make up the borough of Ballybucklebo. They've all been patients at one time or another, but I've no idea how they'll jump."

The chairman rose and banged his gavel until there was silence. "My lord, ladies, and gentlemen. Welcome to this extraordinary meeting of Ballybucklebo Borough Council in the county of Down, which has been called as an advisory body at the request of the Northern Ireland Minister of Transport to enquire into—" He settled a pair of wire-rimmed spectacles on the bridge of a thin nose and read from a sheet of paper. "—the establishment of a safe carriageway between Belfast and Bangor either by straightening the road at a particularly dangerous corner or bypassing the village to the south." He droned on about terms of reference, statutory regulations, keeping of minutes—the kind of red tape that gave O'Reilly simultaneous heartburn, a headache, and an almost uncontrollable urge to head for the Duck.

". . . After a vote tonight, the report of the borough

council will be submitted to the ministry where, of course, the final decision will be taken, although they usually accept an advisory committee's recommendation. Now, to commence the proceedings, may I introduce Mister Ignatius Murtagh, who holds a master's of civil engineering and who is the Down County surveyor and is here to provide impartial technical advice. Mister Murtagh, please stand."

The man in the pinstriped suit rose and set a briefcase on the table to a muted round of polite applause.

"This evening, Mister Murtagh will begin by outlining proposals his department have prepared describing the pros and cons of the alternative routes. Then council members will be allocated five minutes to give a prepared statement or question Mister Murtagh. When they have finished I will entertain a limited number of questions from the floor before asking the audience to leave so council can deliberate in camera."

Another buzz of conversation as neighbour commented to neighbour.

"Makes sense," said O'Reilly. "The councillors, particularly the ones from Ballybucklebo, are going to have to live with their fellow villagers long after the decision has been taken."

"The recommendation to be relayed to the ministry will be reported in the *County Down Spectator* on Friday."

"And everybody in the borough will know by tomorrow morning," O'Reilly said to Kitty, "but I suppose form must be observed."

Mister Baxter banged his gavel and the room grew silent. "If you please, Mister Murtagh?" he said, and sat.

The surveyor opened his briefcase, extracted a sheaf

of papers, consulted his notes, and began in a high-pitched voice, "My lord, ladies, and gentlemen. My department has carried out a full feasibility study and cost analysis of the two options, A and B. Option A involves the compulsory purchase of property at the corner in front of the Presbyterian church, clearing the existing structure, and laying one quarter of a mile of road. The purely mechanical aspects of this option are simple. The ability to purchase is complex. Church property may be exempt. Our lawyers are presently examining the deeds and statutes."

O'Reilly glanced at Mister Robinson. The man's sudden smile was soon followed by a frown, leaving O'Reilly feeling very uneasy.

"Number One Main Street." O'Reilly sat rigidly as Mister Murtagh riffled through his papers. "Under the Town and Country Planning Act of 1947, the building, having been erected within the time frame of 1700 to 1840, is a listed Grade Two structure and as such cannot be modified . . . ahem," he permitted himself a little smile, "although the act is unclear on how to restrict remodelling by runaway lorries."

There was general laughter, but O'Reilly, who was feeling the first stirrings of hope, glanced around to see nothing but sympathetic looks coming his way.

"As I was saying, it cannot be modified except by the granting of planning permission by the borough council." He looked up. "As you can see, if council picks option A, there will be legal work and a great deal more paperwork to be done."

O'Reilly smiled. For the first time in his life, he wholeheartedly approved of paperwork.

Mister Murtagh looked straight at Mister Robinson.

"I gather the minister of the church," then his gaze fixed on O'Reilly, "and the owner of Number One are here. I have no doubt appeals would be launched."

"Damn right," O'Reilly growled in a voice that filled the hall.

"You tell them they'll be in for a fight," whispered Kitty. "I love Number One as much as you do."

"All of this," continued Mister Murtagh, "will require more extraordinary council meetings."

O'Reilly scanned the nine faces behind the table. Apart from Hubert Doran, who was still scowling in O'Reilly's direction, he saw no signs of unrestrained enthusiasm for yet more meetings. All the councillors were busy people. Another negative against option A. He looked at Mister Robinson, who was now successfully keeping a straight face.

The county surveyor continued. "Option B, on the other hand, will involve building a bypass to the south of the village on flat land before the Ballybucklebo Hills start to rise. Approximately one and one half miles of road, starting just before the Catholic chapel at the west end of the village, skirting south of the housing estate, and rejoining the Belfast to Bangor Road three hundred yards past the currently dangerous corner."

Donal Donnelly could be heard saying, "Boys-a-dear, there'll be a brave wheen of ass felt."

"Yes, Mister Donnelly," said the chairman, once the wave of laughter had passed. "It would be a good deal of asphalt, although I would ask you to restrict your remarks to the public portion of the evening."

"Sorry, Your Honour, sir."

When quiet returned, the surveyor continued, "Fortunately, the land in question is under the Agricultural Land Classification Act and rated Grade 5, the poorest quality of nonagricultural land. It is of low economic value, compulsory purchase will cost little, and will be unopposed by the owners. A consortium have submitted a tender. Granting road-building planning permission is likely to be a rubber-stamping exercise."

He paused and drank from a glass of water.

Sounds like no contest to me, O'Reilly thought, fumbling for Kitty's hand beside him and squeezing it.

"My accountants and quantity surveyors have calculated the costs independently," Mister Murtagh continued. "If anyone wishes," he held up his sheaf of papers, "I can provide a detailed breakdown, but if you'll take my word for it?" He paused.

No one dissented.

"Very well, we believe that on a purely fiscal basis, the cumulative prices of property acquisition, planning permission permit fees, and construction costs, allowing in each instance for ten percent cost overruns, option A would be only two thousand pounds cheaper than option B. With apologies to Doctor O'Reilly, some demolition has already been carried out at Number One." The surveyor started to put his papers away.

Despite his worry, O'Reilly managed a grin at the man's little joke.

"That's all I have to say, Mister Chairman."

"Thank you, Mister Murtagh," the chairman said as a polite round of applause echoed around the chamber.

"Could I ask those councillors who have questions to raise their hands?"

Only three hands went up, all from the Ballybucklebo contingent.

Doran sat with arms folded and head cocked to one side. Biding his time like a cat outside a mouse hole, O'Reilly surmised. There'd be some poison from that man before the evening was out, but he'd want to hear what other people had to say first so he could tailor his remarks for maximum effect.

"Very well." Mister Baxter turned to John MacNeill. "My lord?"

The marquis rose. "Mister Chairman, I have no question, but a short statement. We here in Ballybucklebo pride ourselves in taking care of our neighbours. Had my family still owned the land, we would have fought tooth and nail to protect one of our churches and the home"—he nodded at O'Reilly—"of one of our most eminent citizens. We would have sold the wasteland at fair market value, but regrettably we cannot. I ask council to consider the human aspects of this case. And that the land under Doctor O'Reilly's house is leasehold, originally granted by my family. I am not aware at the moment of any conditions or codicils, but tearing down Number One may be more difficult than it now appears. Thank you."

O'Reilly mouthed, "Thank you, John."

The marquis sat, to loud applause.

"Councillor Moloney?"

"Mister Chairman, does the surveyor have any information on the effect on High Street businesses of bypassing a village?"

"I do," he said. "Purely structurally, there is less damage to foundations from vibrations when heavy lorries are diverted from main streets."

"You can say that again," said O'Reilly.

"Thank you, Doctor," said the chairman as the hall erupted into laughter again. "I'll caution you as I did Mister Donnelly."

O'Reilly bowed his head as the surveyor continued.

"There's also less traffic congestion. There can be a drop-off in casual trade, but in a place like Ballybuck-lebo most custom is local anyway."

"Thank you," she said, then frowned and sat.

Oh-oh, O'Reilly thought. She'll not want option B. There was ragged applause led by Willie Dunleavy. The other supporters were all shopkeepers.

Oh well, O'Reilly thought, so much for enlightened self-interest.

"Councillor Bishop?"

Councillor Bishop rose and tucked his thumbs under his lapels. Reflected light flashed from his gold fob chain looped over his waistcoat. "Mister Chairman, may I, in the interests of shortening the proceedings, make a very short statement?"

"Please."

"My lord, ladies, and gentlemen, youse all know I'm a builder. My company couldn't handle a job the size of plan B by itself, so I am chairman of a syndicate that will be bidding to construct the road. We've submitted the quote that Mister Murtagh just referred to. That might seem to put me in conflict of interest."

There was muttering from the crowd.

O'Reilly's heart sank. If Bertie had to withdraw from the in-camera discussion, that would be one less vote for plan B.

Bertie held up one hand, and when silence reigned, said, "But—*but*, I've worked out what plan A would cost, what with demolition and road building. I agree with the county surveyor about the cost. If it is chosen, I will submit an independent tender. That's a job my company can handle alone, so it is. As plan B's more extensive, I'd be a subcontractor to the syndicate, but

I'd likely make the same amount no matter which job I do. I've the figures here and I'll ask council to rule later if I'm eligible to vote. I want no talk about me being swayed by money because I'll say it here and now, I'm with his lordship. People is more important than a few quid."

O'Reilly smiled as applause started.

"I've no qualms about stating this publicly. I'm for a new road in the south, so I am." Bertie sat down.

"Can you believe the change in that man?" O'Reilly whispered to Kitty.

"That heart attack last Halloween must have been a road to Damascus conversion, or else he's becoming even more politically astute than we suspected."

"Cynic," said O'Reilly with a smile.

Mister Baxter rose. "If that's all of the council's public remarks—"

"Hould your horses, Mister Chairman," Hubert Doran said.

I knew this was coming, O'Reilly thought.

"I've something til say, so I have." His voice was harsh. Grating. "All this talk about people's feelings. Very touching. My heart bleeds. That there's Doctor O'Reilly." He pointed. "He's a man just like any other man, not a saint. If it was my house or," he scanned the audience, "Donal Donnelly's house we'd all be sympathetic, but—but there's a small matter of a difference of two thousand pounds. Two thousand pounds." His voice rose. "That's not pocket money and it'll have for til come out of the rates. They'll have til go up. I oppose plan B and I urge you, fellow councillors, til do the financially right thing. O'Reilly'll get compensation. He'll be all right. I've said my piece. Pay heed."

Damn him, O'Reilly thought. It's true, but money doesn't make up for the loss of the memories, the hurt to Kitty and me, and Doran's astute enough to know that.

"Thank you, Councillor Doran," the chairman said. "No more comments from council? Then I'll take questions from the floor now. Kindly raise your hands. Councillor Hare is our honorary secretary." He nodded to a middle-aged man wearing a Donegal tweed hacking jacket and what in Ulster was referred to as a potato face—craggy and lumpy. "I'll ask him to note the order in which hands are put up so we can take questions in order."

This, O'Reilly thought, will be interesting.

There was muted muttering and shuffling of feet but no raised hands.

"Very well," Mister Baxter said. "In a meeting like this it's often difficult to ask the first question—so I'll take the second."

Universal laughter and it hadn't subsided when O'Reilly got to his feet.

"Yes, Doctor?"

"Mister Chairman, you and everyone here know me. And of everyone here, Mrs. O'Reilly and I are the ones with the most vested interest."

"Sorry to interrupt," Kinky was on her feet, "but pardon me, sir, I think mebbe I've some of that vested interest myself, so."

The chairman banged his gavel. "Point of order, Mrs. Auchinleck. Remarks must be addressed to the chair, and Doctor O'Reilly has the floor."

"I'm sorry, sir."

"Mister Chairman," O'Reilly said, "Mrs. Auchinleck

is right. It was remiss of me not to include her. I apologise. I yield the floor, but ask the chair's permission to continue when she has finished." He sat.

"Gracious of you, Fingal," Kitty said quietly.

"You may continue, Mrs. Auchinleck."

Kinky nodded her acceptance. "I've worked all my adult life at Number One Main Street, ever since I came here in 1928. That's nearly forty years, so. I only want to say that his lordship and Mister Bishop are right. People are more important than money." Her voice broke. "If you tear down Number One, you'll break the heart of this Corkwoman who came to live among you and loves you all." She sniffed. "That's all I have to say." Kinky collapsed into her chair and pulled an embroidered handkerchief from her pocket.

Sympathetic murmurings erupted all over the room as Archie bent his head to whisper into his wife's ear.

"Thank you, Mrs. Auchinleck. Doctor?"

O'Reilly was having difficulty controlling a lump in his throat. Once he had, he spoke softly. "Mister Chairman, my thanks to Mrs. Auchinleck, who has been a constant support to me since I came here. I hope you take her plea into consideration. I also want to thank his lordship and Mister Bishop for their kind words. I do not wish to see Mister Robinson evicted. His church is the spiritual home to half the citizens of the borough . . ." O'Reilly saw the minister bow his head in thanks, "but"—O'Reilly put a knife edge into his voice—"nor do Mrs. O'Reilly and I wish to lose our home. I do not believe council will be swayed by sentiment, nor as guardians of the ratepayers' pounds should they be. But they might do well to consider what increasingly heavy traffic will do to the houses on Main Street and the safety of your children if they recommend plan A."

He paused and saw heads nodding among the councillors. Then, staring at each one in turn, but lingering longer on the face of Councillor Doran, he said, "And I now serve notice that Mrs. O'Reilly and I will fight plan A with every means in our power. I have every reason to believe"—the more accurate word was "hope," but they didn't need to know that—"the old lease on our property protects the house from demolition and I expect to be able to produce that document in the imminent future. Council and ultimately the ministry may find that both the church and Number One Main are impregnable. I urge you to adopt plan B without further ado. Thank you." He sat, to more murmurs.

"Thank you, Doctor. We will take your words under advisement," the chairman said.

"Dream on, Doctor," Doran said.

"Councillor, kindly address your remarks through the chair."

Doran shrugged and shook his head.

The minister had his hand up.

"Reverend Robinson?"

"Mister Chairman, I'm sure Councillor Doran has a point, but I wish to thank Doctor O'Reilly for his support and add that as his lease was originally granted so my parish could build a manse on that property, I believe Doctor O'Reilly will have strong grounds . . ."

O'Reilly felt a hand on his shoulder. He looked up to see a woman he recognised as Willie John Andrews's sister Ruth MacCauley, a slim, auburn-haired woman who wore tortoiseshell-rimmed spectacles.

"Can you come quick, Doctor? My brother's taken a turn. He's much worser. All shivery like and awful sore in his lower chest, it hurts til breathe, he says, and he's boked twice."

Oh, Lord, Willie John. The man almost certainly had pneumonia.

"There was no one answering the phone at your house. Maybe your young doctors are both out, but I knew you'd be here. It's only a wee doddle round the corner to Willie John's house so I left him on his own and come over on my bike."

"I'm coming," O'Reilly said, starting to rise. "Do you want to stay and get a lift home, Kitty, see what more is said, or come with me?"

"It could take quite a while before the vote," Kitty said. "I'll come with you. I might be able to help."

"I'll run away on, Doctor." Ruth headed for the door. "I'll be home in no time, but if you get there first, go on on in. The door's open."

"Come on then, Kitty," he said, rising. "The recommendation will be reported in the *County Down Spectator* on Friday, but I'm sure we'll hear on the grapevine by tomorrow." He yelled, "Mister Chairman, I'd like to stay, but I've a patient to see," and not waiting for a reply he followed the two women to the door and the waiting Rover.

25

He Is No Wise Man Who Will Quit a Certainty for an Uncertainty

By the time O'Reilly had parked outside Willie John's bungalow near the corner of Station and Shore roads and accompanied Kitty along the path, Ruth, only slightly short of breath, had pedalled up and leaned her bike against a pebble-dashed wall.

"Come in," she said, opening the front door. She called out, "It's me with Doctor and Mrs. O'Reilly, who've come for til see you, Willie John. He's in here, Doctor," she said, opening a door off the hall.

O'Reilly, clutching his bag, preceded Kitty into a small bedroom. There was no need to explain that Kitty was a nurse. Everyone in the village knew. The room was well lit and smelled of the pungent friar's balsam that O'Reilly had prescribed earlier. A coal-gas fire set in one wall was lit and bluish flames burbled and popped, making the room stiflingly warm. Willie John Andrews lay in a double bed, propped up on pillows, an eiderdown tucked under his chin. Like many Ulster working men, he was wearing his duncher in bed.

"Thanks for coming, Doc—and Missus," he gasped, then grimaced. "Byjizzis, that stings, and I'm foundered, so I am." He was shivering.

O'Reilly set his bag on the end of the bed. He saw how flushed Willie John's face was, although his lips were slate blue. His forehead was damp with sweat and he hardly needed a thermometer to tell that Willie John had a high fever. The man hacked, hawked, and spat into a hanky.

"Let me see that," O'Reilly said. If, as O'Reilly suspected, his patient had pneumonia, it might be due to one of a number of different bacteria. The history of this sudden onset did not suggest tuberculosis. Staphylococcal pneumonia was accompanied by purulent and sometimes blood-stained sputum. The rare Friedländer's pneumonia was caused by *Klebsiella pneumoniae*. O'Reilly remembered thinking as a student how ironic it had been that the self-same organism had killed its discoverer, Doctor Carl Friedländer. It produced sputum that was purulent, but with a greenish colour. Willie John's had a rusty tinge. Almost certainly due to infection with the pneumococcus. Mind you, O'Reilly wasn't going to be like ancient Chinese doctors who made their diagnoses entirely on an examination of the patient's stool. One sputum sample wasn't going to be conclusive. He would do another thorough examination of Willie John's chest.

"Nurse," he said as he fished his stethoscope out of his bag, "give me a hand, please."

While Kitty took off her raincoat, O'Reilly felt Willie John's pulse. Far too fast, at 120. "I need another listen in," he said to the panting patient, who nodded weakly.

Kitty pulled back the bedclothes, removed the pillows, and supported Willie John with one arm while lifting his grey flannel nightshirt with her other hand. There was nothing out of the ordinary when O'Reilly inspected the chest, although the respiratory rate was far too fast. Nor did percussion reveal any dullness. He was not surprised. Even if Willie John were suffering from lobar pneumonia, it usually took twenty-four hours before those signs would appear. "Just breathe as normally as you can, please." He moved the instrument's bell over Willie John's back, listening carefully to each inhalation and exhalation. Pretty much the same as this afternoon, but O'Reilly could persuade himself that the sounds of air entering and leaving the lungs were diminished over the left lower lobe. In the same position he could hear faint creakings like the sounds of boots in fresh snow. That was a pleural rub, caused when two layers of pleura, the membrane that envelops the lungs and lines the chest cavity, rubbing together were dry and inflamed.

For completeness, he examined the opposite side of the chest. No additional findings.

He straightened. "Let's get him comfortable. I'll give you a hand." Together he and Kitty did that, and when her head neared his she whispered, "Left lower lobar pneumonia?"

"How do you know?"

"Don't ever play poker. Your face is a study when you find what you're looking for." She grinned at him.

Damn it all, she was right. They'd been apart for almost thirty years before they'd met again two and a bit years ago, and yet she knew him better than anyone. They were a team. Hadn't she been a great help with Colin Brown a couple of weeks ago? And together they'd delivered Doreen Duggan of a boy last year. Somewhere in the back of Fingal O'Reilly's mind an idea began to form, but his patient needed attention now.

They lowered Willie John back onto his freshly fluffed pillows.

He managed a weak "Thanks."

"How is he, Doctor?" Ruth asked.

"I'm afraid, Willie John, you have a touch of pneumonia as well as bronchitis."

Willie John nodded.

"You'll need oxygen and nursing, lots of fluids, painkillers and antibiotics. With a bit of luck, we'll be getting you on the mend in a couple of days."

"That'd be good, Doc. I feel God-awful right now, so I do. Dead peely-wally."

"You're very lucky Ruth was here, Willie John. She caught it early and you're going to be fine."

"You hear that, Willie John Andrews?" she said, flashing a wide grin at O'Reilly. "So none of that mouldering on about me fussin' over you."

"Och, hold yer tongue, woman." But the look he gave his sister was gentle and full of gratitude.

"Now, Nurse O'Reilly, will you get one hundred milligrams of pethidine ready and five hundred thousand units of benzyl penicillin ready while I go and phone for the ambulance?"

"I will," Kitty said, and headed for the medical bag.

"I'll show you to the phone," Ruth said.

By the time he'd made the arrangements and got back to the bedroom, Kitty was pulling down Willie John's nightshirt and expertly rolling him onto his back before pulling up the bedclothes. A distinct smell of methylated spirits now filled the room. Rubber-capped bottles of medications, a bottle of spirits, a couple of used syringes, and some cotton wool balls lay on the dressing table.

Kitty gave him one of her most dazzling smiles. "I've not been nursing for more than thirty years for nothing," she said. "Here's the form you need to sign telling the hospital what medications the patient has been given. It's filled out. And here's a sick line for Willie John's employers. All you have to do is sign it, Doctor."

"Bless you," said O'Reilly, and signed while Kitty put the gear back in the bag. That idea he'd begun to formulate was really taking shape, but it could wait until they got home. "We'll wait until the ambulance gets here, then we'll be off, Willie John. You try to sleep." O'Reilly inclined his head to indicate that he, Kitty, and Ruth should leave the sickroom. Kitty would check the patient's vital signs in fifteen minutes, but without the equipment in the ambulance that would be here in about half an hour, there was little more a doctor could do.

"Do you want to go back to the meeting, Fingal?" Kitty asked as she closed the Rover's door.

O'Reilly shook his head. "I've said my piece. The vote's being taken in camera, but the results will leak out. I'm sure someone will give us a ring and let us know what happened. I'm worried about how much influence Doran could have, but there's nothing I could say that would sway that man."

"Let's go home, pet," Kitty said. "He may have overplayed his hand."

"I hope so, but . . ." O'Reilly inhaled. "Home it is."

He turned the car, drove the short distance to the lane, and put the Rover in the garage. Together they crossed the back garden, went through the kitchen, warm and redolent of the ginger cake Kinky had baked for dessert that night, and along the hall. The front doorbell rang.

O'Reilly shrugged. "No rest for the wicked. You go on up. I'll see to it."

Bertie Bishop stood on the step. "Evening, Doctor. We just finished up there now."

"Come in, Bertie," O'Reilly said, guessing that the vote had been taken. And judging by the glum look on the councillor's face, it might not be what O'Reilly wanted to hear. He closed the door. "We'll go up to the lounge. Whatever you have to say, I want Kitty to hear, but give me your hat and coat."

He preceded Bertie up the stairs.

"See who's here," he said to a kneeling Kitty, who was poking the fire.

"Bertie." She stood and gave him a great smile. "Please have a seat."

"Thanks, but I'll not be staying. I just wanted til let youse know as quick as possible how things turned out."

"Go on," O'Reilly said.

"It's not black and white. I'm sorry, but they rejected plan B, the bypass. Two thousand pounds is a good bit of dosh. Your man Dornan swayed the vote. He's a very persuasive talker."

"I've said it before, he's a turd of the first magnitude. A miserable wizened-up toad of a man." For a second O'Reilly even forgot about patient confidentiality and blurted, "How his wife puts up with him I've no idea. Before my fight with him—" O'Reilly could picture the scene, the jarring of his knuckles on the man's chin, the venom in his voice as Doran yelled, "I'll get you O'Reilly, you shite." "—she was never out of my surgery. I couldn't diagnose any physical cause for her constant headaches, backaches, tummy upset. Nor could the specialists I sent her to. Typical of a thoroughly unhappy wife. Thank God they've no children. Neither of them are my patients anymore since he and I fell out. Poor old Fitzpatrick looks after the Dorans now."

"I'll not say a word of that to anyone, Doctor."

"Thank you, Bertie."

"There's an election coming and them councillors that's not from Ballybucklebo don't want the voters til think they're not financially responsible."

O'Reilly glanced at Kitty, who was biting her lower lip. He sighed.

"It'll probably take too much legal work to run a road over church property, and again we'd have every Presbyterian voter agin us . . ."

"So they'll recommend expropriation of my house?" O'Reilly felt a chill in his nose tip, a sure sign that he was becoming angry. "Bloody hell."

"Not quite. Between you and Mister Robinson and what his lordship stressed again when it was just the council there, you've got them dead worried about what your lease might say."

O'Reilly frowned. He hoped to God either John Mac-Neill or Mister Robinson could find a copy.

"So," Bertie said, "they compromised. Kicked for touch. It was his lordship's idea. I seconded it. We tabled the vote on expropriating your property, but judging by their comments it would have been four for and only three against. Alice Moloney's on our side. The chairman only votes if it's tied. The best we could persuade them to do was delay making a recommendation to the ministry for a month to give you time til produce that lease." He shook his head. "We all voted for that. There's sympathy for you, sir. It's always a notion to get to know the enemy in politics so I asked Doran on the QT a bit later why he'd not opposed delaying. He said," and Bertie's grimace was fierce, "'Sure won't a month give the good doctor a bit longer to stew in his own juice?' I seen the marquis's face. He'd overheard."

"Doran is a gobshite," O'Reilly said.

"But it gives us a breather," Kitty said. "We'll just have to delay making the repairs, but we can manage."

"By God, you're right." O'Reilly reckoned he felt like a condemned man who had just received a stay of execution. He might just get to keep Number One and put Doran in his box too. Old Doctor Phelim Corrigan's adage back in Dublin in '36, "Never let the patients get the upper hand," had applications under other circumstances and this was one of them.

"If what you said is right, they still may have to recommend plan B," Bertie said. "And there's more. I wish you'd been there. Alice Moloney said it was typical of you, Doctor, even though you probably had the most to lose and might have stayed til the end to make one last try. What did you do? A patient needed you and off you went at once. You should've heard the 'hear, hears,' from all but Doran, when she finished. She didn't tell the other councillors, but her and me had a wee private chat after. She said she near cried when Kinky spoke. She's round at my house now. Her and Flo's starting a 'save our doctor's house' petition, so they are."

"A petition, is it? Jaysus Murphy. I'm very touched," O'Reilly said.

"Aye," said Bertie, "and if it gets enough signatures we'll have a council who will have the Presbyterians agin them and all your patients too if they try til change this corner. I tell you I'd rather fight a campaign as a defender of two good people rather than as an ould Scrooge who was only interested in saving money."

"Thank you, councillor. Kitty and I are most grateful for you letting us know at once," O'Reilly said. "Now, we were just going to have a drink. I know I have you restricted to one pint a day because of your heart, but we could stretch the rules this once. Please join us?"

"Och, no thanks, Doctor. I'd best be getting home."

"I'll see you out then," O'Reilly said, "and thanks again."

⬚

"Here's your whiskey," Kitty said, lifting his glass from the sideboard.

"Thanks." They took armchairs on either side of the fire while Lady Macbeth snoozed on the hearth rug. "Well," he said, "it's not exactly the outcome we wanted, but I think we're in with a chance. I'll get onto John and Mister Robinson in the morning. Leave them both in peace tonight. Even if they could produce the lease now we couldn't do anything with it at nine thirty."

Kitty took a sip from her brandy and stared into the fire. "I must say I'm touched by Alice getting up that petition. Looks like we might have a second string to our bow if the lease doesn't help. Astute of Bertie recognising how the council's stance on this might affect their chances of reelection."

O'Reilly laughed. "In Bertie Bishop's own words he 'didn't come down the Lagan on a soap bubble yesterday.' He is one very shrewd politician of the street-fighter school. I'm very glad he's on our side."

"You know him better than I do, but I have to agree."

"Actually," O'Reilly said, "while it's great to be getting help, there's also the old notion that the Lord helps those that help themselves. I had a thought for our own plan B if we do lose Number One. And I'd hate that."

"Me too, and we know it would break Kinky's heart, but let's hear."

"It occurred to me when we were working together tonight."

"I really enjoyed watching you, Fingal. I have done ever since I saw you care for that poor man Kevin Doherty when he was dying of rheumatic heart failure at Sir Patrick Dun's in Dublin back in 1935."

"And I appreciated your help then, and do you know it gave me a notion." He looked into her eyes, and drank some whiskey. "I know how much you enjoyed the day out searching for Jasper, shopping together, having lunch in the Culloden a couple of weeks ago, dinner with the marquis."

She frowned as if unsure where this was leading. "Of course, Fingal," she said. "I always enjoy my time with you."

"And begod, I enjoy my time with my bride of not so very long ago, and I'd like to enjoy more of it. The pair of us will be sixty soon. 'Time's wingèd chariot,' and all that. Since Barry and now Ronald Fitzpatrick are working with me and the prospects are good for Nonie getting back to work in a couple of months, I'm going to have more time off than I've ever had before and I want to make the most of it," with you, he thought, but wanted her to draw that conclusion herself. People were always more likely to embrace a new idea if they thought it was their notion.

"You've earned it," she said, and sipped her brandy.

"The younger doctors today aren't willing to work singlehanded anymore. They're getting together in things called group practices and they have other professionals attached."

"Midwives, physios, occupational therapists, health visitors," she said. "Some even have professional administrators to fill in the forms. You'd like that."

"I would indeed, and thanks for doing that at Willie John's."

"Doing a bit of nursing tonight was fun."

"It always was with you, Kitty. Remember the day I met you at Sir Patrick Dun's?" He remembered a pair of amazing amber-flecked grey eyes smiling at him.

She laughed. "The day I'd been told to wash the old men's false teeth and I'd collected them all up in one basin. You helped me restore each set to its rightful owner."

"Och," said O'Reilly, "we all did foolish things, but you did turn out a first-class nurse, Sister O'Reilly, and a trained midwife to boot." Now, he thought, give your little speech. "Kitty," he said, "bear with me. I have a lot more free time, but you seem to be working harder than ever and coming home frazzled too many days."

"Are you suggesting I should go part time? Quit? I'll not quit."

"I'd not expect you to. What would you do all day? We've no kids or grandkids and you're not cut out to sit at home being the country doctor's wife, helping out with afternoon teas and charities. I know nursing's an important part of your life, part of who Kitty O'Reilly is, but what would you think of changing jobs?"

She frowned. "Go on."

"What if I was able to get a group practice started in the village? We already have three doctors taking call, and probably a fourth coming back. Nonie deserves her chance. Ballybucklebo has a health visitor who visits patients in their homes to promote healthy living, good nutrition, particularly among the children. And there's Miss Hegarty, the midwife, and Colleen Brennan, the district nurse. I know you're a highly trained neurosurgical nursing sister, but we'd need a nurse or two in the facility, perhaps a second health visitor, and you have the necessary nursing and midwifery experience to do that job." He remembered the night she'd celebrated the arrival of the weekend: "No more committee meetings, no more commuting, no more Belfast rush hours . . ."

"And don't forget the professional administrators to do all the paperwork." She winked at him over the top of her glass.

He laughed. "We'd have to get a budget from the Ministry of Health to build it, take the money Lars says we'd get from the government if Number One is expropriated, build a new house. I could almost argue a case for not living over my work anymore, you having more time off."

She rose and kissed him. "You are a sweet old bear worrying about me." She kissed him more strongly and he felt the tip of her tongue. "I'm no angel, but neither am I a fool to rush in to where the heavenly host fear to tread. So I'll not give you an answer tonight. Let me think on it."

"All right," he said, seeing this very much as a step in the right direction.

"And I'll tell you one thing, if we do open such a practice . . ."

He read her mind. "Of course you can choose the curtains, but," he pulled her onto his lap, "there will be roses in the waiting room."

And Fingal O'Reilly had to wait for a long time until she'd stopped laughing and he could kiss his wife.

26

Fair Stood the Wind for France

The four turboprop engines of the Vickers Viscount seemed to Barry to be remarkably quiet. His initial anxiety—excitement mixed with what he guessed was a normal human response to the prospect of soaring twenty thousand feet in the air—had subsided and he settled back in his port-side window seat to enjoy the experience. He stared down in fascination as the sleek aircraft climbed out of Belfast's Aldergrove Airport. He could see where he'd parked Brunhilde in the airport car park. The pilot set a southerly course to pass over the city. Below him were rows of terrace houses, church spires, and the Lagan winding its way with an occasional flash of reflected sunshine past the gantries of the ship-yards and on to the headwaters of Belfast Lough.

This, he thought, must be how a soaring bird of prey or a mountaineer on the summit of some great peak sees the world. "Amazing." He was barely aware that he had spoken aloud.

"First time up?" the passenger sitting beside him said.

Barry nodded to a middle-aged man in a three-piece grey suit. "Yes."

"Hardly anyone flew before the war," the man said.

"Just the real highheejins. Too expensive. It's really only in the last ten years or so that more and more people are using air travel. I go to London twice a month just for the day now on business. Not like the old days on the smelly old Belfast to Liverpool ferry, half the passengers seasick on a bad night, half of them stocious on a good one, and a wretched six-hour train journey after that. No fun."

"I've never been," Barry said. "To tell you the truth even Belfast's too big for me. I've never really wanted to see London, but I'm off to France now."

"Good for you," the man said. "I hope you enjoy it." He leant forward and peered past Barry. "We're going over Strangford Lough. Have a look and I'll shut up, let you enjoy the view." He sat back and opened this morning's *Daily Mail*.

Barry peered out at glistening mudflats, blue waters with pale stitchings of whitecaps, and many islands. The locals said there was one for every day of the year. One looked like a wishbone from this height, and he wondered if it was the Long Island that Fingal had been on with Doctor Jack Sinton eleven days ago. A vee of geese was passing under the plane's wing. They seemed to be flying backward. It felt strange to be above the birds. Fingal had shot a goose somewhere down there that weekend. Stuffed and roasted by Kinky, it had been delicious.

And here he was hurtling along at several hundred miles an hour, twenty thousand feet above Strangford. He smiled. As Donal Donnelly might have said, "Modern science is a wonderful thing."

On over the Ards Peninsula with its little fields. Barry took a deep breath. That was the Ireland he loved. He'd never been consumed with wanderlust as a boy. When

Dad had come home to Bangor after the war, he'd announced more than once that he'd seen enough of the world in the navy to last a lifetime and Ulster was good enough for him. Family holidays had been taken in Newcastle where Dad had taught Barry to fish on the Shimna River or in Ramelton in County Donegal so they could fish the quiet waters of the River Lennon. Medical school had been all-consuming once the class had left the basic sciences behind and begun their clinical work. What few holidays he got he took in the summer to go sailing. Some of the lads had been given trips to Spain by their parents between passing the final exams in June and starting their houseman's year. Dad and Mum had offered him the chance to go, but Barry had been happy to secure a locum houseman job in the private Musgrave and Clarke Clinic for the month. It had been that money that had bought his Volkswagen.

He'd had plans to visit Patricia Spence in Cambridge in '65 but she'd put the lid on that all right when she'd left him for another man. Water under the bridge. He watched the vista unfold ahead and hugged the thought that in next to no time he'd be landing at London's Heathrow to change to an Air France flight direct to Marseille—and Sue.

Barry looked through the plate-glass window of Arrivées at Marseille-Provence Airport. A plane was taxiing along the main runway, built on reclaimed land out into the waters of the Étang de Berre, an inland sea twenty-five kilometres northwest of Marseille. He joined a queue in front of a uniformed official who, in a very short time, though it seemed like forever to Barry, had dealt with the passengers in front, briefly inspected Barry's passport, and waved him through onto a crowded concourse smelling of Gitane and Gauloise cigarettes.

"Barry. Barry." Sue shouted and waved.

Like in a trick shot in a film, all the other people thronging the hall became blurred, out of focus, and all he could see was Sue waving, her copper hair tossing as she jumped on the spot. Barry, clutching his holdall, started to run and in moments had crushed her in a massive hug and planted a firm kiss on her soft lips. "Sue. Darling." He was trembling.

"I thought your flight would never arrive," she said.

"Heathrow was jammed and it took a while for my flight to get cleared for takeoff." He laughed. "This journey is my first time on planes so it was all a bit scary at first. But I'd have walked and swum the whole way to get here to be with you." He kissed her again. "Now, where's the bus? I can't wait to get you alone."

"We've waited for six weeks, another twenty minutes won't kill you." She laughed, and beckoned to a dark-haired young woman standing at the far side of the concourse. "The bus, once you've caught it, takes at least an hour. My friend Marie-Claude is going to give us a lift in her car. Much quicker."

The young woman, who had the deepest brown eyes Barry had ever seen and an enormous smile, said in barely accented English, "Welcome to Marseille, Doctor."

Barry mumbled, *"Enchanté,"* struggled to try to remember his schoolboy French, then took her hand and raised it to within an inch of his lips.

"It is a pleasure to meet you, Doctor."

"It's Barry. And it's very decent of you giving us a lift, *Ma'm'selle.*"

"It is my pleasure, and you must call me Marie-Claude. Sue has told me a great deal about you."

"All of it good," Sue said with a wink. "Marie-Claude teaches with me and has a little Citroën Deux Chevaux. It's the most popular car in France for underpaid folks like schoolteachers. She'll run us to our *pension*." She grabbed Barry's hand and started pulling him toward the exit.

They left the terminal building and walked under a Mediterranean sky of blue where the sun, while not scorching, certainly took the chill off the air.

"Here's your magic carpet," said Marie-Claude, opening the rear door. "Hop in, Sue, Barry. I'll play chauffeur so you can sit together."

Barry climbed aboard and sat on a simple wooden slatted bench. The 2CV was not Citroën's luxury model. He clutched Sue's hand and felt the length of her thigh pressed against his. Control yourself, boy, but his thoughts went to their first sweet lovemaking in her flat in Holywood the day after their engagement last year.

"Corner of Rue Beauvau and Rue Saint-Saëns," Sue said. "We're practically in the Vieux Port and not far from the Canebière, the main street."

"And," Marie-Claude said, pulling out of the parking lot, "it's almost a straight run down the A 55. I'll have you there in twenty minutes."

Barry smiled at Sue and was rewarded with a beaming green-eyed one in return. Twenty, twenty-five minutes and he'd have her to himself. It would be no imposition to be polite to this French girl on the journey. Barry turned back and said, "Thank you, Marie-Claude."

"It is always a pleasure to do a favour for your fiancée,

Barry. Sue has become a great asset to our staff. We shall miss her when she leaves next month."

And I'll be very happy to have her back, Barry thought. The car was passing through a built-up area. "Big place, Marseille."

Sue laughed. "It's bigger than Ballybucklebo, that's for sure. Marseille is a wonderful place and I am going to show you all the sights." She increased the pressure on his thigh. "All of them."

Barry swallowed and tried to concentrate on what Marie-Claude was saying.

"Sue's correct about Marseille. It is a wonderful place. I have lived here all my life," said Marie-Claude. "Look out there to your right. We are passing the modern port, which is not very exciting, but out in the bay are the four islands of the Frioul archipelago, and the Chateau d'If is on one of them. And that's the Basilica of Notre Dame de la Garde on the top of that hill directly ahead."

Barry peered through the windscreen at a massive white building, its square campanile revealing a belfry with a statue of the Madonna and Child on top, and a lower tower surmounted by a dome.

"The first church on that site was built in 1214," Sue said.

"You couldn't ask for a better guide than Sue," said Marie-Claude. She drove the car through 360 degrees around a small lake. "Vieux Port to your left . . ."

Barry saw a narrow harbour with fleets of private pleasure vessels tied up at fingers. Four-storey terrace houses, all with wrought-iron balcony railings and opened louvered shutters, stood at the harbour's head.

"We're on the Quai de Rive Neuve now," Sue said. "We'll be at the *pension* in a couple of minutes."

Barry was still staring out at the harbour and inhaling sea and fish smells. He'd read about a daily fish market on the Quai des Belges at the head of the harbour. The car turned right, then after three more quick turns pulled up at the kerb.

"Here we are," Marie-Claude said.

Barry let himself out, walked around the small car to open Sue's door, and helped her out. "Thanks for the lift, Marie-Claude," he said.

"My pleasure," Marie-Claude said. "I'll be off. See you next week, Sue, but if you need anything between now and then just let me know."

"We will," Sue said. "*Ciao.*"

Barry watched the little 2CV drive away, trailing a small plume of blue exhaust fumes. "Decent lass, your friend," he said.

"She is," said Sue, "and knew to get off-side at once," she winked, "because she understands that . . ." It was a spot-on imitation of Marlene Dietrich: "Ve vant to be halone."

He found her wink bordering on the lascivious and laughed at her accent.

"I've already registered us and even if it is only four o'clock I really would like to go up to our room and lie down."

His pulse started to race as if he'd run here from the airport. "I think," he said, and swallowed, "that would be a very good idea."

Barry, spent, drowsy, and deeply in love, sat in a chintz-covered armchair in their second-storey room. The bed was tossed and untidily covered by a duvet. When he looked outside, beyond the roofs of houses, the Quai de

Rive Neuve, and the mouth of the Vieux Port, he saw the now-darker waters of the Golfe du Lion waiting for the sun to slip down and bring dusk's soft blanket to Provence's Bouches du Rhône and the marshy Camargue to the west.

Sue sat in front of a dressing table mirror, rhythmically brushing her mane. Now she wore an open-neck white silk blouse and bottle-green mini when not an hour ago she'd been wrapped in nothing but Barry's embrace. "You look lovely," he said, consumed by her beauty. Seeing her, still tasting her.

"Thank you," she said, "and thank you for loving me, Barry. Please don't ever stop."

He rose and dropped a kiss on her crown. "Never," he said. "How could I? I promise."

"So do I—promise to love you always," she said. "It is so good to have you here. And it'll not be long now until we're wed. Mum's been going round like a bee on a hot brick making arrangements for next month." She stood, faced him, kissed him chastely, and said, "I must say after all that—uh—exercise, I've suddenly got an enormous appetite. I'm starving."

"Me too." He smiled. "You know the town. Where to?"

"The whole of the Vieux Port is awash with great little fish restaurants. There's one called the Chope D'Or . . ."

"The golden chop? Or perhaps the golden shop?"

She chuckled. "No, silly. The Golden Tankard. It's just on the far side of the Vieux Port. Six-minute walk. They do super *moules et frites*."

"That I can translate. Mussels and chips. Sounds good, but I'd like to try some *bouillabaisse*."

"So you shall," she said.

The light in the room dimmed and Barry turned to watch the last of the sun sink beneath the horizon, and all over the city as far as he could see, streetlights and apartment lights, shop windows and cafés came to life. All he could hear was the snarling of traffic, the honking of horns, and the demented buzzing of a multitude of mopeds. The *nee-naw, nee-naw* of a police car in the distance was not a sound to be heard in Ulster. It was all very foreign to a young man who had never been out of Ireland in his life.

She handed him his sports jacket and picked up a heavy cardigan. "It can get a bit nippy once the sun has gone down."

He slipped on the jacket. "Ready?"

She nodded.

He took her hand and they set off.

Barry could not remember ever having been happier. He skipped as they crossed Rue Pytheas and swung her hand as a sixteen-year-old might swing the arm of his first love. Around them, the crowds swirled.

Sue pointed to a large building on their left between the wide Quai du Port where they strolled and the water. "That's the city hall, built in the seventeenth century, and that great wide street to your right heading uphill is the famous Canebière. We're on the Quai des Belges. Not far now."

"You seem to know your way round pretty well," Barry said. "You did say in your letters you'd done lots of sightseeing."

"And reading too," she said. "Did you know there's evidence that this part of France was inhabited by Paleolithic man? Some cave paintings east of here are said to have been done between twenty-seven and nineteen thousand years B.C."

Barry whistled.

"Ancient Greeks arrived about 600 B.C. from what today we call Turkey and named the place Massalia. It's been an important seaport ever since."

"And now we're on Rue de la Republique," Barry said, looking up to the street sign. "Even with my grammar school French I can translate that."

"This is an important street. Five hundred volunteers left from here to march to Paris in 1792 to support the Revolution. And guess what marching song they were singing?"

"'La Marseillaise'?" Barry laughed. "Trust the French to compose an anthem that's a damn sight more cheerful than 'God Save the Queen.'"

Sue smiled. "Okay, I'm officially off duty as a travel guide. Here we are, 32 Quai du Port. La Chope D'Or."

They stopped outside a low railing. Tables were arranged on a patio in the open air, but only two were occupied by patrons, well bundled up in heavy overcoats. One couple were accompanied by a large shaggy dog that sat on one of the wicker chairs. The sign above the restaurant's picture window, white letters on a bright blue background, read Brasserie *LA CHOPE D'OR Crêperie*.

Sue led the way inside. The place was packed and the sounds of conversation and laughter rose and fell, punctuated by the *boing* of a spring closing a door that, judging by the coming and going of waiters with loaded trays, led to the kitchen. Barry breathed in the aromas of garlic, onions, thyme, fresh fish, and Turkish tobacco. He was definitely in France.

A waiter greeted Sue like a long-lost friend, showed them to a table for two in the window, pulled out a chair so Sue could be seated, and with a flourish spread a spotless white napkin on her lap. *"Les menus."* He set two down. *"Et quelque-chose à boire?"*

"Barry?" Sue asked.

I'd love a Guinness, he thought, but said, "When in Rome. What are you having?"

Sue ordered a carafe of the house white and the waiter left.

Barry turned to stare out over the harbour and south to where Notre Dame de la Garde, lit by floodlights from below, stood on its hill surveying the scene. He turned back to Sue. "It's lovely," he said, "and you are lovely. Very lovely, darling."

She inclined her head and smiled. "Thank you, Barry."

He looked into her eyes and took her hand, and for the second time that day, the people all around them faded.

The waiter reappeared, coughed discreetly. He poured for each of them from a carafe. Sue sipped. *"Très bien."*

Barry presumed that the rapid-fire conversation between the man and Sue was to establish that they needed more time to study the menu. He left.

"You know I'm not very good at languages, but I think I detect quite a nasal quality to the waiter's speech?"

"Pierre's a local," Sue said. "The French spoken here is much harsher than that in Paris."

"I thought there was something different. Our French teacher at school, Mister Marks, used to say, 'Laverty, *vous parlez français comme une vache espagnole.*' You speak French like a Spanish cow."

Sue laughed and squeezed his hand and said in a low voice, "But you make love like an Italian called Casanova."

Barry glowed. He raised his glass, sipped the cool, crisp wine, and said, "I love you, Sue Nolan."

She said, "And I love you, Barry." She lifted her menu. "And I think, prosaic as it sounds, we really should think about ordering."

Barry smiled. "Let's," he said.

Sue said, "I'm going to have some pâté to start with, then the mussels."

Barry said, "*Bouillabaisse* for me. The local fishermen invented it here."

"No starter?" Sue said.

He shook his head.

She leant across the table and whispered, "I'm taking you sightseeing tomorrow, but with what I have in mind for later this evening I really would suggest half a dozen raw oysters."

Barry started back in his chair. "What?"

"You heard me," she said, and her smile broadened, her right eyebrow lifted, and she half turned her head, never letting her gaze leave his eyes.

And Barry Laverty, feeling himself aroused, laughed and shook his head. "Shameless hussy," he said, "but you have a point. Let's make it a dozen."

27

One of Those Telegrams

"So," said Barry, buttering a fresh croissant, "what'll we do after breakfast this fine Thursday morning?"

He and Sue were sitting at a table for two in the small dining room of their pension. Three more tables were occupied. The hum of conversation was muted, the air perfumed by the aroma of freshly brewed coffee and newly baked baguettes.

"Another *belle journée de printemps*. Do you know what that means, Barry?" she said with a wink.

"I do, Miss Nolan, soon to be Mrs. Laverty, and even if it was bucketing down, it would still be a lovely spring day as long as I'm with you." He looked over at her, admiring her fawn-coloured sweater and how it complemented her copper hair, then laid his hand on hers on top of the white linen tablecloth.

She laughed and turned her hand so she could hold his. "You are sweet," she said, and lowered her voice, "and a terrific lover."

Barry blushed. Last night, contentedly full of oysters, *bouillabaisse,* and several glasses of the Chope D'Or's vin blanc, he had walked her back to the pension and taken her to bed, softly, gently, with none of the urgency of their first lovemaking. His only thought on waking had been how wonderful it was going to be for the next five days finding this beautiful warm creature beside him every morning and, once they were married next month, for the rest of his life.

"I know," she said quietly, as if he had voiced every thought he had just had. He felt his face colour again and yet it was oddly reassuring to know that someone could read him so well, know what he was thinking and feeling. He looked over at her. "Just thinking about it leaves me speechless, Barry. I love you." She smiled at him, squeezed his hand, and let the silence hang for long moments before saying, "You asked me what'll we do after breakfast?" and inclining her head.

He chuckled, nodded, and said, "We could, but perhaps we should do a bit of sightseeing first."

She laughed. "All right. There's so much to see and a lot of it's in easy walking distance. We could go to La Vieille Charité first. It's about a twenty-minute walk. The old building was originally an alms house, but now there's a museum with all kinds of archaeological specimens and a gallery with African and Asian art."

Not entirely Barry's cup of tea, but he knew how much archaeology fascinated Sue.

"Then on the way back it's not far from there to Rue Henri Barbusse and the Marseille History Museum. There are some marvellous old Roman ruins there."

Barry tried to look enthusiastic. Maybe she wasn't as good at reading his mind as he thought.

"Or," she said, and giggled, "knowing how absolutely fascinating you find old ruins, I thought I might surprise you—"

"Oh?"

"I've booked one of the local fishermen to run us out to the islands for the morning. I'm told the grouper fishing's very good out there and I've heard a rumour that you love to fish."

Barry laughed. "You, Sue Nolan, are an awful tease rabbitting on about your ruins. That's a wonderful idea to go fishing. Thank you." He frowned. "But will it not be terribly expensive chartering his boat?"

"It would be," said Sue, "except he's Marie-Claude's uncle. He's taken me and her out lots. He knows I've learned about boats and he often lets me steer. And before you ask, no, she'll not be coming with us."

"You," he said, "are a very thoughtful woman."

"We've only got five days. I didn't think you'd like to spend them in musty old museums. On Saturday, Marie-Claude's going to run us out to the Calanques, east of here. They're like mini-fjords. Very pretty. But today after we come in from fishing, we'll head to the Canebière for a leisurely lunch."

"Sounds like a pretty full morning," he said. He looked her right in the eye. "After all that fresh air we might need an afternoon nap."

"Indeed, sir, we very well might, and it's only five minutes from the bottom of the Canebière back to here." She dabbed at the corner of her mouth with a napkin and said, "If you've had enough breakfast . . . ?"

"I have."

"I'd suggest we get started."

They retraced their steps of last night along the Quai des Belges where the fish market was in full swing. As they passed the fishermen and their stalls surrounded by busy buyers, Barry admired the row upon row of gleaming silver fish, fresh from the Mediterranean Sea. He inhaled. With those smells there could be no mistaking this place for anything other than what it was.

"Those big ugly ones with thick lips are groupers," Sue said. "That's what we're after today. And the flat olive ones with red spots and brown blotches are flounders, but those two are the only ones I recognise."

"Those silver ones with two dorsal fins and bluey-green stripes are mackerel," Barry said. "My dad used to take me fishing for them when I was little."

"We were lucky, weren't we? Both to have dads that took their kids on outings? Some of the poor little mites at school never seem to see their fathers. But mine was great. He taught me to ride," Sue said. "I was a slow learner, but he's a wonderfully patient man, is my dad." Barry heard the deep affection in her voice. "I wonder how he and Mum are. We'll nip down and see them as soon as I get home. I'm sure everything will be under control for our big day, but I'd just like to be sure."

"March the twenty-eighth," said Barry. "Roll on."

Sue smiled at him and squeezed the hand she was holding. "Barry," she said, pointing to a middle-aged man with a face engraved by the sun, the winds, and the rain, "this gentleman," she bowed, "is *mon ami* Marius Dupont." He looked like a man who had spent a lifetime in the open air. He stood in front of his small boat moored to the stone pier and accepted Sue's hug with a quiet dignity and a fatherly affection. "He's going to help us enjoy this morning's part of our holiday."

The way she stressed "morning's" left no doubt in Barry's mind that they would need no outside help this afternoon.

"Monsieur Dupont," said Barry, and shook the man's calloused hand.

"*Bienvenue au Marseille, m'sieu le docteur,*" Marius said, and busied himself with his dock lines.

"I'm afraid Marius doesn't speak any English, but he's a wonderful boatman." She chatted away with the fisherman in what seemed to Barry to be effortless French. He cast a sailor's eye over the little craft. She was beamy, with both bow and stern coming to points, a design that seamen called a double-ender. She was about twenty-five feet long, open fore and aft, with a windowed structure near the stern that was covered by a flat roof. The gunnel, a foot-wide band encircling the boat, and the interior were painted sky blue and the rest white. A large reel was mounted on the prow. Her name painted on her stern was *Ange de la Mer*. Barry could translate that. *Sea Angel*. "Hop aboard, Barry."

He did, aft of the deckhouse, and held out his hand to help Sue.

Once aboard, she fiddled with levers and valves on the large inboard engine as if to the manner born. Cranking on the starting handle with a grunt, she smiled up at him as the engine came to life with a bang and a rumble, then took her place on the starboard-side thwart beside Barry.

Marius meanwhile had cast off the dock line and jumped aboard. He said something to Sue then with a wave and a shy smile moved into the deckhouse, took the wheel, and guided the little craft away from the quay.

"He says as he doesn't have English he's quite happy to run the boat. Leave us alone to blether away."

Barry wondered if Sue might not have asked Marius for that courtesy. There was nothing shy about Sue Nolan.

The water in the harbour was flat calm, and the *Sea Angel* pushed ahead at a steady five knots, passing ranks of moored luxury yachts.

The harbour mouth was guarded by two huge stone forts, one on each side.

"That's Fort Saint Nicholas to port and Fort Saint-Jean to starboard. There were fortresses there built by the Knights Hospitaller of Saint John in the twelfth century. Louis XIV extended them in the seventeenth. In more modern times, Saint-Jean was where recruits to the French Foreign Legion were housed before being shipped to Algeria for basic training."

The boat began to pitch gently as it encountered the Mediterranean waves, but the wind was light and the sun shone overhead. The engine's note changed as Marius increased speed to, judging by the way the wind of their passage ruffled Barry's hair, ten knots.

"The Frioul archipelago is two miles offshore," Sue said.

Twelve minutes at ten knots, Barry thought. Lord, but it was good to be out in the sea air with Sue, far away from coughs and colds and doctors who fell asleep while attending to their patients. Out here he could see the humour of the situation with Nonie, get perspective on the possibility of Fingal and Kitty losing Number One Main.

"Four islands," Sue said. Barry gave himself a little shake and looked to where Sue was pointing, resolving to no longer think about Ballybucklebo for the rest of his holiday. "That one's called Tiboulan, which is Provençal for 'small piece of island,' and I'm sure you know about 'If.'"

"With its famous chateau immortalised by Dumas

père in *The Count of Monte Cristo*. You told me you'd visited it."

"Pretty dank and musty indoors. Not somewhere I'd like to have lived," she said, and shuddered.

"You'll not have to," Barry said, "but if you like the bungalow I wrote to you about . . ."

"Oh, yes, Barry, tell me more about it," she said, and her green eyes sparkled.

"It's no distance from the village on the Bangor side. Completely private, on its own little peninsula."

"So I can sunbathe and get an all-over tan," Sue said, raising an eyebrow.

Barry felt an immediate frisson. "Only in the summertime," he said with a laugh. "The rest of the time you might end up with hypothermia like Andy did when he cowped that dinghy in January, but there's a lovely fireplace in the lounge. I'll get you a bearskin rug to curl up on in the winter."

Her chuckle was throaty and, glancing at Marius to make sure his back was turned, she kissed Barry. "I love you," she said.

"And I love you . . . and you are going to love the view from our first home. Just a small garden and a rocky shore then all the way across Belfast Lough to the Antrim Hills."

Her sigh was contented. "I think," she said, "you've been very clever, Doctor Laverty. I can't wait to see it."

"First thing we'll go and look at once you're home," Barry said. "I'll line Dapper up to give us a viewing."

"Lovely," said Sue. "Lovely, and speaking of houses, what's the word on Number One Main?"

By the time Barry had explained about the council meeting, the decision to give O'Reilly time to locate any original leases, and the real possibility he and Kitty might lose their home, the engine note had slowed.

"*Pardon*," Marius said, moving past them and going for'ard.

Barry watched as the man lowered an anchor hand over hand. Then he began preparing three rods and reels.

"We're on the fishing ground now," Sue said. "And that great pile," she pointed inshore, "is the notorious Chateau d'If."

Barry looked up at an irregular shoreline of white rocks surmounted by high walls surrounding a plateau. On it perched a small lighthouse with a red domed roof and behind that he could see three circular towers, one taller than the other two, linked by a wall surmounted by large gun embrasures.

"It was built as a fortress," Sue said, "but was turned into a prison. Thirty-five hundred French Huguenots were locked up there simply for being Protestants." She shook her head and Barry knew she was thinking of her work with campaigning for civil rights for the Catholic minority in Northern Ireland. "I wonder when the human race is going to stop persecuting people just because of how they worship." She exhaled and smiled. "And we're not going to talk any more about that on your holiday. We're going to catch ourselves a grouper. Marius, of course, will keep the catch and sell it to the restaurant I'm going to take you to for lunch."

"Grouper," Barry said. "I once read a book called *Diving to Adventure,* by a man called Hans Hass. He used to spear them when he was snorkelling in the Med. You saw what they looked like in the market. Huge mouths and they can weigh up to fifty pounds. They hide under overhanging rocks."

"I'll bet you," said Sue, "one or two won't be able to hide from Marius."

And she'd been right.

Barry had been idly jigging his bait up and down when something the size of a midget submarine hit. The reel shrieked and the line was stripped. Barry, well experienced in the ways of brown trout, was caught by surprise, but soon recovered. He pointed the rod tip up so the line never went slack, which would have given the fish the opportunity to throw the hook. It took fifteen minutes of alternatively reeling in the line like a madman then letting the fish run before he was able to bring the monster alongside the boat for Marius to gaff. Which he did, muttering, *"Bon. Très très bon."* When put on the boat's scales, the fish weighed twelve kilos.

"Lord, I've got aches in muscles I never learned about in anatomy class. I think after lunch, Sue, I'm going to need a massage."

She was still giggling when her reel began to scream.

By twelve Marius had landed Barry and Sue and two large fish on the quai. Marius stayed behind to see to the boat as Sue and Barry headed for the restaurant. By one thirty, they were well fed on *langoustine* and were walking along the Canebière. Pedestrians and pigeons milled on the footpath; Renaults, Peugeots, and Citröens competed with mopeds and Vespa scooters for road space. And all, at least to Barry's eye, were driving on the wrong side of the road. French drivers were not shy about using their horns.

"I'm glad you were there to translate, love. The *Cuisine*

Algérienne on the menu had me stumped. I don't know what I would have ended up eating without you."

She laughed. "Okay, class, time for a review: *couscous* is steamed semolina, *merguez* is a lamb sausage with cumin and hot peppers, and *shakshouka* are poached eggs in a chili pepper sauce."

"And you were right about that semolina pastry, what's it called, *makroud*? Yummy." He held Sue's hand and listened to the sounds of traffic, the hoarse, shrill cries of gulls. They turned left onto Cours Jean Ballard. The street was deserted so he stopped, forcing her to stop too, wrapped her in a great hug and kissed her long and hard, tasting the honey, dates, and cinnamon of the dessert they'd just shared. "I love you, Sue Nolan," he said, "and I'm the happiest man in France. Come on." He set off at a trot, tugging a laughing Sue after him. "Here we are." He stopped at the door to the pension and opened it to let her enter first. He noticed a 2CV parked near the door.

Sue inclined her head. "Thank you, kind sir," she said, and went in, smiling broadly.

As Barry followed he saw Marie-Claude standing wide-eyed in the foyer. She was a nice girl, but his plan had been to have Sue to himself this afternoon. He didn't need someone playing gooseberry.

"Sue," Marie-Claude said, "a telegram came to the school for you. I-I know everyone back in Ireland thinks you are in school today." Marie-Claude's gaze darted to Barry and back to the telegram still in her hands.

"I thought it must be urgent. I brought it straight here. I was going to leave it with the concierge, but you arrived before I could." Marie-Claude thrust the flimsy into Sue's waiting hands.

Barry felt his irritation turn to concern.

Sue ripped the telegram open, read, clapped a hand to her mouth, and whispered, "Oh God. No." Tears were already welling in her eyes and spilling over as she handed Barry the message.

He read aloud. "*Dad had heart attack Stop In Waveney Hospital Stop Come home Stop Love Mum.*" Dear God.

Marie-Claude gasped. "Oh, Sue, *je suis désolé.* I'm so sorry," she said. "I knew it must be important, but I hoped it wouldn't be bad news."

"Thank you," Barry said, moving to Sue and putting an arm around her shoulder, drawing her close into the protection of his chest. "Darling, we'll have to go home at once."

"Yes, yes. As soon as possible. Oh, Barry."

"Pack your valises," said Marie-Claude. "I can drive you to the airport. Someone will cover for me at the school. There's a four o'clock flight to London that Air France made a fuss about introducing last year. You might be able to get on it. And don't worry about your classes. I'll explain. They'll understand."

28

As the Heart Grows Older

Barry took Sue's hand and together they walked into the entrance hall of the Waveney Hospital. He could sense her trembling. The hospital smells of floor polish and disinfectant hadn't changed since he'd worked here in 1965. His eyes felt gritty and his chin was rough with stubble. The flight yesterday afternoon from Marseille to Heathrow had been uneventful, but they had had to wait until seven the next morning to catch the early flight to Aldergrove.

He looked over at her now, seeing anxiety and frustration etching their marks on her smooth skin. They were still pretty much in the dark about her father's status. The telegram had been short and to the point. Such was the nature of telegrams. She'd phoned her parents' home last night as soon as they were in the London terminal and spoken to an aunt, who'd come to the farm to answer the phone so Irene Nolan could stay close to her husband's bedside. All Sue's aunt could say was that he'd been admitted and according to the hospital was "comfortable." Sue had cried her relief standing at an airport call box as Barry held her close, protecting her as best he could from the rush of commuters laden with luggage and briefcases and shopping bags. At least they knew Selbert Nolan had been alive at 5 o'clock last night.

Barry had hoped he could give Sue more assurance by using his professional status to find out more details. But knowing hospital procedures, he was none too sanguine. With his last few coins for the pay phone he called the hospital and got no more information than "He's comfortable." A request to talk to a junior colleague on duty had been denied.

By then Sue was up to high doh and there was nothing practical he could do to comfort her. Neither slept much that night.

They left the plane at Aldergrove at last and he'd hustled her to his car and driven for half an hour along the A26 to the Cushendall Road in Ballymena and the hospital. O'Reilly would have approved of Barry's utter disregard for the speed limit. Sue was breaking her heart and the sooner he could get her to the ward and get some concrete information, the better.

They stopped at a desk labelled INFORMATION, where a receptionist sat behind a low glass partition. The mousey-haired, tired-looking woman lifted her eyes from a copy of *Film Review*. "Yes?"

"We'd like to see Mister Nolan. I'm Doctor Laverty and this is Miss Nolan, his daughter. We've just flown in from Marseille."

The receptionist consulted a list. "He was admitted yesterday. Heart attack. He's on the men's medical ward . . ."

Sue sighed a deep sigh of relief and he squeezed her hand. So her dad was still alive. Coronary patients could die rapidly after the initial event. Not knowing the details and not wanting to scare her he'd been pretty circumspect in his explanations to her on the way here.

The woman pointed to her right. "Down that there corridor for a wee ways, then first on your left." She hesitated. "It's only immediate family or the patient's own doctor outside visiting hours, sir."

"I'm engaged to Miss Nolan."

"That's different, so it is."

"Thank you," Barry said. "Come on, Sue. It's not far." Having done a year's obstetric training here he knew his way around the place. He turned to his left and started to walk quickly.

"Oh, Barry, I-I hope . . ." Sue said. She didn't finish the sentence as he navigated her around a porter in a brown grocer's coat pushing a tea trolley and two uniformed nurses heading the other way. She stopped suddenly, almost causing a collision behind her.

"What is it, Sue?"

Tears glistened in her eyes. "Mum and Dad mustn't know that we were together in Marseille," she whispered. "I know they're very fond of you, but . . ."

He tugged her gently toward the wall, out of the stream of human traffic. "As far as they'll know, you called me from Heathrow and I picked you up at the airport. All right?"

She nodded and he squeezed her hand gently. They continued down the hall.

Barry recognised a sign above a pair of varnished double doors. MEDICAL WARD. "In here." The Waveney was a general hospital and didn't have wards specialising in cardiology like the Royal.

Barry immediately saw a uniformed junior sister sitting with her back to him and went straight up to her.

"Good morning, Sister. I'm Doctor Laverty and this is Miss Nolan."

Sister rose and turned. She inclined her head and smiled. "Hello, Doctor Laverty. I was a staff nurse in the Royal in '62."

He noticed the oval silver and green Royal Victoria Hospital badge on her apron shoulder strap. Nurses traditionally continued to wear the emblem of the hospital where they had trained.

"I'll be damned. Sister Bette Robinson."

"What brings you here?" said the nurse.

"My father," Sue said, looking out to the twenty-four-bed ward, eyes scanning, searching. "He-he was admitted yesterday."

"Yes, of course. With a coronary. He's doing well, Miss Nolan. Your mother's with him. I'll take you to them." The wooden-floored ward was well lit by tall windows. Men lay in iron-framed beds, each with a set of earphones hung beside the bedhead so the patient could listen to the radio. Others sat in dressing gowns and pyjamas on plain wooden chairs. Nurses and ward orderlies bustled about their duties. There were bunches of daffodils in vases on two tables in the centre of the ward.

"Here," Sister Robinson said, stopping where curtains hanging from an overhead rail had been closed around a bed halfway down the ward. She pulled one curtain back. "Go on in."

"Go ahead, Sue," Barry said. He followed her through the curtains, then closed them behind him. Sue was hugging her mother, who had risen from a plain wooden chair.

"Mummy, oh, Mummy," Sue said, "I'm so sorry." A tear glistened, then slid down her cheek.

"There, there," Mrs. Nolan said, rummaging in her handbag and giving Sue a hanky as she must have done a thousand times when her girl was little. "We're sure your dad's going to get better. There he is, you see. Large as life."

Sue sniffed, managing a weak smile as she walked to the head of the bed. "Daddy." Sue bent over and kissed his forehead. "Oh, Daddy. I'm so sorry you're sick." Her voice quavered.

"Hello, Barry," Mrs. Nolan said. "Thank you for picking Sue up at the airport."

He inclined his head. "Glad I could help. I'm sorry for your troubles."

Mrs. Nolan returned to her chair.

Selbert Nolan was a big man. His normally ruddy farmer's cheeks were pallid, but at least there was no cyanosis, so no heart failure. His cheeks had deep lines gnawed in them by his years exposed to the bitter Ulster winds. The green plastic tubes of oxygen cannulae disappeared into each nostril and the flow of the gas made a soft hissing. His breathing was slow and regular. A glass bottle on a gallows above the bed dripped what Barry assumed to be a saline/heparin mixture through a red rubber tube into an arm vein. Anticoagulants were given to prevent more clots forming.

He had managed a weak grin when he saw his daughter. "Aye. It's no' much fun, but I think I'll be all right." The man's voice was weak, slurred, and his pupils were tiny.

Morphine, which constricted the pupils, a quarter grain every six hours for pain control, was part of the treatment.

A cable, which Barry knew carried wires from electrodes called "leads" attached to Selbert's arms, legs, and chest, ran to a yellow box on a shelf above and be-hind the patient's bedhead. A monitor in front of the box gave a continuous display of cardiac electrical activity. To Barry's relief the spacing of spikes in the tracings was perfectly regular.

Sue sat on the left side of the bed and smiled up at Barry from her chair. The frown lines that had been almost constantly on her forehead had fled. Then she turned back to her father, and the love Barry had heard yesterday when she'd called him a very patient man was deep in her green eyes. "Barry's been wonderful," she said.

He smiled inside, the relief on behalf of this girl he loved so dearly filling his chest. Now Sue had actually seen her father, he knew some of the uncertainty about a loved one's condition had been removed. And it was the uncertainty that was always hardest to bear. Soon he would excuse himself and have a word with Sister Bette Robinson, one professional to another, about his father-in-law-to-be.

"You must be tired, Mum," Sue said. "You've been here all night."

Mrs. Nolan shook her head. "Och well," she said, "it could hae been worse. I had a few naps and this morning, one of Dad's nice doctors, I think he's called a registrar, I didnae get his name"—her Antrim accent, sibilant and full of old Scots usage, was very obvious—"he and I had a wee word earlier the day. He explained that we're no' out of the woods yet, but it's the first twenty-four hours that're critical and we're nearly there, hey."

"I'm no cardiologist, but that's what I've been taught," Barry said. "If you'll excuse me, I'll go and have a word with his nurse. See if I can learn any more."

"Go ahead, Barry," Sue said. "I'll stay here. Keep my folks company."

Barry let himself out through the curtains.

Bette Robinson was alone and hunched over a broad wooden desk, making notes. He smiled to himself when he realized her posture hadn't improved since he'd worked with her at the Royal. "I suppose you'd like to hear about Mister SN? I've pulled his chart. I know you want to explain things to the family. I still remember we all thought you were a bit odd at the RVH spending all that time trying to tell patients information they probably couldn't understand anyway."

Barry shrugged. "Actually you'd be surprised how much the average patient does take in, but we have time in general practice. I know how busy hospital doctors are. I want to set the Nolans' minds at rest as best I can."

"Fair enough. Have a pew."

Barry perched on the wooden chair.

"Let's see, farmer, aged fifty-four. Married. Two children . . . We admitted Mister Nolan yesterday at noon and made a working clinical diagnosis of myocardial infarction with no arrhythmias. This was confirmed with electrocardiographic findings and the usual enzyme tests." She opened the chart and showed him a long strip of narrow pinkish graph paper where a central black-inked line was interrupted at regular intervals by upward and downward spikes.

Barry smiled. "Tell me what it means," he said. "I always had trouble reading those things and we don't do them in general practice."

"The heart muscle is damaged at the back of the heart."

"I see. And you treated him with—?"

"Morphine for pain relief. He's getting an IV infusion

of heparin ten thousand units every six hours. We'll start him on an oral anticoagulant, dicoumarol, in a couple of days. Complete bed rest, naturally. Assuming no complications."

Barry mentally listed heart failure, arrhythmias, thrombo-embolism, and rupture of the heart, any of which could be fatal. Much as he believed in honesty with patients and their families, he'd keep those to himself for a while.

"He'll need that for about four weeks before we let him home, then he'll be able to get up a bit more every day and back to work in three months. He'll need weekly follow-up here as long as he's on the anticoagulants. Long-term outlook?" She shrugged.

"Thanks, Bette," he said. Much of what she'd told him he'd been pretty sure he already knew, but it was good to have it confirmed by a senior nurse who dealt with these cases day and daily. It seemed that for the present it was likely that Mister Nolan would recover, but no one could foretell what his future might hold.

Barry would explain to Sue and her mum when they all got home, but for now he thought it tactful to give the family privacy. And he was curious about Bette Robinson, whom he had last seen walking out for a short spell with Jack Mills back in '62. "How are you, Bette? When did you come to the Waveney?" She'd not been on the staff in '65.

"Grand," she said. "I married Jim Montgomery last July. Do you remember him? He was a year behind you and Jack Mills, and he came here in '64 as a houseman. Now he's a surgical registrar. The move to the Waveney got me a promotion to sister too."

"I do remember him. And good for you, Bette. On both counts."

"And you, Barry?"

"I'm a GP in Ballybucklebo. Working with Fingal O'Reilly and—"

"Doctor Fingal Flahertie O'Reilly," Bette said with satisfaction. "Irish rugby international—Jack Mills thought the world of him—and we knew at the Royal he was one of the last of the breed of old-style GPs. Well done, Barry. I'll bet he's a great teacher for you."

"He is. I'm loving the work. And then last year I got engaged to Sue Nolan."

"She seems like a lovely girl."

"She is, and I'd better get back to her and her family. Thanks for the gen."

"Anytime. Just ring me and I'll clue in the other sisters about who you are so you'll be kept up to date with progress if I'm off duty."

"Thanks, Bette."

Once inside the screens, he saw that Selbert Nolan had drifted off. Sue was sitting staring at her father. Mrs. Nolan was knitting, her needles clicking, not quite in rhythm with the constant passage of the intermittent upticks in the green lines on the cardiac monitor.

"Hello again, Barry," Mrs. Nolan whispered.

He nodded.

Sue turned and smiled at him.

"Now that your father's resting, Sue, why don't you and Barry go home. He's doing as well as can be expected and I can keep him company. You've had a very long journey, and you must be tired. It's only a few miles back to the farm."

"Are you sure you don't want us to stay, Mum?"

"I'll be fine, pet, and I'll phone if there's any change. There's a phone booth in the corridor. Go on, the pair of you. Barry, take Sue home, let her get a bath and a rest, and I'm sure she can make you a good Ulster fry for your lunch, hey. If I didn't know better, I'd think neither of you had had a decent night's sleep or a scrap of decent food since Sue got the news in Marseille yesterday. But, ah, that's love for you. Thanks again, Barry, for picking up our wee girl from the airport."

Barry scratched his whiskers and looked at Mrs. Nolan. She had returned to her knitting and did not have the look of a woman harbouring a secret. Barry smiled. A bath and shave sounded very good. And if Mrs. Nolan was happy to let them go, why not. Their staying would serve no practical purpose. After nearly a whole day of airport and aeroplane food, a fry sounded even better. He knew Sue's cooking of old.

"I've our motorcar," Mrs. Nolan said, "so I'll come on later once he's woken up and we've had a wee word together. It's Friday. Perhaps you can get the weekend off and stay with us for a few days, Barry. Although I'm worried about Selbert, we do need to talk about the wedding plans too. I'm no' sure March the twenty-eighth is a starter anymore."

29

And Talk of Many Things

Barry looked around the big farmhouse kitchen with its red-tiled floor and whitewashed walls of rough plaster that were splashed with afternoon sunlight. A plain Welsh dresser stood against one wall, blue willow-pattern china plates arranged in rows on its shelves, a black cast-iron Aga range bulked against another.

"I grew up in this house," said Sue, holding a teacup in both hands. "I can't remember a day that Dad and Mum weren't here." She sighed. "It seems so empty to-day. Lonely."

She rose from the kitchen table, looked at him, and pursed her lips. "I'm so glad you're here, Barry. I didn't mean—"

"I know what you meant. Of course I do. You're still very worried about your dad. It takes more than a hot bath, a good meal, and a nap to get over a shock like that."

Sue looked as if she might come over to him, but then seemed to change her mind and instead put her cup on his plate and started gathering up dishes.

"It's more than twenty-four hours now since his heart attack," Barry said, "so the time of maximum danger is over. I'd be very hopeful of his recovery now." He used his most professional voice, as if Sue was simply the daughter of a patient. Barry had known for years the therapeutic value of a completely professional opinion. To add more weight as he spoke, he did not smile. He kept a niggling concern to himself. Hopeful in the short term, he thought, but fifty-four was young for a first heart attack. Time would tell.

Sue nodded and said, "Thank you. That is good to know . . ."

He saw her lips start to say, "Doctor." Good. He was sure she was reassured.

Moving to her side, he folded her into a gentle hug. "Your mum will be home later, and your dad should be discharged reasonably soon. And if it helps, I'm here."

"I know." She nodded. "And it does help. A lot." She took his hand and started to walk to the door. "But I'd really like to get a breath of fresh air. We seem to have been cooped up in planes and cars and"—she shuddered—"hospitals forever."

Barry understood. He unlatched the door. "Where to?"

"Let's go down to the river. It's always peaceful there."

They crossed the dry mud farmyard where brown hens pecked among scatterings of straw. A white rooster with scarlet comb and wattles was perched on a fence-post lording it over his harem by crowing loudly. At the far side was a row of thatched, single-storey outbuildings with green-painted doors. A faint smell of cow clap came from what must be a byre, and beyond were small fields, either pastureland lying fallow awaiting the spring ploughing or brown with stubble where a crop had been harvested last autumn.

"We're a mixed farm: poultry, barley, pasture for a

couple of horses, and a small dairy herd. Twenty Friesians." She stopped and bent to pick up a heavy work glove. She tutted. "Dad's always dropping them. Careless man. Just be a tick."

Barry waited until she'd trotted over to one of the sheds and come back empty-handed.

"I was telling you about our farm. It's a family business, passed on from father to eldest son. My brother, Michael, and I pitched in from when we were each about six. That's when Mum taught me to gather up the eggs every day. I've been hooking up cows to milking machines since I was ten."

They passed a corrugated iron shed with open double doors. Barry could see a red Massey-Ferguson tractor inside. Assorted farm implements, none of which he recognised, hung from the walls. The upper half-door of a smaller building was open, the lower shut. A frantic barking began from within.

Sue shook her head. "Poor Max." Barry knew the Nolans had been charged with the unenviable task of looking after Sue's unruly springer spaniel while she was away. "I love him dearly, but I simply never got the hang of training him. You'd think I'd be better at it, seeing as I'm a teacher." Barry watched as Sue shook her head and the ghost of a sweet smile brushed her lips. He loved that she could smile at herself, even today. "You stay, Max. We'll go for a walk soon," she said. "He'll be fine. Fred Alexander, the neighbour who's looking after the animals, fed him when he milked the cows. And Max and I had a lovely nap together this morning."

Sue and Max had napped on her old single bed while Barry had bunked out on the Nolans' sofa. As Barry had dropped off to sleep he had envied Max.

"Right now I just want to be with you," she said.

"Fine by me," Barry said.

"Here." She opened a gate in a hedge at the bottom of the yard, let Barry through, followed, and closed the gate. They walked round the edge of a field full of stubble from where last season's corn had been reaped. Barry could imagine it three months from now with the long dark furrows and the scent of freshly turned earth filling the air.

"Thank you, Barry, for being here. You are a great comfort, you know."

Barry shrugged. "I love you, and sometimes being a doctor comes in handy for those closest to you. I believe there's a line in the wedding ceremony, to love and to cherish in sickness and in health. You're heartsick right now." He knew he didn't have to explain any further.

She stopped and kissed him before they walked on.

Overhead the sky was studded with slowly drifting fluffy clouds that cast shadows over the low hills. A small flock of cawing rooks flapped past, heading toward a row of pollarded willows that Barry guessed marked a riverbank. The Nolans' farm lay to the south of the Braid River. A blackbird in the hedge gave its low-pitched fluted warble, which changed to an alarm call of *pook-pook-pook* as the humans approached.

"And speaking of weddings, I know our plan had been for you to finish your term in France on the twenty-third of March when the schools break up the day before Good Friday, then wait until Easter's over and get married on the twenty-eighth—"

"So we could have a ten-day honeymoon on Easter break before I'm back to work at MacNeill Elementary. But Dad has to get better first. I know."

"Most patients are back at light work within three months," Barry said, "and that takes us into May. How about we postpone the ceremony until your summer holidays in July?" He stepped over a clod the plough's blade had dumped last year onto the pathway skirting the field. He stopped, faced her, and put a hand on each of her shoulders. "I don't really need a wedding. As far as I'm concerned, after our night together in Marseille I feel completely married anyway and it will be 'til death do us part,' ceremony or no ceremony."

She smiled. "You're right, darling. We are man and wife, now and forever." Her eyes shone. "I don't need a minister to make it true, but it would kill Mum and Dad if we 'lived in sin' without the church's blessing." She kissed him. "When term starts again in Ballybucklebo and I'm back in my flat in Holywood, you can come and . . ." She grinned at him, cleared her throat and said, "visit me." The implied promise was clear.

Barry took her in his arms. "I know," he said, "and it will be wonderful." Inside him his heart sang. He took her hand and they walked on, finally coming to the end of the field. "Over here," Sue said, indicating a stile in a low dry stone wall.

Barry clambered over and gave Sue a hand. He turned and saw a horse at the far end of the field.

"Look, there's Róisín. Rosebud. She's what's called an Irish Sport Horse. She's tough but as gentle as a kitten." Sue laughed and beckoned to the horse, who came cantering toward them, her mahogany coat glossy, her tail, mane, and ear edges shiny black.

The horse slowed her pace as she drew abreast, lowered her head, and nuzzled Sue. Barry looked into great liquid brown eyes and smelled the tangy, earthy scent of horse. Sue took something from her pocket and, keeping her hand flat, offered it to the horse, which rolled back her big lips and took the sugar lumps. Sue stroked the animal's cheek. "Dad taught me to ride on Jessie's mum, Kyran. She was black and her name means 'small dark one,'" she said. She lowered her voice. "It didn't matter how busy the farm was, even at harvest time, Dad always found time to give me a jumping lesson. I loved it. Still do. You know I'm a member of the North Down Pony Club. Michael tried it, but didn't like it, and Dad never forced him. He's a very understanding man, my father."

Barry heard a daughter's love in those words. "You'll be riding with him again soon enough," he said, and was pleased by her comforted smile. He wondered what kind of a father Barry Laverty might make when or if they started a family.

"Go on," Sue said, slapping the animal's rump, "off you trot, Róisín."

The bay galloped to the far side of the field, kicked up her heels, and whinnied.

"Full of the joys of spring, that one," Sue said with a little grin. "I remember her as a foal, all spindly legs and a big head. Young animals are darlings."

"They are." He hesitated, then, "Sue," he said, "perhaps this isn't the right time to discuss this, but, you know, we've never actually talked about whether we're going to have a family or not."

She frowned. "Och, Barry. You must know I love kids. That's why I'm a teacher. And you did that training in obstetrics. I just assumed we would. I thought it was one of the reasons people got married." She touched his arm and looked into his eyes. "Barry?"

"I know you love kids and, well, I do too, but I sometimes wonder about this world we're in right now. The Cold War getting hot. We came so close to World War Three during the Cuban Missile Crisis five years ago.

Maybe it would be, I don't know, selfish? Irresponsible? To start a family." He realised it was the first time he'd ever acknowledged his niggling uncertainty.

Sue opened the gate they'd come to and let Barry through, joined him, and closed the gate.

They were now in a meadow bordering the Braid. Lime-green pussy-catkins hung from every branch of the row of willows. The river was in spate with brown rolling waves tumbling dead tree branches over the shallows and making a rushing noise.

"I had a wonderful childhood, you know, Barry. Dad didn't go to war. He was here, growing food for people. But Mum's told me how her friends were saying the same thing about having children in 1939 because there was going to be a war. I'm so glad my folks and yours paid no attention."

"Me too," he said. Life now without Sue Nolan would be unthinkable. "I know you'll make a marvellous mother."

"Even with poor Max as an example?" Sue laughed and pulled a catkin from a willow tree, rolling it between her fingers.

He laughed. "Even with Max." The laugh died. "But I'm not sure what kind of father I'll be. I was taught in medical school that we learn those skills very early in life from our own parents. I was five before I really met my dad. Mum kept telling me he'd got three weeks' home leave when I was nearly three, but . . ." He shrugged. "And I didn't have any brothers or sisters."

"You, Barry Laverty, are going to be an amazing father. You're kind and funny and wise." Sue wrapped her arms around him and kissed his neck. "Our love will see us through. I truly believe that, Barry. Now, you were telling me about that wonderful bungalow that might suit us. I'd like to see it before I go back to France—I've still got six weeks to do over there. Do you think one of the bedrooms would make a good nursery?"

It was abundantly clear how Sue felt.

They'd come to the riverbank. He cast a fisherman's eye on the water, not sure what to say next. Come May, with the river in its summer calm, there'd be big brown trout in a deep pool under those willows, waiting for insects to fall off the leaves. Would he someday come down to this river with a small child to watch a mayfly hatch on a soft evening, silent but for the gentle splash of rising fish sending concentric circles outward. He could feel the weight of the child in his arms, perhaps wriggling to be on the ground and saying, "Let me down, Daddy. I want to look at the fish."

"This is a beautiful place, Sue," he said.

"I know. I can see our children here, Barry. You're standing on that bank with a fishing rod in your hand casting, and a little blond boy with a cowlick is right beside you. I'm a country girl, and I always will be," she kissed him, "and that's why I'll be happy to be a country doctor's wife and mother to his children."

Barry swallowed, steeled himself, looked at the riverbank—and took a leap of faith. "And I will be happy to be your husband and father to our children and, yes, there would be room for a nursery in the bungalow."

"Oh, Barry, I'm so glad. Thank you," she said, and kissed him. "I think we should have at least two kids."

"I agree, but maybe not right away?"

"Heavens no. I'd have to give up my job, and if we do buy a house we'll need my income for a while too."

Barry nodded and felt a sense of relief. There was no hurry. They'd let the river of life flow on. Suddenly, having children with Sue felt like the most natural thing to do in the whole wide world.

"Thank you for coming for a walk and talking about . . . important things, Barry. It's helped me to stop worrying about Dad, if only for a little while. And I'm glad you had the courage to say what you said about starting a family."

"Good, and I'm glad," he said.

"But I think we should head back home now. Mum may be back and she might like a little company."

"I'm sure she will, Sue, and now we've had this chat we can set her mind at rest about the wedding."

Mrs. Nolan sat at the kitchen table drinking a cup of tea.

"You're home, Mum. How's Dad?" Sue asked.

"He's awake, feeling better, and he was able to have a cup of tea. He remembers that you two were there today and sends his love. Sister says he's still not out of the woods, but he's on his way, they'll let us know if his condition changes, but she'd appreciate it if we kept the visits to regular hours now. His rest is an important part of his recovery. Officially he's 'comfortable and improving.'"

Barry recognised the standard hospital euphemism taken from a list that included "critical," "seriously ill," "condition guarded," "improving," and "much better." The staff never divulged details. He was glad he could use his position, if necessary, to get more accurate information. "I think by 'comfortable and improving' they mean he's over the worst part."

Sue sent him a grateful smile.

"Thank you, Barry. That is a comfort," Mrs. Nolan said, "and they told me he'll probably be home by mid-March."

"I'll have to go back to France to finish my exchange, Mum, as soon as Dad's a bit better, but I'll be back the twenty-third or twenty-fourth of next month to help out here."

"Good," Mrs. Nolan said. She frowned. "And what about your wedding?"

"Barry and I have decided to postpone it until Dad's back on his feet. We'll pick a day in July."

"I think that's very wise and generous of you both. Thank you. And Dad will be pleased. Now sit down, you two. Tea?"

"Not for me, thanks," Barry said as he sat at the table, but Sue went to the dresser, brought a cup, and poured for herself before sitting.

"We really don't mind waiting to get married, Mum, until Dad's really at himself again. I want him to give me away."

"He would have been heartbroken to miss that," Mrs. Nolan said.

"And," said Sue, "I'll be home from France for good soon. I can help out here in the Easter holidays, get down from Holywood for a few weekends during the summer term . . ."—her look told Barry that they would be the ones when he was on call—"and I'll be able to help with the wedding preparations when I'm on my summer holidays."

Mrs. Nolan smiled. "The pair of you have thought this through pretty well. Thank you, byes." She sipped her tea. "I'll call Reverend Wallace this evening. Explain about the change in plans. I'm sure he'll understand. Thank goodness the invitations havnae gone out yet, hey." She drank more tea and said, "It does make a lot of sense. Coping with your dad's illness will be quite enough for us for a while."

"But we'll all be fine, Mum. You'll see," Sue said. "And we'll keep the farm going too." She glanced at her watch. "Now, Barry, what size shoe do you take?"

Barry frowned. What on earth had that to do with the price of corn? "Eight," he said.

"That's lucky. My brother takes eight and a half. They'll fit you. It'll soon be time to get the cows for their afternoon milking," she said, "and I don't think you'd want to go tramping through any sheugh in your good shoes."

As Barry put on the loaned Wellies, he again had the same feeling he'd had at the river with Sue. That what he was doing was the most natural thing in the world.

30

I Ofen Looked Up at the Sky an' Assed Meself the Question

K itty looked east round the long crescent of golden sand lapped by the waters of Belfast Lough. Helen's Bay Beach was deserted, even on this sunny Saturday, and they'd had the place to themselves while Arthur had a good long swim in the chill waters. Fingal took Kitty's hand and they began to stroll back to the Rover.

"Hall Campbell brought us past here when we went mackerel fishing last year. Remember I showed you the old fort at Grey's Point with its six-inch guns? The battery's just behind where we're standing." He pointed in the opposite direction. "The first little peninsula that way is Wilson's Point and away farther round is Ballymacormick. Bangor and Ballyholme lie between those two. I should have named them when we were walking toward them."

"Fingal, sometimes people don't always feel like blethering. I understand."

They hadn't spoken much as they'd strolled, hand in hand, along the quiet stretch of damp sand, Arthur running ahead and splashing into the lough, idly chasing the dunlin and ringed plovers that danced along the shoreline.

Now almost to the car, she turned to him. "Who was Helen?"

"Helen?"

"You're a million miles away, aren't you, love. Helen. Of Helen's Bay." She was studying him intently. She probably suspected he was worried about not hearing from the marquis about the lease, and although he was grateful for her concern, it irritated him that he was letting it show.

"The wife of one of the marquis's progenitors. He wanted a village built here as a seaside resort back in the mid-1800s when sea bathing was becoming popular and the railway opened between Belfast and Bangor. Her son built a tower on the estate in her honour too. There's a replica of it at Thiepval in France as a memorial to the Ulstermen who fell at the Somme in 1916."

"And speaking of the marquis," said Kitty gently, "you're worried, aren't you, that we haven't heard from him since the council meeting?"

"I am. Bloody marquis," O'Reilly mumbled. "I know we're close friends, but John MacNeill is not in my good books at the moment. It's three weeks since the lorry went through the dining room wall, five days since council made a decision in principle to expropriate our home. With a stay of execution while Mister Robinson and the marquis look for the original lease, I know, but that month will go by quickly."

He held open the Rover's door for her. "Hop in."

"And you, you great lummox," O'Reilly said as he grabbed a towel from the backseat and began towelling the big dog dry. "You should know better than to be chasing those shore birds. This is a protected area. What would your uncle Lars think?"

Arthur's eyebrows peaked as if to say, "Ah, come on, boss, it was only a bit of *craic*."

O'Reilly knew he sounded tetchy, he'd been growly all morning, but he was worried and had been getting progressively more so the last few days. He held the back door open and a sandy Arthur Guinness climbed in. O'Reilly shut the door.

He put the car in reverse and, staring over his shoulder, guided it along to where an open gate allowed him to back into a field. O'Reilly drove out through the gate and turned left, heading for the main road. "Damn, damn, damn," he muttered under his breath, barely recognising he'd spoken. He turned right onto the main road where the traffic was much lighter than on a working day. "I've been cross as two sticks all morning. I'm sorry, Kitty." He changed down and pulled out to pass a lorry, then tucked back into his own side of the road.

"And you didn't sleep well last night. I heard you get up twice." She patted his arm. "It's not like the marquis to be inconsiderate. He knows how much this means to you—to us. Look out, Fingal. A cyclis—"

"I missed him," O'Reilly said. "I always do." In the rearview mirror he saw a man in a thick brown wool sweater and duncher wobble then straighten up. "No harm done. Keeps them on their toes." He sighed. "I spoke to the reverend yesterday. He's not had any luck so far, but he's going back up to Church House on Fisherwick Place in Belfast next week to hunt about some more."

"He's doing his best for us," Kitty said. "Gives us something to hope for."

O'Reilly liked the way she said "us." "At least I know what's going on with the minister's enquiries, but John

MacNeill hasn't phoned, and he promised he would, no matter what the news, good or bad."

"And the uncertainty's killing you?"

"It is. And I of all people should bloody well know better. It's the same for every patient, every patient's loved ones. The not knowing before a diagnosis is made and a plan of treatment outlined drives most people up the walls." He glanced to his left, saw they were passing the ornate wrought-iron gates of Ballybucklebo House, and instinctively slowed down. "I've seen it happen for thirty-five years and now I'm letting the same get to me."

"My guess is that there's no news," Kitty said, "and John knows how important this is and doesn't want to disappoint you. He's just like my father. Hates disappointing people. Why do you think the marquis sits on so many committees?" She laughed. "He's probably got Thompson and Myrna and old Mister O'Hally digging through dusty old boxes right now and only wants to give you good news."

O'Reilly sighed. "You're probably right. What should I do? Just bide? Do a Mister Micawber and hope something turns up?"

"Welllll . . . You could."

"Mmmmh." His grunt was not one of acquiescence. "Why not take the bull by the horns?" he said. "I've been picking up the phone for the past couple of days, then putting it down. I don't want him to think—" O'Reilly shook his head.

"You don't want him to think you can't cope with not knowing and you don't want to offend him by making a move that he promised to make and hasn't."

"That's right." He signalled for the next left turn and then with a squealing of tyres made a tight U-turn on the deserted side road. "No time like the present."

Kitty clutched the edge of the seat and said nothing.

Returning to the main road, he floored the accelerator, barely paused before making a right turn across the Belfast-bound traffic, and in moments was heading up the long curved gravel drive to Ballybucklebo House, past the lopsided topiary. He braked outside the great front door.

"Well, you seem to have made a decision."

"I have. I see no reason not to drop by. John MacNeill is still one of my patients, and he has hypertension. Come on in with me. I need some moral support."

They mounted the short flight of broad steps. "And if you keep driving like that he won't be the only one with high blood pressure," Kitty said. But she was smiling. "As Cissie Sloan would have said, 'I near took the rickets.' You must learn to slow down."

"Sorry," O'Reilly said, trying to sound contrite as he shoved on the brass bell-push, "but I was in a hurry."

"Dear old bear," Kitty shook her head, "whenever are you not?"

The front door opened. Thompson, his lordship's valet/butler, stood, firmly at attention, a silver tray tucked under his left arm.

O'Reilly half expected the old chief petty officer to salute. The man always used O'Reilly's naval rank.

"Surgeon Commander and Mrs. O'Reilly. How may I be of service? And please come in."

O'Reilly, holding his ground, said, "Thank you, Thompson, but no. Is his lordship at home?"

"I regret that no, sir, the marquis and Lady Myrna are out at the moment."

"Oh. I see." O'Reilly now regretted his impetuousness. Face-to-face with John MacNeill he was sure he could have passed this off as a routine drop-in. The pressure didn't really need remeasuring for another two months, but it would have been easy enough to laugh, remark that he must have got the dates wrong, take the readings, and work the question about the lease into the conversation. Now he felt awkward and off-balance.

"Will there be a message or would the surgeon commander prefer to leave his visiting card?" The silver tray was proffered.

O'Reilly shook his head. "Left my cards at home, Thompson. Off duty today. Actually I'd prefer it if his lordship didn't know I'd called." Standing on the man's doorstep, he suddenly appreciated that not only did he not want the marquis to know how agitated he was, he didn't want John MacNeill feeling under pressure to find that damn lease.

Thompson frowned. Swallowed. Then took a deep breath, obviously steeling himself to face the unexpected situation. O'Reilly took in the man's usually neat appearance and noticed a small smudge of dirt on his forehead and the faintest tracery of a cobweb on the shoulder of his black coat. "It is a somewhat unusual request, sir. I am expected to notify his lordship of all callers. All callers."

Bloody hell. He was putting this man on the spot, but it couldn't be helped. "Thompson, you and I are both old *Warspites*." That was how men who'd served on the same naval vessel referred to each other, regardless of rank. "As one to another, I'd rather he didn't find out I'd been here."

"May I be so bold, sir, as to inquire whether this has to do with the lease situation?" Thompson's face was expressionless.

"It has, Thompson, and I know what I'm going to ask might contravene the butlers' code"—If there was such a thing. O'Reilly had no idea—"but Mrs. O'Reilly and I are eager to speak to the marquis. I don't suppose . . ."

A small smile began on the butler's lips. "They have to attend a meeting at the Ulster Folk Museum in Cultra. They just left a few minutes ago, sir. The meeting's not until three, but I believe there was some horse demonstration they wished to observe."

"Thank you, Thompson. I think perhaps Mrs. O'Reilly and I will just nip round to the museum. See if we can bump into the marquis there, accidentally, on purpose, as it were. And if you don't mind—"

"Mum is the word, sir." Thompson's smile had reached his eyes. "As one old *Warspite* to another."

"Thank you," O'Reilly said. "Thank you very much."

Thompson nodded. "And if that will be all, sir, I'll return to my duties. Good day, sir, madam." The butler retreated inside, closing the heavy wooden door behind him.

It wasn't until they had reached the main road and were heading for Cultra that Kitty said, "I seem to remember Bob Beresford calling you 'The Wily O'Reilly.' Appealing to the man's loyalty to an officer? That was a pretty impressive display of thinking on your feet."

"Perhaps not the best use of rank, but it had to be done. I just hope to God we see John and Myrna," O'Reilly said. "Old Number One's been my home since before the war. More than twenty years."

"And mine since we got back from our honeymoon. I know that's only seventeen months, three weeks, and four days . . ."

She'd been keeping count too? Dear Kitty.

". . . but I love the old place. I don't want to leave it, not one bit, and nor does Kinky, but I suppose if we must . . ." She touched his shoulder.

"I've been thinking about the plan B we talked about last Saturday and how I feel about Number One. It was the place I yearned for as a safe haven all through the war." A snatch from a tune called "The Enniskillen Dragoons" flitted through his mind.

when these cruel wars are over, I'll be home in full bloom . . .

And the wars had been cruel. Planes ablaze tumbling from the skies, ships blowing up, victims of shells, torpedoes, bombs. Huge warships sinking into the sea. Men on both sides maimed, burned, dying. O'Reilly had not returned to civvy street in full bloom. He'd returned a changed man. A scarred man, a grieving man, his new bride dead and five years buried. But at least Ballybucklebo had provided him with a calm refuge and Number One and dear old Kinky their safe place.

He indicated for a left and turned into the drive to the Ulster Folk Museum, pulled into the car park, and stopped the Rover. "It's not quite as cut and dried as I first thought."

"It rarely is. You having mixed feelings?"

He nodded. "There are memories, of Ballybucklebo and Number One, that involve Deirdre and old Doctor Flanagan, and a young Kinky Kincaid. Bittersweet memories. Then, my love, you came along and filled the place and filled me and made me happy, but sometimes I wonder, does the thought of those memories of mine not bother you?"

"I do not begrudge you Deirdre, Fingal O'Reilly. You loved her dearly and were shattered by her loss." Kitty's voice was matter-of-fact. "There's always been a place in your heart for her. I've always known that, but I'm not jealous."

"Thank you."

Nodding her head slowly, she continued, "Those memories might get to me, if I let them, but I don't. I had my own past. Remember?"

"I do," he said, "and it bothered me for a while, but not anymore." He stared through the windscreen, then said, "For the last couple of days I've been wondering. We made a new start in July '65 when we married, and it's been wonderful. Would it be such an awful thing if we did lose Number One and had to make a complete break with my past?"

Kitty took her time answering. "I don't know, Fingal. I honestly don't know. Apart from the effect on us, I keep thinking of Kinky. She'd have no place in a modern group practice in its own building. And if we were to build another house I'd prefer something smaller. She might not need to come every day, and the place has been her home a lot longer than yours. Still, she has her own home now. Perhaps she might think it wouldn't be such a bad thing to break with the past herself. It was a sanctuary for her, as well, after her husband died."

"Aye, it was," he said. "It's what I said, the whole bloody thing's not cut and dried, and anyway it's probable we'll not have the choice." He shook his head and made a growling noise. "Even so, I want to know what, if anything, John MacNeill knows about our future, and we're not going to do that sitting in a car park." He opened the door. "Let's look for him and see the museum at the same time. I'm told it's very interesting, but do you know? I've never been here once in the three years since it opened."

31

God Made the Country
and Man Made the Town

Ten minutes later, he and Kitty, in company with other sightseers, were strolling along a tarmac path toward the early-twentieth-century town of "Ballycultra," reconstructed from buildings brought from all over Ulster. "Each one disassembled brick by brick, numbered, and then rebuilt on this site," said O'Reilly, reading from the guidebook.

Kitty stopped. "Listen."

From overhead came a glittering song, rising, soaring, as pure and bright as diamonds.

"What an exquisite sound."

"Skylark," O'Reilly said. "The museum's farm deliberately plants crops to provide habitat for them." He smiled. "I only know because it's one of Lars's pet projects. The species has become threatened by modern agricultural methods."

O'Reilly led the way along a cobbled street of grey terrace houses. "There's a horseshoeing demonstration in a few minutes. I reckon that's what Thompson was referring to. We've time to take a gander at the village before we head there."

The first shop was a grocery. Wares in tins and bottles were displayed in the window: Coleman's Mustard, Tate and Lyle Golden Syrup, Lipton's tea, Jacob's Cream Crackers. The slogan *H. Rawlinson, Purveyor of Fine Groceries and Sundries since 1878* had been painted in a semicircle of gold letters high on the glass and in smaller letters below *By appointment, supplier of China teas to the Twenty-Sixth Marquis of Ballybucklebo.*

"Fingal? Do be tactful about how you ask the twenty-seventh about the lease."

"Of course I will. I am the soul of tact, my dear."

Kitty made a comic face and O'Reilly laughed. She knew him so well. But he promised himself he would not let his temper get away with him. They stopped in front of the open door. A smiling mannequin with an up-curved waxed moustache and brilliantined dark hair with a centre parting stood wearing a full-length brown apron. Glass-topped counters displayed rows of bottles, each containing boiled hard sweeties: clove rock, brandy balls, bull's-eyes, gob-stoppers. A coal fire burned in a small black grate.

"I remember shops not much different from this when I was growing up in Holywood in the 1910s," O'Reilly said.

"And of course you would remember that era so much better than I." Her chuckle was throaty. "Since you're older than me."

O'Reilly laughed. "By two whole years, madam."

They walked past other open doors of what the guide-book said was a street of typical city terrace houses. He noted a spinning wheel in one, an HMV gramophone with a horn and the famous trademark of Nipper the dog in another. It stood on a table next to a treadle-operated Singer sewing machine. Ma had had one for her maid, Bridgit, in the big house on Lansdowne Road, Dublin, before the war.

At the end of the street was a small school. A teacher and her class, each pupil clutching a slate and chalk, all sat behind lift-top desks, each with its own ceramic ink-well inset at the right front corner. It must be the kind of outing the schools arranged as educational treats for the kiddies. They were being addressed by a bespectacled school ma'am, her hair in a severe bun, a white blouse with mutton-chop puffed sleeves and a cameo over her left breast, flared grey skirt over black high-button boots. All very Edwardian. Behind her, pinned to a wall, was a map of the world with the British Empire coloured red.

"Come on, Kitty," he said, "time to be heading on. Says here," he consulted the guidebook map, "the farm and smithy are at the end of this street." He led her over the cobbles to a five-bar gate that opened onto a rutted lane with grass growing up the centre. To the left a great leafless oak towered over a dry stone wall. A single massive brown and white Hereford bull with a ring through his nose stood thrashing his tail and chewing his cud in the surprisingly warm winter sunshine. O'Reilly wished he could feel as contented as that animal, but the anticipation of getting news from the marquis was creating a queasiness in the pit of his stomach. The almond scent of whin flowers filled the air, coming from several clumps in the field, and he breathed in the fragrance, hoping it would calm him.

"Good Lord." Kitty pointed to the ditch, where a small rotund creature with a pointed snout, beady eyes, and its body covered in spines was trundling along. "Who is that odd little fellow?"

"Hedgehog," said O'Reilly, remembering Marge

Wilcoxson at Twiddy's Cottage in Fareham in 1940 with her trio of orphans, Riddle, Me, and Ree. She'd been hand-rearing the spiny little creatures, and her huge Old English sheepdog Admiral Benbow had paid for his curiosity more than once. "They usually hibernate from November to March, but they do change nesting sites during that time. Maybe the sun woke this one up."

"I've seen all kinds of interesting things with you—badgers, woodcock, hedgehogs. Thank you, Fingal."

He paused to watch the little animal sidle under the hedge before saying, "I love the country and I love showing it to my city girl." He stole a quick glance up and down the lane. No one in sight. He turned, and kissed her. "And I love you, Mrs. O'Reilly. Now," he said, "let's go and see how a working horse is shod and beard the marquis in the process." He laughed. "I'll always remember what a Dublin patient who hated his job said. 'Jasus, Doc, the only animal that works is the draught horse . . . and you know what part of its anatomy it turns to its labours? Its feckin' arse.'"

And, both laughing, Doctor and Mrs. O'Reilly walked into the farmyard to join the small crowd, which to O'Reilly's delighted relief counted among its numbers John MacNeill and his sister, Myrna.

They were in a high-ceilinged barn at the front of a small crowd of sightseers, many of whom were children. Sun streamed in through the open double front doors and between cracks in the plank walls. O'Reilly could see a half-full hayloft above his head and a ladder leading up. Of eight stalls three were occupied, and tack and nose bags hung from the walls. There was a smell of hay and horses.

"There they are, Fingal. Now please, please be discreet. The marquis is a busy man. I'm sure you can find a way to get the conversation around to the lease without—"

"Halloooo, O'Reillys." Myrna's cultured contralto voice cut like a huntsman's horn through the buzz of conversation. She gestured to them to join her and John at the front.

They snaked their way through the crowd. "Fingal, Kitty, what a delightful surprise." O'Reilly knew the marquis was skilled at sounding delighted even when he was not, but today he did not sound convincing. In fact, he looked distinctly uncomfortable as he stared down at his boots.

"Everyone's told us what a great spot this is, sir, and we've never been," O'Reilly said. Some of the crowd were a bit too close for O'Reilly to be informal in his address. "It's a fine day so we thought we'd take a shufti."

"I hope you were impressed with Ballycultra," the marquis said.

"Very," Kitty said.

A heavy anvil sat front and centre beside a small forge where charcoal glowed cherry red and bellows waited to bring it to greater heat. The tools of the farrier's trade—hammers, pincers, nippers, tongs, hoof knives, and nails—lay in ranks on a workbench. Assorted sizes of shoes filled galvanised buckets under the bench. A bucket of water stood by the anvil.

"John was on the steering committee when the folk museum was being organised," said Myrna.

The marquis nodded. "The folks who run the museum are always on the lookout for new properties. We've come to discuss donating two of our eighteenth-century labourer's cottages. They're not needed now since we've had to let some staff go, but their upkeep costs money. Myrna and I are meeting with senior museum administrators at three."

"I think that's wonderful," Kitty said, "and I'm sure the cottages will be accepted."

"They will. We've kept them in good repair over the years," Myrna said. "I'm just here to keep John company. I had hoped Lars would be here too, but the wretched man is back in Portaferry this weekend tending to his precious orchids. Sometimes," she said, "a girl could despair when she's put aside for a bunch of exotic flora." She chuckled. "Still, he'll be back tomorrow evening."

O'Reilly glanced at Kitty, who nodded once. She too, must have detected the fondness in Myrna's voice. He truly hoped matters were progressing on the romantic front for his big brother. But as he smiled at the Mac-Neills, inwardly he was seething. Did John simply not want to discuss the matter? O'Reilly inhaled. It looked like he was going to have to come to the point and ask directly. "John—"

"Fingal, I think I know what you're going to say. Look, I've wanted to call every day this week. I know how important the lease is to you, but I'm afraid my files are not quite as, well, quite as organised as I might wish and—"

"What my brother is trying to say, Fingal, is that while he is a very conscientious steward of his land, he would never get a place as an efficiency expert. John is mortified that he has not found that lease, Fingal. He's had Thompson going through every desk drawer, file cabinet, and pigeon hole in the house. And Simon O'Hally's clerk is doing the same at his office."

"I'm so very sorry, Fingal, Kitty," the marquis said. "Lars and Simon have been going through all the documents pertaining to the National Trust transfer as well, but of course we don't own the land Number One is built on anymore so it hasn't turned up in those files. But my father's policy was never throw anything away if it pertained to the estate and there's stuff all over the house."

"It will be my retirement project to create a proper archive one day," said Myrna.

"I kept hoping each day that something would turn up—"

"Look," said Myrna. "There's Norman. He's one of the curators. I think he's going to introduce Paddy."

"My lord, my lady, gentlemen . . ."

Good old class system, O'Reilly thought, and shook his shaggy head. The same class system that had stopped him from owning the land upon which Number One sat. The marquis, Myrna, and perhaps O'Reilly were being recognised—a purist might argue that a physician hardly qualified as a real gentleman unless he were landed. But the formal welcome did not extend to the presence of lesser females or working men.

"I am Norman Bowe, one of the curators here. Welcome to our demonstration of traditional horse-shoeing." He beckoned to a man wearing a duncher, open-necked blue shirt with its sleeves rolled up, and a full-length leather apron that was split from the lower centre almost to the man's crotch and the flaps held in place round his legs by leather straps. "I'd like to introduce Paddy Jackson, our farrier, who will explain about horseshoeing, which is now a dying art. He will then demonstrate on one of our working plough-horse mares. Paddy."

The farrier stepped forward. O'Reilly had twice had to treat the sixty-seven-year-old man for burns, an occupational hazard of his trade. Fingal looked over at Kitty, who raised her eyebrows and took his hand. He swallowed down his disappointment and prepared to enjoy the little show. Paddy removed his duncher, lowered his bald head, and said, "My lord, lady, and how's about ye, Doc?"

"We are all very well, thank you, Paddy," the marquis said, "and we'll be seeing you soon again because Myrna's horse, Ruby, will be needing a new set, but I'll be in touch. Do carry on with your work."

"Right. Thank you, sir," said Paddy. He grinned, reset his duncher, and launched into what must be an oft-repeated routine. "You might ask why does a horse need shoes? Wild horses don't need 'em, but wild horses don't carry riders or pull heavy loads, and doing that and walking on cobblestones and tarmac causes wear and tear on the hooves. So ever since the ancients domesticated the animals, we've been working out ways to protect the hoof."

He bent and from the bench lifted a leather tube above an oval metal plate. "This here is a replica of what we think a Roman hipposandal looked like. 'Hippo' was Latin for horse. Up in Belfast the theatre the Hippodrome is called for the places Romans used to race horses, and 'hippopotamus' is Latin for 'river horse.' Anyroad, the horse wore the hipposandals like boots and them and stirrups was what gave the Roman cavalry the advantage over their enemies."

"That's something I didn't know," O'Reilly whispered to Kitty. "Hipposandals. Hmh."

"It's likely the very first nailed-on horseshoe appeared about 500 B.C.," Paddy said, "and cast bronze ones with six nail holes began to be used in Europe about 1000 A.D. In 1835 an American called Henry Burden made a machine that could turn out sixty steel shoes an hour." He paused, surveyed the crowd, and said, "And here endeth the lesson. No more dry history. I'm off now for til get the horse from her stall and I'll show youse how a shoe is put on."

There was a polite round of applause and a buzz of conversation began.

"He's quite the character," the marquis said. "Paddy was one of the last farrier quartermaster sergeants in the British Cavalry. Inniskilling Dragoon Guards. Served in the first war and in India. Used to do a lot of work for us, but of course we've had to reduce our stable considerably. I'm glad I was able to get him a permanent position here. He loves his work. I do so wish I could help *you*, Fingal."

"Ulster, or at least North Down, is going to miss the MacNeill dynasty," Kitty said quickly.

The marquis sighed. "Perhaps. The title will carry on through my son, Sean, and his heirs and successors," the marquis said, "and after I'm gone Myrna, if she wishes, and Sean, will have permanent use of a comfortable private suite in the big house. Unless of course she decides to move out."

"Look, " said Kitty, "why don't you and Myrna come for dinner on . . ." She glanced at Fingal.

"Tuesday," O'Reilly said. "Barry will be on call."

"Come on Tuesday. As a gesture of friendship, to show you there are no hard feelings about the lease. We know you've done your best—"

"We haven't given up, Kitty. We're still looking, aren't we, John? Well, we're not personally." She laughed.

"Indeed we are. And in fact I unearthed another box from the attic just this morning. Thompson's going through it now. God knows what's in it, although I suspect it's just more dance cards and menus and quite possibly a complete set of copies of *The Illustrated London News* going back to its first edition in 1842. But you never know."

"I'll give you a ring on Monday, shall I, when John's had a look at his diary," Myrna said. "And perhaps Lars will be back by Tuesday and he can join us. Thank you. We'd love to—"

She got no farther. Paddy Jackson had reappeared, leading a huge horse by a halter.

The mare's body was reddish brown, her face, lower legs, and feet white, her fetlocks and shanks covered in long dense hairs called feather.

"She's called Brianna. It means 'Noble,'" Paddy said, "and she's due for shoeing." He pointed to a little girl in the front row. "Would you like to pet her?"

"Yeth pleath." She went and stood beside Paddy. She was dwarfed by the great animal.

"What's your name?"

"Elithabeth, but everybody callth me Lithie, tho they do."

He lifted her up. "Now, Lizzie, with the loveable lisp," he said, "let Brianna sniff your hand."

The child did, and the great equine nostrils flared.

"Now stroke her cheek."

The child did and the horse sighed with pleasure.

Paddy set Lizzie down. "Off you trot. Right," said Paddy, "I took off her old worn shoes yesterday." He walked her in a half circle so her rump faced the audience, turned his back on her, and lifted her left hind leg between his own legs, gripping it with his thighs. He pointed to the oval hoof. From its rear edge, a raised triangle ran for two-thirds of the way to the front edge. He pointed. "That there's called the frog. The front of the bottom's the sole and," he ran his finger round the periphery of the front and sides, "them there's the walls. You can see it's darker than the sole and divided from it by a thin, lighter strip." He replaced the hoof on the ground. "You, sonny," he said, nodding at a schoolboy wearing a Bangor Grammar School royal blue and yellow ringed cap, "Any notion what the light bit's called?"

"The white line, sir. My daddy has a cob for riding, like."

"Dead on. And it's very important because on the walls' side of the white line there's no feeling. None at all, and that's where we put the nails to hold the shoe on."

He nodded to another little girl. "Now, sweetheart, what happens when Mummy takes you to the shoe shop?"

She looked at her feet, fidgeted, turned one foot in.

"She's dead shy, so she is," a woman who must be the girl's mother said.

"That's all right," Paddy said, "I'll tell youse. You pick out the shoe youse like and then try it on for size. That's what I'm going til do." He scanned the audience. "I need a helper."

The shy girl buried her face in her mother's skirt.

Paddy looked at Myrna. "If you'd be so kind, your ladyship? You've helped me often enough up at the big house."

She walked up to Paddy.

"You just hang on til her halter til I've got the first shoe fitted, then me and one of the other lads'll finish off."

While Myrna gentled Brianna, Paddy brought back a selection of steel shoes. "Last night when I used pincers to get the old shoe off, I trimmed the walls with nippers and the sole and frog with a hoof knife. I'm glad we don't need that when we get new shoes, but it doesn't hurt the horse." He laid a series of shoes of increasing size on the hoof then held one up. "That's the boy," he said, "but it's not quite the right shape." He moved to the forge, set the shoe on the coals, and worked the bellows. When he was satisfied, he brought the red-hot shoe to the anvil using long-handled grippers and beat the glowing metal with a heavy hammer. Sparks flew to fade and die.

O'Reilly remembered a snatch of a Longfellow poem: "Children . . . love to see the flaming forge, and hear the bellows roar." Certainly these youngsters were enraptured.

Paddy brought the still-hot shoe and laid it on the hoof. "Got it first time," he said, removing it as O'Reilly smelled singeing keratin.

"Now we cool and quench it." He plunged the steel into the bucket of water with a great hissing and bubbling and gouts of steam rising.

"Three more steps," the farrier said. "Nailing, clinching, and rasping."

In very short order he had laid the shoe on the hoof and driven in seven nails. Their points stuck out through the walls, pointing away. He cut off each sharp point in turn and used a clincher to bend the nail down to lie flush against the hoof. Finally he took a rasp and smoothed off any rough edges where shoe met hoof. He replaced the foot on the ground. "Only three more to go," he said, "and you know, when you've seen one you've seen 'em all." He removed his duncher and made a little bow before straightening and saying, "Thank youse all very much for coming, and that concludes this afternoon's demonstration. I'm sure you'll all fancy a nice cup of tea in the Tea Room."

There was a polite round of applause and the little crowd began to break up.

Myrna turned Brianna over to a youth and rejoined her brother and O'Reilly and Kitty. "Neatly done, Paddy," she said as he bent to his work on the other rear hoof. He touched the brim of his cap and looked up. "Thank you, ma'am. And thanks for your help."

Myrna looked at her watch. "John, you and I must trot. It's nearly three. Fingal, Kitty, we hope to see you on Tuesday. I'll phone." She grabbed her brother's arm and hustled him off as the man tried to stammer out his good-byes and another apology.

"Well, I suppose that's that," said O'Reilly. His shoulders slumped. "They've been looking for days and nothing's turned up. Two hundred years is a long time for a piece of paper to survive."

"That is not that, Fingal. Not by a long chalk. Didn't the marquis himself quote Winston Churchill when we were looking for Jasper last month? 'Never, never, never give up,' he said, and I for one don't plan to."

32

Home and Beauty

Oh my, Barry, the house is in such a lovely spot. It's just the way you described it, on its own little peninsula." Sue was turning through a complete circle, looking around her and smiling. "Very private." He pulled her to him and she looked around her quickly, then kissed him under a midmorning spring sky where the eggshell blue was interrupted only by a high, narrow vapour trail heading west. To America or Canada. "Very private," she repeated.

"Through here." Barry opened a black wooden gate in a low, whitewashed wall. It surrounded the modest, whitewashed bungalow with its grey slate roof and faded brown trim. "We're at the back of the house right now." The garden had a few bedraggled herbs and a shrub or two but was mostly the kind of coarse, hardy grass that grows on sandy soil and, to Barry's secret relief, required little maintenance. Gardening had never been one of his hobbies and Sue had never expressed an interest.

Right now, she seemed more interested in the small bird running across the grass. Its underbody and face were white, its cap, short beak, and bib black. A narrow tail, as long as its body, twitched up and down incessantly, giving the bird its name, wagtail.

He footered with the key before he was able to unlock a back door painted a fading brown. "Hmmm," said Sue. "I'm sure we could paint that door a more cheerful colour. Perhaps yellow?"

"Go on in," he said, and followed Sue into the kitchen. She stopped abruptly in front of him.

"Excuse us. We're terribly sorry," she said. "We didn't mean to intrude."

"Oh, dear. I told you, you should've got up earlier, Lewis." A woman shook her head. "The ould goat insisted on staying up for til watch *Late Night Line Up* and then I couldn't get him out of bed this morning." Her words might sound harsh but her smile was all forgiveness. "Come on youse in, dears. Don't mind us. I'm Gracie Miller and this here's my husband, Lewis, who sometimes thinks he's Rip Van Winkle." The couple, who both appeared to be in their mid-seventies, were finishing a late breakfast, and the kitchen was redolent with the smell of toast and coffee. They were O'Reilly's patients, but Barry had seen the retired postman for follow-up last year after he'd had a cataract removed at the Royal. "Mister Frew told us the house would be empty," said Sue. "We can come back later if you'd like."

But not much later, Barry thought. He had to get her to Aldergrove to catch her flight back to Marseille at one fifteen.

"How's about ye, Doctor Laverty, Miss Nolan." Lewis's wispy, sandy hair was neatly combed and the grey eyes behind spectacles, the left lens of which was made of thick convex glass, did indeed look tired. He rose from the table and gave a courtly bow to Sue. "Gracie thought you were coming at nine thirty, but I thought it was eleven thirty. As usual she was right. We was just finishing our brekky. Don't mind us. You tear away and get a good look at our wee home." There was the hint of a catch in his voice as he sat.

His wife, a small woman with iron-grey hair done up in a bun, and tortoiseshell-framed spectacles, popped out of her chair the same time her husband sat and Barry had to stifle a smile. She began buttoning her woolly blue cardigan and smoothing her grey skirt. "Youse'll be wanting a wee cup of tea in your hands before youse look around," she said.

Barry detected a note of urgency in her voice. He looked at Sue and gave her a quick nod. Another ten minutes was neither here nor there. "That would be lovely, Mrs. Miller," he said.

"You see til them, Lewis, dear," she said. "I'll only be a wee minute." She trotted off with small swift steps to the kitchen door.

Lewis Miller laughed. "My Gracie's dead house proud, so she is. She'd be mortified if youse seen the bedroom with the bed not made."

"Mister Miller, in my line of work, you see plenty of unmade beds, mostly with people in them, but if your wife is more comfortable making it, we'll not stand in her way."

"Thanks, Doc." Lewis Miller busied himself pouring two cups. "Milk and sugar's on the table. Help yourselves and have a pew."

Barry and Sue sat. "Your house is certainly in a lovely spot," she said.

"It is that. And do you know we've been in it since we got wed in 1917." Lewis sighed. "I tried for til join up with the Ulster Division in '15 and do my bit to fight the Boche, but I'd flat feet and weak eyes. They wouldn't have me. Said being a postie was a valuable job, and I suppose it was. Most of my pals volunteered and not too many come back."

"But you tried," Barry said, and made his voice reassuring. "Hardly your fault the army wouldn't take you."

"I suppose so." He smiled and said, "Thanks, Doc. Anyroad, it's our golden anniversary this year."

"Congratulations, Mister Lewis. We wish you many more." Sue was sipping her tea, but glancing round the room. When last he'd been here with Dapper, nearly a month ago, Barry had been content to note that the place had one of the recognised facilities of any modern house, a kitchen, much in the way a man buying a car would take for granted that, yes, it had four wheels, without paying much attention to the make of the tyres. Sue was taking in more details: the plain but bright white cabinets, the tiled worktop that looked in good condition, the multipaned windows looking out onto the back garden.

"You've a lovely view from your kitchen window," Sue said.

"Aye," said Gracie Miller as she rejoined them to stand beside her husband. "Us women spend a lot of time at the kitchen sink. Mind you, my Lewis always helps out washing the dishes. That there window above the sink has a great view out at the heath and that row of elms. They're beautiful in the summer when their leaves open, and with the kitchen facing south they provide shade. And a windbreak in the winter. The garden's not up to much but it's hard to grow things in this sandy soil. We tried. Och," she said. "It seems like no time at all since our wee girl, Joy, was out there in her pram. She's all grown up now. Married and lives in a big house in Portrush. She has a flat for us in it. That's why we're moving. To be nearer her and her husband and our grandchildren, even if they are both teenagers now. It's dead kind of her, and all," she said and took a deep breath, "but I'll miss this wee place, so I will. A powerful lot. And sixty miles is a brave long ways away, so it is." She looked around her kitchen. "All the memories," she said.

She pointed to a shelf bearing a row of four mugs, each decorated with the coat of arms of the British royal family. "They give all the schoolchildren—I was just ten then—that one of Edward VII in 1902 for his crowning, way before Lewis and me got married. Since we got wed, we've seen two kings come and go, and our queen, Elizabeth, have her coronation in 1953. That was on the telly. It was dead on, so it was, all them dukes and earls and thon great big woman, Queen Salote of Tonga. It was coming down in stair rods in London and yet there she was, riding in an open carriage, smiling and waving. She was grand, so she was."

"I remember her," Barry said.

"I hope Doctor Laverty and I see our fiftieth anniversary," Sue said.

"Aye, and with plenty of bairns too," Lewis said. "Not just the one, like us."

Barry frowned and said, "Is it fun being a father, Mister Miller?"

Lewis Miller reached out to take his wife's hand and nodded. "Next to being wed to my Gracie, it was the greatest thing in my life. Our Joy lived up to her name right and proper, so she did. At first we was puzzled, you know, that there was no weans. Then after a couple of years we went til see Doctor Flanagan and he sent us til see Professor Johnstone, him that got a knighthood in

1938, up at the Royal. But no matter what tests the doctors done, they never found out why."

Unexplained infertility, Barry thought. A frustrating condition with no diagnosis and no logical cure. Today, specialists were using injections of gonadotrophic hormones or the new fertility pill clomiphene citrate, but the results were contradictory. It was hard to tell if any pregnancies were a result of the medications or had simply happened spontaneously. He glanced at Sue and saw her frowning.

"And then, glory be," Lewis said, "about two weeks shy of her thirty-ninth birthday didn't Gracie get up the spout, and our wee Joy was born in 1931."

"I'm glad for you both," Sue said. "I love children. I can't imagine not being a mother one day."

"Well," said Lewis, "it's not my place to give a learnèd man advice, but no harm til yiz sir, once you and Miss Nolan's married, don't leave it too late, and if the wee ones do come, make sure you spend time with them. They're only kiddies for a very short time. They grow up quare nor fast."

"We'll take your advice, won't we, Barry?" Sue said.

Barry thought back to the commitment he'd made on the riverbank at the Nolans' farm three days ago. He still wasn't sure he felt comfortable with the idea of being a father, but Sue was waiting for a response. He had no choice but to smile and agree.

"Now," said Lewis Miller, "we'll be running along so you can take a good long gander at the place. Just leave the keys on the hall table. I've got the other set. Come on, old girl." He stood, took his wife's arm, and headed for the front door.

Gracie stopped and with her eyes glistening said, "I'll

miss this wee place sore, so I will. So many memories."
She turned and walked slowly away.

Barry heard the front door close.

"What a lovely couple," Sue said. "I hope they're
making the right decision. Mrs. Miller seems more than
a bit cut up about leaving."

"After fifty years I'm not surprised," Barry said.
"They've spent their entire adult lives in this house. But
it sounds like they've got a good situation waiting for
them in Portrush, close to their daughter and grandchildren. Now, I think we should get a move on so you can
see the rest of the place."

"Aye-aye, sir." Sue quickly inspected the kitchen.
"Good. Lots of storage space. Nice cooktop, four burn-
ers," she said, opening the oven door. "Good oven. I
noticed two Calor Gas liquefied natural gas cylinders
outside as we came in. It's efficient and cheap. I like to
cook with it."

Barry, whose only familiarity with a cooker had been
with Kinky's great range back at Number One, bowed to
Sue's expertise and was delighted that she approved
so far. He had fallen more for the private location and
the view.

She looked under a shelf. "Now that's a very convenient place for a small refrigerator and it's a Frigidaire—
good brand. She peered under the worktop. "Oh-oh."

Barry frowned. That didn't sound good.

Sue straightened and dusted off her hands. "I think
the washing machine must be one of the original Hoover
models from the fifties. Top loader, with hoses to attach
to the hot and cold taps at the sink. No spin dryer, but
with a wringer, and I noticed a clothesline in the back
garden."

Barry relaxed. "I'm sure we could get a more modern one, and maybe a dryer too, if there's room."

Sue frowned. "They'd need to be rewired and plumbed in."

Barry chuckled. "Not only did God create woman, he also gave us Donal Donnelly, and if he can't do the jobs himself, he'll find us a good sparks and a plumber. I don't think we need let that put us off."

She smiled. "It wouldn't have, but it might make a difference to the price we offer. Wiring and plumbing will cost money."

Barry laughed. "Right enough," he said, "Broughshane's only a couple of miles or so from Ballymena."

Sue frowned. "I don't see what that's got to do with getting the price of the house down."

"They do tell," Barry said with a grin, "that a Ballymena man would wrestle a bear for a halfpenny. I suppose it applies to Broughshane girls too."

"You are a buck eejit, Barry Laverty." She kissed him. "That's one of the reasons I love you. Now, come on, show me the rest."

He happily stood back while she approved of the bathroom, although she thought the pink fittings looked more 1957 than '67. After looking at the two smaller bedrooms, she announced, "The one at the back of the house will be ideal for a nursery, and then when number two comes along . . ." Sue hesitated, bit her lower lip. "Barry, how many folks are like the Millers and have trouble getting pregnant?"

It was his turn to pause. The most recent figures suggested the rate was as high as one in ten couples and he didn't want to scare her. "We don't start to worry until they've been trying for at least two years, unless there's something screamingly obvious in the history like the man having had mumps as a teenager, and I haven't, or if the woman has a history of tubal infection . . ."

Sue shook her head.

". . . or irregular or no periods."

She grinned. "You could have set your calendar by mine even before I went on the pill."

"I'm sure we've nothing to worry about," he said. Damn it all, he hoped he'd get the hang of it when the first child was born—in a few years.

"In which case number one will be promoted to the bedroom at the front of the house and number two will get and keep the nursery. Meanwhile, we've room for guests if, for instance, Mum and Dad want to pop up from the farm or your pal Jack Mills wanted to stay. What do you think, Barry?"

He smiled, pleased that his opinion was being sought. Here in rural Ulster, the care and feeding of babies was very much considered to be women's work, and as such it was right that Sue should decide about things like nurseries. But wasn't it typical of her not to take complete charge? To make him feel he had a contribution to make. "Sounds good to me," he said, "and we'll certainly need that washing machine. I've done my bit of handwashing nappies when I was a student in the Royal Maternity nursery." He wrinkled his nose.

"I'm told modern mums use disposable ones now," Sue said.

"Bloody good thing," Barry said, "because I hear modern dads are expected to help with the changes. At least after RMH, I do know how." He led her into the biggest bedroom. The bed was newly made and the curtains had been left closed. He decided, for good reason, not to open them. "How do you like this for us?"

"Certainly big enough," Sue said, "and," she opened

double doors in a built-in wardrobe, "good hanging space, some drawers, but we'll need a dressing table for socks and undies." She moved to the curtains and began looking for the cord to open them. "I'm sure the Millers wouldn't mind if we—"

Barry moved closer to her, took her hands in his, and said in a low voice, "And what kind of bed would you like in this room, soon-to-be Mrs. Laverty?"

"Well, Doctor Laverty, I'd really love a big old-fashioned brass bedstead, and you in it to wake up to."

He held her close, kissed her, and said, "I do love you." He laughed. "But don't you go getting me all hot and bothered. You've a plane to catch and more of the house to see." Barry had, by stopping her from opening the curtains, deliberately done exactly as Dapper had and kept the best until last. "One more room," he said, and led her back along the hall. "Ta-da." He ushered her into the combination living-dining room.

Even practical Sue stopped dead and simply stared through the great picture window with its vista from shore to shore of Belfast Lough and the Antrim Hills interrupted only by one of Kelly's ubiquitous coal boats on its way to discharge its cargo on Bangor's Central Pier. The little vessel was dwarfed by an anchored bulk-carrier.

Her mouth opened, but no words came. She gasped, her green eyes sparkled, and a single tear ran down her cheek. She turned to him. "Barry," and her voice was barely above a whisper, "I've seen the highheejins' mansions on their own promontories overlooking the Copeland Islands down at Donaghadee, but I've never been in a place with such a lovely view. Never in my whole life. I love it." She moved to him, nestled in his arm, and held her mouth up to be kissed.

He needed no encouragement. He kissed her long and soundly before letting her go so she could say, "And I love you, Barry. Thank you for finding such a perfect spot."

"It is, isn't it?" he said. "I knew, as soon as I saw it, I just knew you'd be impressed." He took her hand and led her out through the front door. A perimeter path of white and black oval stones surrounded a trimmed lawn. The little garden was thirty feet from the house to another low, whitewashed wall. Beyond the wall fifty yards of coarse marram grass stretched to where jagged rocks tumbled fifteen feet to the shore. "Listen," he said. Only the harsh cries of gulls and the piping of oystercatchers interrupted the regular *swoosh* of rollers tumbling onto the rocks below. All else was silence. No traffic. No chattering people. No transistor radios. She was standing in front of him and he wrapped his arms around her shoulders and rested his chin on the top of her head. They stood like that, listening, neither moving. Finally, Sue stirred in his arms.

"Do you remember Nina and Fredrick?" she said softly.

"I do. Wasn't he some kind of baron?"

"He was. From Denmark. They sang this beautiful song,

Listen to the ocean, echoes of a million seashells
Forever it's in motion . . .

"And it is. I love the sea, Barry. Can you imagine coming home here after a rotten day? Such peace. Look." She pointed. "What are those birds?"

He saw, bobbing on the waves close to shore, a small flock with black heads, backs, and wings but with white bellies and chests, paddling along and diving from time to time. One surfaced with a tiny silver fish wriggling in its beak.

"Guillemots," Barry said. "I never knew much about birds until I started taking walks with Fingal. People often mistake them for storm petrels, he says. He's quite the authority on waterfowl."

Sue listened to their high-pitched piping call. "I think," she said, "the birds here will make very nice neighbours."

She looked down, then up. "Here I am picturing us living here, and I haven't even asked how much the Millers are asking for it. Can we afford it?"

He nodded. "Five thousand, but Dapper reckons I could get it for four thousand eight hundred." He chuckled. "Less the price of fitting a new washing machine, of course. I need a ten-percent down payment and I've shares in a company called Baker Perkins that my grampa left me when I was nine. They're worth more than that now."

"Oh, Barry. Your grandfather's inheritance. Should you use it?"

"I can't think of a better way," he said.

"So, you'll buy it," she said softly.

"No, *I* won't. We will. I want it to be jointly owned." He was going to say, so that if anything happens to me you'll still own it. But given her dad's recent coronary, he decided to let that hare sit. Sue was satisfied her dad was mending well. Four days had passed since his heart attack, and he no longer required morphine. She had said her cheerios to him during visiting hours yesterday. Even so, she'd been quiet on the hour it had taken to drive here from Broughshane and Barry knew that Selbert Nolan was never out of her thoughts for long.

"That will be my wedding present to you, darling, and we've lots of time. It's not coming on the market until April."

Sue spun, stared at the bungalow, turned, and looked at the view again. "It'll be wonderful, Barry. I just know. Thank you."

"And," he said, "thank Dapper for thinking of us and letting me see it first." He glanced at his watch. "Now, we need to get you to Aldergrove. You head on round the house and I'll leave the keys inside and lock up when I leave."

He rejoined her in the Volkswagen. "I'm so glad you like it, pet. While you're away I'll get on with lining things up so we're ready to buy it as soon as it comes on the market. And I'll keep you posted by letter." Remembering Lewis Miller's look and his wife's tears when she'd said how much she was going to miss the place, he hoped to God the Millers didn't change their minds about selling.

Before he could start the engine, she leaned across, kissed him firmly, and said, "And all the while I'm gone I'll be able to think of us, in July, snug in our nest. Just the three of us."

Barry frowned. "Three? Three?" After all that talk about babies—Oh my God, was Sue—

She laughed. "That's right. Three. You, me—and Max."

"Oh," said Barry. "Yes. Max." He switched on, put the car in gear, and drove off. "I'd quite forgotten about Max."

33

You Are a Bachelor

Lars took a deep breath as he shifted uncomfortably in the hard wooden chair. "Bear with me, Finn. I need your advice on something and I will get to the point, but first remind me how long you and John Mac-Neill have been friends?"

"Since he and I both ended up on the rugby commit-tee. Just after the war. We found we'd some mutual interests—rugby, shooting, both ex-servicemen—and once you get to know him, he's an all-round sound man."

"So, you've known him almost twenty years. Long enough to feel comfortable with the man."

O'Reilly nodded. "You know," he said, "if you can forget, and it's not always easy in public, that he is a peer of the realm, sits in the House of Lords, in private he's one of nature's gentlemen. I am very fond of John MacNeill and I am delighted that you are being of such great help to him and his family. You've never men-tioned before about feeling uncomfortable working with the MacNeills."

"I know. They've been extremely gracious and genu-inely kind. But there is that social gap."

"There is, and it's a huge divide between a country

solicitor or a GP and a marquis and his family. Kitty and I are aware of that. Try never to overstep the mark, but we are having them here for dinner on Tuesday and you're invited. Myrna was going to tell you when John had checked his diary to make sure he'll be free."

"Thank you. I'll enjoy that." Lars, who had been on his way to the big house, had arrived on the Number One Main doorstep saying he needed advice, and O'Reilly had led his brother into the surgery and shut the door.

Now Lars pushed his left fist against his closed lips, pulled it away, and repeated, "That social gap. They seem unaware of it, but I still feel uncomfortable not calling him 'sir' or 'my lord,' and I'll never get used to being waited on by his servants. I know I have a housekeeper, but I hardly think of her as a servant." He got up, paced, turned, and said, "Finn, I don't know what to do. I think . . . I think . . . well, the truth is I think I've fallen in love with Myrna."

"That's teetotally marvellous, or as one of my Dublin patients might have said, gameball and ter-feckin'-rific. I'm absolutely delighted." O'Reilly reached for his pipe and before lighting up said, "Have you told her?"

Lars shook his head. "That's what I need advice about. Look. Myrna moves with the *Ulster Tatler* set, garden parties at Hillsborough Castle, and Buckingham Palace. Rides to hounds with the horsey mob. Royal Ascot. The Boat Race." He looked into his brother's eyes. "She has a doctoral degree in chemistry, is a senior academic at Queen's, mixes with some of the cleverest, best-educated people in Ulster. See what I mean?"

O'Reilly nodded and puffed his pipe. Good listeners did just that, listened. He said nothing.

"Who am I? I've a bachelor of law degree, work as a

small-town solicitor, grow orchids, and work for the RSPB and the National Trust." He collapsed into the chair again. "I know the queen's the RSPB's patron, but I'm never likely to meet her. Most of the members are ordinary folk. My life is ordinary."

"And you're trying to say, sorry to be blunt, that you're not good enough for the daughter of the twenty-sixth marquis, is that it?"

Lars hung his head and said in a low voice, "Sounds pathetic, I know. I mean, it's 1967. She probably sees me as an equal, and yet I can't shake this feeling of, well, of, just not being good enough."

"And you've not told her you love her?"

"Good lord, no. Wouldn't dare. You know how she is. Full of laughs and fun and flirting. But I just don't know if that's how she is with everyone—or just with me."

O'Reilly got up, walked from the desk to his brother, and put an arm around his shoulder. "I've known Myrna almost as long as I've known John, and truly, Lars, she's come alive since you came to Ballybucklebo House."

"Do you really think so? Sometimes I find it hard to trust my own judgement when it comes to women."

"I do understand a little, big brother. You were sore wounded when Jeannie Neely turned down your ring on Christmas Eve years ago back in Dublin." O'Reilly sat down on the wooden chair beside his brother.

"I was, and it hurt for a very long time. I'm pretty well over her now . . . I mean, of course I am. It's just that . . ."

"And I'm pretty well over Deirdre," O'Reilly said, "but a taste still lingers. I know and feel for you, Lars."

"I-I pretty much gave up on women, Finn, after that.

I've got very set in my ways, happy with my own company, a few men friends, you and Kitty, my orchids, my birds, my dogs. It was hard to meet women. They were so often clients, or wives of clients, or daughters of clients. Now, thirty years have gone by. I don't even know how that happened." He shook his head and smiled. "Time. It's healed the wound, but it's also made me, well, complacent really, content with my lot. I don't want to be rejected again, but I think I could face it. There's another thing though." He hesitated.

O'Reilly said, "Go on."

"I couldn't say this in front of Kitty, that's why I wanted to speak to you privately. I don't know much about the really intimate side of love. Jeannie and I never . . . well, you know. A lot of us when we were students went to Monto once or twice . . ."

"Dublin's red-light district. Rumour has it that when he was Prince of Wales, Edward VII lost his virginity there. You were in good company."

"I suppose so, although wasn't he something of a ladies' man? I have to say I didn't much like it."

"I imagine a lot of men feel that way about prostitutes and find it's different when they fall in love with the right woman."

Lars nodded. "I did meet an English widow in Villefranche about ten years ago. We were both a bit lonely, attracted to each other, and she and I . . ." He hung his head.

"Um," said O'Reilly, "it's our very Victorian upbringing showing. I don't think sensible people give a tinker's damn now what two unmarried adults get up to in private."

"Honestly?"

"Honestly."

"Beatrice stopped coming to France six years ago. I did miss her and miss it, the sex, for a while, but . . ." He sighed. "Somehow it didn't seem very important to me. But now Myrna arouses feelings in me, she's been married, knows what to do . . . and I feel . . . I feel . . . damn it, I feel so bloody inadequate." He spat out the last words.

"Hmm," said O'Reilly, aching for his brother. "Listen." For an experienced physician, no body function was embarrassing. "You already know what to do; you say Myrna gets you excited, she's certainly experienced. I reckon the pair of you won't have any difficulties in that respect." He clapped his brother on the shoulder. "I don't really know what to say about the social differences. They are there. I'll admit barriers are breaking down, but old habits die hard. Even if John is my friend, there will always be that gap. But I'll also tell you that we get round it. Myrna might be willing to try. From a few things she's said to Kitty and me, I do believe she has feelings for you. Yes, she's animated and very friendly. But truly, brother, I think you've brought that out in her."

Lars managed a weak smile. "Really?"

"Of course really."

"Gosh. Thanks, Finn," Lars said. "Thanks a lot." He lowered his head again. "So you think I should take a chance?"

There's the rub, O'Reilly thought. He'd been taught in medical school that the first tenet of offering counsel is do not make others' decisions for them. Still, Lars clearly wanted direction, and his sister-in-law, as it happened, wasn't so squeamish when the truth was staring her in the face. "Tell you what," he said, "I fully understand why you'd not want to mention sex in front of Kitty, but why don't we get a woman's perspective on the social side of things. She already suspects, just like me. Would you feel comfortable talking to her about how you feel?"

"Yes, Finn. Yes, I would."

"Right," said O'Reilly, "my belly thinks my throat's cut and she's making scrambled eggs on toast. When Kinky's off we use the kitchen for a dining room. Saves traipsing up and down stairs. Shall we?"

A smiling Lars nodded and followed his brother. "Suddenly I feel extremely hungry."

"Help yourselves to tea," Kitty said. "I've the eggs, butter, and milk beaten and the chopped chives and grated cheese ready to drop in." She poured the scramble into a saucepan, put it on the range top, and with her back to them, began to stir. "So," she said, "have the brothers O'Reilly solved the riddle of the universe?"

"Not quite," said O'Reilly, "but Lars has confided something in me and asked me what to do and I'm not quite sure how to answer. We'd like your help. I'll let Lars explain."

"Fair enough. If I can."

Lars swallowed and said, "Kitty, I'm becoming very fond of Myrna."

Kitty's voice was level when she said, "Fingal and I've suspected that and we think your feelings are returned. And we are very happy for you both." She kept on stirring.

"I really wasn't sure if she cared for me, but you and

Fingal have helped me to hope. The other trouble though is she's noble and I'm a commoner. I haven't dared to speak to her about it."

Kitty turned from the stove, nodded, then said, "I know what you mean. The first time Fingal took me to Ballybucklebo House I confess I was overawed, but both John and Myrna have a happy knack of putting folk at their ease. Tallagh in Dublin, where I was reared, is not Belgravia in London. My dad was a scholarship boy. Pulled himself up by his bootstraps." Kitty went back to her stirring, mixing in the cheese and chives. "Sorry. Can't have it burn," she said, then turned back. "I'm a bit of a socialist at heart. I had a discussion three weeks ago with John MacNeill about how, as my dad says, 'It's ill divid,' meaning there is quite a distance between the rich and the poor. You were there, Lars. Remember how charming John was? Didn't rear up one bit."

"But," said O'Reilly, "you, dear Kitty, do have a habit of speaking your mind and then regretting it later."

"Ooh," said Kitty, "you mean like when I said yes when you asked me to marry you?"

O'Reilly laughed. "Nice one. See, Lars, how a happily married couple can enjoy slagging each other?"

Lars laughed. "I've got to admit she did get you with that one."

"It's all right. I still love her."

Kitty laughed. "I'm not worried about Fingal taking offence, but I was worried about John," she said. "And now with this lease situation. Well, I just want to be sure the friendship is unharmed. So we're going to treat the MacNeills and you to a special dinner on Tuesday." She pushed the bread into the toaster and pulled three hot plates from the oven. "But that doesn't answer your question, does it, boys?"

" 'Fraid not," said O'Reilly, "and we'd like a woman's perspective."

Kitty kept stirring. "I truly don't think the divide will matter that much. It's not as if you were not a professional man, respected in Ulster. The nobility don't always have to marry their literal peers. Princess Margaret married a commoner."

"But if it all pans out, Lars, I don't think Her Majesty will make you an earl like she did Lord Snowdon," O'Reilly said.

"Good thing too," Lars said. "I'd always be feeling sorry for the poor ermine that was used to trim my robes."

The toaster popped and Kitty put the toast on three plates and buttered it. "I'll not tell you what to do, but I'll say this . . ." She started spooning the scrambled eggs onto the toast. "Fingal and I came to love late in life and it's wonderful." She set plates of lunch before each man, went and brought back her own, and sat. "I've no regrets." She leaned over and kissed Fingal. "And I know very well neither does your brother." She picked up her knife and fork and said, "I know I said I'd not tell you what to do, but I do think it's worth the risk, Lars. Now let's tuck in before it gets cold."

"Just what the doctor ordered," O'Reilly said, still savouring the tang of the old Cheddar cheese.

The back door swung open and Kinky, propelled by the stiff northeasterly, was blown into the kitchen, her best hat askew. "Whew, that's a ferocious capful of wind out there. I believe the geese will be flying backward. Good afternoon," she said, "and hello, Mister Lars. I'll not disturb you. I've just popped in after church. I want to collect some pots of strawberry jam I made last summer, so."

"Help yourself," O'Reilly said, "and while you're at it, Kitty and I have a great favour to ask. Will you sit for a minute?"

"I will," she said, and shook her head when Kitty gestured to the teapot.

"We've invited the marquis, his sister, and Lars for dinner on Tuesday. Drinks at six thirty, sit down at seven fifteen. I'm sorry about the short notice, but we'd like you to cater it for us."

Kinky sat back, frowned, and put a fist on one of her not inconsiderable hips. "I don't know at all, not at all, so, but I suppose if it's what you truly want, sir, I will stay and cook." By her tone she'd rather have faced the Spanish Inquisition, but loyalty even in the face of the perceived idiocy of her employer had always been her long suit. She tutted and said, "But a real lord and lady should not be taking their tea with yourself and Kitty and your brother Lars crammed round a couple of collapsible card tables in the upstairs lounge. It won't do, sir. It will not do at all, so."

"I'm inclined to agree, Fingal," Kitty said. "I wasn't thinking when I invited them. I forgot we've no dining room. Should we perhaps not postpone?"

"I'd rather not," O'Reilly said. "I've already been after John about finding that old lease and I know he's feeling responsible. I don't want to rub his nose in the situation by having to cancel because we have no dining room." He turned to Kinky. "Come on, Kinky. I know you are the very divil for the social niceties and we all admire you for that, but it is our turn to have his lordship round, the dining room is still out of commission, and we certainly can't entertain in your kitchen and expect you to cook and serve . . ."

"Saving your presence, sir," she said, squaring her shoulders, "but I do hear that the Culloden has a fine kitchen and private function rooms, so."

"It does," Kitty said, "but it doesn't have Kinky Auchinleck working the ovens and stove. I know Fingal's told you before how very much the marquis looks forward to your cooking."

Kinky blushed and smiled. "Welllll," she said, "maybe a slap-up feast would make up for the utterly throughother seating arrangements."

O'Reilly chuckled. He'd have said "plebian," but the Ulster "throughother" gave a much better sense of careless untidiness.

"Indeed," she said, "I've had an idea. My dining room table seats six. It's not heavy bog oak like the one under wraps here, and a couple of men like Donal Donnelly and Dapper Frew could bring it round on Tuesday afternoon if Donal could get the loan of Mister Bishop's little lorry."

"We couldn't possibly, Kinky," said Kitty, "but it's a very generous offer."

It was clear to O'Reilly that Kinky's mind was made up. He decided that discretion was the better part of valour and kept his mouth shut.

Kinky harrumphed. "It does not be the place of a part-time housekeeper to tell the mistress of the house her business, but, Kitty—"

At least she hadn't reverted to the formal "Mrs. O'Reilly," for which he was thankful.

"I'd die of shame. My doctor and his family crammed round . . . ?" She shook her head. "No. Archie and I can manage on a couple of shmall tables until ours is brought back on Wednesday."

"Thank you, Kinky. I think it's a splendid idea," O'Reilly said.

"It is, so," Kinky said, clearly still not entirely mollified.

"And what would you suggest, Kinky, for the menu?" Kitty asked.

Kitty, you may like to speak your mind, but you can also be the soul of tact, O'Reilly thought.

"Well," Kinky said, "let's see. I'd start with melon balls and ginger. Easy to prepare and have ready. Fish?" She tapped a crooked finger against her lips. "I do think fresh plaice—and Hall Campbell's the fisherman for them—lightly bread-crumbed and grilled. Main course?" She beamed and her dark eyes sparkled. "I've not done one for a while, but my friend, Emer Cullen, God rest her, who'd worked in the Café de Paris in London before she took service with the marquis's father, taught me to make beef Wellington. I'll have Mister Mawhinney get me a well-aged fillet steak, but he'll have to get the pâté de fois sent down from Belfast. I'll see him on my way in tomorrow. I'll make the *duxelles* and puff pastry myself. Roast potatoes, champ, and seasonal vegetables. And for dessert? Sure, that's wee buns. A good sherry trifle. I know for a fact the marquis loves my sherry trifle. It's not fancy, like crêpe suzette or crème brûlée, but when it comes to his puddings, the marquis is a simple man. I'll make that on Monday, and I'd want a few plates of After Eight chocolate mint thins to go with the coffee."

"I'll buy some," O'Reilly said, "and I'll look after the drinks." He realised he was salivating.

"Kinky, how on earth can you manage all this by yourself?" Kitty asked.

O'Reilly knew Kinky could handle the cooking; he was more concerned about all the traipsing up and down stairs.

Kinky's snort was almost derisive. "I cannot, but I'll have a grand helper, so. I'll cook, but Archie will serve. I'll just come up once when the main course is ready. It does please me to examine the slices of beef to make sure I got them just right."

"Kinky, you are a gem beyond price," Kitty said. "I don't know what we'd do without you. Thank you."

Kinky, all smiles, double chins quivering, could only say, "Och, get on with you, Kitty, flattering a poor Cork-woman," but O'Reilly knew she was glowing with the compliment.

34

A Feast of Wine on the Lees, of Fat Things Full of Marrow

O'Reilly, his scuffed brown boots as highly polished as they could be, was dressed in his Sunday-best tweed three-piece suit. Two bottom buttons of the waistcoat were undone. He had decided to wait for their guests in the surgery and steal a few moments of peace after the excitement of the preparations. Last night Kitty, freshly coiffed and manicured, had sat him in a chair in the kitchen and done her best to trim his shaggy mop. And this evening he'd shaved for the second time today. Friends they may be, but there was still that lingering sense of a class gap, and Fingal O'Reilly wanted to make John and Myrna feel they were being treated with respect.

Kinky, God bless her, had run round like a bee on a hot brick vacuuming, polishing, and doing her cookery preparations. At the last minute she had changed into what must be her best dress, a string of pearls and a brand-new spotless white starched apron under her old pinafore. The apron was for her appearance later upstairs.

She'd been busy for the past two days preparing the feast, and in slightly more than forty-five minutes, Archie would be serving the first course on the Auchinlecks' dining table, which Donal and Dapper had lugged upstairs and set up in the lounge two hours ago.

He took a quick look at his watch, then bounced out of his chair and strode across the hall. The dining room door was resolutely closed and he pushed it open and peered inside.

The plywood and canvas patch still plugged the jagged hole in the brickwork where the lorry had come through, tearing up several floorboards in its passage. Dust sheets covered the old bog oak dining room table and the sideboard, both of which had escaped damage. The five undamaged chairs had been taken upstairs. The lorry had smashed chair number six to matchwood. The sheets, the carpeted floor, and the crystal chandelier were covered in a patina of brick dust and the smell reminded O'Reilly of the bombed streets of Portsmouth in 1940 after a Nazi air raid.

Would it stay like that until wrecking balls and diggers came and knocked the whole house over like a pile of children's wooden blocks? He hoped not.

The front doorbell rang and O'Reilly shook off the image of the house disappearing in a cloud of dust, backed out of the room, closed the door, and opened the front door to usher John MacNeill, Myrna, and Lars into the hall.

"Fingal," John said, "grand to see you." The marquis looked behind him, performed a nimble sidestep and, to O'Reilly's dismay, allowed Arthur Guinness, only recently banished to the backyard, to charge past and race upstairs.

"Damn that dog. I told him to stay in his kennel," O'Reilly said.

"Don't be silly, Fingal," Myrna said with a laugh. "It's

cold out there. We've got our animals all over the big house. Please, we're all friends here. Don't concern yourself about Arthur. And that includes you too, your ladyship." She bent and picked up Lady Macbeth, who had just appeared from the kitchen. The little white cat purred and immediately deposited a fine layer of snow-white fur on Myrna's black Persian lamb coat. "You'll not object, Fingal, if I bring her up? She's such a darling and there's something homey about having a cat in the room."

O'Reilly felt himself relax. "No objections at all."

As he took off his camel hair overcoat, John MacNeill nodded at the shut dining room door. "I hope we're not putting you to a great deal of trouble. I know the dining room is still, ahem, nonoperational."

O'Reilly shook his head. "Not at all. I'll have to ask you to excuse us for feeding you upstairs, but I think you'll find Kinky's meal to your liking."

"Anything Kinky has cooked," said Myrna, who was being helped out of her coat by Lars, "I would eat from paper plates on my lap sitting on a chair in your waiting room, Fingal."

Lars, shy, humourless Lars, laughed so hard he might have just heard a Bob Hope one-liner.

O'Reilly wondered if his brother had spoken to Myrna. Judging by the look that passed between them, he had his hopes. "Let's go upstairs." He had promised Kitty earlier not to ask about the original lease, but John said, "And I must apologise, Fingal. Still no luck on your behalf."

"I understand," Fingal said, "and let's call that subject closed for tonight." Disappointed as he was, there was no point raking over cold coals. He collected the three coats and hung them on the coatstand. "After you, Myrna. Kitty's waiting for us."

Kitty stood by the sideboard, a gin and tonic in her hand, his Jameson on the sideboard's top beside a row of decanters and a Waterford cut-glass water jug. O'Reilly again admired the knee-length black sheath dress he'd zipped her into only half an hour ago, sheer dark tights, black patent leather pumps. Sexiest woman in the six counties, he thought as she and the guests exchanged greetings and he took their drinks orders; dry sherry for Myrna, whiskey and water for both Lars and John.

"Come and sit down," Kitty said, inclining her head to a semicircle of chairs arranged around the fireplace. Arthur Guinness had made himself at home in front of the fire. "And please excuse Arthur, but I hadn't the heart to chase him."

"Perfectly all right," John said. "Finn McCool, my red setter, thinks he has squatter's rights on that piece of territory in our house."

There was laughter and as the usual formalities were seen to and Myrna set Lady Macbeth on the carpet, Kitty waved a hand to encompass the room. "Kinky has done a wonderful job."

Wine tables stood between each of five armchairs, their surfaces dotted with small dishes of almonds and potpourri. Later there would be After Eight chocolates for when the company returned to the fire to take their coffee and after-dinner drinks.

Lars sat on the extreme left, with Myrna next to him. O'Reilly sat in the middle, already helping himself to some almonds. He was flanked by Kitty and John. "So she has. I've always liked this room," said Myrna, taking a sip of her sherry and studying the marble chimneypiece, which glowed in the firelight.

"Do tell, John," said Kitty. "Did the folk museum accept your cottages?"

John MacNeill smiled. "They did indeed, and they'll look after the disassembly, transport, and reconstruction on their premises. One less thing to worry about."

Myrna looked at Lars. "And your brilliant brother, Fingal, has tied up everything to do with giving the estate to the National Trust at the appropriate time. The paperwork will be all signed, sealed, and delivered by next Monday."

"It is a very great load off one's shoulders," said John MacNeill, "and it is panning out just as we described the night three weeks ago when you and Kitty came to us for dinner."

"We are delighted," Kitty said, "aren't we, Fingal?"

O'Reilly, who had just popped another almond into his mouth, nodded.

"And," said Myrna, "we're going to celebrate. Tell them please, Lars."

Lars's thin moustache curved up as he smiled, before saying, "Myrna, and Simon O'Hally, and I have been nose to the grindstone since last December. You all know I have a place in Villefranche-sur-Mer?"

"I didn't know that, Lars," John said.

"I went there for a holiday fifteen years ago. I just fell in love with the place. It was small, only about five thousand people lived there then, and I found a seafront apartment not far from the old Chapelle Saint Pierre. Wonderful views of the harbour." He looked down. "Finn can tell you I don't usually act on impulse but . . . I bought the flat and I've been going there every year since."

"And Fingal and I intend to come and visit you someday soon," Kitty said. "Both of us need to slow down a bit."

O'Reilly registered Kitty's comment with pleasure but didn't let his eyes leave Myrna's face. There was such delight, excitement, and fondness there, he felt fully convinced that matters really were moving ahead. He snaffled another almond.

"You'll be most welcome," Lars said, "but not until later in the year, because Myrna and I are going there to take a fortnight's break soon after her Hilary term is over at Queen's in March and before Trinity starts in mid-April."

"That's wonderful," Kitty said.

"It is a bit risqué, we know," Myrna said, "but we're not children, no parents to worry about upsetting, and we're only telling our families. Damn it all, it's not 1867. It's 1967. We want to get to know each other better, don't we, Lars?"

"Very much so," Lars said, smiling.

"Fair play to you both," O'Reilly said, "and you're right, the Puritans are long gone." Something caught his attention. He looked over at John MacNeill. His face was puce and he was emitting strange strangling noises. Was the marquis having apoplexy at the thought of his sister going off with a country solicitor? Then he realised the man was choking. O'Reilly leapt to his feet and slapped John MacNeill firmly between the shoulder blades. He coughed mightily and a soggy spray of petals flew across the room. He dragged in a great gasping breath.

O'Reilly was getting ready to clout John again when the man held up his hand.

"I'm . . . I'm all right," John managed, and hauled in

another lungful. "Sorry about that," he said, rising, heading to the sideboard, and pouring himself a glass of water. "I ate a handful of potpourri thinking it was almonds. Silly me." He effected a weak laugh. "I'm fine. Thanks, Fingal."

"Are you sure you're all right?" O'Reilly asked.

"Right as rain," he said. "Please do excuse me. And excuse my theatrics at your news, Myrna dear. I'll admit it took me somewhat by surprise and I wasn't paying attention to what I was doing. But I couldn't be happier."

"Another good reason to be thankful it's 1967," Myrna said. "Belting a peer was probably treason back in good Queen Bess's day. 'Off with his head.'" She smiled at O'Reilly.

"I doubt it," O'Reilly said. "Us doctors were always given a bit of leeway if we were saving nobilities' lives. The chap who founded my old teaching hospital in Dublin, Sir Patrick Dun, got his knighthood for treating King William III for a shoulder injury the night before the Battle of the Boyne in 1690." He could feel the slight tension in the room dissolving.

There was a discreet cough from the doorway where Archie Auchinleck, hair neatly combed and parted, resplendent in a black bow tie, starched white waistcoat, and dinner suit, white towel neatly draped over his right arm, was setting a tray on the sideboard.

"My lord, lady, Mister O'Reilly, Doctor and Mrs. O'Reilly, if you'd please be seated?" The man nodded to the bay of the bow window where his own dining room table stood under a spotless white linen tablecloth. Five places were set for a four-course dinner, the best silverware and cut glass polished and sparkling.

While Kitty seated the guests, O'Reilly went to the sideboard, where two bottles of Blue Nun Liebfraumilch were in ice buckets. He opened one as Archie served the first course. It's a great pity, he thought, given that the MacNeills' affairs were now in order and the very clearly developing romance between Lars and Myrna, that he didn't have a bottle of champagne. Oh well. Maybe, just maybe, he'd be able to open one if things worked out for them here at Number One.

As they tucked into the melon balls, John remarked, "I suppose this may not be very salubrious dinner conversation, but that was a terrible thing two weeks ago, those three American astronauts dying when their capsule caught fire on the launch pad."

"Dreadful," Kitty said. "Poor men."

"You'd not get me up in one of those tin cans for love nor money," O'Reilly said.

"You'd not fit, dear," Kitty said, "and I'm sure they have maximum weight allowances." She smiled sweetly.

"You minx," O'Reilly said, and joined in the general laughter.

Archie cleared the melon and served the fish course.

"Straight from the sea this morning," Kitty said.

"They really are scrumptious," John said. "Despite the downturn in the MacNeills' fortunes, if Kinky ever wants a new job . . ."

"Don't you dare even suggest it, John MacNeill," O'Reilly said.

The conversation became lively and wide ranging, from the recent change in the leadership of the Liberal Party to a near riot at Heathrow when teenagers swarmed through the airport to see the American pop group The Monkees.

"The lead singer, Davy Jones, was apparently nobbled by some love-struck young woman, and the poor lad isn't even an American," said Fingal, shaking his head.

Lars laid his knife and fork precisely parallel to each other beside the bones of his plaice to indicate that he had finished. "Stardom," said Lars, "is a dangerous profession."

Archie quietly and unobtrusively cleared away plates.

O'Reilly went to the sideboard and returned with a decanter full of Chateauneuf-du-Pape. "I'll be carving in a minute, John. Will you do the honours?"

"Of course."

Archie was setting a large oval Delft platter bearing the beef Wellington surrounded by roast potatoes. Dinner plates were being kept warm on a sterno burner. Kinky had a tray with tureens and a gravy ewer, which she rapidly distributed around the table. She curtsied to the marquis and said, "My lord."

"Arise, madam," John said with a teasing tone in his voice. "That's not necessary, Mrs. Auchinleck. Myrna and I are simply guests of this house, and fortunate indeed to be eating your delicious fare."

She blushed. "Thank you, sir. It does be my honour and great pleasure, so."

Kinky would never lose her awe of the gentry, O'Reilly thought as he half listened to a subdued murmur of conversation from the table. He inhaled the gentle aroma of puff pastry done to a rich brown perfection. It was not quite overpowered by the aroma of baked beef filet. He lifted the carving knife and steel, and with a rapid grating sharpened the blade.

"I'll not try to teach my granny to suck eggs," whispered Kinky, who, perhaps a little less in awe of the marquis, was now standing at O'Reilly's shoulder, "but please cut generous slices, sir."

"I will." He skewered the meat through the pastry and made his first incision. The knife slid effortlessly through the crust as steam escaped and small flakes fell onto the dish. He cut on. "Kinky," he said, "it's like carving butter." And he wasn't being flattering. The knife simply slid through the meat. He laid the first slice on its side, noting the evenness of the surrounding pastry, the paleness of the layer of paté spread on very thin pancakes, the duxelles, and the fillet, brown on its outside and pink at its core. "Kinky Auchinleck," he said, "this is a thing of beauty. It's perfect."

"Well," she said, head cocked to one side, "I am pleased to hear you say that, sir, but to my eye the centre might have taken a minute or two more."

O'Reilly laughed. "You are the world's greatest perfectionist, Kinky Auchinleck, and we love you for it."

She coloured again and lifted a dinner plate. "Do you please be putting a slice and two roasties on here, sir, so Archie can serve the marquis."

In no time everyone had been served their beef Wellington and had helped themselves to champ, gravy, and vegetables.

Kinky and Archie had vanished.

John cut his first bite of beef, as did all the others. A blissful look crossed his face as he swallowed.

O'Reilly savoured the mix of flavours—the tenderness of the filet steak, the piquancy of the paté de fois gras. When he'd been in Bremerton in World War II, while *Warspite* was being repaired in the great U.S. shipyard after a direct hit by a German bomb, he'd once heard a Texan workman say in great approval of something,

"Sell muh clothes, shoot the hound, Momma. I'm goin' to heaven." And that just about summed it up.

"So," said Kitty, "tell us more about your trip to Villefranche."

Myrna put down her knife and fork, dabbed her lips with a napkin, and said, "Lars and I have been working together for several months and during that time we have been growing . . . closer." There was fondness in her smile to him and he replied in kind.

"It seems that my belonging to the peerage has inhibited the dear old sausage from saying anything. Silly man. I have to get you to understand that I am not one bit impressed with my accident of birth. I consider professionals like lawyers and doctors my equals, of course, and I also feel as John does about skilled people. Paddy Jackson the farrier *is* streets ahead of us when it comes to shoeing horses. Now that's not to say he'll be dropping into the big house for cocktails, but we really do believe that each individual should be respected for their skills."

"It certainly came as an eye-opener to me," Lars said. "Fingal and I do come from a very traditional background. It'll take me a little time to get used to Myrna being as happy with her horses and country folk as she is with her society friends, so I thought a bit of time away would be a good start. If she wants to see some of her friends while we're in Villefranche, Nice is only eight kilometres away and Monte Carlo seventeen, with a very good rail service to both."

"And John and I do have friends in both, although I think I shall be perfectly content to see the sights of Villefranche," Myrna said. "I'm told the views from Mont Leuze are spectacular and the hike up excellent exercise."

"I for one am delighted," John said. He raised his glass. "Here's to you both."

O'Reilly and Kitty drank. "To Lars and Myrna."

Good old Lars. He had taken the plunge, and if the way Myrna kept glancing at him and her obvious delight in their plans were anything to go by, his feelings were returned and damn the social gap. It would be interesting to watch his elder brother's transformation from solitary, self-sufficient bachelor to, if it all worked out as O'Reilly fervently hoped it would, married man.

"Now," said O'Reilly, wishing he could undo his waistband, "would anyone care for some more beef?"

There was a series of polite refusals.

"Then," he said, "I'll nip down and ask Archie to clear off the wreckage and to bring up the dessert."

John forestalled him. He rose. "Let me go," he said.

"Don't be daft—" O'Reilly began.

"Carry on, John," Kitty said. "We like our guests to feel right at home. Lars, Myrna, I'm sure I can speak for Fingal when I say we wish you the very best. We really do."

Myrna reached across and took Lars's hand. "So," she said, "do I."

John reappeared with Archie and to O'Reilly's surprise Kinky in tow. Archie bore the trifle and Kinky had taken off her apron. She was glowing, O'Reilly assumed with pride.

"Now," said John, "I would like, with Doctor O'Reilly's permission . . ."

"Please," O'Reilly said. John never forgot his manners.

". . . for both you and Mrs. Auchinleck to join us for some of this delicious-looking trifle and a glass of wine. I'm sorry I can't ask you to the table. There are only five places, but, here," he said, beginning to move the two closest armchairs so they were included in the small circle of the dining table.

"Oh, my lord, we couldn't." Kinky looked genuinely dismayed and yet at the same time even prouder than she'd looked a moment ago.

"No, I insist." He waited while Archie served the company, seated her, and then poured a glass of white each for himself and Kinky to accompany their helpings of trifle.

"I should like to propose a toast, so please charge your glasses and rise," said John MacNeill, twenty-seventh Marquis of Ballybucklebo, getting to his feet and raising his glass. He waited until everyone was ready and turned to face Kinky and Archie. "Please drink with me to tender our sincere thanks and admiration to Mrs. Maureen Auchinleck, the finest cook in Ireland . . ."

Kinky blushed and smiled.

" . . . and to Mister Archibald Auchinleck, who has so ably abetted his wife in serving with great panache this incomparable feast."

Archie bowed.

"I haven't tasted beef Wellington with such an exquisite texture and flavours . . ."

He was interrupted by Myrna calling, "Hear him. Hear him."

" . . . since my father's cook passed away."

The company echoed the toast and drank. The applause was long and loud.

O'Reilly sat and tucked in. No doubt, John MacNeill was one of nature's gentlemen when it came to dealing with people. He could "walk with kings nor lose the common touch."

O'Reilly saw Lars bend and whisper something to

Myrna, who smiled and quite unselfconsciously patted his arm.

Kitty caught Fingal's eye and smiled.

He smiled in return and settled back into his chair. What a wonderful evening, he thought. John and Myrna perfectly at their ease in this old house of his and Kitty's. Lars and Myrna on the brink of a romantic adventure. Kinky and Archie smiling up at the marquis, laughing at something he had just said. Coffee and brandy or whiskey would follow, adding another layer of warmth to the evening. He sighed. The time had passed so pleasantly he had for the whole time forgotten the threat to Number One. Surely the blasted lease must show up soon. Mustn't it? He wanted more evenings just like this one. Many more.

35

The Game's Afoot

Barry wanted John D. MacDonald's new book, *One Fearful Yellow Eye*. He was quite the fan of MacDonald's "salvage consultant" Travis McGee and his live-aboard houseboat *The Busted Flush,* and a quiet read of the new book was part of the plan for his evening off. He and Jack Mills, who he'd be seeing soon, would rather have been out with the ladies in their lives. It was, after all, Saint Valentine's Day. But Sue was still in France, and Helen, despite Jack's most persuasive arguments in favour of the saint, was studying for her next professional examination, the fearsome Second MB.

Erskine Mayne's book and stationery store on Donegall Square West, across from Belfast City Hall, was large and quiet. The current proprietor was the fifth member of the Mayne family, originally from Scotland, to be running the old establishment. The ancient wooden floors were well worn, and the high ceilings were embellished with ornate mouldings.

People spoke softly to the store assistants as if they were in a library, and the place had that smell of dust and paper unique to bookstores and library stacks.

Barry had spent many happy hours here wandering the logically laid-out and well-posted passages between bookshelves, but today he would have to find his book without delay. He was meeting Jack at the Queen's Squash Club for a quick game and then a bite to eat and a pint. Barry was looking forward to seeing his old friend, but he was of two minds about the squash. He'd not played for some time, but Jack had phoned and said he needed some exercise to keep his mind off women. His exact words had been "My seminal vesicles are so full I've got lumps behind my ears." Barry had laughed and hadn't bothered to correct Jack's faulty understanding of anatomy. It had never been his long suit.

Barry found the book in *Crime Fiction,* arranged in a row beside MacDonald's seven earlier McGee novels, all of which Barry had read. He picked up a copy and headed for the cash register. The tall angular man just ahead of him was wearing the kind of Gannex raincoat made popular by British prime minister Harold Wilson.

The man turned and smiled at Barry. Ronald Fitzpatrick raised his brown trilby hat, his voice barely above a whisper. "Good evening, Doctor Laverty. How are you?" Fitzpatrick wore his gold pince-nez firmly perched on his nose, but his prominent Adam's apple was hidden under a sorbo-rubber Stamm collar.

"I'm fine, Doctor Fitzpatrick. Just buying a book," Barry replied, sotto voce.

"Me too; several in fact," Fitzpatrick said, holding them under his left arm. "I'm sorry I've not seen more of you, Doctor Laverty, since you all so kindly invited me to join your on-call rota. I am so enjoying the extra time off. I hear you've been spending your extra time making some very exciting plans." The man readjusted his pince-nez and looked conspiratorial. "Fingal keeps me up to date on news."

"Yes, I'm getting married soon. My fiancée and I are arranging the details of, we hope, buying a seaside bungalow near Ballybucklebo and I'll be enjoying my off-duty even more when Sue gets back from France next month."

"I wish you success with your purchase and every happiness in your marriage," Fitzpatrick said. "I never did marry. Ah, well." He sounded wistful, but then his expression changed. "Dale Carnegie says feeling sorry for ourselves and our present condition is not only a waste of energy but the worst habit we could possibly have. Now, Doctor Laverty, I'm so glad I bumped into you. I'd be very grateful for your advice."

"If I can help," Barry said, wondering what sort of advice his colleague might want.

Fitzpatrick ran a finger under the upper rim of his neck brace and turned his head from side to side. "They should call this thing a damn collar, not a Stamm collar." His dry laugh was subdued and Barry realised that dour Doctor Fitzpatrick had cracked a joke. Fair play to him. "I find it hard to express just how grateful I am to you, and Fingal, and Doctor Bradley when she was there and now Doctor Stevenson, for caring for my patients when I was, ahem, incapacitated. I am even more grateful to be permitted to join your on-call schedule."

He had been in the rota since the first of February. "I think it's working very well," Barry said, "particularly with Doctor Stevenson only able to work on site . . . at least until she gets the go-ahead from her specialist to drive again."

"It is, and I wish a speedy recovery for her, but may I explain what advice I need? I have been buying books for Fingal, Kitty, and yourself that I hope will reflect your special interests."

"That's very kind, but there's no need—"

"I'd shake my head if I could, but I choose to disagree. Now it's to be a surprise, but I've some books on wildfowling for Fingal, a excellent tome about the French Impressionists for Kitty, but I'll not tell you what yours is. And please keep this to yourself."

"Of course," Barry said.

"I need to know what pastimes the two young lady doctors might have."

Barry thought for a moment. He remembered Nonie being excited about going to see a Sam Thompson play and Jenny he knew used to attend the annual performance of *Swan Lake* at Belfast's Grand Opera House and had made several trips to Sadler's Wells in London. He said, "I'm not altogether familiar with their hobbies, but I'm pretty sure Nonie'd enjoy a book about Irish theatre and Jenny? Ballet."

"Thank you. Thank you very much." He held his right index finger against his lips. "Now, not a word to our colleagues."

Barry nodded.

"It was so pleasant running into you like this. May I call you Barry?"

"Of course."

"And I'm Ronald," he said. "Now, please don't let me detain you. I must go and complete my purchases." And with that he lifted his hat, turned, and went off looking at the signposts and muttering, "Irish Theatre. Irish Theatre."

Barry chuckled and headed for the counter. Their new associate certainly was different, even a little strange, but the more Barry saw of the man, the more he recognised depths he hadn't suspected. He hoped their new cover arrangement would continue to be successful, particularly now that before the year was out he'd be a married man.

◫

Jack had beaten Barry to the squash club. He was sitting in the men's changing room wearing a white shirt, white shorts, white knee socks, and white guttees. The room was warm and smelled of sweat, and steam from the showers. As Barry approached, carrying a hold-all, Jack said, "How's about ye, ould hand?" in a perfect Belfast accent. "Fit and well you're looking, so y'are."

Barry was not such a good mimic as Jack, but came close with, "Dead on, mate, and all the better for seeing your lovely self."

They both laughed. As Barry was changing, he said, "You'll have to start easy, Jack. I'm not as fit as I used to be and I haven't played since we were housemen. I'm rusty."

"It'll come back, and you owe me. You beat me in that last game in three straight sets. I may have a bit of an edge too. Helen's making me quit smoking along with her," he said. "She's more of the scientific student than I ever was. She's read the 1956 British Doctors' Study that links smoking with lung cancer and heart attacks, and the 1966 follow-up paper. She's convinced it's true."

"We had to read the '56 one too," Barry said, "remember?"

"Aye," said Jack with a grin on his countryman's face, "but I never understood the terms like prospective cohort study, multivariate analysis, and 'p' values to express statistical significance. The only vital statistics that ever interested me were 36-24-36."

Barry laughed. "Right," he said, lacing up his shoe, standing, and putting on plastic lensless eye protectors. "Into the court and warm up the balls." He led the way from the changing room to a walled court, held the door open for his friend, and closed it behind them.

Other games were in progress and the courts area was noisy with the thumps of balls off walls, thudding of feet on the court surface, and occasional cries of "Good shot."

"I'll warm them," Jack said, for which Barry was grateful. He wanted to conserve his energy for the match.

Jack moved to the service box of the back left quarter and began hitting a small black rubber ball off the front wall between the lower service line and the upper out line and returning it with a series of accurate volleys. Cold balls had little or no bounce, and this made them die when they bounced off a wall.

"How's Helen?" Barry asked, and it wasn't a simple politeness. Barry hadn't seen Jack since they'd lunched in the Causerie a month ago, when all had not been sweetness and light between his best friend and Helen Hewitt. Barry was concerned.

Jack kept on pasting the ball, but the sounds of it striking the wall did not prevent Barry hearing his answer. "Worried, scared. The exams're in two weeks. She's really hitting—" He slammed the ball with his racquet. "—the books."

"All exam candidates are scared. We know. We lived through it. I mean how are things—"

"Between me and Helen?"

"Between you and Helen."

Jack grabbed the ball. "This one's nearly ready," he said, then inhaled, scratched his head, and looked Barry in the eye. "You told me to give her her head, let her get on with her studying, not insist on seeing her, and she'd thank me if she passed."

"Have you?"

"I didn't need to. We went out once more last month." He blew out his breath against pursed lips. "She's not the first girl I've told 'I love you,' not by a long chalk." He looked Barry right in the eye again. "But it's the first time I've meant it." He served again. His stroke was vicious and the now nearly warm ball ripped back past Barry's head with only inches to spare.

"Go easy, Jack," said Barry. "You nearly hit me."

"Sorry," Jack said, "I wasn't concentrating." He lowered his voice. "I was thinking about the night I told Helen I loved her. And you're the only other person I've told that to, hey."

"It'll go no farther, but that's terrific, Jack. What did she say?"

"I was running her home to the women students' halls of residence and I parked in the grounds. I kissed her and told her." His serve was more accurate and his forehand returns were powerful. "And she kissed me back, said I'd dumped her once . . ." Another smashing volley. "That she was taking a chance this second time around. Thought she might fall in love with me. Thought she was close . . ."

"I'd say that's pretty bloody promising."

Jack caught the ball. "This one will do," he said, pocketing it. "Then she said, 'But'—and Barry, it's a big 'but'—'until the exams was over, love has to wait.'" With another ferocious forehand, he began to warm up another ball. "Any other girl and it would have been *adios, sayonara,* toodeloo, there's more fish in the sea, but damn it all . . ." The words came in a rush: "I'm daft about Helen. Bugger." He'd struck the ball at an angle and had driven it into a corner where it slid to the floor. Jack walked over and picked it up.

"As one of my patients might say, it's sticking out a mile, old friend," Barry said. "And there is a bright side, you know. Before Patricia and I broke up, I spent weeks agonizing over whether she had another fellah in England. She had. It hurt. You know that. But you don't have that worry. If Helen Hewitt says she's working, she's working." He wondered if Helen were also playing a bit "hard to get." He had always thought Helen was a keen observer of human nature, and that she had the measure of Jack Mills, Barry had no doubt. But he kept that thought to himself.

"Thanks." Jack inhaled deeply and backhanded the retrieved ball. "And we did have the conversation about the Protestant-Catholic thing." He caught the ball and bounced it in front of him. "This one's warm enough. She's not been to mass once, at least since I've been seeing her. She's not devout, and it doesn't bother her one bit. Her dad, who's a bit of a Republican, might be difficult. My parents, they're country folk. Old ways die hard, but if she does say she's in love with me, we'll work it out somehow. We'll have to. What are you smiling about, mate? This is serious."

"I know, I'm sorry. It's just that, well, the refrain from 'There's a Place for Us' from *West Side Story* started playing in my head."

"Daft bugger. You romantics." He laughed.

"One step at a time, eh?" said Barry.

"That's her." Jack grinned and caught the ball. "And that's her too. This one's ready. Spin for service?"

"Fine. Go ahead. I call 'up.'"

Jack's racquet stopped spinning and, to Barry's delight, the Spalding trademark was facing up. "My serve," he said. "Three sets, first to nine?"

"Sounds good."

Without speaking, Barry moved into the service box of the right back quarter, waiting for Jack to take up his position in the opposite back quarter. "Ready?" The minute Jack assented, Barry slammed in his first serve. It ricochetted back and Jack returned it with a searing volley. Barry retreated and let it bounce once before slamming it so it left the front wall at an acute angle and next hit the left side wall and flew into the back of the court where Jack had no chance to return it.

"Point to you," Jack said, "and still your serve."

By the time the first set ended, nine to seven in Barry's favour, he was sweating rivulets, his legs felt like rubber, and each inhalation burned in his chest. He already knew he was the craftier player—he had always been better at calculating angles and estimating the force required to make a return drop so it barely made the back quarter before bouncing twice. But Jack, as befitted a man who played rugby football in the second row, relied on what was known in Ulster as "good old brute force and ignorance," and Barry had no doubt he'd be worn down. "I need a breather," he said. "I told you I wasn't fit."

"All right," Jack said. He was breathing as if he'd had no more exertion than a summer stroll.

"You're—" Barry gasped, "in fine fettle, Mills."

"I bloody well ought to be," Jack said. "No more fags. Gym twice a week and a good cross-country run once. I have to do something in my time off, and other girls are out of bounds." He grunted. "Strictly out of bounds. Jaysus, the things I do for love." He laughed. "At least I'm not taking cold showers. Yet."

Barry laughed. "Remember there was a rumour at boarding school that they put saltpetre in our tea to 'suppress bodily urges'?"

"Didn't suppress mine," Jack said. "Remember when we had the combined dance with Victoria College? That little blonde, remember, the one who looked like Brigitte Bardot . . ." He made a strangling noise of great pleasure.

"Mills, you are incorrigible, and I do not remember the blonde who looked like Brigitte Bardot. But I do hear you," Barry said, "and believe me, sticking to a woman you love is worth it, and if exercise helps?" He grinned. "Kipling said it very well. 'Take a large hoe, a shovel also, and dig til you gently perspire.'"

"I'd rather be doing something else that requires breathing heavily and sweating profusely," Jack said.

"All right," Barry said, "in this purgatory of yours, there must be an end in sight. The first step is the exam itself, that many-headed Hydra of papers, and practical and oral exams. How long did you say until it starts?"

Jack, now bouncing a ball up and down off his racquet, said, "The first written paper is at nine on Monday, March the sixth, in the Whitla Hall. The tests go on all week and the results will be posted in the cloisters at Queen's sometime after six on the evening of Friday, March tenth."

Less than two weeks before Sue would be home, Barry thought.

"And you'll be taking her to the party after." It was a long-hallowed tradition that the junior anatomy students threw a bash for the senior ones so the successful could celebrate and the unsuccessful could drown their sorrows.

"I will." Jack missed, dropped the ball, and had to chase it across the court.

Barry's breathing had now settled but he was happy to prolong his rest. "But you'll not be seeing her before?"

"Don't think so. I mean, if she wouldn't come out on Saint Valentine's . . ." He started bouncing again.

"Then get a florist to send her a big bunch of flowers—"

"Hey, I just sent her some chocolates this afternoon."

"Doesn't matter. Send her the flowers and a good-luck card on the Friday before the exam. I'll bet she phones to thank you."

"All right. You'll be bankrupting me, Laverty but, by God, I'll do it. I should have thought of it myself. Thanks, Barry."

Barry shrugged. "When I think of how you've held my hand."

Jack changed the subject. "But I'm not holding it now, brother. My serve, I believe. Right side."

Barry moved to the centre of the back left. Jack's service was a screamer that Barry couldn't reach, never mind return. Perhaps the repressed energy of Jack's enforced celibacy was being directed into that hard little black missile. Barry gave the ball to his friend, vowing to be on his guard.

The returning bounce of Jack's second serve hit Barry's thigh. "Yeeeow. That bloody well stung," he said. "I'll have a bruise like a soup plate tomorrow. You don't know your own strength."

"Sorry," Jack said, and sounded not the least contrite. After eleven more rallies in which Jack had Barry scampering round the court like a liltie on amphetamine and twice having to make a dive to avoid being hit again, the score stood at nine to four in Jack's favour. Barry, bent over, hands on knees, was hauling in fiery lungfuls. "Enough. I'm whacked. Banjaxed. I couldn't go a third set. You win. Mercy."

Jack held his hands aloft like a victorious prize fighter and announced, "The winnah," and adopted a Muhammad Ali accent. "Float like a butterfly. Sting like a bee. I am the greatest."

"Greatest . . . bollix if you . . . ask me," Barry said, his breath slowly returning.

Jack laughed. "Och, Barry. Thanks for the game. It took me out of myself for a while. Gave me a chance to let off steam. And thanks for listening. No hard feelings. The pints are on me tonight after we've had our showers."

"I'm your man," Barry said.

"And," Jack said as he opened the door out of the court, "in a couple of weeks I'll need some more moral support. How'd you like to come to the post-exam party with us? For old times' sake. I know you'll have to go stag, but . . ."

Barry laughed. "I don't mind going alone, just as long as you promise me that this time you'll not try to let down the tyres of a police car—with the rozzers still inside."

It was Jack's turn to laugh. "They let me off with a caution, remember? I wonder if they would again, now that I'm a respectable doctor and all. But I do promise. I just want you there to celebrate if things go well for Helen, and, I hope, for Helen and me . . ."

The words "and try to cheer me up if Helen blows me out," were left unsaid.

36

᠄᠄᠄

Desires and Petitions of Your Servants

The rotund Presbyterian minister wore his white dog collar under a dark pullover beneath a Harris tweed sports jacket. He managed to look both welcoming and apologetic when he held out a hand to O'Reilly at the door to the parish hall. "I can only say I deeply regret that, to date, my search of the church's records has failed to turn up any trace of the original lease. Perhaps tonight's proceedings might bring you a little comfort."

"We hope so," Kitty said. "The marquis still has had no luck either."

And, O'Reilly thought, Bertie Bishop phoned last night to say that Hubert Doran has been canvassing like billyoh for the council to recommend compulsory acquisition of Number One.

"It's a shame," said Mister Robinson, "but all's not lost yet. You have a lot of support." He waved a hand to the packed room. "We've admitted as many folks as the hall will hold, but had to turn a lot of people away."

Conversations buzzed, and heads turned to take notice of the newcomers. O'Reilly saw elbows nudging ribs and more heads turning to stare in his direction. There was a vague smell of dust and floor polish, but no hint of stale tobacco. Smoking was not permitted on church premises.

"It is quite the turnout, Reverend," O'Reilly said. He could see over the heads of the standing-room-only crowd to a small stage at the far end. Seated on it behind a long table were Alice Moloney and Flo Bishop, the prime movers in organising the petition to "Save Our Doctor's Home." Bertie Bishop sat with the platform party, his thumbs hooked behind his lapels, a look of satisfaction on his face as he surveyed the crowd.

"I'm chairing this meeting," Mister Robinson said, "and I'd like you and Mrs. O'Reilly to join me on the platform."

"It's very generous of you, Mister Robinson, considering that the probable decision to demolish Number One guarantees that your own property will be spared," O'Reilly said.

"Doctor, we want to save both your house and the Lord's house. After all, as Bertie Bishop said, 'People is more important than a few quid.' I concur, for, 'The love of money is the root of all evil—'"

"First Timothy six verse twelve, I believe."

Mister Robinson smiled sympathetically. "Och, Doctor O'Reilly, the stress of the situation is telling on you. It's six ten, but six twelve is good counsel as well. 'Fight the good fight of faith, lay hold on eternal life, whereunto thou art also called, and hast professed a good profession before many witnesses.' The scriptures always show the way. What else are we doing here but fighting the good fight of faith for a good profession . . . before many witnesses." He moved his outstretched hand, palm up, in front of him as if passing a benediction over the assembly. Mister Robinson had always had a touch of the theatrical about him and the evening's packed house was bringing it out.

"I do think it would be a sin to see you dispossessed for the sake of a small saving to the council's budget. And I am not alone in thinking so."

"Thank you," Kitty said. "It's certainly very gratifying to see all the people here."

"If you'll follow me?" Mister Robinson began to walk along a central aisle between row upon row of folding chairs.

O'Reilly, Kitty at his side, followed.

Notice boards on one wall held announcements of meetings of the youth club. The local Wolf Cubs, Brownies, Boy Scouts, and Girl Guides used the hall for their weekly events, and posters of their activities added bright colours. Progress along the aisle was slow because they had to keep stopping to acknowledge greetings and expressions of support from well-wishers.

"How's about ye?" Donal and Julie Donnelly said together.

O'Reilly calculated quickly. Today was February 20, so she was twenty-one weeks. Her distended belly was obvious now. Barry would be seeing her for an antenatal visit soon.

"Evening, Doc and Missus," said Gerry Shanks, Mairead by his side.

"Good luck, Doc," said Lenny Brown.

"We're rooting for you," added Connie, "and wee Colin sends his regards."

"No surrender. Not an inch. This we will maintain." Willie Dunleavy, a staunch member of the Orange Order, was using their slogans of stubborn intransigence to any suggestion of change. He stuck two thumbs up.

"Back on my feet now, Doctor." Willie John Andrews, his pneumonia cured, was sitting with his sister, Ruth. "Got home last Tuesday."

As they neared the front of the hall, O'Reilly noticed a banner hanging from the front of the committee table. An embroidered bush in flames stood above the motto, *Ardens Sed Virens,* "burning but flourishing," the emblem of the Presbyterian Church in Ireland.

Kinky and Archie were sitting in the front row. Kinky sported her favourite green hat. "In all the years I've been here," she said, "I've not missed a Monday-night meeting of the Women's Union, except when I had that awful tummy trouble two years ago, so, but every member, every last one, agreed that having this meeting tonight to try to save Number One was more important than ours. They gave the place up for you and Kitty, and," she stifled a small sob, "for me." Her voice hardened and she set her jaw. "I do not want us to lose our home, sir, even if," she clutched Archie's arm, "Archie and I do have our own home too."

O'Reilly wasn't quite sure what to say to comfort her. He managed to pat her arm and murmur, "We're not going down without a fight, Kinky, and it looks like the whole village is fighting on our side too."

"They are, so. And that awful Mister Doran shouldn't think he can go at us like a bull at a gate." Kinky's agate eyes flashed.

O'Reilly felt choked. "I hope you're right," he said. "Now Mister Robinson wants Kitty and me on the platform. Keep your chin up, Kinky. It's not over yet." O'Reilly led Kitty onto the stage.

Bertie, who was sitting on the nearest chair, rose and indicated that O'Reilly and Kitty should sit to his right. Flo and Alice Moloney both gave the O'Reillys beaming smiles as Mister Robinson took his seat between Bertie and Flo Bishop.

"How are youse both?" Bertie asked.

"Well," O'Reilly said, "but anxious, and very gratified by the support that's been drummed up for us. We've had no luck finding the original leases. It looks like the petition will be our last chance."

Bertie shook his head. "I think you've known me long enough, Doctor, to know that I usually like to have another card up my sleeve. But I'll say no more about—"

He was interrupted by Mister Robinson rising, banging a gavel, and calling, "Settle down now, please. Settle down. I'd like to call the meeting to order."

"Like thon Yankee fellah said, 'It ain't over til it's over,'" Bertie whispered as conversation tailed off in the hall. He winked.

"Ladies and gentlemen. Ladies and gentlemen," Mister Robinson said, "I want to thank you all for coming out tonight in support of our senior and much-respected physician, Doctor O'Reilly, and his charming wife, Sister Kitty O'Reilly."

There was a round of applause.

"Thank you. Now you may ask why did the committee call this meeting? After all, everyone knows that a petition has been circulating and those who have signed it are showing their support for the plan to bypass the village rather than tear down our belovèd doctor's home. Normally a petition is simply handed in for council's information, and we can only hope they'll take notice and act on it. But we decided we wanted a more tangible show of support for the O'Reillys, and we also continue to need your help."

"Youse done good, so youse did, I think," Mister Coffin, the undertaker, called from the floor.

"Thank you, sir, we appreciate that, but I'd ask the audience to keep questions or remarks until later when anyone who wishes to speak will be given the opportunity to do so."

A subdued murmuring of assent.

"First, I'd like Councillor Alice Moloney to report to you on where the petition stands. Alice?"

Alice Moloney rose. O'Reilly could not recall her looking as well as she did this evening. It had taken her a while to recover from her illness of two years ago, but tonight, in a two-piece suit of palest blue, a ruffled cream blouse, and a matching blue pillbox hat, she looked ten years younger than her fifty-four years. Even in the garish light of the parish hall, he could see more than a glimmer of the girl who had fallen in love in India thirty-five-odd years ago with a subaltern in Skinner's Horse. "Good evening," she said. "We of the committee want to thank you—you who are here this evening and all those who signed—we thank you from the bottom of our hearts. As of now we have collected one thousand, two hundred and sixty-two signatures. That's sixty-eight percent of our one thousand, eight hundred and fifty-six citizens of voting age, according to the 1961 census."

There was much applause and cries of "Wheeker," and "Dead on," and, "Sticking out a mile."

O'Reilly glanced at Kitty, who was staring, damp-eyed, at the enthusiastic crowd. She reached out her hand beneath the table and clasped his. He cleared his throat. A distinct lump had formed and he could feel the tears prickling in his eyes.

Mister Robinson—wisely, O'Reilly thought—let the expressions of pleasure continue uninterrupted. They subsided and Alice Moloney said, "We'd love it to be one hundred percent, although that's probably unrealistic, but we still need as many as we can get, so we want every one of you to have a word with your friends and neighbours. Copies for signature will be in my shop, Mister Bishop's building company's office, the Mucky Duck, the tobacconist's, and the newsagent's on the housing estate until the first Monday in March."

"Mister Chairman," Donal Donnelly called, "I think it's up til each and every one of us here til firmly grasp the thistle on this one . . ."

It took a second for O'Reilly to realise he meant "grasp the nettle."

". . . and do what Miss Moloney asks."

Cries of "Hear, hear" followed, with one particularly loud voice saying, "Ouch, Donal. I don't know which would be worse—a thistle or a nettle. Good thing there's a doctor in the house."

"Settle down now, settle down," Mister Robinson said with a broad smile, "and thank you, Donal."

Alice Moloney waited, then said, "Council have their meeting two Mondays hence, March the sixth, at seven o'clock in the evening, when the petition will be presented and given, we hope, due consideration. So we will keep it open until noon that day. The last decision taken on February the sixth was to postpone recommending the issuance of a compulsory acquisition order until the March meeting. As I said, that's still two weeks away. We do have time to get more signatures. Please all do your very best to get more signatories. Thank you all again." She sat, to huge applause.

"And we thank you, Miss Moloney," Mister Robinson said. "Now," he said, "while I'm sure Doctor O'Reilly is busting to say a word of thanks, I have another speaker. Mister Bishop, the floor is yours."

Bertie rose, hooking his thumbs behind his lapels in his characteristic stance. "Right," he said, "I'm dead proud of what Miss Moloney and my wife Flo has done. I only helped out a wee bit and I think the petition should do the jibby-job, so I do. But I do want to caution you that while the petition is admirable, it's still true that money talks."

"The penny is mightier than the sword," Donal Donnelly yelled.

"Well, I hope it doesn't come to that, Donal," Bertie said, "I certainly hope it doesn't. But if council changes its mind and opts til go south, everyone's rates will need to go up to cover the cost, and that will weigh heavily with the councillors. I don't want til pour cold water on our hopes. I just want to be clear about what we're up against and back up Miss Moloney's request. Every signature counts." He paused to let that information sink in.

O'Reilly glanced at Kitty, who was no longer smiling. Kinky, in the front row, looked tense.

"Any comments or questions for either Councillor Moloney or Councillor Bishop?" Mister Robinson asked.

Hands went up.

"Mister Shanks?"

Gerry Shanks rose and said, "I don't see why it has til go on the rates . . ."

A chorus of boos echoed through the hall.

"Houl your wheest, Gerry."

O'Reilly did not recognise the forceful voice telling Gerry to shut up.

"Now hold your horses. Hang about," he said, "I'm not done yet. I'll bet youse that if we did a door-til-door whip round, passed the hat like, we'd raise the ready in no time flat." He sat, to a chorus of now approving noises.

"Councillor Bishop?" Mister Robinson said.

Bertie said, "That's a very nice suggestion, Gerry. It shows the kind of support we know we have for each other here, but, and I am speaking as a member of council now, things must be done through the proper channels. That's how councils work. It's not a charity. I'm in favour of the bypass, but I do want to bring a wee touch of realism into the proceedings."

"Thank you, Councillor," said Mister Robinson drily. "You've certainly done that. I for one would much rather see any increase in lorry traffic diverted away from the village main street. One of our hymns says, 'The church's one foundation is Jesus,' and that is true in the spiritual sense. I mean no blasphemy when I say that First Ballybucklebo Presbyterian's worldly foundations are very old bricks and mortar that do not benefit from the passage of what politicians in England are starting to call Juggernaut lorries because of their size."

More heads nodding. A few loud chuckles.

"Yes, Cissie Sloan?"

Cissie rose. "I've a wee question for Doctor O'Reilly. I'm not very good at public speaking. Mind youse I did once give the toast to the bridesmaids at my cousin Jenny's wedding back in '56 . . . or was it '57?" She frowned, then smiled. "It was '56, so it was. That was the year them Hungarians reared up agin the Russians and—"

"Forgive me, Cissie, but your question?" Mister Robinson asked.

"Right enough. Doctor, if they do knock down your house, where'll we go for corn if we need a doctor?" She sat.

"Doctor O'Reilly?"

"Good question, Cissie. I don't think, if the worse comes to the worst and we do have to go, I don't think any demolition would be started until Mrs. O'Reilly and I have found somewhere to live and I have found alternative premises for the practice. Doctors Laverty, Stevenson, and I will still look after you all."

"'At's a great comfort, so it is. We don't want to lose any of youse, sir," Police Constable Mulligan called. "Sorry for speaking out of turn, sir."

"Thank you, Officer," O'Reilly said, and remained standing. "Now," he said, "I don't want to cut off any more questions or statements, but seeing I have the floor, I want to take this opportunity to say how very deeply touched Mrs. O'Reilly and I are by the way that Councillor Moloney and Mrs. Bishop have organised the petition on our behalf, how you have all come out tonight to give us your support. No one could accuse me of ever showing false humility, but I am humbled and touched to the quick. If I were alone I think I might shed a tear." He felt Kitty's hand slip into his and heard her whisper, "I know what you mean."

"And, damn it all—pardon me, Reverend—but sometimes petitions do sway councils, Councillor Bishop. I appreciate your comments, but I won't let them stop me hoping for the best and that Mrs. O'Reilly and I and, bless her, Kinky Auchinleck, and the young doctors are still carrying out our duties in Number One long after the bypass is completed."

The cheers and applause were deafening.

O'Reilly waited for silence then continued, "And finally, may we thank Mister Robinson for the use of the parish hall, and for so skillfully chairing the meeting. Thank you all."

He sat, to resounding applause, and when it had died, Mister Robinson rose and said, "I believe that now concludes our business. Please do try your best to get more signatures, and let us give three cheers for the petition. Hip-hip."

The three hurrahs rang into the rafters and when they had died, the assembly began to break up.

O'Reilly turned to Bertie. "Thank you, Bertie. I know it wasn't easy being the one to have to bring the voice of reason to the proceedings."

"I just hope the petition works," Bertie said.

"You said you'd another line of attack up your sleeve, Bertie," O'Reilly said. "I don't want to twist your arm, but—?"

Bertie shook his head. "Doctor," he said, "I'm not good at the quotes like you, but there's one about secrets shared not being secrets anymore. I've been in politics for a brave wheen of years. No harm til youse both, but it's up my sleeve now and it'll stay there unless I really need it." He grinned. "There is one thing I can do up front though. I'll give Mister Baxter a ring tonight. Tell him there's already near seventy percent in favour of the southern route. Ask for the meeting and the taking of the vote to be open til the citizens. That might sway a vote or two our way."

"Fair enough," O'Reilly said. He inhaled deeply. "Thanks for that, but . . ." He exhaled. "It's still going to be a very long two weeks until the next meeting of council."

37

In the Valley of Decision

Hello, Doctor, dear," Kinky said. "I'm getting your tea ready."

O'Reilly had just returned from a home visit to the sight of Kinky, her eyes streaming, standing at her chopping board, chopping and sniffing.

"Kinky Auchinleck. Please don't cry. Everything will be fine. Really."

"Get away with you, Doctor. It's the onions. They do make a body's eyes water. I'm not worried about this evening at all. Now, if you're looking for Doctor Laverty—you were looking for himself, were you not?" She inclined her head to the door to his quarters. "He's working on his little boat, so."

"Thank you." He'd not ask Kinky, either about why she wasn't worried about this evening nor how she knew he was looking for Barry. O'Reilly shook his head, felt a shiver travel up his spine, and crossed the kitchen. He knocked on Barry's door and opened it when a voice said, "Come in."

"Coming up for a jar, Barry?"

"Love to," Barry said, rising from his worktable to join O'Reilly. "Smells good, Kinky," Barry said as he and O'Reilly headed for the hall, where they met a jubilant Nonie Stevenson coming in through the front door. She was carrying what looked like an overnight bag. "Fingal, Barry," she said, and the words poured out, "I've just driven down from Belfast. I saw Doctor Millar this afternoon and guess what?"

O'Reilly opened his mouth to speak, but Nonie laughed and said, "I never was very good at telling stories. I just gave it all away by saying I just drove down from Belfast. It's exactly four weeks and three days since I started taking the lowest possible daily dose of amphetamine. I've not had a single daytime episode since. He had said it could have taken a couple of months to get me stabilised, but he's sure we've done it in one. Doctor Millar's amazed, says it's the fastest recovery he's ever seen, and is confident my narcoleptic episodes are under control. I'm sleeping better at night too, and you'll probably not believe this, but I'm not craving tobacco anymore."

"I am absolutely delighted," Barry said, "and congratulations about the fags. I quit four years ago. It was bloody murder."

"Thank you," she said, "I can believe that. The first couple of weeks were hellish." She looked from man to man and said, "I want to celebrate my cure now . . . well, not actually a cure. The narcolepsy will never go away, but it's under control. It's under control, and I want to celebrate that in a special way."

"Go on," said O'Reilly.

"Now don't laugh, but I'm still feeling guilty about having been difficult about swapping call. I promised not to let that happen again, and it won't."

"We know that, Nonie," O'Reilly said, his voice level.

She lowered her head. "Thank you. It is comforting to be trusted."

Barry nodded.

Nonie said, "And I can never repay you, Fingal, for keeping me on with limited duties until I recovered—"

"That, Doctor Stevenson, is a load of bollocks," he said with a broad smile. "Any decent person would have done the same. You were ill and the last thing you needed was to lose your job at the same time."

"Well, you and Barry have been more than decent about it, and so I want to start paying back right now." She lifted her bag. "I've got my toothbrush, my jammies, and the book Doctor Fitzpatrick so kindly gave me, *John Millington Synge and the Irish Theatre*." She giggled and held up the overnight bag.

O'Reilly glanced at Barry and saw a look of amazement cross his young friend's face.

Nonie's tones brooked no argument. "Whoever is on call tonight isn't anymore. I am, and I will be every fourth night and weekend from now on, and I'll take my share of home visits too."

Barry laughed. "Good for you, Nonie. I was on tonight, but I'll be perfectly happy to have the night off. I'm only a few hours away from finishing my model ship, and I had planned to work on it this evening while I was waiting for any emergency calls."

"Your model that, but for the grace of God, I nearly completely finished off for you in January."

"Water under the bridge," Barry said with a smile. "We didn't know you were sick then."

"Thanks, Barry." Her smile was open and beautiful.

Barry turned to O'Reilly. "I'd like to come to the meeting with you and Kitty. I'm as anxious as you are, Fingal, to find out what's going to happen."

"'Anxious' is the right word," O'Reilly said, "but it'll be over soon, and there's a pressing practical matter. If you two would like to go on up, I'll join you in a minute for that predinner tot, but I'll need to ask Kinky to 'throw another spud in the pot.'" He turned back to the kitchen as Barry and Nonie climbed the stairs.

"I have a favour to ask please, Kinky," he said, inhaling the scents of beef, onions, and carrots stewing. "But I also have some great news for you about Doctor Stevenson."

"Oh?" Kinky said, turning from where she was making suet dumplings.

"Doctor Stevenson has been cleared by her specialist to come back to work full time."

"Now that does be grand news altogether," Kinky said. "I am very pleased, for I think her a nice young *cailín*, so."

"And she's going to—"

"Take call tonight, sir?"

"Well, yes, how did you . . . Never mind. Kinky, she'll need—"

"Feeding, sir. There will not be any difficulties. I've made plenty of stew." She began to grate the suet for another dumpling. "Kitty will know when to put the dumplings in. I'll set another place upstairs. And it will not stop me getting home to feed Archie and myself and still have plenty of time to get to the March council meeting on time. We'd not miss that for love nor money. I've a notion you'll be pleased, sir."

He felt the hairs on the nape of his neck rise again. Kinky Auchinleck, lately Kincaid, née O'Hanlon, had inherited the gift from her mother. And she'd said he'd be pleased. There was still good reason to hope.

O'Reilly's, Kitty's, and Barry's heels clacked across the parquet flooring of the packed town hall. Old councillors, some with muttonchop whiskers, others bearded or wearing high wing collars and cravats, still looked down with dignity from a few ancient daguerreotypes. Their dour looks matched O'Reilly's mood.

Conversation was muted and O'Reilly felt the intensity of the sympathetic stares directed at him and Kitty. In contrast to the lighthearted air of the church hall meeting—at least before Bertie had had his say—the atmosphere was subdued.

He ushered Kitty and Barry into a seat in the front row beside Kinky and Archie and noted that his housekeeper was again wearing her prized green hat that O'Reilly had given her two years ago. O'Reilly bent and said to Kinky, "I have to tell you, Kinky, that beef stew with dumplings beat Bannagher. Thank you."

She smiled. "You're welcome, Doctor. And I hope it'll not be the last one I do cook at Number One. My wish is for many years to come in my kitchen, so."

"We all wish for that," O'Reilly said.

"We certainly do," Barry agreed.

O'Reilly sat, and looked up to the dais where the nine-member council sat at the table. John MacNeill nodded to O'Reilly and Kitty from his seat beside the chairman, Mister Robert Baxter. John, at least, was one staunch ally. So were Bertie Bishop and Alice Moloney, but that was only three votes. O'Reilly sighed.

And there, scowling at O'Reilly like a gargoyle on a cathedral, was Hubert Doran. No question about how he'd vote. Could he bring four councillors with him? Five would make the majority. The man's gaze shifted from O'Reilly to a small woman sitting near Kinky. Mrs. Hubert Doran. Brought her along to savour his triumph?

O'Reilly wondered. She had a careworn face, deep crow's-feet at the corners of her pale eyes, and frown lines scored on her forehead. She wore a headscarf over lank, untidy hair, was wrapped in a grey overcoat, and clutched a handbag on her lap.

Mister Baxter rose, used his gavel. He did not need to call for quiet. The room was hushed immediately. "My lord, ladies, and gentlemen, it is time to call this meeting of the Ballybucklebo Borough Council to order. Tonight our agenda is very straightforward. We must first approve the minutes of the last meeting. These have been circulated to council. Are there any additions or corrections?"

No one spoke until the other woman councillor, Sinead Monaghan, a rosy-cheeked market gardener, said, "I move acceptance."

"Seconded." This was from Wilson Grahame, a farmer whose lands marched with Reggie and Lorna Kearney's. O'Reilly had diagnosed his inguinal hernia four years ago and arranged for its surgical correction.

"All in favour?"

Eight hands were raised.

"Motion carried."

Mister Hare, the potato-faced secretary, licked his pencil and made notes.

The chairman continued, "Tonight we will confine the agenda to a single item." Mister Baxter paused and looked down to O'Reilly. There was sympathy in the chairman's brown eyes.

O'Reilly did not like the look of that. A smile would have been preferable.

"The question of alleviating traffic congestion on the bend outside Number One Main Street. At the last meeting it was proposed to recommend the compulsory purchase of Doctor O'Reilly's property and straightening of the road. In view of very strong representation by three council members, that as the land had originally been leased by the MacNeill family to the Presbyterian church there may have been codicils protecting buildings on the property, the council voted to postpone the final decision until tonight to allow sufficient time for a search for that lease. It has not been presented to council."

"Nor will it be, I'm afraid, Mister Chairman." The marquis shook his head. "And I believe Mister Robinson has not found the church's copy either."

O'Reilly saw the minister in the audience nodding his agreement.

Doran grinned and twitched his head at O'Reilly in an "I told you so" gesture.

"In that case," Mister Baxter said, "under ordinary circumstances, in light of the previous decision, we would have no choice but to proceed with our recommendation. However, notice has been duly filed two weeks ago of fresh information for council's consideration tonight. A petition was presented at the town hall office at one P.M. today, the minute we reopened after lunch." He held aloft a sheaf of papers. "It asks that council reverse its earlier decision and pick the option to bypass the village to the south.

"I wish to make it clear that unlike the last meeting, where we took questions from the floor, tonight if necessary we will permit only a closing statement from the party directly involved, Doctor O'Reilly. General questions and comments from the floor will not be entertained."

Quiet murmuring, but no challenge.

"Thank you. Now, I apologise to council that the

figures have not been circulated among them. Some staff stayed late to complete the independent scrutiny and verification of numbers. Counting one thousand, five hundred and ninety-one signatures and matching them to our electoral rolls, a total of one thousand, eight hundred and fifty-six names, takes time, and I was handed those numbers moments before coming in here."

A chorus of in-drawings of breath, "Oohs," "Ahs," and a lone man's voice saying, "Boys-a-boys, thon's a brave wheen of yea votes, so it is."

O'Reilly thought he recognised the speaker's tones, and it was confirmed when Baxter said, "It is, Donal Donnelly. It is, and the 'yeas' represent eighty-five percent of eligible voters living in the villages and townlands that constitute the borough."

O'Reilly whistled. Eighty-five percent. Amazing. He looked at council. Bertie and Alice and John were smiling, as well they might. Four of the other five members had looks of frank amazement. Doran folded his arms across his chest, his face expressionless.

Kitty whispered, "We might just be in luck."

O'Reilly hoped so.

"In order to open this for discussion by council," Baxter continued, "I am prepared to entertain a motion either pro or con the petitioners' request," the chairman said. "Yes, my lord?"

John MacNeill stood. "It is my belief that every one of us here was elected to represent the views of our constituents. I strongly suggest that these overwhelming numbers must be heard. I therefore propose a motion that 'This council rescind the vote to recommend expropriation of Doctor O'Reilly's house and instead advise the ministry to bypass the village to the south.'"

Both Bertie and Alice Moloney rushed to second the motion.

"Proposed by the Marquis of Ballybucklebo, seconded by . . . ?"

"Miss Moloney," Bertie said.

She acknowledged with a smile.

"Have you got that, Mister Hare?"

The secretary nodded.

"The motion is now open for discussion."

"Thank you, Mister Chairman." The marquis took his seat again.

"That petition," said Sinead Monaghan, "says a great deal of the esteem in which our doctor is held, but I'm sorry, I can't be persuaded by sentiment. Councillor Doran has advanced cogent arguments in favour of the cheaper option. These are hard times economically, and I for one do not want my rates raised. Unemployment, inflation, slowdowns in the shipyards, linen mills closing . . . I think we must do what is most economically sound."

O'Reilly watched Mister Hare, Wilson Grahame, and Mister Warnock, a tall, angular, hook-nosed man with close-set eyes who ran the Ballybucklebo ironmonger's, all nodding. Not good.

By the way Bertie was scrutinising the faces of his colleagues, he was drawing the same conclusion.

"Mister Chairman?" Hubert Doran asked.

"Yes, Councillor."

"The numbers on that there petition is very persuasive," he said, his tones level and reasoned, "but with all due deference to our doctor and his family, we was also elected for til be fiscally responsible. Two-thousand-quid difference is not til be sneezed at. It's a brave clatter of money, so it is. At the heels of the hunt, it all boils down to pounds, shillings, and pence. Now youse all know me. I'm a simple farmer—"

"Simple my ar—" Donal yelled from the floor. "You could buy and sell half of us here. Why the hell have you taken a right scunner at our doctor?"

"He's right," "Dead on, Donal," were two remarks O'Reilly heard over the general hubbub.

Bertie smiled broadly at Donal.

"Mister Donnelly," Baxter said, and pounded with his gavel. "Mister Donnelly. Silence. Silence or I'll clear the hall."

The muttering slowly subsided.

"Please continue, Councillor Doran."

"I've no axe to grind against O'Reilly," Doran said.

O'Reilly noted the omission of his title.

"Why would I have?" His smile at Donal and then at O'Reilly had all the sincerity of a crooked bookie rooking a punter and relishing it. "But I will vote against, and urge my fellow councillors to do the same."

Low mutterings from the audience began.

Sinead Monaghan looked at Wilson Grahame and both of them looked at O'Reilly and shook their heads. He could not determine if what he took for sympathy in their gaze was because they intended to vote for the motion or they were sad because they felt they must vote against.

"I think we can surmise how his lordship, Miss Moloney, and Mister Bishop feel," the chairman said. "But do any of the rest of you have statements to make?"

Heads shook.

O'Reilly tensed.

"Mister Chairman?" Bertie said, rising.

"Yes, Councillor."

"I greatly respect Councillors Monaghan and Doran's respect for the taxpayers' money."

O'Reilly tensed. He felt Kitty take his hand.

"Youse all know that I'm no slouch when it comes til protecting my own do-re-mi."

Universal laughter.

"My record of protecting the taxpayers is clear too." He paused and his gaze swept council. "I agree with most of what Mister Doran said, but I'd like to challenge one wee remark he made. I asked him after the last meeting why he hadn't opposed the decision to give the doctor time to produce the lease, seeing as how he supported the motion that would mean the doctor's house would be acquired and demolished." Bertie glared at Councillor Doran. "Did you or did you not, sir, say," he raised his voice, "'Sure won't a month give the good doctor a bit longer to stew in his own juice'?"

A wave of gasps and "No" ran through the room. Bertie pointed a finger at Doran.

Doran's face was reddening and a vein throbbed at his temple.

"'Sure won't a month give the *good* . . .'" This time the sarcasm was even heavier than in the first telling. "'. . . doctor a bit longer to stew in his own juice?'" Bertie repeated. "And that's from a man with no axe to grind? Rubbish."

"I never said no such thing. Prove it, you great glipe." Doran sneered at Bertie. "You're on his side so you're just making that up."

"Order. Order," the chairman yelled. "Remarks will be addressed through the chair, and language will be parliamentary."

O'Reilly saw the very deep frowns on the faces of the

four councillors who had seemed ready to vote with Doran. Ulsterfolk have a deeply ingrained dislike of liars.

"Mister Chairman," John MacNeill said, "if I may?"

"Please."

"I was present. I overheard that conversation. Mister Bishop is repeating it verbatim. Mister Doran is guilty, in parliamentary language, of a terminological inexactitude."

Winston Churchill, 1906, O'Reilly thought. It took a moment for the members of the audience to realise that John MacNeill was calling Doran a liar. But now the racket of catcalls and stamping feet was deafening. It took several minutes for quiet to return.

Mister Baxter said levelly, "Have you anything to say, Councillor Doran?"

The man hung his head.

O'Reilly stole a look at Mrs. Doran. He saw the slightest suggestion of a smile beginning. This was probably the first time she'd seen anybody stand up to the little gobshite.

"Very well," said Baxter, "I will ask council to take into consideration that Mister Doran's motives in opposing the motion are less pure than he has led us to believe. If no one has anything more to say?" He waited. "Then I call the question on the motion to be indicated by a show of hands, reminding you that as chairman I will not be voting except in the event of a tied vote."

O'Reilly squeezed Kitty's hand, held his breath. He noticed that Barry had both fists tightly clenched.

"Those in favour?"

Up went seven hands.

"Begod, we've done it," O'Reilly said, once he had exhaled.

"Against?"

Councillor Doran did not move.

"The motion is carried by seven votes to one abstention, and the ministry will be so notified tomorrow."

The hall erupted into applause and shouting.

Mrs. Doran rose, came to where O'Reilly was sitting, and said, "It's about time my husband got his comeuppances." She smiled shyly at O'Reilly. "If it's all right with you, sir, would you take me back as a patient?"

"Of course, Hester," O'Reilly said.

"Thank you, sir." She turned and, with shoulders braced, walked away.

I'll be damned, O'Reilly thought. Good for you. Then he leant over and kissed Kitty, and Kinky Auchinleck said just loudly enough for O'Reilly to hear, "I was not concerned, but I will say, I am very pleased for you and Mrs. O'Reilly, sir. Indeed I would go as far as to say, I do be over the moon, so." Still the hall buzzed as excited people exchanged their views with their neighbours.

Mister Baxter banged with his gavel. "Silence. Silence."

The noise gradually subsided.

"As that concludes the business for . . ."

"Excuse me, Mister Chairman," Bertie Bishop said, "but Doctor and Mrs. O'Reilly have been living with a bloody great hole in their house for six weeks. I don't think we should make them wait another four til the next meeting of council. The house is listed Georgian, and the builder, that's me, has til apply for planning permission to council before he can begin reconstruction. Council can give that approval now if it so wishes because the existing structure will not be modified in any way, shape, or form from its original before the accident."

That was music to O'Reilly's ears.

"New curtains," Kitty whispered with a smile.

Bertie continued, "The ministry have never ever turned down a recommendation for road work by this council before. I'm willing til take a chance this time and at least get a start made on the work before they have accepted this one."

Mister Baxter nodded. "It is irregular, but you do have a point. Is any member of council opposed to giving that permission?"

No one moved.

"Mister Doran?" said the chairman.

Doran scowled but held his peace.

"Very well. The necessary papers will be issued tomorrow, Mister Bishop, and I will use my position to expedite a rapid decision by the ministry."

Bertie grinned at O'Reilly and Kitty.

"And now," said the chairman, "I will entertain a motion to adjourn."

O'Reilly paid little attention to the council going through the procedural motions. He was jubilant. Kitty and he would see out their days in good old Number One Main Street, with Kinky happy at her work. "Damn it all," he said, "once the dining room's done . . ." he made a half bow to Kitty, "and you've hung your new curtains, I think we'll have a party to celebrate its reopening, and everyone who worked so hard for us will be invited."

38

Gaudium, What Joy Is in It

"Less than an hour to go until they post the results of Second MB," Jack Mills said, shifting in his chair so he was closer to Helen Hewitt.

"You're going to be fine, Helen. I just know it," Jack said.

"Lord, I hope so," Helen said. She looked into Jack's eyes, and Barry heard a wistfulness in her voice that was soon replaced by something more down-to-earth. "One of the questions on the anatomy paper was a stinker, 'Describe in detail the functions of the rotator cuff of the shoulder during the act of lifting a bucket of water,' and I think I got the wrong results in the physiology practical exam yesterday. I always hate footering about with Douglas bags to collect expired breath for analysis."

"Me too," Barry said. "I was all thumbs." He sipped his pint. Barry hoped Helen passed for her own sake, but he also understood how much Jack was counting on it. In a phone call last week, his friend had confessed again that he was desperately in love with her and couldn't wait for her results to be announced. "I don't know if it's any help, Helen, but when Jack and I were writing exams, our classmates who were sure they'd aced the test often hadn't, and those who were worried stiff that they'd failed, like you are, usually had passed."

Jack nodded. "Often the confident ones hadn't studied enough and couldn't recognise how much they didn't know, and the worriers knew very well the breadth and depth of what they were meant to have learned, and it scared them. But take it from someone who's been there. You sure as hell do know your stuff."

Helen managed a weak smile. "Thanks, boys." She sighed. "But I wish the time would pass." She moved in her upholstered armchair and toyed with a vodka and orange. Her natural beauty was marred by the blue-black bags under her eyes. Her red hair was untidy and lank. "I don't think I've slept much all week." Her laugh was brittle.

They were waiting, as was traditional, in the Club Bar on University Road, a short walk from the Queen's University campus. The Club was favoured by medical students in their preclinical years, and this five-day marathon of written, oral, and practical exams just finished today, Friday, March 10, would decide who among them would remain preclinical students and who would move on to the teaching hospitals.

Most of the students in the predominantly male class were next door in the men-only, spit-and-sawdust public bar. The lounge bar where Barry sat with his friends was carpeted and better furnished with comfortable chairs, individual tables, mirrors behind the shelves of bottles, and a marble-topped bar. The room admitted women and their escorts—and mine host, the silver-haired Mick Agnew, charged a premium for drinks served in the premises, as was the custom in lounge bars all over Ulster. Some of Helen's classmates had brought their girlfriends, and one table was occupied by seven unattached young women, classmates all, Helen had said, awaiting their fates.

Conversation was subdued. Cigarette smoke blued the air. Drinks that on a normal Friday night would have been swallowed greedily were sipped. Barry felt the tension in the air like a viscous substance, making everything duller, slower, heavier.

He overheard one woman at the all-female table saying, "Did you hear what happened to Curly Gurd?"

"No. What? What happened?"

"He was convinced there'd be a physiology question on the red blood cell so he boned up on it."

"How could he know?" said one of the girls, her gaze darting around the room.

"I don't know. But he said he didn't study all that much else because he was so sure."

"There was a question about the blood system all right, but it was 'Discuss the function of the arteries.'"

"So what did Curly do?"

"He wrote, 'A function of the arteries is to carry red blood cells and their functions are . . .' and he described them in great detail."

"Poor man. He'll have ploughed." There was sympathy in the brunette's voice, but tinged with a touch of the "rather him than me."

Barry caught Helen's eye and she smiled wanly. "You heard that," he whispered.

She nodded. "Curly's an eejit. There are no shortcuts."

A man at the next table remarked, "Poor old Barney Walsh. Daft bugger took amphetamine so he could stay up all night and cram, sat down to the first paper, wrote his name at the top, and then spent the three hours writing it over and over again. He didn't show up for any more. He'll be repeating a year."

Barry, seven years removed from the ordeal, could still shudder at the thought of what a time of stress the examinations had been.

"This waiting's killing me," Helen said. "Can we please go over to the cloisters now?"

"It's only twenty to six," Jack said, "but a bit of fresh air won't hurt, and we'll walk slowly." He finished his pint, rose, and pulled Helen's chair out so she could stand.

Barry downed the rest of his pint and followed. He noticed that Helen's vodka was only half drunk.

The sun would set in about forty minutes and the light was fading. Streetlamps cast long shadows, and across the road the lights in the window of The University Café, better known as Smokey Joe's, threw their brightness across the road where red double-decker corporation buses vied with motorcars and bicycles.

Barry was pleased to see Helen reach out for and take his friend's hand.

They passed rows of three-storey brick and stucco terrace houses, then crossed University Square. To their right was the Georgian façade of Queen's Elms, the men's halls of residence where Barry and Jack had lived when they in their time had studied for and passed the exam Helen had just taken.

To their left, behind cast-iron railings, stood the main building of the old university designed by Sir Charles Lanyon and opened in 1849. Queen's University Belfast had been one of three Queen's colleges, the others in

Cork and Galway, established to give higher education in Ireland to Catholics and Presbyterians. Previously, the privilege of advanced learning had been available only to Anglicans at Trinity College, Dublin.

Barry, as ever, admired the Tudor-Gothic main building. He was proud of his alma mater, so proud that a numbered print of a painting of it hung in his quarters at Number One. He followed Jack and Helen through the gates to the courtyard in front of the building, its rosy brick and cream-coloured sandstone glowing in the dying day, electric lights burning behind high arched windows in the front of the building. They passed the war memorial, a bronze winged Victory supporting a stricken youth, and on to the passage through the high arched front double doors beneath the central square tower. Thin tapering spires topped each of its corners and from a flagpole on the roof the Union Flag drooped limply.

In twos and threes, students and their supporters were drifting through the great marble-floored atrium toward a door at the back that led to the cloisters surrounding the quadrangle. Many of the medical students could be recognised by their six-foot-long red, yellow, white, and black British Medical Students' Association scarves.

"Through here," Barry said, holding the door for Jack and Helen.

A crowd had formed, encircling a glass-fronted notice board on the cloisters' back wall. Farther along, light spilled from mullioned windows.

Jack said, "The examiners are having their meeting in there."

Helen drew in a very deep breath.

"Sometimes a very good mark in one subject," said Jack, "can compensate for a poor mark in another and the student be given an overall pass."

"So even if you didn't do too well in anatomy, Helen, you could still have compensated," Barry said.

She gave him a weak smile of thanks.

Barry looked round. He didn't know any of the students except Helen. A tall man with a fair moustache and wire-rimmed National Health Service granny glasses peered through the glass of the notice board and yelled, "Nothing yet."

Disappointed murmurs ran through the crowd.

Barry usually thought of himself as a stable person, but like everyone else he hated waiting for results. Medical tests for a patient, deliberations of a jury, exam results. It was part of life, he supposed, but they had to be some of the most painful experiences to live through. That struggle of trying to close your mind to the possibility of a dreadful outcome, yet being rational enough to try to make plans if such were the result. The need to present a carefree façade to the outside world. The unspoken preparations for breaking unwelcome news to loved ones. He nodded. You went through all of that and if the result was the one hoped for, the relief and joy were overwhelming.

Jack put his arm round Helen's shoulder. "Won't be long now, and you're going to be fine. I just know it."

Barry heard the confidence and the hope in his friend's voice.

The crowd was shifting, drifting back. Students and their supporters were nudging each other, pointing. "Look," a loud voice said. "He's here."

"Give the fellow room. Let the dog see the rabbit."

A middle-aged man in the livery of a hall porter had

appeared through a door beside the lighted windows. His boots rang on the cloisters' flagstone floor. He lifted a key on a chain attached to his belt, unlocked the glass-fronted case, pinned a long sheet of paper to the corkboard, closed the glass, and locked the case.

"Ladies and gentlemen," he announced to reverent silence, "the results of the second professional examination for the degrees of bachelor of medicine, bachelor of chirurgerie, and bachelor of the art of obstetrics in this year of 1967 have now been posted. Good luck." He withdrew.

The crowd surged forward. "Look after Helen, Barry." And as if piling into a rugby maul, Jack forced his way forward through a milling crowd. Already there were yells of, "Begod, I passed."

"Me too."

"Oh shite."

The young woman who'd been telling the story of Curly Gurd stood laughing while tears ran down her cheeks.

Barry felt Helen tense beside him, saw her screw her eyes tightly closed. Jack was forcing his way back and he was grinning from ear to ear. He stood in front of Helen and said, "Congratulations, Helen . . ."

Barry could sense that she was shaking. Saw her green eyes open wide.

"Not only have you passed in every subject . . . you took first prize in physiology. So much for your worrying about the Douglas bag. Oh you beauty, Helen Hewitt. You did ace it. Well done."

She gasped, grinned, and said very quietly, "Thank you, Jack. Thank you very much. And thank you for being patient while I studied."

Jack shrugged. Smiled.

Barry said, "Well done, Helen. And a prize too. My God, that is grand. Congratulations."

She blew out her breath through pursed lips. "Oh Lord," she said, "I'm all atremble."

"Come on," said Jack, taking her hand. "You need to see this for yourself." He led her up to the front of the now-thinning crowd, and Barry watched as Jack pointed to the middle of the list where she would be able to read her results. She flung her arms round Jack's neck and, careless of the bystanders, kissed him long and hard. Hand in hand they moved back to where Barry waited.

"It's true," Helen said, "I really did pass." She grinned, looked up at Jack and back to Barry. "And," she said, "I know how close you two are, but I don't know if Jack told you, Barry, but I've been keeping him waiting for months and I've a promise to keep and I want you to hear too." She turned to Jack and said, "Jack Mills, you lovely, understanding, patient man, I was heartbroken when you dumped me—"

"I'm sorry, Helen. I was—"

She held up a hand and shook her head. "But, but, I took a second chance and I'm very glad I did. I love you, Jack Mills, and I always will."

Jack's whoop echoed through the cloisters and he grabbed her, swung her round in a circle with her feet off the ground, and kissed her soundly.

Barry's heart filled for his friend.

"Now," said Helen, taking Jack's and Barry's hands, "there are phone boxes in the students' union. I want to phone Dad and Doctor O'Reilly. Your boss, Barry, helped get me my scholarship from the marquis. And I'll write a thank-you letter to the marquis, lovely man that he is, tomorrow. But once I've made my calls tonight, there's a party and I want us all to go and celebrate."

"Now there," said Jack Mills, "is one hell of an idea." And his laughter, like his whoop, filled the quadrangle with peals of unfettered joy.

39

Come Live with Me and Be My Love

Movement in the grass caught Barry's attention. Two hares were standing on their hind legs, long ears laid back, boxing furiously until one leaped into the air then dropped to all fours and took off bounding like a frenzied liltie. For a moment, Barry had forgotten where he was—that the animals were two of the famous Aldergrove hares that, for reasons no naturalist could explain, had made the runways their home. He stood behind the plate-glass window of Aldergrove airport staring out to the tarmac to see if he could catch another glimpse of the long-legged, rangy creatures, dozens of which roamed the area. Sue's flight from London was due in ten minutes. Ten interminable minutes, it seemed, and he had welcomed the comic distraction. For the last week he had thought today might never come, but it had. It had, and soon he'd be holding his love in his arms. She'd be back home here in Ulster with him where she belonged. Where from the first time he'd told her he loved her, she'd always belonged.

He caught another flash of long ears poking above the grass. Mad March male hares, Barry thought. Their mating season was now, late March, and for reasons that did not surprise him he thought back to his night with Sue in Marseille and lamented how their holiday had been cut short. How long might it be before he could get Sue to himself in a private place?

He tried to distract himself by examining the British United Airways jet aircraft parked near the terminal building. BUA had started Belfast's first jet service in January 1966. The plane was different from any other Barry had ever seen, with a streamlined nose and its two engines mounted at the rear of the fuselage. Perhaps, he thought, with his appetite for foreign travel whetted by his short trip to France, he could whisk Sue off to somewhere exotic for their honeymoon in July.

He was aware of the high-pitched whine of aero engines and a brassy announcer's voice on a loudspeaker so distorted he missed pretty much everything except the critical, ". . . arriving at Aldergrove from Heathrow . . ." That was Sue's plane coming in to land. He shifted from foot to foot.

The twin-engined propellor-driven British European Airways aircraft touched down, taxied, and turned off the runway to come to a halt outside the terminal. The propellors changed from spinning discs reflecting the sunshine to slowly turning individual blades and then stopped. Ground crew ran a wheeled staircase to the front of the craft, where a door in the fuselage opened and a stewardess, neat in her Hardy Amies uniform of blue jacket and skirt, blue hat, and white gloves, stood smiling on the staircase's upper platform. Passengers started to disembark.

He waited to catch his first glimpse and, oh joy, there she was pausing at the top, with one hand shielding her eyes from the sun that made her copper hair glow. She trotted nimbly down and joined the crocodile of passengers moving toward the entrance to the building.

Barry ran to the door. Already the entrance, a single glass door, was becoming clogged with people so impatient to meet loved ones that as soon as they came through the doorway there was hugging and excited talking. The little family groups forming held up later arrivals and kept them waiting on the tarmac. "Excuse me, excuse me." Barry was not shy about forcing his way past. The second she appeared, he grabbed her hand, dragged her aside, and hugged and kissed her as if he'd never have another chance. "Welcome home, darling. God, I've missed you," Barry said, hoping that at last his pulse rate would start to slow. He released her, holding her at arm's length. She was glowing. "I love you."

"Oh, Barry, I love you too, and it's lovely, lovely to be home. I've missed you so. I'm home for good now. No more exchange teaching for me." It was her turn to kiss him before saying, "Now let's get my bags and head on down to Broughshane. I'm dying to see Mum and Dad too."

"I must say, Barry," said Selbert Nolan, "your colleagues and the nurses in the Waveney were all powerful nice to me, but I'm very glad they let me out two weeks ago. My Irene's cooking beats the hospital kitchen's by miles. That lunch really hit the spot. Them brown trout came straight out of the Braid. The season opened last month and your man Fred Alexander's a dab hand with a fly rod. And never you worry, son. Any time you want onto my water, just ask."

"Thank you, Selbert," Barry said. "I'll take you up on that one day soon."

Selbert Nolan laughed. "Fishing's one way to get outside, and right now for me it's great til be in the fresh air after being cooped up in thon hospital."

Barry and he sat on a bench at the side of a field that had been set up as a practice arena for training horses to compete in shows. Several jumps with red-and-white-striped cross bars were arranged in a circle where they alternated with fencing hurdles made of woven withies.

Sue, wearing a black hard hat, green cotton shirt, jeans, and riding boots, sat astride Róisín, her Irish Sport Horse. For the last half hour, while Barry had chatted with his father-in-law-to-be, he had been torn between trying to listen to words, not hooves on grassy ground, and keeping an eye on Sue. As he watched with his heart in his mouth, she and Róisín had soared over the jumps.

"Thon wee girl of mine sits a horse very well," Selbert said. "I started teaching her when she was six. She won a fair wheen of jumping trophies when she got older. I think she misses it, but I know her job takes up a lot of time."

"It's only a forty-minute run from the bungalow we hope to buy to Broughshane," Barry said. "She can come out any time she likes if she needs to ride."

"I'm pleased to hear that," said Selbert, rising. "Thanks for bringing her from the airport, Barry."

"My pleasure," Barry said, "and I'm sorry I'm going to have to take her away tomorrow, but Doctor and Mrs. O'Reilly are having a party to celebrate the rebuilding of their dining room."

"You two go on and have fun, hey. I know she'll be down to see us again soon."

"She will."

"Good. Now you and Sue enjoy the rest of the afternoon. I'm away off home for my nap. We'll see you at teatime." And with that, he began his walk back to the farmhouse, leaning on a blackthorn stick. Barry studied his soon-to-be father-in-law. The man was taking measured paces. They weren't the long, businesslike strides Barry remembered from when he and Selbert had taken walks together before the man's heart attack, but nor were they an old man's shuffle. Barry reckoned Selbert was making a good steady recovery.

He turned back to watch Sue. At last. Apart from the drive down in the car when in the midst of all their catching up he'd taken the opportunity to park for a moment on a side road so he could kiss her properly, Barry'd not really been alone with Sue since she'd arrived. Tactful of her dad to take himself off.

Barry rose as Sue walked Róisín over to him. She dismounted and, holding the reins in one hand, kissed Barry. He was excited by the taste of her, but her faint perfume was overpowered by the strong smell of horse sweat. Róisín tossed her head and whinnied.

"Come on," said Sue, "let's take a walk down to the bluebell wood. The flowers don't come out for another month or so and it's very beautiful then . . ."

"You are very beautiful now," Barry said, kissed her, and took her hand. "Come on, show me the way."

They left the paddock and wandered beneath a cloudless sky along a dry earth lane. Grass grew along its middle and the blue flowers of speedwell trailed from gaps in a dry stone wall on one side. Two small tortoiseshell butterflies, their red wings edged by black spots at their fronts and blue spots round the sides, sunned themselves on one of the wall's upper stones. A little grey rabbit—soft and round and toylike, very different from the athletic hares he'd seen boxing earlier—hopped along ahead. The blackthorn hedge on the other side of the lane was leafless but covered in masses of white, star-shaped flowers and the warm air was heavy with their delicate scent. A small flock of birds perched in the hedge, each about six inches from beak to tail, with bright yellow heads, darkly streaked backs, and yellow underparts. One sang "A little bit of bread and no cheese," increasing the volume and length of the last two notes.

"Yellowhammers," Sue said. "Pretty wee things."

Barry was quite content simply to hold her hand and walk beside her in silence. They turned off the lane and onto a path through a wood where buds were ripening on broad leafless beech trees. The ground was springy underneath.

"You go ahead," Sue said. "There's not room for us and Róisín side by side."

Barry led and Sue, with her horse walking behind her, followed until they came to a grassy clearing surrounded and screened by the trees.

Sue moved beside Barry. "You should see this place when the flowers are out," Sue said. "Acres of the brightest blue."

"Let's come down and see it next month," Barry said, feeling the nearness of her.

"Yes. Let's." Sue stopped and loosely wrapped Róisín's reins round a low branch.

At once the horse began cropping the grass, making tearing noises as she pulled bunches free.

Sue turned to Barry and looked into his eyes.

He was speechless, drinking in the loveliness of her: copper hair, sparkling green eyes, soft lips with a hint of coral pink lipstick smiling over even white teeth. Lips opening for a tender kiss that became more urgent by the moment.

He held her to him, gently at first, his hands on her back feeling the muscle beneath her shirt, then more tightly, his chest against the soft firmness of her.

Together they sank to the grass and he felt its softness a springy cushion where the white-starred flowers of wood anemones and wild garlic gave their scents in counterpoint to Sue's light perfume.

He took off his sports jacket and made a pillow for her head and lay beside her, propped on one elbow, marvelling at the radiance of the woman he loved.

He stroked the side of her face and said, "Sue Nolan. I love you. I have loved you from the evening I saw you at the school Christmas pageant, although I didn't recognise it then. I knew it the day you nearly drowned . . ."

"And you rescued me," she said.

"Because I couldn't bear the thought of a world without you. I loved you then, I love you now, and I will love you forever."

"Thank you, darling Barry," she said with longing in her voice. "And I love you, from the bottom of my soul." She crooked one arm around his neck and pulled his lips onto hers.

And Barry Laverty made love with Sue Nolan on a bed of grass under a blue sky etched with a tracery of bare branches as an unconcerned horse ignored them and dined at her leisure.

40

Our Revels Now Are Ended

Barry finished knotting his black Old Campbellian tie with its narrow green-and-white diagonal stripes and boar's head motif, turned down the collar of his white shirt, and put on his blue blazer. "Will I do?" he asked.

Sue, looking lovely in red heels, taupe tights, a red tartan pleated mini, and cream angora sweater, was perched on a chair in Barry's quarters at Number One Main Street, thumbing through a book. The light from the window sparkled from her engagement ring as her fingers moved.

She cocked her head, scrutinised him, and said, "Very nicely, sir. I think I'll keep you."

"Eejit," said Barry with a grin. He turned and noticed what she was reading. "Interesting?" She had been flicking through a tome entitled *The Masting and Rigging of English Ships of War. 1625–1860* by James Lees. It had been Ronald Fitzpatrick's gift to Barry last month, along with *Morning Flight* and *Wild Chorus* by the naturalist Peter Scott, beautifully illustrated with the author's own oils of wildfowl for Fingal and the 1966 *Impressionism and Post Impressionism, 1874–1904* for

Kitty. The books for Nonie and Jenny Bradley had been chosen with equal care.

"Not really," she said. "Not my cuppa, fore t'gallants, buntlines, and mizzen backstays, but I know how much you enjoy your modelling. You made a fantastic job of your *Rattlesnake*. I'm proud of you."

The finished model sat in all its three-masted glory inside a perspex display case crafted by Donal Donnelly.

He crossed to her, took her hand, and gave her a chaste kiss. "Thank you. My next project's going to be HMS *Victory,* Lord Nelson's flagship at the Battle of Trafalgar in 1805."

"No," she said, "your next project's taking me to the party. Come on." She opened the door to the kitchen, where Kinky and Archie were putting the finishing touches to the nibblers for the evening's affair. "Can we help you with anything, Kinky?" Sue asked.

Kinky whipped off her apron and smiled. "Thank you, Miss Susan. If you'd be good enough to carry through that plate of cocktail sausages, and you, sir, those stuffed mushroom caps, I'd be grateful. Archie and I'll see to the rest when we come through." She heaved a sigh of deep contentment. "It does be a great relief that old Number One is as good as new and won't be pulled down."

"And right and proper," Barry said, "that you and Archie are coming to the party as guests."

"Well," said Kinky, "we'd have been pleased to serve, but everything's ready, folks can help themselves, and Donal's going to be barman, so there's not much for us to do. And it is an honour to be invited, so."

"After thirty . . . how many?" Barry said.

"Thirty-nine years since I first came here to look after old Doctor Flanagan. It was 1928 and me only nineteen," Kinky said.

"After that long it's no more than your due, Kinky Auchinleck. You're family." Barry lifted the plate. "See you soon," he said, and with Sue by his side, headed for the hall.

The door to the surgery was shut and the surprise for Kitty that Barry, at O'Reilly's request, had bought today was hidden in there. On his boss's signal, it would be presented to Kitty.

The dining room door was open and the smell of fresh paint not yet gone. As he'd promised, Bertie Bishop's construction crew had started work the day after the council meeting. It hadn't been much of a gamble. The Ministry of Transport had ratified the council's recommendation within three days. For ten days, the house had rung to the sounds of hammering and sawing and smelled of wet cement, wood shavings, sawdust, fresh paint, and turpentine.

Barry let Sue precede him.

"How's about youse both?" Carroty-haired Donal stood beside a sideboard laden with drinks and glasses. He wore green elastic garters to hold his shirt cuffs up and a white tied-at-the-waist apron. "What'll youse have?"

"Sue?"

She shook her head. "I think later, Donal, thanks."

"Me too. How are you, and how're Julie and Tori?" Barry did a quick calculation. Julie'd be twenty-five weeks now.

"I'm grand and Julie's blooming, so she is. Tori's growing like a dandelion in springtime and she's impatient til meet her baby brother."

Barry refrained from suggesting that Julie might be carrying another girl. "Gotta put these down, Donal." He moved to where the old bog oak table held pride of place in the centre surrounded by six chairs and set down his plate beside Sue's. "Kitty found a near match in a Belfast antique shop for the chair that got smashed by the lorry."

"Quite the spread," she said, cocking her head and surveying the array of dishes.

"Any time you ask Kinky to cater," O'Reilly's words preceded him through the door, "you'd think she'd started with five loaves and two small fishes and ended up with enough to feed five thousand." He wore the trousers and jacket of his tweed suit, but was tieless.

"I'll not bore you with chapter and verse," Barry said, still enjoying their duelling quotations game, "but the story is the only miracle to be reported in all four gospels."

"But Matthew and Mark also reported the feeding of four thousand," O'Reilly said, with a look on his face which said, "Game, set, and match."

Barry laughed and shook his head.

"Evening, Doctor," Donal said. "The usual for yourself and Mrs. O'Reilly?"

"Please," O'Reilly said. "And your hands are empty, you two."

"A glass of white, please." Sue turned to Kitty and said, "Where did you get that dress? It's quite stunning."

Barry had to agree. The jade-green silk set off Kitty's eyes and silver-tipped black hair to perfection. While the women chatted on about fashion, Barry put in his order for a small Jameson. "I'll go," he said when the front doorbell rang.

"Come in," Barry said, greeting the Bishops, the first

guests to arrive. "Good to see you both." Neither wore coats, but Flo sported a white conical hat like those once worn by Chinese coolies, tied under her chin with a diaphanous white scarf. The evening was mild as April approached. The sun had just sunk beneath the distant blue Antrim Hills, leaving a soft glow of early twilight to limn the steeple of the Presbyterian church across the road against the satin evening sky.

"Grand evening for the time of year it's in, Doctor," Bertie said, ushering Flo into the hall.

She took off her hat with some ceremony and handed it to Barry, who carefully hung it on the hatstand. He wondered if the creation was one of Alice Moloney's and then saw the woman herself walking toward him from the direction of her flat over the shop and saw Doctor Fitzpatrick's angular shape coming the other way. He was wearing his protective collar. "Go on into the dining room," Barry said to the Bishops. "I'll welcome some other guests."

Barry heard the greeting noises, glass clinking on glass behind him, as Ronald Fitzpatrick doffed his trilby and bowed to let Alice go before him through the front door.

"Good evening to you both," Barry said. "May I introduce you to Doctor Fitzpatrick, Miss Moloney?"

Alice smiled and said, "Pleased to meet you, Doctor."

Fitzpatrick nodded, stooping his tall frame into a small awkward bow. "It is my pleasure."

Barry pointed to the dining room. "Please go through," he said. He'd seen Lars's motorcar turn into the lane and knew he and Myrna would let themselves in through the kitchen. The only invitees missing were Lord John MacNeill, who had had to attend an emergency meeting in Belfast for one of his many charities, and Nonie, who with graciousness had offered to take call tonight and was out on a maternity case. Her medication was still doing its job.

Barry went into the now-crowded dining room to pick up his drink. Donal was serving O'Reilly his second. "Wee Colin Brown was out the other day with Murphy til visit Bluebird," he overheard Donal saying. "'I'm going til Bangor Grammar School in September,' says he til me. And says I til him, 'You work hard like a good man. You was quare and smart getting your Eleven Plus, so you were. It's no time now to be resting on your sorrels." He nodded at his own sagacity.

O'Reilly was turning puce trying not to laugh.

"My whiskey, please, Donal," Barry said.

"Here y'are, Doctor Laverty, sir." Donal handed over the glass.

Barry glanced around and then said softly, "I was sitting beside Doctor O'Reilly at the meeting on Monday and I nearly died when you yelled out what you did. Then I thought I saw Bertie Bishop grin in your direction. Just between you and me and the wall, did Bertie put you up to it?"

Donal sucked in his cheeks and cocked his head. "Mister Bishop did have a wee word before the meeting," he said, sotto voce. "Says he til me, 'Donal, I need a hand for til get at your man Doran the night. You and me's going til get the vote in Doctor O'Reilly's favour.' 'Aye?' says I. 'I love a good caper, so I do. You know that, sir, and I'd do anything for Doctor O'Reilly after all he's done for me and mine. Ask away, sir.' Says Mister Bishop, 'After Doran's had his say, and he'll be supporting demolition of Number One, you yell out you want til know why he's picking on our Doctor O'Reilly. That's all. He'll rise til the fly and swear he's not, and

An Irish Country Love Story   433

then I've something he said that'll half scupper him. He'll have til deny it.' I said to Mister Bishop, 'It'll be your word against his then. No harm til you, sir, but I don't see how that'll help much.' Mister Bishop laughed. Says he, 'Will the council doubt his lordship's word too?' 'Bejizzis,' says I. 'You're setting up the ould one-two punch, aren't you?' I reckoned they must have had something cooked up between them. Anyroad, a wink's as good as a nod til a blind alley. 'I'm your man,' says I, and between the three of us, we put Doran back in his box, so we did."

Barry chuckled. "And nailed the lid shut. Thanks for telling me, Donal. It'll go no farther." It wouldn't be Ballybucklebo if Donal Donnelly wasn't wrapped up in some scheme or other. Barry turned and surveyed the big room. Kitty and Sue were in conversation with Bertie and Flo in the recess of the bow window. New curtains were bunched with ties at their middles to tethers on the walls.

Ronald Fitzpatrick, with a glass of Bass ale, and Alice Moloney, holding a Cantrell and Cochrane brown lemonade, stood deep in conversation nearby. He seemed to be hanging on her every word. "And you actually met Mahatma Gandhi? In person? How positively intriguing. You must tell me all about it. I'm fascinated by the Orient. I grew up in China."

"Hello, Barry," Lars said. "Dry sherry and a whiskey water please, Donal."

"Lars. Myrna." Barry's eyes widened. Myrna, whom he had always taken for a bit of a blue stocking, had had her hair done: short, curling under her chin with a parting on the left and a fringe diagonally across her forehead. She wore a lilac pantsuit with a hint of cleavage between wide lapels and slim trousers over flat heels.

Elegant yet sexy. Lars, Barry noticed, was hovering protectively over her and smiling frequently.

"Barry," Myrna said, accepting her sherry from Lars, "have you got a minute?"

"Of course."

More laughter from the bay window, where Kitty and the Bishops were all on their second drink. Fitzpatrick too, was laughing his dried-leaves chuckle. He snatched off his pince-nez.

"Lars has had an idea. You know he has a place in Villefranche?"

"Yes."

"He was wondering . . . Hello, Sue."

Sue had appeared at Barry's side.

"Don't let me interrupt," she said.

Lars picked up where Myrna had left off. "We know you two are getting married in July. Have you plans for a honeymoon?"

Sue shook her head.

"How would you like to have my place in Villefranche for a couple of weeks?"

Barry could see himself yesterday staring at a jet and thinking about whisking Sue off in one. "Sue?"

"It would be wonderful," she frowned, "but, well, we are hoping to buy a house in April . . ."

"Broughshane's very near Ballymena, where the natives are renowned for their frugality," Barry said, taking Sue's hand between both of his.

"Heavens. I wouldn't charge you," Lars said with a laugh. "It would be our wedding gift to you."

"Our wedding gift." A few days ago Fingal had mentioned to Barry how pleased he was that Lars was becoming so attached to Myrna. That "our" sounded like a deep mutual attachment indeed. "Having your place would be wonderful, Lars," Barry said. "Thank you. I'll have to talk to you about the actual arrangements, but—"

O'Reilly had moved to the head of the table and was banging a spoon on a glass.

At the same time Nonie appeared and whispered to Barry, "Normal confinement. Baby boy. Mother and child are doing well. Am I on time?"

"Right on time. Fingal's about to speak."

"Right," said O'Reilly. "I'm not one for speechifying, and as everyone here knows, Number One has been under threat of demolition for eight weeks. But thanks to the hard work of a few, and the solidarity of the many, Kitty and I will be able to stay on here in the home we love with Kinky looking after us as she has always looked after me. Doctor Barry Laverty can have his quarters until he moves out to marry his beautiful schoolmistress Sue Nolan, and the latest addition to the O'Reilly family, Doctor Nonie Stevenson, who I am very happy to say is better now, will be fed and lodged here on her on-call nights." He took a pull on his second whiskey as Bertie and Flo clapped.

"I've only a wee bit more to say, so hold your applause til I've done, but it's us should be applauding Flo Bishop and Alice Moloney, who got the petition going. And cheering the thousands who signed, and Lord John MacNeill, Councillors Moloney, Bishop, Hare, Monaghan, Warnock, and Grahame, who voted in favour. Thank you. Thank you all."

Everyone was clapping mightily now, and Barry looked around this now-familiar room, as familiar and as treasured as his own parents' dining room, and the site of so many of Kinky's wonderful meals. I hope, he thought, reaching for Sue's hand again, that when I've been here as long as you, Fingal Flahertie O'Reilly, I have the love and respect of the whole village too.

Bertie Bishop said, "Doctor, sorry til interrupt, but can I ask a question?"

"Fire away."

"Would you consider running for council? There might be a vacancy." Bertie grinned. "I heard tell Hubert Doran could resign."

"You what?"

"Aye, he's 'having second thoughts about his civic duty,' according to my sources. If anybody's been stewing in his own juice for the last couple of weeks, it's that gob—"

"Bertie, remember your blood pressure," said Flo.

"Thinking of resigning. I'll be damned," said O'Reilly. "Thank you, Bertie, for the offer. But you'll have to look elsewhere if you need a successor. I'm no politician. Now, I've still some people to thank. Donal, thank you for running the bar. Have one yourself."

"Thank you, sir." Donal poured himself a half-un.

"And thank you, Kinky and Archie, for all the fine grub."

Kinky smiled.

"A couple of last things," O'Reilly said. "Kitty and I have agreed to disagree about new curtains, but," he walked over to the window, "if, Bertie, you and Flo, will move out of the bay?"

"Right you are, Doctor. Come on, Flo. Shift your chassis, woman."

O'Reilly motioned Kitty to stay, bent and, with a flourish, undid the curtains' lashings, the signal for Barry to carry out his task. As he left, he heard, "Will you do the honours, Mrs. O'Reilly?" and two perfect teal-blue velvet curtains swished into place to another round of applause.

Barry hastened back with his burden only partially hidden behind his back and slipped it to O'Reilly as the curtains were reopened to let the stars smile down through the window onto the celebrants.

"Finally," said O'Reilly, "unbeknownst to any of you, for some time in this household my dear wife and I have been having our own minor war of the roses. Kitty had her way in the waiting room and has changed the wallpaper, all but for Donal's magnificent rose mural—"

Loud laughter.

"And tonight, to help her celebrate her curtain victory, I have a gift that comes with all my love." He solemnly presented her with a large vase containing two dozen red roses.

"Oh, Fingal, they're exquisite. Thank you." Kitty accepted her gift and sniffed the flowers' perfume.

"Let me set it on the sideboard," O'Reilly said. He did, turning the vase through 180 degrees to reveal, painted in bright colours against the jade enamel, one massive tea rose. "And," he said, "when the last rose of summer has faded, the vase will stay."

Barry Laverty, *Doctor* Barry Laverty, looked from O'Reilly to Kitty, their love for each other so clear. It was a love that had lasted long after the last rose of summer had faded. And this house, this village, these friends helped sustain that love. I'll never leave here, Barry suddenly vowed. I love you dearly, Sue Nolan, I love Number One Main Street, I love Ballybucklebo, I love Ulster, and, damn it all, I love you, you great untidy, crusty bear of a man with a heart of corn, Fingal Flahertie, the Wily O'Reilly.

AFTERWORD

by Mrs. Maureen Auchinleck

Here I am again, sitting at home with Archie. He's reading the *Belfast Telegraph* and I'm sat at my kitchen table, pen in fist, writing out more recipes for your man Patrick Taylor to put at the end of another yarn about the doings of the folks of Ballybucklebo. I've six for you this time: mussel and seafood chowder, pork in mustard sauce, beef Wellington, ginger biscuits, buttermilk scones, and hard fudge.

And, bye, I've some exciting news. With a bit of help from Doctor Laverty, Patrick Taylor, and Dorothy Tinman, I'm getting my very own *Irish Country Cookbook* published next February. Do keep an eye out for it, so.

And here are this book's recipes.

• MUSSEL AND SEAFOOD CHOWDER

450 g / 1 lb. shellfish such as mussels, scallops, and
    shrimp
225 mL / 8 oz. dry white wine
700 g / 1½ lbs. white fish such as cod, haddock, or
    snapper
425 mL / 15 oz. milk
1 teaspoon fresh thyme leaves
1 bay leaf
113 g / 4 oz. smoked streaky bacon

1 tablespoon olive or sunflower oil
28 g / 1 oz. butter
1 leek
1 shallot
1 small carrot
700 g / 1½ lbs. potatoes, peeled and finely diced
112 mL / 4 oz. cream
1 tablespoon fish sauce (optional)
A handful of chopped parsley

First, clean the mussels and, using a sharp knife, remove the beard. That's the little tufty bit on the shell. Bring the wine to a boil in a saucepan, add the mussels, cover with a lid, and cook for about 4 minutes. Discard any that did not open and remove most of the rest from their shells, leaving just a few for decoration. Set aside the cooking liquid.

Simmer the white fish in the milk with the thyme and bay leaf for just a few minutes until cooked but still firm. Remove the fish and set to one side. Discard the bay leaf and season the cooking liquid well with salt and freshly ground black pepper.

Now chop the bacon and sauté in the oil and butter for about 1 minute till crisp. Add the finely sliced leek, shallot, carrot, and diced potatoes. Cover and cook gently for a few minutes, without browning. Add the cooking liquid from the mussels and the white fish and simmer all together until the potatoes are soft and breaking up. Then add the scallops and shrimp. They will only need a very little time to cook so watch that you do not overcook them or they will be rubbery.

Now add the fish and the cooked mussels together with the cream and fish sauce. Season to taste and add chopped parsley. If the chowder is too thick just add some more milk or water, and adjust the seasoning if necessary.

Serve with my wheaten bread and butter and this will be a substantial meal on its own.

• PORK IN MUSTARD SAUCE

700 g / 1½ lbs. apples, peeled and thinly sliced
4 slices of pork loin or pork chops trimmed of fat
15 g / ½ oz. butter
60 mL / 2 oz. dry white wine
75 mL / 5 tablespoons Dijon mustard
227 mL / 8 oz. thick cream
salt and pepper

Set the oven to 400°F, 200°C, or gas mark 6. Butter a casserole dish big enough to spread the pork slices side by side. Cover the base with the thinly sliced apples and bake for 15 minutes in the oven.

While the apples are cooking, place the salted chops with the remaining butter in a pan over a medium heat and cook until they are nicely browned on each side. This should take about 15 minutes.

Now remove the apples from the oven and place the pork on top of the apples in the casserole dish. Place the pan back on the heat, add the wine, and deglaze the pan until the wine has reduced by half. Pour this over the pork in the casserole.

In a bowl, mix the mustard into the cream, tasting as you go, add some salt and pepper, and pour the mixture over the pork. Return the dish to the oven and bake for a further 25 minutes or so.

This is delicious served with champ and just about any other vegetable that you like.

• BEEF WELLINGTON

1 kg / 2 lbs. 4 oz. fillet of beef, trimmed
Small bunch of thyme leaves
Sea salt and freshly ground black pepper
1 tablespoon olive oil
2 tablespoons strong English mustard or prepared
   horseradish
500 g / 1 packet frozen puff pastry
1 egg (to glaze)

Duxelles
Splash of truffle oil
3 shallots, finely chopped
1 clove of garlic
450 g / 1 lb. Crimini/chestnut mushrooms
1 tablespoon finely chopped parsley

First make the duxelles. This is the layer between the beef and the pastry.

To a little truffle (or olive) oil in a medium-hot pan add the chopped shallots and the crushed garlic, then add the mushrooms and cook until all the moisture from the mushrooms has evaporated. Now add the chopped parsley.

Now dry the fillet of beef with kitchen paper and sprinkle on plenty of salt, the thyme leaves, and freshly ground black pepper. In a frying pan heat a tablespoon of olive oil and, keeping the pan at a hot temperature, sear the beef on all sides and each end. Now spread either the mustard or horseradish over the entire fillet and leave to rest, wrapped in clingfilm, to chill in a refrigerator. This may be done up to 24 hours ahead.

When you are ready to cook the beef, set the oven to 220°C / 450°F.

Roll out the puff pastry to a size that will completely wrap around the beef, plus an extra inch or two for sealing. Spread the duxelles over the pastry. Lay the beef on top, then fold the pastry round it and moisten and seal the pastry edges. Brush the pastry with the beaten egg and decorate with a sharp knife to make a crisscross pattern. Sprinkle the pastry with some coarse sea salt to help it to crispen.

Now bake for about 30 to 35 minutes, then remove from the oven and allow to rest for 10 to 12 minutes. Then, with a really sharp knife, cut into slices and serve.

Kinky's Note:
When I made this for the marquis I added another step to the recipe, but it really makes the dish much richer and is probably more suited to a very grand occasion, so.

What you need is a portion of pâté de foie gras, a tablespoon of brandy, and some very thin cooked pancakes or crêpes. Then you put a layer of pâté, softened with the brandy, onto the pancakes and place this, pâté side up, between the pastry and the duxelles.

• GINGER BISCUITS

85 g. / 3 oz. plain flour
½ teaspoon bicarbonate of soda
1 teaspoon ground ginger
60 g / 2½ oz. sugar

85 g / 3 oz. rolled oats
Ginger root, about 2 inches, peeled and chopped or
   grated finely
100 g / 4 oz. butter
1 tablespoon syrup (golden or maple)
1 tablespoon milk

Preheat the oven to 150°C / 300°F. Line 2 large baking tins with baking parchment. Put all the dry ingredients and the fresh ginger into a large bowl and mix together. Melt butter, syrup, and milk in a saucepan over a low heat and mix into the dry ingredients. Pop it into the fridge for about 5 minutes until it has firmed up and cooled.

Now put heaped teaspoons on the baking sheets, very well spaced apart, as they spread while cooking. Flatten the top of each biscuit with the back of a spoon and bake until lightly browned.

This can take between 10 and 20 minutes, depending on your oven. Now you need to let them cool on the trays, otherwise they would disintegrate. When they are cool enough to move, transfer to a cooling rack and store, when cold, in an air-tight box.

Kinky's Note:
Ginger keeps very well in the freezer and is easy to grate whilst frozen.

• ULSTER BUTTERMILK SCONES

225 g / 8 oz. plain flour
2½ teaspoons baking powder
Pinch of salt

½ teaspoon bicarbonate of soda
56 g / 2 oz. sugar
85 g / 3 oz. butter, at room temperature
1 egg, beaten
4 to 5 tablespoons buttermilk

Preheat the oven to 200°C / 400°F and line a large baking sheet with greased baking parchment.

In a bowl, sift the flour with the baking powder, salt, and bicarbonate of soda and add the sugar. Cut the butter into the flour mixture and rub in with your fingers. Then stir in the egg and a tablespoon of buttermilk. Gradually work in the rest of the buttermilk to make a dough. Different brands of flour may use more or less buttermilk, so do this slowly, as you may have too much or may need to add more. When it all comes together in a soft dough it is ready to be kneaded and rolled out on a floured work surface. It should be about 1 inch or more thick. Now take a cutter or a small downturned glass tumbler and cut out rounds about 1½ inches in diameter. You should end up with about 12.

Arrange the scones on the baking sheet and brush with a little egg yolk mixed with a little milk to give the scones a golden top, or you could simply dust them with flour.

Bake for about 10 minutes and cool on a wire rack.

This is the recipe that I gave to Maggie MacCorkle.

• FUDGE

115 g / 4 oz. butter
397 g / 14 oz. condensed milk
150 m / 4 oz. milk

1 teaspoon salt
2 teaspoons vanilla essence (optional)
455 g / 16 oz. Demerara sugar

Line a 30 × 20 cm baking tin with parchment.

Melt the butter in the condensed milk and the ordinary milk over a low heat in the biggest, heaviest-bottomed pan you can find. Add the salt, vanilla (if using), and gradually add the sugar. Stir until the sugar has dissolved. Then turn the heat up high and watch that the mixture does not boil over. Continue to boil for about 10 to 15 minutes, stirring often and making sure that the bottom of the mixture is not burning. The colour will change from a creamy white to a shade of light brown and the temperature will register about 240°F / 116°C. A drop of the mixture dropped into icy-cold water will form a soft ball of fudge.

Beat with an electric mixer for about 5 minutes and pour into a baking pan about 30 cm × 20 cm or 12″×7″. Leave to cool and when almost but not quite set, mark into squares with a sharp knife. When cold, cut up into squares.

GLOSSARY

I have in all the previous Irish Country novels provided a glossary to help the reader who is unfamiliar with the vagaries of the Queen's English as it may be spoken by the majority of people in Ulster. This is a regional dialect akin to English as spoken in Yorkshire or on Tyneside. It is not Ulster-Scots, which is claimed to be a distinct language in its own right. I confess I am not a speaker.

Today in Ulster (but not in 1967 when this book is set) official signs are written in English, Irish, and Ulster-Scots. The washroom sign would read Toilets, *Leithris* (Irish), and *Cludgies* (Ulster-Scots). I hope what follows here will enhance your enjoyment of the work, although I am afraid it will not improve your command of Ulster-Scots.

acting the lig/maggot: Behaving like an idiot.
aluminium: Aluminum.
amadán: Irish. Pronounced "omadawn." Idiot.
and all: Addition to a sentence for emphasis.
anyroad: Anyway.
arse: Backside. (Impolite.)
at himself/not at himself: He's feeling well/not feeling well.
away off (and feel your head/and chase yourself): Don't be stupid.

aye certainly: Of course, or naturally.

back to porridge: Returning from something extraordinary to the humdrum daily round.

bang your drum about: Go on at length about a pet subject.

banjaxed: Ruined or smashed.

banshee: Irish: *beán* (woman) *sidhe* (fairy). Female spirit whose moaning foretells a death.

barging: Telling off verbally or physically shoving.

barmbrack: Speckled bread. (See Mrs. Kinkaid's recipe in *An Irish Country Doctor*.)

beat Bannagher: Wildly exceed expectations.

bee in the bonnet: Obsessed with something.

bee on a hot brick: Rushing round at great speed.

been here before: Your wisdom is attributable to the fact that you have already lived a full life and have been reincarnated.

beezer: First rate.

bettered myself: I rose in the world by my own exertions.

between the jigs and reels: To cut a long story short.

biscakes: Biscuits (cookies).

bisticks: Biscuits (cookies).

bit the head off: Gave someone a severe verbal chastisement.

blether/och, blether: Talk, often inconsequential/ expression of annoyance or disgust.

bletherskite: One who continually talks trivial rubbish.

blow out: End a romantic affair, or a feast.

boke: Vomit.

bollix: Testicles. (Impolite.)

bollixed: Wrecked.

bonnet: Hood of a car.

bookie: Bookmaker.

boot: Trunk of a car.

bore: Of a shotgun. Gauge.

both legs the same length: Standing around uselessly.

boys-a-dear or **boys-a-boys:** Expression of amazement.

brave: Very.

British Legion: Fraternal organisation for exservicemen (veterans).

brogue: a) A kind of low-heeled shoe (from the Irish *bróg*) with decorative perforations on the uppers, originally to allow water to drain out. b) The musical inflection given to English when spoken by an Irish person.

bull in a china shop/at a gate: Thrashing about violently without forethought and causing damage/ charging headlong at something.

bye: Counties Cork and Antrim pronunciation of boy.

cailín: Irish. Pronounced "colleen." Girl.

camogie: A stick-and-ball team game akin to hurling, but played by women.

candy apples: Apples dipped in caramel glaze.

candy floss: Cotton candy.

can't for toffee: Is totally inept.

casualty: ER department of a hospital.

champ: A dish of potatoes, buttermilk, butter, and chives.

chemist: Pharmacist.

chips: French fries.

chissler: Child.

chuntering: From the Scots. Waffling on interminably.

clap: Cow shit.

clatter: Indeterminate number. See also **wheen**. The size of the number can be enhanced by adding **brave**

or **powerful** as a precedent to either. As an exercise, try to imagine the numerical difference between a **brave clatter** and a **powerful wheen** of spuds.

cobbler topping: A circle of scones (see recipes) placed on top of a stew or a dish of fruit and baked in the oven. Those used on a stew are made savoury with the addition of herbs and cheese.

cod/codding: To fool/fooling.

collogue: Chat about trivia.

collywobbles: Vague feeling of being unwell.

come on on in: The second "on" is deliberate, not a typographical error.

comeuppance: Served right.

Cookstown sausage: Thin pork sausages made in Cookstown, County Tyrone.

corker: Very special.

course: From the ancient sport of coursing, where quarry is started by dogs and pursued by the hunters who run after the dogs.

cowlick: Hair hanging diagonally across the forehead.

cowped: Capsized.

cracker: Exceptional.

crayture: Creature, critter.

crick: Sprain.

cross/cross as two sticks: Angry/very angry.

cruibín: Pickled pig's trotter eaten cold with vinegar.

cup of tea/scald in your hand: An informal cup of tea, as opposed to tea that was synonymous with the main evening meal (dinner).

currency: Prior to decimalization, sterling was the currency of the United Kingdom, of which Northern Ireland was a part. The unit was the **pound** (quid), which contained twenty **shillings** (bob), each made of twelve **pennies** (pence), thus there were 240 pennies in a pound. Coins and notes of combined or lesser or greater denominations were in circulation, often referred to by slang or archaic terms: **farthing** (four to the penny), **halfpenny** (two to the penny), **threepenny** piece (thruppeny bit), **sixpenny** piece (tanner), **two-shillings** piece (florin), **two-shillings-and-sixpence piece** (half a crown), **ten-shilling note** (ten-bob note), **guinea** coin worth one pound and one shilling, **five-pound** note (fiver). In 1967 one pound bought nearly three U.S. dollars.

dab hand at: Very skilled.

dander: Short walk, or literally, horse dandruff.

dar dar: Noise made by little Ulster boys in imitation of handgun fire.

dead/dead on: Very/absolutely right or perfectly.

decked: Knocked down.

desperate: Terrible.

didn't come down the Lagan on a soap bubble: Used to indicate that the subject is worldly wise.

dig in the gub: Smack or punch in the mouth.

dig with the left (foot): A pejorative remark made about Catholics by Protestants.

donkey fringe: Bangs.

do-re-mi: Tonic sol-fa scale, but meaning "dough" as in money.

dosh: Money.

dote: (v.) To adore. (n.) Something adorable.

dozer/no dozer: Stupid person/clever person.

drumlin: From the Irish *dromín* (little ridge). Small rounded hills caused by the last ice age. There are so many in County Down that the place has been described as looking like a basket of green eggs.

dulse: A seaweed that when dried is used like chewing gum.

duncher: Cloth cap, usually tweed.

eejit/buck eejit: Idiot/complete idiot.

fair play/fair play to you: Fair enough/Good for you.

feck (and variations): Corruption of "fuck." For a full discussion of its usage see author's note in *A Dublin Student Doctor.* It is not so much sprinkled into Dublin conversations as shovelled in wholesale, and also used in Ulster. Its scatalogical shock value is now so debased that it is no more offensive than "like" larded into teenagers' chat. Now available at reputable bookstores is the *Feckin' Book of Irish*—a series of ten books by Murphy and O'Dea.

ferocious: Extreme.

fillet steak: Beef tenderloin.

fillums: Ordinarily I avoid using phonetic spelling, but there is no way round it if I am to render the Ulster propensity for inserting the extra syllable "um" into films, movies.

Finn McCool: *Fionn* (blonde) *mac* (son of) *Cumhail* Cumhal), a mythical Irish hunter and warrior. His deeds and those of his followers, the Fianna, are the basis of the Finian cycle of Irish legend.

flex: Electrical plug-in cord.

footer: Fiddle about with.

for all the marleys: Everything riding on a desired outcome. See also **Losing your marleys.**

foundered: Frozen.

gag: Joke or funny situation. Applied to a person, humorist.

gander: Look-see.

git: Corruption of begotten. Frequently with **hoor's** (whore's). Derogatory term for an unpleasant person.

glipe/great glipe: Stupid/very stupid person.

go away with you: Don't be silly.

gobshite: Literally, dried nasal mucus. Used pejoratively about a person.

go for corn: Have no idea what to do.

going spare: Losing it.

good man-ma-da: Literally, "good man my father." Good for you. A term of approval.

grilled: Broiled.

gurning: Whingeing. Whining.

gurrier: Street urchin, but often used pejoratively about anyone.

guttees: Canvas-topped gym shoes with rubber (originally gutta percha) soles. Known in England as plimsols.

half-un (hot): Small measure of spirits. (Irish whiskey, lemon juice, sugar, cloves, diluted with boiling water.)

hames: Literally, "testicles." To make a hames of is to mess up.

ham-fisted: Clumsy.

hammer and tongs: Fighting fiercely.

headsplitter: Hangover.

headstaggers: Take leave of one's senses.

heart of corn: Very good-natured.

heel(s) of the hunt: When all's said and done.

heifer: Young cow before her first breeding.

higheejin: Very important person, often only in the subject's own mind.

hirstle: Wheeze in chest.

hirple: Stagger.

HMS: His/Her Majesty's Ship.

hobbyhorse shite: Literally, sawdust. To have a head full is to be extremely obtuse.

hoovering: Generic use of the name of a brand of

vacuum cleaner, to denote using any vacuum cleaner.

hold your horses: Wait a minute.

hot press: Warming cupboard with shelves over the hot water tank.

hould your peace: Keep your mouth shut.

houl' your wheest: Hold your tongue.

how's about you?: How are you?

humdinger: Something exceptional.

I doubt: I believe, if accompanied by a negative. "I doubt we'll no' see him the night" means "I believe we'll not see him." Otherwise, standard English meaning.

I'm yer man: I agree and will cooperate fully.

in the stable: Of a drink in a pub, paid for but not yet poured.

jag: Jab by an injection needle.

Jezebel: A scheming, promiscuous, fallen woman, named after the biblical (II Kings) wife of Ahab.

Job's comforter: Biblical. Someone whose well-meaning advice in time of adversity makes matters worse.

juked: Dodged.

kick for touch: Tactic of putting the ball out of play in rugby football to slow the play and possibly gain field advantage. In other usage prevaricate, compromise.

kilter: Alignment.

knackered: Exhausted like a worn-out horse on its way to the knacker's yard where it would be destroyed.

laugh like a drain: Be consumed with mirth.

learned: Ulsterese is peculiar in often reversing the meanings of words. "The teacher learned the child," or "She borrowed [meaning loaned] me a cup of sugar." "Reach [meaning pass] me **thon yoke**."

length and breadth of it: All the details.

let the hare sit: Let sleeping dogs lie.

liltie: Irish whirling dervish.

lip: Cheekiness.

losing your marleys: Losing your (marbles) mind. See also **For all the marleys**.

madder than a wet hen: Very angry.

marmalize: Cause great physical damage and pain.

midder: Colloquial medical term for midwifery, the art and science of dealing with pregnancy and childbirth, now superseded medically by the term "obstetrics."

mitch: Either play truant or steal.

more meat on a hammer/wren's shin. Descriptions of a skinny person.

more power to your wheel: Words of encouragement akin to "the very best of luck."

muffler: Long woollen scarf.

muirnín: Irish. Pronounced "moornyeen." Darling.

my/your/his shout: My/your/his turn to pay for the drinks.

neat: Of a drink of spirits, straight up.

no flies on: An astute person.

no goat's toe: One who has a very high and often erroneous impression of one's self.

no harm til you, but: I do not mean to cause you any offence, usually followed by, but you are absolutely wrong.

no slouch: Very good at, a "slouch" being a useless person.

no sweat: Nothing to worry about.

not a bad head: A decent person.

not at yourself: Unwell.

och: Exclamation to register whatever emotion you wish. "Och, isn't she lovely?" "Och, he's dead?" "Och, damn it." Pronounced like clearing your throat.

off side: Out of the line of fire or out of sight.

on the pour: Of a pint of Guinness. There is an art to building a good pint of Guinness and it can take several minutes.

on the QT: Privately.

ould hand: Old friend.

oxter/oxtercog: Armpit/help walk by draping an individual's arm over one's shoulder.

paddy hat: Soft-crowned, narrow-brimmed, Donegal tweed hat.

Paddy's market: Disorganised crowd.

peely-wally: Scots, but used in Ulster. Under the weather. Feeling unwell.

petrol: Gasoline.

piece: Bread and spread, as in "jam piece."

playing gooseberry: An unwanted third person during a romantic encounter.

ploughed: Of an exam. Failed.

power/powerful: A lot, very strong.

punter: Bettor on horses or dogs.

pupil: In Ireland and Britain "student" was reserved for those attending university. Schoolchildren were referred to as "pupils," nor did graduation occur until after the granting of a university degree.

quare: Ulster and Dublin pronunciation of "queer," meaning "very" or "strange."

rag order: Dublin slang for untidily dressed and coiffed.

rapscallion: Mischief maker.

rates: Municipal taxes.

rear: Of a child. Bring up.

rear up: Take great offence. Become angry and pugnacious.

restful on the eye: Usually of a woman. Good-looking.

right enough?: Is that a fact?

rightly: Very well.

RMS: Royal Mail Ship.

rook: Black bird of the crow family.

rooked: Cheated out of money or paying too much.

rozzer: Policeman.

rubbernecking: Being unduly curious.

ructions: Violent argument.

said a mouthful: Hit the nail on the head. Are absolutely right.

Sassenach: Gaelic term originally applied to Saxons, now used, usually in a bantering fashion, by the Scots and Irish to mean "English."

saving your presence: I am about to insult you, but please don't be offended.

scared skinny: Terrified.

scrip': Script, short for "prescription."

see him/her?: Emphatic way of drawing attention to the person in question even if they are not physically present.

shenanigans: Carryings-on.

sheugh: A muddy place often fouled with cow clap.

shufti: Military slang, from the Arabic. Look-see.

sick line: Medical certificate of illness allowing a patient to collect sickness benefit.

sidhe: Irish. Pronounced "shee." The fairies.

skelly: Take a quick look at.

skinful: One of the 2,660 synonyms or expressions for "drunk." (*Dickson's Word Treasury,* 1982)

skitters: Diarrhoea.

skivers: Probably derived from "scurvy." No-good wastrels.

sláinte: Irish. Pronounced "slawntuh." Cheers, your health.

so I am/he is/it's not: An addition at the end of a sentence for emphasis.

sound/sound man: Good/good, trustworthy man.

sparks: Electrician.

spirits: Of drink, any distilled liquor.

spud: Potato. Also a nickname for anyone called Murphy.

stew in your own juice: Worry and be bothered about something with no hope of resolving the situation by your own efforts. Often you have been the cause of the situation in the first place.

sticking out/a mile: Good/excellent.

sticking the pace: Showing no signs of aging, fatigue, or decay.

sting: Hurt.

stocious: See skinful.

stone: All measurements in Ireland until decimalisation were Imperial. One stone = fourteen pounds, 20 fluid ounces = one pint.

stoon: Sudden shooting pain.

surgery: Where a GP saw ambulatory patients. The equivalent of a North American "office." Specialists worked in "rooms."

swinging the lead: Malingering.

take a scunner: Really have it in for someone.

take someone out of themselves: Get their mind off their troubles for a while.

take the rickets: Have a great shock.

take the strunts: Become angry or sulk.

take yourself off: Leave me alone.

take yourself off by the hand: Don't be ridiculous.

tanned: Spanked. As in "getting his arse tanned."

targe: Woman with a very sharp tongue. A scold.

tear away: Get on with it.

terrace: Row housing, but not just for the working class. Some of the most expensive accommodation in Dublin is found in terraces in Merrion Square, akin to low-rise rows of attached town houses.

tetchy: Irritable. Bad-tempered.

that there/them there: That/them with emphasis.

the day: Today.

the hat: Foreman, so called because his badge of office was a bowler (derby) hat.

the wee man: The devil.

thole: Put up with. A reader, Miss D. Williams, wrote to me to say it was etymologically from the Old English *tholian,* to suffer. She remarked that her first encounter with the word was in a fourteenth-century prayer.

thon/thonder: That/over there.

thran: Bloody-minded.

throughother: Slovenly. Carelessly untidy.

throw another spud in the pot: Add more ingredients to the upcoming meal because of the arrival of an unexpected extra guest.

til: To.

'til: Until.

to beat Bannagher: Explanation unknown, but means exceptionally.

tongue's hanging out: Very thirsty.

tousling: Beating up, either verbally or physically.

townland: Mediaeval administrative district encompassing a village and the surrounding farms and wasteland.

turd: Piece of faeces.

Ulster overcoat: Heavy-duty double-breasted overcoat.

up one side and down the other: A severe chewing-out.

up to high doh: Really strung out.

warm: Well-off.

wasters: No-good wastrels.

wean: Pronounced "wane." Little one.

wee turn: Sudden illness, usually not serious, or used euphemistically to pretend it wasn't serious.

wet the baby's head: Have a drink to celebrate a birth.

wheeker: Terrific.

wheen: An indeterminate but reasonably large number.

where to go for corn: Completely at a loss as to what to do.

yellow man: A crunchy honeycomb toffee associated with Ballycastle, Northern Ireland.

yoke: Thing. Often used if the speaker is unsure of the exact nature of the object in question.

you know: Verbal punctuation often used when the person being addressed could not possibly be in possession of the information.

you me and the wall: In strictest confidence.

your man: Someone either whose name is not known, "Your man over there? Who is he?" or someone known to all, "Your man, Van Morrison."

youse: Plural of "you."

zizz: Forces slang. Nap.